Lighting the Shadows of Joshua Clay

A Story of Blood and Salvation

Book Two of The Scrollbearer Saga

Written by:
J. Scott

Published by Sparky Bites Publishing under the J. Scott Publishing imprint

ISBN (Hardcover, 6x9): 978-1-968023-16-4

ISBN (Hardcover, 7x10): 978-1-968023-11-9

ISBN (Paperback): 978-1-968023-10-2

ISBN (eBook): 978-1-968023-12-6

First Edition, May 2026

Lighting the Shadows of Joshua Clay: A Story of Blood and Salvation

Book Two of The Scrollbearer Saga

Written by J. Scott

Cover Design by J. Scott

Characters Created by J. Scott

Revised and edited by J. Scott

For more information, visit sparkybitespublishing.com

This novel continues the saga first envisioned in the poem The Darkened Light of Joshua Clay, originally written in 1988 and registered under copyright in 2018 by the author. While the poem served as the spark, Lighting the Shadows of Joshua Clay builds upon the world it began—expanding its story, deepening its characters, and carrying the legacy forward into a new chapter of The Scrollbearer Saga.

Printed in the United States of America

To my wife—

for carrying more than your share so I could carry these words.

For listening when the story spilled out,

and for holding me together when I felt undone.

And to all who encouraged me,

who gave me time, patience, and grace—

this book is as much yours as mine.

The Echo

You were not sent to carry the toll, but to bow beneath it.

For pride bears light as burden, but grace bears it as breath.

And so the light did not flee. It waited—for your surrender.

(from the Scroll of the Covenant, Fragment VII:9)

Table of Contents

Prologue: The Fire That Remains

"It's necessary to go through the fire to be tempered and refined."

When my father said that, he wasn't trying to make suffering meaningful. He was naming a condition. Fire does not negotiate. It does not care what you intended to become. It reveals what will endure and leaves the rest behind.

For a long time, I thought the fire was finished.

When Joshua Clay fell and the scroll slipped from his hands, the world did not end gently. Light tore through the Withering—not like judgment, but refusal. The Veins split beneath us, seams opening too fast to hold. The ground buckled. Darkness did not retreat; it unraveled where the light passed through it.

I remember the sound of it most.

Not the bell.

Not the shouting.

The tearing.

The dark does not die quietly. It resists and clings, trying to drag the world with it when it cannot stay. The light answered without cruelty and without compromise. Where it moved, there was no room left for negotiation.

Prologue: The Fire That Remained

Joshua screamed "Redemption" when the God-Forsaken Bell rang—and the dark seized him, claiming its due. Not in anger, but in law.

It was not a prayer.

Not a plea.

A declaration spoken too late—

and yet not too late at all.

I saw the moment the scroll left his hands. Not thrown. Not offered. Released. For a heartbeat, it hung between him and the ground, its light flaring once as if something essential had been interrupted.

Then Joshua was gone.

Seized is not the right word. Neither is lost. He was claimed.

By every law that governs the crossing of realms, Gillie and I should have followed him. We had entered another's Withering. We had bound ourselves to his burden. If he fell, we were meant to fall with him. The Severing does not weigh intention. It answers only outcome.

I waited for the pull.

That inward collapse.

That certainty.

The moment the ground gives way and there will be no return.

It did not come.

The light surged outward instead.

It moved through the army of the dark and the shapes that wore bodies unraveled mid-motion. They did not explode. They emptied. What remained struck the earth like husks already forgotten.

The force drove me to my knees—not in reverence, but survival. My chest burned. My vision whitened at the edges. I remember tasting iron and thinking, absurdly, that this must be what lightning feels like from the inside.

When the light receded, I was still breathing.

That unsettled me more than the destruction.

The ground held us.

The air did not reject us.

The scroll did not fall silent.

For a moment, I thought perhaps the law had bent. That something had gone wrong in a way no one anticipated.

But the longer I remained upright, the clearer it became that this was not error.

It was restraint.

The world bore the marks of fire. Ash lay thick in the low places. Stone radiated heat where light had passed through it. Nothing rushed to become whole. Everything held itself still, as if listening.

The scroll rested against my back—warm, steady. It did not pull forward. It did not release us. It simply remained.

Gillie stood beside me, hands shaking, face streaked with soot and light. She pressed her palm to the ground, as if expecting it to give way.

When she looked up, her eyes were not afraid.

"They land feels different," she said. Not healed. Not broken. "Like it knows something happened."

She was right.

The world had changed—but more than that, it was aware. As though it had witnessed something it would not forget.

Fire does not always destroy what it touches. Sometimes it leaves behind something far more demanding: what remains when destruction fails.

Tempering is only the first trial. Refining takes longer. It asks whether what survived the fire can endure being shaped.

Prologue: The Fire That Remained

The light had moved through the world. That much was certain. But it had not withdrawn. It lingered in the Veins, in the ground, in the silence that followed the reckoning. It lingered in us.

We did not move.

Not from fear.

Not from uncertainty.

Something had not released us.

The fire had passed.

The reckoning had spoken.

What remained was weight—the kind that waits to see whether it will be carried forward or laid down.

If this was the tempering, then what came next would reveal something harder than survival.

The light had ended the war.

It had not yet answered what would be built in its name.

And it had not finished asking its question.

The Uneasy Calm

Where Light First Took Root

The first morning didn't come with ceremony. It crept in quietly, the light spreading over the fields like someone checking for a pulse. It wasn't bright enough to blind or warm—just enough to show what remained.

The sky was washed-out gray, the color of exhaustion. Ash filled the furrows where crops once grew, and when the wind turned, it carried the smell of smoke and rain, like the storm hadn't decided whether to leave.

We'd called it the end, but the word didn't fit. Endings don't set you free; they only clear the wreckage so something else can begin. The ground gave a small sigh—not of relief, but of readiness—as if it remembered how to receive weight again. Blades of grass bent under the new light, trembling but alive. The sun didn't flood the valley; it asked to come back in.

And it was evening, and it was morning—the first day had passed.

The fields stirred but did not yet trust themselves to green. Mercy moved like a hand learning its strength, touching what it could and leaving the rest for later. Each gust chose between ruin and recovery. Shadows withdrew to the edges, close enough to listen. Morning shone more brightly than it felt. Light isn't always fullness. Sometimes it is exactly enough to take one step you couldn't take yesterday.

We took that step.

Our legs still ached from the year of running.

The scroll leaned—subtle, sure—and the ground answered with a faint hum beneath our feet, the kind that doesn't promise anything but asks you to keep moving.

Gillie watched the horizon and said, "One step is still a road, if it knows where to go."

We didn't speak about signs or destinies. We watched the light test the furrows and let our feet agree.

We hoped, quietly and against our own caution, that Joshua might rise with it. Not easily. Not clean. Hope came carefully, knowing it would ask for more than belief if it were answered. His absence made the air sound like a hymn missing its last note. None of us spoke his name. It wasn't forgetting. It was disbelief. We had watched him drop the scroll, turn toward the dark, cry for redemption—and still the ground took him. The sound of it had not left our ears.

We didn't speak his name that morning, but the day kept arranging itself around the space he left.

The scroll remained.

It hadn't finished with us. Its weight did not accuse. It summoned. The page had turned, but the story hadn't closed. Its bindings pressed like a question against my shoulder: Carry breath where ash sits. Re-thread what the Veins forgot. Stand where water remembers how to open.

We weren't walking home. What we had called home seemed to burn with him, and what remained did not receive us the same.

None of us could say what home meant anymore.

The fields stretched where we remembered them, the sky opened as it always had, yet something underneath had changed. The ground felt thinner, the air closer, the colors too deliberate—as if the world had been rebuilt from memory and not quite in the right order.

The Bearing looked like the land we left, but it breathed differently now. Aware of us.

The Withering had followed—not as fire or shadow, but as a quiet distortion in everything that lived. What had been healed carried a faint reflection of where we'd been, as though two realms now shared the same breath.

We walked as though recognition might return if we pressed far enough, that some tree line or streambed or stone worn by feet would greet us and say we had arrived. But every turning felt borrowed, each familiar shape laced with unease, as though the land remembered us differently than we remembered it.

We hoped for a world to walk home into. We found only echoes—reminders we belonged, and reminders we did not.

The scroll allowed us to sleep, but only barely.

For the last year we spent in Joshua's Withering, we were denied rest. The moment we stopped moving, the whisperers came. They filled the air, crowding into our thoughts until every memory turned against us. Their voices didn't simply speak; they bled. To stand still too long was to invite them in, and once they entered, they made a home of your silence.

Sleep wasn't rest there—it was surrender.

We later understood that it was Joshua's doing, though not in the way he meant. When he still walked the living world, he had prayed that his conscience would never grow quiet again—not until he had made right what he'd broken. In the Withering, that prayer became law. The whisperers enforced it, punishing any pause, any breath that resembled peace.

But here, something had changed.

The ground still remembered his torment, yet it no longer obeyed it. The scroll quieted the whisperers when it drew near, pressing their voices back into the soil. At night, the world didn't scream. It listened.

And in that hush, we found room for something we hadn't dared name before.

Rest.

Not comfort. Not forgetting. Just enough stillness to stand again. Sometimes it even allowed laughter—small, uncertain, the kind that sounded borrowed from an older world. But it never allowed us to stay still. When we lingered too long, it tugged the way a compass tugs toward north—quietly, insistently—reminding us that stillness and obedience were not the same thing, though many had died believing they were.

For a while we let silence do the counting.

The Veins still remembered their three parts—pause, passage, promise—and so did we. Our breaths were stitched with loss we hadn't yet spoken. We knew that if we lingered, Joshua's ruin would plant itself where witness should stand. If we moved, maybe the Word would breathe again where people had traded breath for ash.

The days blurred together at first—gray mornings, hollow light, the sound of our own footsteps keeping time. The land didn't fight us anymore, but it didn't welcome us either. It only watched.

By the second night, the quiet had grown so wide it felt like it might swallow our thoughts. Even the wind stopped trying to explain itself. That's when we began to notice something beneath it—faint, regular, like a pulse through the soil.

On the third day, the hum rose clear—a thin, steady thread, almost swallowed by quiet. Those who leaned close flinched, as if melody had lifted a cover from what they already knew.

The sound felt like soil remembering seed.

Gillie slowed beside me, her gaze fixed on the scroll where it rested against my shoulder. "It's speaking," she said softly. "Not words. Just a weight that wants to be heard."

I stopped. "You hear it?"

She nodded once. "Not to all of us. Only to me, right now. May I?"

I turned slightly so she could reach.

Gillie touched the scroll—careful, almost apologetic. Her other hand brushed the knife at her side. She let it hang loose and whispered, "Still unbalanced."

The word landed heavier than it weighed.

"What did you say?" I asked.

Her eyes stayed on the horizon. "Still unbalanced." The way she said it, I couldn't tell if she meant the scroll beneath her palm or the blade at her hip—or both, as though naming two burdens at once.

"The scroll doesn't lean to balance us," I said. "It leans to guide us."

She didn't look up. Her fingers drifted from the scroll to the knife, tracing the worn grip. "I wasn't talking about the scroll," she said.

She drew the knife halfway from its sheath, not in threat but curiosity. The metal caught the light and gave it back like a breath. "I keep thinking it's going to talk to me," she said quietly. "Every time I touch it, I expect it to say something different. Like it's waiting for the right moment—or the right reason."

Her thumb followed the spine of the blade, slow and uncertain. "Maybe it remembers something I don't. Maybe that's why it feels heavier some days."

"If it took," I said, "it may still owe."

She looked at me then. "You don't think blades can give back."

"I don't think they were made to," I said. Then, quieter, "Unless the taking was never the point."

The wind stirred the ash at our feet, faint but familiar. She watched it swirl before adding, "If Joshua could find peace, maybe the knife would stop listening for it through me."

She slid the blade back into its sheath like she didn't trust her own hands.

The silence that followed wasn't heavy. It was listening.

We did not yet know which of us would finish what had begun.

But the ground already did.

Her voice thinned. "But Joshua fell, the scroll endures, and the blade is still unbalanced. I'm still unbalanced."

She went quiet then. Her thumb circled the hilt, slow and thoughtful, as though the leather grip might confess something she'd missed. The motion kept time with her breathing—small, searching turns that said more than words could.

For a while I thought she was finished. But her breath deepened, steadied. When she spoke again, it wasn't to me. It was to the weight itself.

"It's been this way since the beginning," she said. "I was a child when it was given to me."

The knife shifted in her hand; her fingers found the balance point without looking.

"A man I didn't know pressed it into my palm. He called it the Balanced Blade. Said it wasn't for death, but for life… or something like that."

She hesitated—eyes narrowing, head tilted slightly—as though replaying words that had worn thin with time.

"He told me it would feel heavier to one side until it found its balance again," she said. "I keep waiting for that. For it to feel lighter."

I watched the knife catch what little light was left—dull, steady, almost breathing.

"For life," I repeated softly. "I don't know how a blade can be for life. It's made to divide things that belong together."

She looked down, listening.

"Maybe that's what balance costs," I said.

Gillie's gaze lifted. She studied me first, then the edge. The silence between us folded once, twice, before she finally spoke.

"But the world is balanced, isn't it?" she said. "We have life, so we have death. We have light, so we have dark. Every weight should find its counterweight."

Her eyes flicked toward the scroll. "But this… this feels like the blade. Tilted. Heavy. Maybe it should give something back for what it took."

The air tightened—not tense, but aware. I held her gaze.

"It plants," I said quietly. "What sinks looks like loss, but a seed sinks the same way. Maybe what's hidden now will rise later as life. I don't know yet."

Her mouth tilted—not quite a smile, not quite surrender.

"Then let's hope the soil was ready."

Somewhere behind us, the path we'd taken felt closed, though no sound marked the moment. It wasn't a gate or a tearing—just the quiet knowing that whatever had carried us out of the Withering was gone now. The Vein had sealed itself, not in defiance, but in mercy.

We stood again in the pace of the living. Even here, the trees bent from habit, and the grass grew cautious, as if light itself was still learning how to stand.

The Uneasy Calm

We moved. Not toward a city—toward a threshold. The scroll seemed to guide our feet more than the roads did: heavier when we strayed, lighter when the line beneath us held. At dawn it tilted east, by noon it steadied north, and by late day the pull lay straight as a buried cord. When it slackened, we rested. When it pressed, we rose.

We slept where the ground agreed to hold us—once beside a windbreak of thorn that knew how to keep sheep honest; once under a stand of poplar with leaves that whispered the old alphabet; once in a quarry that had learned to be quiet for stonecutters and was willing to try for us. We kept no big fires. A kettle warmed on coals; grief warmed the rest.

The night rebuilt itself in pieces. First the crickets returned, then an owl somewhere far off, then smaller sounds—the shuffle of creatures testing the edges of our camp. The world wasn't silent anymore, just cautious. The rhythm felt new and familiar at once, like hearing your own pulse after too long underwater.

Sleep came lightly. It didn't take us completely, just enough to rest without forgetting where we were. It was the kind of sleep that still listened for danger, the kind none of us had known in Joshua's Withering.

Sometimes Gillie stood in the dark, holding her knife toward the faint starlight. She wasn't sharpening it. She was waiting. Her head would tilt as if listening for words she might have missed before. The blade never answered, but she looked less alone when she tried.

A thin thread of smoke drifted toward us before dawn, and the scent of it carried a kind of memory. From the hedge came a figure—her clothes gray with ash, a scroll pressed tight to her chest. When she spoke, her voice was coarse, like bark cracking after fire.

"The flame still speaks," she said.

Gillie stepped forward and took her arm before her knees could fail her. The ground seemed to ease under them both, softening as if it remembered mercy.

Only later did we learn her name—Miriam, the one said to have walked through fire and lived. People claimed the smoke from Joshua's ruin had scattered across the land, and that she was where one ember chose to rest. We didn't name it then, but a steadiness entered with her—the kind fire learns when it stops devouring and starts guarding.

At first light a figure appeared on the ridge above our fire—barefoot, hair tied back with leather, his silence deliberate. He stayed there long enough for us to wonder if he would turn away. Then he descended, sat near the coals, and watched the flame without a word.

"I know his name," he said finally, eyes still on the fire.

No one asked which name he meant. Gillie broke off a piece of bread and handed it to him, and that was enough.

Tomas was quiet and certain—one of those who believed the act of remembering was a kind of worship. Something in the air recognized him; memory stood up straighter, as if a forgotten name had turned its head.

By midmorning, the fog thickened until we could hardly see the path ahead. Then, through the mist, a sound—low, steady, beautiful. A voice humming a tune that bent the air itself. The fog rolled back as if to listen. A woman stepped forward, and for a heartbeat the ground vibrated beneath our feet, following the rhythm of her song.

Gillie met her halfway. The hum faded into stillness, but its echo stayed.

Sera's voice carried memory. The world didn't just hear her—it recognized her. Her tone found seams in the day the way light finds grain in wood—patient, exact, repairing as it moved.

Later, while crossing near a stream, something moved beneath the water. A man rose from it slowly, grief running from his arms like the river had refused to keep it. His palms were darkened by lines that caught the light like unhealed scars. He said nothing, but his silence carried weight. That night he wept beside the fire without shame. By morning, the soil where he'd slept was damp and dark, and small green shoots had broken through. Miriam touched them and whispered, "Mercy."

That was Eliah, whose tears grew roots. His sorrow didn't bloom—it repaid what the fire had taken. Where his grief touched soil, loss stopped performing and started planting.

We heard the next one before we saw her—the reeds shifting in small whispers. A woman stepped through, cautious but unafraid. "I got lost in the song," she told Gillie, "but your quiet pulled me back." Gillie reached for her hand, and the air seemed to pause, waiting for them to finish what had already begun.

Her name was Nadya, and she carried silence like others carried light—steady, invisible, essential. Silence gathered around her like a cloak that warmed instead of hid; we didn't know it then, but some wars end only where quiet keeps its vows.

Evening found us with another. One moment the road was empty, the next there was a man walking beside me, mid-sentence, as though continuing a thought he'd started miles ago.

"It matters," he said, "whether the bell is tolled or heard. One marks the moment. The other carries it." He smiled faintly at his own reasoning.

That was Rowan, whose words always seemed to arrive before the meaning did. His speech felt unfinished on purpose, like a road that knows it will meet a bridge.

The last figure waited longer than the rest, keeping distance until the sun sank low. He watched us for some time before stepping from the shadow of a bent tree. When he joined us, the air steadied—not brighter, just surer, as if a table had found its fourth leg. He said nothing, and no one needed him to. Gillie's nod was small but certain, and something unseen released its hold on the air.

That was Cassian, the anchor none of us asked for but all of us needed. Weight redistributed itself when he stood with us—packs rode easier, arguments rode lower. The ground seemed to accept our footprints more willingly, as if it finally recognized the pattern we were making.

For the first time, our number felt complete, though none of us said so. The air steadied. Even the wind seemed to pause between breaths, listening. We didn't know what would come next, only that the road no longer felt borrowed.

Others came and went—faces I can't recall, prayers I never learned. They followed for a while, drawn by the same pull. We didn't claim them, and they didn't claim us. They walked in our dust and called that enough.

Once, a man stepped too close and tried to kneel in the scroll's shadow. Gillie shifted—not angry, not permitting—and he understood. Reverence could be as dangerous as defiance if you didn't know which one you were practicing.

When the last of them turned away, the silence that followed didn't feel empty. It felt like permission. For the first time since the Withering, we stood without waiting for the ground to tell us what to do. The horizon offered no sign—no tower, no city—but the pull beneath our feet gathered direction the way rivers find slope.

We began to move again. Nine sets of footsteps settled into measure—not perfect, not rehearsed, just honest. No one called the pace, yet somehow we shared it.

Cassian kept to the edge, his eyes scanning ahead; Nadya lingered near the back where quiet could hold the group together; Rowan muttered half-sentences the wind kept stealing; Tomas matched his stride to Gillie's without realizing it; Sera walked near the middle, her hum low and steady. Miriam's cloth brushed her fingertips as she walked. Eliah followed the sound of her steps like water finding its echo.

At some point the strap shifted into her hands, and she didn't give it back.

Gillie walked just ahead of me. The scroll leaned against her back like a heart that hadn't yet decided whether to rest or march. I stayed close enough to feel its pulse through the air.

There was no leader. There was only movement.

The way north rose before us—not familiar, but certain. It didn't feel chosen; it felt necessary. North didn't feel like a decision; it felt like obedience. We walked not because we understood where we were going, but because the light behind us refused to let us stand still.

The ground softened beneath our feet, rich but uncertain, as if learning to trust us again. The wind brushed our faces with warmth that wasn't quite blessing. It was testing us.

We spoke little. Words felt small compared to what we carried. The air was not watching us—it was remembering us. That's why we walked the way we did—not to conquer what lay ahead, but to keep from breaking what had begun to heal.

Sometimes the scroll tugged faintly, measuring our pace. When it leaned forward, we followed; when it eased, we rested. The rhythm was simple. The meaning never was.

The farther we walked, the more the air changed. Ash gave way to clay, then to the faint sweetness of grass trying again. The sun rose higher but didn't burn. Every step felt both borrowed and returned.

Once, I looked back and saw our trail stitched across the slope like handwriting—nine sets of footprints pressed into earth that hadn't known trust in a long time. They didn't wander. They held.

The scroll grew heavier—not from distance but from attention. Gillie noticed first. "It's restless," she said, brushing the strap. She took the satchel from me, and the air steadied as if a chord had resolved.

We crossed water without ceremony and passed places that didn't want witnesses. Some ground wanted only to be left alone, and we honored that.

When the trees closed over the road, light filtering through in narrow bars, a hum lived in the soil itself—steady, low, as if the earth kept its own heartbeat now. Gillie slowed. "This isn't where the fire burned," she said quietly. "This is where the light took root."

The words landed heavy. A woman covered her mouth. A boy knelt and pressed his palm to the soil. Even the birds tested silence and kept it.

Gillie placed her hand flat to the ground. "It doesn't feel angry anymore."

"No," I said. "Because it isn't theirs anymore."

"The light?"

"It found a place to stand."

"Then why us? Why not Joshua?"

"Because we stayed," I said. "We carry what he dropped."

"To keep silence from winning."

"And to bring light where they forgot it was real."

"They'll come for this."

"They always do," I said, touching the scroll. "But they can't burn breath."

We left the grove slowly. Beyond it, meadow opened—haystacks leaning like sleeping giants. A farmer fingered a bell-shard and looked away. A windmill turned once without wind and stilled itself as if in prayer.

By the time the road leveled into plain, the air had warmed. Gillie fell in beside me. "Do they know why they're here?"

"No," I said. "Not yet. Maybe they're following what the light saved."

She nodded, tightening the strap across her shoulder—not to show strength, but to share its weight.

We made camp early on a ridge above a dry creek. Nadya checked our hands for tremor; Sera tuned her hum until the quiet felt whole. Cassian marked first watch with his boot. Travelers paused at the edge of our light, offering nothing, asking nothing.

The scroll rested beside us, its weight finally level.

"Will it ever be full again?" Tomas asked.

"Full enough," Gillie said.

We slept under wind that sounded like itself—no voices, no weight. Only the motion of mercy returning to its rhythm.

Before dawn, the scroll pressed lightly against my shoulder. We rose together and faced north. The way ahead was open.

Some said the roots of the first Humming Tree reached this far, carrying light through the veins beneath the ground.

Standing there, I believed them.

The Missing Flame

We left the grove in silence, the hum fading behind us until it was only a memory against the air. Each step away felt like peeling back from warmth. The trees thinned, and the sounds of life—wind, breath, the faint creak of branches—returned slowly, cautious, as if unsure whether they were allowed to speak again.

Gillie glanced back once, catching the last shimmer through the leaves.

"It's quieter already," she said.

We didn't look back again. Some places ask to be left whole.

The hum lingered faintly beneath our steps, then gave way to the hush of the forest beyond. What waited ahead felt different—unanswered.

The path narrowed. Light dimmed without clouds. Moss spread deep underfoot, damp and dark, clinging to bark and boot. Branches hung low with mist. The air smelled of stone and rain. Our footsteps softened, uncertain, as if the ground resisted giving our echoes back.

Rowan slowed. "Feels like walking through someone's memory," he said. "Like the forest is trying to remember our sound."

"Then walk softer," Cassian said from behind him. His cracked bell tapped once against his leg—a dull note swallowed by fog.

Gillie moved ahead, steady but tense, her hand brushing the knife at her side. The blade caught what little light remained and turned it gray.

Miriam lifted her cloth and coughed. "Burnt sap," she said, rubbing ash from her fingers. "These trees remember fire."

Nadya crouched beside a root, palm pressed to the soil. "So does the ground," she said. "It's still warm."

From the back, Tomas rolled a coin across his knuckles. "Warmth without flame isn't comfort," he said. "It's what's left."

Ahead, Sera began to hum. The sound was small—barely breath—but it threaded through the leaves. The trees answered with a faint vibration.

"They're answering me," she said.

"Or finishing what you started," Gillie replied.

Sera shook her head. "No. They're correcting."

The air tightened. Mist sank lower. Even Rowan went still.

"We're not welcome," Cassian said.

"Maybe not unwelcome," Eliah answered, rubbing river ash between his palms. "Maybe we're being watched."

"Feels like judgment," Gillie said.

"Or mercy," Miriam said quietly.

The scroll pressed faintly against my back—aware, not heavy.

The trail dipped around a stone rise slick with moss. The smell thickened—smoke, personal, like something recently burned and not yet mourned.

"Smoke," Rowan said. "But no fire."

"Not yet," Nadya murmured.

The path opened suddenly into a clearing. The trees stopped hard at its edge, roots tangled into shadow. Ash grayed the ground. Oil clung close to the dirt.

A man sat on a flat stone near the center—robes the color of soil, beard streaked with white. He brushed ash from the rock with slow, precise movements that left no mark. He didn't look like the one tending the small fire near the edge.

"There's nothing sturdier than a stone to build on," he said without looking up. "Fire licks it. Rain thins it. Years lean on it. Still it bears."

"Stones don't choose their weight," Cassian said.

"Neither do most of us," the man replied, almost kindly.

Miriam's cloth smoldered faintly. Sera's hum faltered. The scroll went taut across my shoulders.

The forest leaned in—not threatening, just listening. The scroll held, tight and attentive, as if the ash under his hand matched a grief it already knew.

Gillie stopped. She didn't touch the knife, but the air leaned toward it anyway. Her eyes narrowed—not suspicion alone. Recognition. Not of him, but of the burden he stood inside. Weight, felt before it was named.

Near the clearing's edge, a smaller fire struggled to hold shape. An old man tended it carefully, movements precise, as if the flame might shatter. He didn't turn when we approached.

"You came later than I expected," he said.

"You knew we were coming?" I asked.

"Not who," he said. "Just that someone would. The roots feel it first. Then the air."

Gillie's gaze went to the stones before him—a ring, blackened and mended by hand. Ash filled the center. In it lay a shard of bell metal, jagged and dulled, less placed than rescued.

"Is this a shrine?" she asked.

"Not memory," he said. "Grief."

"For whom?"

He tipped oil into the ash. The smoke darkened, sharpened.

"For the one who burned," he said. After a pause: "For the one who burned so others might live."

The company went quiet. Not shock—recognition catching up.

"Joshua," Gillie said.

The air pulled tight. The trees shifted; the ground felt close beneath our feet. The scroll pressed faintly against my back. Cassian's hand went to his bell. Rowan's breath caught. Miriam pressed her cloth to her chest.

The old man watched the smoke. "Fire purifies," he said. "It also consumes." He let the thread of it climb. "Some wounds burn too long without light. When it touches them again, they can't tell if it's mercy or memory."

"You think he's lost," Gillie said.

"I think he's not burning anymore," the man answered. "That's not the same thing."

No one spoke.

A young pilgrim stepped forward—mud on her knees, a white stone scorched at the edges. She placed it in the ring of ash. "My sister said he once spoke, and the dark listened," she whispered. "Now, when we say his name, the silence listens too."

The man turned toward me. From his sleeve he drew a small coin, worn smooth, and set it beside the shard.

He didn't ask me to take it. The scroll pressed against my shoulder—gentle, firm. I reached forward. The coin was warm—old, but not dead.

"What's this?" I asked.

"The thirteenth," he said.

Nothing more.

No one spoke for a long moment.

The word settled. The scroll stirred faintly.

Gillie's brow tightened. "Who are you?"

He rose slowly and set his palm on the rock, not to clear ash, only to be certain it remained. As he shifted his weight, he leaned briefly on a staff—wood worn smooth where a hand had rested for many years. His step followed, measured but sure, favoring one side. Not hesitation. Accommodation.

"My name is Cephas now," he said. "For the stone that bore the weight, and did not turn away when the bell fell."

He tapped the stone with two fingers. The sound went down through the roots. "Faith without weight is wind," he said. "What endures carries fire and silence both."

He looked past us. "There was a prophet who promised rain to a land taught to be quiet. Some say he walks again. If he does, it won't be for altar or ash. It will be to rinse the ground itself."

Leaves turned pale. The scroll braced against my back.

"Foundations crack," Cassian said.

"Even roots forget soil," Rowan murmured.

"Some say he walks in darkness," Cephas said. "I say he walks through it. The difference is the return."

"Return to what?" Gillie asked.

"I've spoken what was given," he said, turning. "The rest is for another hour."

He walked away. The air loosened behind him.

I closed my hand around the coin. The warmth was steady.

"He knew more than he said," Gillie murmured.

"Or said it elsewhere," I answered.

Reckoning rarely arrives with thunder. It begins as hunger.

We left the clearing without speaking. My mouth felt full of ash. Smoke thinned into gray threads. The forest rustled, uncertain.

Gillie kept a few steps ahead. "We shouldn't have come this way."

"Why?"

"That wasn't only an old man," she said. "It was a warning that knew how to sound like comfort."

"He gave us a coin."

"One more weight," she said quietly. "That's what frightens me."

The group drew closer without speaking. Sera hummed once, stopped, then tried again. Nadya brushed the ground. Eliah followed, eyes wet but steady.

The forest seemed to close in, curious. Roots lifted slightly underfoot. Branches brushed shoulders and hair. The ground gave just enough to remind us it was listening.

Her gaze met mine. "What if we're not here to carry the scroll?" she asked. "What if we're here to finish what Joshua couldn't—what he began, but never reconciled?"

Somewhere deep, wood moved like a hinge. Leaves trembled.

"It isn't about finishing," I said, keeping my voice steady. "It's about not letting the end be the last word."

Gillie looked down at the scroll. The wrappings had begun to fray where her fingers worried the fabric. Loose threads hung like nerves. "I wish he'd told us more."

"He did," I said. "Just not in the way we wanted."

The circle loosened. Sera's hum steadied. Cassian lowered his arms. Nadya pressed her palm to the ground and murmured a few syllables we didn't know. Eliah took a long breath and let it go.

Gillie drew her cloak close, crisp and certain. "Then we walk."

We did.

The ground felt different—awake, not hostile. Stones held. Roots reached downward instead of up. Even our shadows stayed beside us.

Behind us, the smoke was gone. Ahead, the forest found a rhythm. Not a song yet, but trying. Our steps fell into it without effort.

The coin warmed in my hand, then settled back into my pocket. It didn't guide; it agreed. When the scroll shifted against my back, the coin answered with one faint beat. Then stillness.

"Through, not in," Rowan said softly.

"And the difference is the return," Sera answered.

We came to a stand of elder trees once burned. Blackened trunks rose into green crowns. New shoots pushed through old ash. Gillie touched one as we passed.

"Balanced," she said.

"Balance is slow," Nadya replied. "But it lasts."

The light ahead didn't brighten, but it cleared. The air felt clean—like water remembering how to move. The scroll rested in its bindings, no longer arguing. Ready.

For a time, no one spoke. The woods filled the quiet. Insects worked under bark. Water moved against stone.

At a bend, the path split around a massive tree, its heart long burned out. The outer trunk lived on, thick and sound. We passed through the hollow one by one. Gillie paused, hand on the wood. Eliah followed and let two tears fall. The tree accepted them.

Beyond, the air cooled—not for comfort, but clarity. It stripped pretense and asked for stillness. Cassian answered it first, squaring his shoulders, giving a single nod.

Miriam lifted the edge of her charred cloth. A thread of ash drifted free. She watched it settle, then pressed her fingers to her chest.

Tomas crouched by a thin stream, turning the coin once before pocketing it. "Still counts," he murmured. "Still answers."

The air shifted again—steady, exact. Not mercy. Readiness.

Sera spoke at last, quiet but sure. "We'll see him again."

"Maybe not as we expect," Rowan said.

"Maybe not as he expects," Nadya added.

The trail rose. The forest opened. Light came through more evenly now. The breeze smelled of pine and dry grass.

At the ridge, the land spread out—field and hill, touched by late sun. Not promise. Distance. And distance was enough.

Gillie looked back, counting without counting. Her hand rested on the scroll. "We keep walking," she said. "We don't mistake fear for mercy."

Eliah asked, "And if the road asks for more than we have?"

"Then we lend it grief," Miriam said. "Grief can be spent without turning false."

Rowan smiled, crooked. “And we don’t waste what children saved for us just to sound brave.”

Gillie nodded once. “That too.”

We started down the slope. The trees didn’t follow. They waited.

The scroll stayed quiet—not sleeping, listening. When the weight shifted against my back, the coin answered once. Then stillness. The path ahead drew itself together—narrow, clear.

Wind crossed the hill and left our names alone. We stepped into it as we were.

Night came without spectacle. No fire. The earth was warm enough. The scroll lay between us, its bindings rising and falling like breath. I turned the coin once. It didn’t point. It agreed.

Gillie rested her hand on the satchel strap. In the hush, Sera tried a single note. It held.

“The dark isn’t empty,” Gillie said.

“No,” I answered. “It’s waiting.”

We let it wait.

And we listened back.

The Weight of the Scroll

Dusk gathered not as shadow but as breath. The air thickened, soft with water and fading gold. Ahead, the sound of a stream reached us before we saw it—thin, quick, certain. After hours of wind and whispering branches, its voice startled us. The water ran clear through roots and fern, swift as if it still remembered where it was meant to go.

Once, rivers here had carried rot, black and sluggish, the Withering leaking through their beds. This one ran clean—but not innocent. It bore the memory of what had poisoned it, like a scar that had learned not to close.

Clean didn't mean safe. As the light fell, the surface turned from silver to iron. A ripple of dread moved through me, uninvited, like muscle remembering an old wound before the mind caught up. I thought of the swamp—the stillness before the dark began to move—and the smell of smoke that never quite leaves. Sometimes memory walks ahead of you.

The stream neither rushed nor pleaded. It listened. Stones beneath the surface were pale and smooth, shaped by patience. Moss clung to the banks, thick and wet. The quiet wasn't empty. It was attentive.

Gillie set her pack beneath a broad tree whose roots flared like open hands. She dipped her fingers into the water. Droplets clung briefly to her lashes before falling back, as if choosing to return. She shivered. Cold, or something deeper—I couldn't tell.

I pressed my palm to the moss. The scroll rested along my spine—no pain, only awareness. The coin in my pocket pulsed once, warm and steady, answering the current. The stream seemed to notice, altering its voice by a fraction.

"It's quiet," Gillie said.

"Too quiet?"

She shook her head. "Careful. Like the water doesn't want to speak wrong in front of what listens."

We stayed until the sky deepened to ash and indigo. Then we made camp beneath the roots. The hollow felt shaped for us—wood arching overhead like ribs. The air carried a faint metallic taste, the kind that lingers after lightning—like rain striking iron and not yet deciding whether to cleanse or scar. Our fire was small, its crackle apologetic, as though flame itself knew it was a guest.

It allowed it. In the swamp, silence had meant danger. Here, it felt like permission. Rest wasn't retreat—it was the mercy required to stand again.

The Uneasy Calm

Gillie lit the fire herself. The first spark flared like a sigh. The flame caught, small but watchful. Its light ran across the scroll's clasp, drawing out a faint gleam.

Most slept soon after. Those who stayed awake did so quietly. Nadya watched the water, prayer-cord looped around her hand. Rowan traced circles in the dirt but left them unfinished. Cassian stood at the edge of the light, testing his stillness.

Gillie moved closer to the scroll. She knelt and set her fingertips against the bindings—not to test, but to apologize.

Then she opened it.

The clasp released with a sound so small it might have been breath. She lifted one corner of the parchment.

The air froze.

Even the stream hesitated. The flame narrowed toward her hand.

The page wasn't bright—it lived. Light passed through it the way heat moves through stone, slow and deliberate.

"It's heavier today," Gillie whispered. Her hands trembled—not with fear, but obedience. She lowered the page and closed the clasp. The motion cost her a breath.

"I know," I said. "It's waiting to be answered."

The silence that followed wasn't absence. Bark creaked softly. The fire snapped once, then stilled.

"I used to think it was just record," she said. "Holy, but finished."

"It remembers," I said. "And it still has will."

"Then it can grieve."

"Yes. And it can hope."

From her bedroll, Miriam murmured through the charred cloth at her chest, "Fire still speaks when ash pretends to sleep."

The scroll pulsed faintly in reply. The coin warmed at the same moment.

We sat shoulder to shoulder. The fire burned low. The scroll rested—not bright, not dark—aware. The stars arrived slowly. Somewhere, a night bird missed its note and tried again.

Gillie traced the bindings. "It feels like restraint," she said. "Like a voice holding its breath."

"Restraint isn't absence," I said. "Sometimes it's trust."

"The scroll?"

"It never stops watching. It knew Joshua. It knows what followed."

Her face tightened. "Then it must hate what it sees."

"It can't," I said. "It was made with breath, not vengeance. That breath hasn't left it."

She nodded. "Then it obeys."

"It obeys," I said, "and it waits to finish what it was sent to finish."

"Then why the ache?"

"Because it still believes in him," I said quietly. "It mourns. It wants to be carried where it belongs."

Gillie stared into the flame. "Hope that outlives failure doesn't ease pain."

"No," I said. "It deepens it. But that's the kind that heals."

If Joshua ever rose again, it wouldn't be by will or name. It would be because the Word remembered him—the same Word that remembered us.

A wind passed through camp. Not warm, not cold—present. The moss lifted and settled again.

Gillie rebound the scroll, every fold exact. The clasp closed like a promise meant to reopen. Beneath her hand, the parchment stirred—not command, not warning.

From the stream, Nadya spoke without turning. "It asks who carries who."

Gillie leaned back against the roots. "I don't think it's warning us," she said. "I think it's asking if we're sure."

"Sure of what?"

"Of carrying him too."

No one answered. The fire burned to a low, steady core. Beneath it all, the air hummed faintly—the same resonance that lives beneath every bell.

I didn't sleep. Not from fear—because she was right. The scroll wouldn't speak of itself. It would speak of him. Of Joshua. And of whether we had the strength to bear what he left behind.

The coin in my pocket pulsed once, then cooled. One slow beat—then stillness. Not urging.

Across the stream, the water's song shifted. It carried the rhythm of something larger, like breath drawn through hollow stone. For a moment, the stars above flickered in time. I thought of Cephas's words: Faith without weight is wind. The scroll pressed gently against my back, as if agreeing.

Gillie lay still beside the fire, eyes open, catching its dim glow. I could tell she wasn't asleep. None of us truly were. The others stirred now and then—Rowan muttering fragments of dreams; Cassian rising once before settling again, his bell silent; Miriam clutching her cloth until ash dusted her fingers. We weren't listening to the forest. We were listening for what lingered behind it.

At some hour between night and dawn, the flame fell to ember. The stream spoke louder.

I rose and went to its edge.

Moonlight bent through the current, breaking into ribbons of light. Beneath the surface, stones bore faint grooves—not writing, but marks left by weight. One gleamed briefly, shaped like a broken circle. A bell's shadow.

I touched it. Cold, but not dead. The scroll shifted across my shoulders. The coin answered—two beats this time, then stillness again.

Behind me, Gillie spoke softly. "It listens to where we stand."

"So do I," I said.

We stood together, the stream between us like a boundary that refused to divide. Dawn gathered behind the trees, pale and patient. When the first light touched the water, it scattered instead of reflecting, as if the world didn't yet trust its own image.

Gillie crouched and pressed her palm to the current. "It remembers him," she said.

"Then remembering may be the road," I answered. "Not what we leave behind, but what still knows how to speak his name."

She looked up. "And if that's true?"

"Then we're already on it."

We stayed until the light thickened enough to show our breath. The others began to wake. Cassian smothered the last ash with moss. Miriam whispered a brief prayer—something about flame learning to forgive its smoke. Rowan traced the stream's surface as if writing on air. Nadya wound her cord tight again.

When the scroll was lifted, the air shifted, as though the trees themselves inhaled. The weight wasn't heavier. It was awake.

Gillie shouldered it, eyes closed for a moment, brow resting against the strap. Then she said, "North."

No one questioned her. The direction felt given, not chosen. The road ahead leaned, like something long prepared finally being lifted.

We crossed the stream one by one. The water reached our ankles, then our knees, cold enough to remind us we were still flesh. Each step stirred silt that drifted downstream like loosened memory. When I crossed last, the coin warmed again—three pulses, then silence.

I looked back once. The current was already erasing our passage.

Even healed ground remembers iron.

Gillie's Unease

"The light came through," Gillie said finally, her voice low, more thought than speech. "But it didn't end the war. It only moved it."

She drew her cloak closer, as though trying to keep the words from escaping. "We thought the fire was finished—that when he fell, the shadows fell with him. But darkness doesn't die. It waits. It learns. It finds new silences to speak through. What we faced was only one form. It will return in another."

We stopped beneath a humming tree scarred long ago by flame. Its trunk was split wide, its roots spread like open hands bracing against remembered heat. Mist coiled around its base, and sap glistened along the seams. The moss there smelled faintly of iron, as though it fed on memory more than soil.

The sound it made was uneven—tones rising and breaking halfway, a rhythm that didn't quite trust itself. Between each note was a pause that felt longer than silence, and the mist gathered in those gaps like thought turning inward. It wasn't the tree that was faltering. The wound ran deeper. I felt it through the soles of my boots—the Vein beneath us cracked, trembling. The tree only sang what the ground remembered: a broken rhythm. Every note cost it something.

The pilgrims who had followed from afar—the ones with ash on their wrists and bits of bell-metal hanging from cords—began to drift back. No one told them to leave. Some roads release what they were never meant to keep.

Gillie sat in the crook of a root, knees drawn close, her cloak wrapped tight. I stayed near. The scroll lay against my back, not heavy but aware. Its stillness felt like concentration. The air carried a taste of metal, steady and submerged, like iron under water. Moss clung to her sleeve as though it wished to hold her there. Small sounds moved in the brush, but nothing crossed the ring of roots. Even the air felt divided—warm where I sat, cool where she lay—as if the tree remembered two lives and could not decide which to keep.

Her breathing slowed. Sleep took her the way frost takes glass—slow, deliberate, uninvited but certain. Her fingers twitched. Her lips moved once, shaping a name too faint to catch. I thought it might have been Joshua—or something older, buried in the cadence of prayer.

Then her face tightened. Her hands clenched, unclenched. Her chest stopped rising for a long, thin moment. The mist around her deepened, faintly pulsing with her breath. Sap brightened along the trunk. The hum slipped into three notes—one silver, restless and sharp; one gold, full and trembling; one iron, deep and broken. They wove together, not as music, but as meaning waiting to be understood.

Gillie stirred, breath caught in her throat, eyes fluttering beneath their lids. She turned as though listening to a voice just beyond reach, and then—without sound—her mouth opened in a silent cry. Her head tilted back; the tones fractured. The tree answered once with a single, strained hum that climbed and broke like a sob. The air folded around her, holding its breath. Then she inhaled sharply, eyes flying open, hands gripping the root beside her.

"Gillie," I said, reaching toward her. "You're all right."

She blinked, orienting herself, the dream still clinging to her voice. "It wasn't just a dream," she whispered. Her hand went to the scroll, tracing its edge, fingertips trembling but deliberate. "It felt like it knew I was there—like it wanted me to see."

"What did you see?" I asked.

Her voice came haltingly, searching for language that didn't exist yet. "I was standing in a place that wasn't ground—more like a memory pretending to be land. The air was cold in a way that didn't touch my skin but settled behind my ribs. Every step I took disappeared before I could hear it. The air didn't move unless I breathed. It was silver at first, then gray, and every color kept turning in on itself, like light folding into shadow."

She rubbed her palms together. "There was a figure across the space. I tried to walk toward him, but every step pushed him farther away. The distance grew, even when I ran. The world stretched between us, pulling apart. I tried to call out, but—" She paused, swallowed. "My mouth wouldn't open. My jaw moved, but the sound stayed locked inside, like my throat had forgotten words. I could feel them building under my tongue—burning—but nothing came out. My teeth ached from holding what wouldn't break loose."

Her eyes unfocused, chasing the vision. "He was wrapped in flame, but it wasn't burning him. It folded inward, like breath that couldn't leave. The fire was his shape, not his punishment. It smelled like rain striking iron—clean and scorched at once. And behind him…" She looked toward the scroll. "…it was there. Floating. Not on fire, but alive. Its pages were open, and light hung above them in thin bands, like cords of gold trying to hold it together. The light kept pulsing—strong, then weak—like a heart that didn't want to stop."

She breathed out slowly. "I knew it was Joshua. Not because of his face—I couldn't see that—but because the air remembered him. The silence around him felt reverent—and wounded. I wanted to reach him. I tried again. I felt my ribs strain, but no sound came. My hand lifted, and the world tilted toward me, but I couldn't close the distance. The harder I tried to speak, the farther he drifted back. The flame around him folded tighter, and I felt it closing me out."

The night had gone utterly still around us. Even the tree's hum was listening.

Gillie continued, her voice low but steady now. "The scroll followed him—not out of loyalty, but pity. It wasn't chasing. It was waiting. And then the sound came."

"Sound?" I asked.

"Three notes," she said. "One sharp and silver, one gold and heavy, one iron and broken."

Her fingers pressed harder into the scroll's binding. "I woke just after that. It felt like being pushed out of a river."

I waited until her breathing steadied. "And what do you think it meant?"

She looked at the ground for a long moment. "I think the scroll's remembering—not what's been, but what hasn't yet. What it will lose if no one carries it forward."

"You saw him," I said quietly.

She nodded. "He didn't speak, but I knew what the silence meant. It wasn't anger. It was waiting to be forgiven."

Her voice softened. "It felt like the dream was using the scroll—or maybe the scroll was using me. I can't tell the difference anymore."

Nearby, Rowan murmured backward numbers in his sleep. Miriam turned and pressed the cloth tighter to her chest. Even asleep, they carried the echo of what had entered the air.

Gillie's eyes lifted toward the stars. "When the light broke through, I thought it was over," she said.

"It only moved," I answered.

She nodded. "They're gathering again—not to reclaim what they lost, but to stop us from carrying it forward. To keep us from finding whoever comes next."

The tree gave a low tone, clearer than before.

"What if the scroll isn't just a record?" she asked.

"It isn't," I said. "It's will. And it isn't finished."

"Then it needs more than memory," she said. "It needs messengers."

She looked back to me. "The dream showed a man who once carried the light but no longer spoke its name. The scroll followed him because it still believes he might choose again."

"And the question?" I asked.

Her voice fell to a whisper. "Whether we'll carry the light he left—or follow him into whatever he's become."

The tree answered with a clean note. Gillie leaned back, eyes tracing the thin light between branches. "We aren't just walking through what was," she said. "We're shaping what's next."

The scroll rested between us, not as relic or burden, but as vow. And in the Withering, vows don't fade. They travel.

The air tightened—the stillness before weather. The scroll didn't pulse; it settled, sure of its place.

The war hadn't ended. It had shifted.

We were no longer only witnesses.

We had become part of the answer.

And somewhere beyond the Veil, something dark began to count.

Ash and Iron, Bread and Light

The First Followers

Morning found us on the move, the echoes of Gillie's dream still clinging to the air like something half-remembered. The world hadn't answered yet what to do with what she'd seen.

The stream fell behind us until its talk was only damp on our boots. A thin path left the bank and climbed through brush. It ran north, narrow as a scar—not a road made by feet so much as a mark pressed into the earth. Dawn carried the stillness forward, the air thin and watchful, as though it had forgotten how to rest.

Dust lifted with each step. The wind carried warm smells—turned soil, hearth smoke, fresh bread—but under it lay a metallic edge, like rain on iron. Even before we saw the houses, the air felt rehearsed, as if the land had practiced a welcome we hadn't asked for.

Gillie walked a little ahead, the scroll tight across her back. It didn't thrum or shift. It simply held itself, tense as a breath not yet released. It hadn't rested, only quieted—listening harder than before.

Sera hummed under her breath. Rowan muttered a half-proverb backward and let it die. Tomas kept his hands in small fists and moved his lips without sound. The others came on in the kind of quiet that gathers weight as it goes. Gillie didn't speak of the dream. She didn't need to. It walked behind her, setting the pace as surely as the road.

Then the village showed itself.

Two roads crossed in a wide meadow. Whitewashed cottages leaned close. Gardens kept neat rows of herbs and flowers. Chickens scattered across clean yards. Smoke climbed from chimneys with the good smell of oak. A stone well stood bright at the center, rope and pulley polished by many hands.

Children played. Mothers leaned from windows. Men came in from the fields with easy shoulders.

It looked untouched, as if grief had walked past and chosen not to enter.

But the light was wrong.

It lingered too long on eaves, catching corners it shouldn't reach. Shadows arrived late, as if the sun had to tell them twice where to fall. Laughter rang like bells struck with a glove—pleasant, empty at the center. The air was still and careful. It carried voices too far, like someone wanted us to hear before we arrived.

Even the chickens kept their distance from the altar stones.

Gillie touched the binding on the scroll. "They're waiting," she said.

She didn't say what.

The answer came sooner than we expected. A woman hurried toward us, arms full of flowers. She pressed them into Miriam's hands. "He promised beauty would return," she whispered, voice trembling like she was finishing a prayer, not offering a gift. Miriam's jaw set hard, as if the petals stung.

A man followed with a round loaf. "Bread," he said to Gillie, "from Joshua's blessing." His eyes shone—devotion aimed at a name. Gillie bowed her head, then set the bread on a low wall once he turned. Her fingers stayed on the crust a heartbeat longer—not hunger.

Unease.

As we stepped into the square, the shape of things came clear. This wasn't welcome. It was rite. A low altar stood at the center, stones stacked and scrubbed. One word carved deep across the face, gouged and recut until the rock could hold nothing else: **Joshua.**

Children circled it, humming. At first it sounded like a game. Then the notes lined up around syllables. The name sat inside their tune.

Joshu-a. Joshu-a. Joshu-a.

Not play. A litany with little voices.

Gillie stopped. Her lips parted and closed. Her hand found the knife hilt—not to draw it. To steady herself.

An elder stepped forward. Clean robe. Trimmed beard. Eyes polished like river stones. His smile was warm in the way of a man who is certain.

"You've come," he said. His gaze slid past us to the scroll. "The shadows are gone. Light has returned. We walk in Joshua's name."

"And the Word?" I asked.

"The Word walked with him," he said, widening his hands as if blessing us. "Now we walk in him. His silence was a gift. His fall, a sacrifice. The Veins took his toll. In his wound the world was healed. So we speak his name, because his name reminds the world how to breathe."

People straightened. A murmur rose—not scattered, but trained. "His silence was gift. His fall was sacrifice. His name is life." The refrain filled the square until stone and throat seemed to chant together. A woman pressed her child's brow to the carved letters and breathed "Joshua" against his skin. Another man bent and set his forehead on the altar as if waiting for a pulse to meet his. The creed wasn't faith. It was memory spoken until it lived in the bone.

The scroll didn't flare or cry out. It only grew tight against my back, a weight that ached behind the ribs. Something that had once sung was being sung over. Gillie's jaw set. She glanced at me with the question she wouldn't voice: *Do they not know? Or have they chosen not to?*

The children kept circling, their hum like thread, binding the name to the stone. Their faces were open. The rhythm was not. We did not turn away. Leaving then would have meant leaving the children in that loop, unchallenged. So we stayed.

Evening came slowly, the light lowering itself into the square until candles began to replace it. Flames shivered in windows and along the paths, and the people moved among them as if rehearsing joy. Food appeared—fruit, grain, stew, bread torn and handed to us. They pressed bowls into our hands like that, too, was part of what must be done.

Then they sang.

Not to Breath. Not to Flame. Not to the Word—only **Joshua.**

They sang his fall as victory, his silence as salvation, his burden as a crown. His name threaded every verse—not servant, not witness, but light itself. The harmony was strong and empty all at once, like bells struck without wind in them.

The Seven shifted. Sera's hum faltered and fell quiet. Rowan whispered words out of order, tugging at the edges of the villagers' song as if he could loosen it with misalignment. Tomas pressed his fists to his chest and mouthed, *That's not his name.* Miriam crushed flower stems in her palm, their scent sharp and bruised, tiny sparks of heat flickering against her wrist. Cassian crossed his arms and fixed his gaze on the scroll, daring it to remain still beneath a pressure that had begun to take an edge.

"This isn't worship," Gillie whispered. "It's mimicry in a bright coat."

The scroll pulsed once at her words, a brief tremor along my spine. It stung—not pain, but a tight acknowledgment of something wrong.

Gillie leaned close, her voice barely air. "This is how darkness survives," she whispered. "But what's done in the dark… always comes to light."

When the last verse drained out of the villagers, the silence that followed wasn't reverence. It sagged across the square, thin and empty, like voices had been poured into a vessel that couldn't hold anything sacred. For a moment, nothing moved. Then the ground shifted beneath us.

It started faintly—a soft click under the altar, the gentle settling of stone, a tremor slipping through the seams between paving stones. The air leaned downward as if listening. The sound deepened, not shaped by any human throat but rising slowly through the earth itself, patient and steady. It felt like a breath that had been trapped too long finally exhaling.

The stones carried it upward, a low ache threading through the soles of my boots. The sound wasn't loud. It didn't need to be. It was the kind of grief that has learned how to endure when no one is willing to hear it.

Miriam stopped crushing the petals. Rowan's whisper died halfway through a syllable. Tomas's mouth opened as though to speak, but no words came. The weight of that quiet lament pressed itself through marrow, a sorrow older than any voice in the square.

A boy in the children's circle paused mid-step. He tilted his head, brow furrowing at the tremor beneath his feet. Before he could ask anything, his mother touched his shoulder, turning him back toward the altar with a practiced, gentle insistence. The children resumed their humming, the chant wrapping back around the carved name as if nothing beneath the stone had stirred at all.

Gillie's breath caught beside me. "They don't hear it," she whispered.

"No," I said. "But the scroll does." The weight across my back tightened—not violently, not warning, but with the quiet recognition of a wound reopened. A single thought surfaced before I could stop it, quiet and unbidden: the Hollowing. The ground answered with another slow, aching pulse, as if acknowledging the name.

Before I could speak it aloud, a voice near my shoulder caught the word on its breath. Rowan—still pale, still listening to the stones—murmured, almost to himself, "The Hollowing…" His eyes met mine, wide and unsteady, and I gave the slightest nod. The earth had taught him the name the same moment it taught me.

The lament didn't challenge the villagers' chant, and it didn't fade as the people drifted back toward their doors. It simply stayed—quiet, persistent, weeping through stone and root. It was grief born from what had been forgotten, a sorrow the land had held alone for far too long. One by one, the candles in the windows guttered, their light thinning as if even flame didn't wish to linger in the square.

None of us spoke after that. The Seven kept to the edges of the dark, listening with the kind of stillness you only see when something sacred or dangerous has settled over a place. Gillie stood with her hand on the scroll, her fingers unmoving. Sera drew her cloak tight. Rowan turned his ear toward the stones more than once, as if the lament might shift into words. Even Cassian—unshakable Cassian—watched the altar with a heaviness that didn't belong to him.

The night wore on without changing. The weeping beneath the square remained steady, unhurried, the kind of sorrow that had waited years to surface and refused to slip back into silence now that it had been heard. The villagers didn't notice. Their chants rose and fell in practiced waves, thinning only when exhaustion pressed too heavily on their throats. Candles guttered, flames bending low, as though even fire wished it could slip away from what it illuminated.

We stayed at the edge of the square, the Seven gathered close, listening to a lament that did not belong to any living mouth. No one spoke. The scroll lay heavy against my back—listening, bearing, remembering. The cold found us, creeping through cloaks and breath. The sky began its slow graying, stars dimming to pale scratches above the roofs.

When the villagers finally drifted toward their homes, they did so with a quiet, satisfied certainty. Their rite had not ended; it had simply shifted. Doors shut softly. Windows dimmed. But none of them looked at us as they passed. Whatever they believed Joshua had done, they believed it had been done without us.

Only then did we move—but not to leave.

A woman stepped from the last lit doorway and held up a hand, palm marked with ash. "Come," she said softly, almost reverently. "The remembering continues."

We followed because to remain in the square alone would have felt like standing in a story that had closed its page. The path she led us toward bent away from the altar and into the far edge of the village, where a ruined wall rose like a broken spine against the first thin breath of dawn.

Ashen Devotion

The villagers moved ahead without beckoning, their silence shaped by ritual more than speech. Reverence had become reflex here—something worn smooth in the bones. Even the children had stopped humming, their small mouths set as if waiting for a cue none of us could hear.

The clearing lay just beyond the last row of homes. Ash pressed into the soil so deeply it no longer stained hands or hems; it rose only in thin gray sighs with each step, carrying a scent not of fresh burn but of something older, something that had burned long ago and refused to leave the memory of it behind.

A woman knelt in the center and touched ash to her brow. Others followed—brow, lips, chest—each gesture identical, practiced, unhesitating. When they finished, they turned toward us and waited. Gillie did not answer their waiting. Her gaze flicked to the scroll across my back; her jaw tightened. She knelt, pressed her palm to the ground, and rose with her hand unmarked. No ash. No vow. No surrender.

A few of them flinched as if the refusal had made the air colder.

The elder from the square stepped forward as though he had been waiting for that exact refusal. His voice carried the weight of countless repetitions. "Ash remembers. Ash redeems. What was burned was offered. What was consumed returns as life. Joshua bore the fire—so we carry what it left behind."

The village answered as one: "We bear his ash. We carry his fire. We walk in his name." Their hands moved in perfect rhythm—forehead, mouth, heart. Even the children mirrored the movement, their solemn faces tracing devotion learned long before understanding.

Sera's hum broke, caught between awe and dread. Rowan muttered a proverb backward—"Ash washes only the hand that scatters it"—and let it die. Tomas watched the elder with the guarded stare of a child who knows something essential is being twisted.

"The Veins weep no longer," the elder continued. "The toll was paid. Silence is broken. Joshua fell, and in falling he lifted us. His ash is seed; his name our harvest."

A boy smeared ash across his cheeks and looked to his mother. She nodded, whispering the name again, and again.

The scroll pressed flat and heavy against my back. Not glowing. Not warming. Grieving.

"This isn't devotion," Gillie whispered. "It's possession."

Ash sifted from the elder's raised hands, drifting like winter that refused to melt. His gaze settled on me. "Will you take the mark? Will you remember the fire that saved you?"

I did not answer.

Gillie stepped forward and laid her fingers on the scroll's clasp. "The fire did not save," she said, voice steady and soft. "The Word carried us through."

A ripple went through the clearing—sharp breaths, a hiss, a shuffle of feet. The elder's smile thinned into something shaped more by certainty than grace. "The Word spoke through him. Without him, there is no light."

Gillie didn't meet his argument. She held his gaze with silence sharp enough to cut.

That night, fires rose around the square—not for warmth or cooking, but for feeding something unseen. The villagers circled them and sang Joshua's name until the syllables lost edges and blurred into a rhythm that sounded more like marching than worship. Their faces glowed in the shifting light, struck with a kind of practiced ecstasy.

We stood apart. Miriam held her charred scrap of cloth as if waiting for the right flame to leap from it and straighten the world. Cassian folded his arms and kept them folded. Sera covered her ears, though no one else seemed to think the sound could wound. Rowan laughed once—too sharp, too hollow—then caught the sound in his hands and whispered a backward proverb into them, as if he could smother the echo. Tomas sat cross-legged, rocking slightly, whispering, "That isn't his name," over and over.

The scroll lay hot against my spine—heat without fire, memory without speech.

"If this spreads," Gillie said, voice thin beneath the chant, "they won't need the Word. They'll believe the fire is enough."

"Or the ash," I said.

She turned her face toward the flames. Shadows pooled under her eyes. "And when ash becomes god," she asked, "who will speak for the living?"

Near midnight, the chant frayed at the edges. Voices cracked. Throats rasped. Still the marks were renewed—forehead, mouth, heart—as if sleep might wash them away. Then another sound rose, thin as a thread under the fires.

Not wind. Not song.

Weeping.

It seeped up from beneath the square—muffled, ancient—like sorrow carved into the stone. No words. Only the ache of a wound that doesn't forget what happened above it. The villagers only sang louder, drowning the weeping with devotion.

We heard.

The ground trembled—small, steady—as if roots strained against masonry. Ash whispered across the paving like breath from hidden lungs. Hairline cracks murmured to each other. The air tasted of buried soil and old heat. The land grieved out loud beneath a liturgy that denied it.

Miriam's tears cut clean paths through the gray on her face. Rowan's mouth shaped words but made no sound. Tomas clutched his chest. "Stop," he whispered. "Please stop." Sera folded to her knees, hands clamped over her ears though the villagers' chants had never touched her.

"The ground remembers," Gillie said softly. Her eyes shone—not with fear, but with a knowing older than speech.

The scroll answered with a faint pulse. Not comfort. Not warning. Recognition.

We didn't explain it. We bore it.

By dawn, the fires had collapsed into heaps of ash. The villagers woke hoarse but satisfied, their hands blackened to the wrist. Morning brought its own false certainty, and they wore it like a badge. They did not look for us. Their rite had closed its circle.

We left quietly. Smoke thinned into a pale sky. The square smoldered. The altar sat cold and sure, the carved name unspent.

"They think they carry him forward," Gillie said, pulling her cloak tight.

"They carry ash," I answered.

The scroll rode heavier than before. Not waiting. Not warning. Mourning.

The road out bent toward the broken wall again. The earth beneath our steps held its low cry, patient and steady as breath through clenched teeth. None of us spoke—not because words failed, but because the Word we carried said nothing, and we would not lay speech like a lid on what the ground refused to hide.

To stay would have made our silence look like agreement.

To argue would have fed a fire that only consumes.

So we turned north—neither victors nor fugitives—bearing a grief that did not belong to us alone.

The land had kept the truth. The scroll kept its silence.

And we walked on.

The Scroll Remains

By the time the sun climbed past the low branches behind us, the village had become nothing more than a faint smudge in the southern distance. A thin column of smoke still drifted up from its fires, but the chant that had filled the night had finally fallen quiet. We had been walking for hours, and yet the air still carried a faint aftertaste of what had been spoken there—not the Word, not truth, but a name repeated until even silence took its shape.

The quiet that followed wasn't comforting. It sat low in the chest, the kind that lingers after leaving a place where something has gone wrong but no one inside seems willing to admit it. The scroll pressed steady against my back, the pressure less like weight and more like attention. It had absorbed what the villagers refused to hear, and now it sorted through the remnants in its own way.

Gillie walked a few paces ahead, her shoulders squared, one hand resting near the knife at her belt. She wasn't expecting danger, but something in her posture said she wasn't willing to assume it was gone either. The Seven followed in a loose string behind us.

Rowan broke the silence first. He kicked a stone down the path and muttered, "Ash that crowns is no crown. Ash that saves only saves when someone agrees to wear it." His riddles usually circled back on themselves. This one fell straight.

Miriam walked with her scrap of parchment pressed to her chest, her limp more pronounced today. She breathed in shallow pulls, as if the land itself had taken something from her. Eliah kept his palms open as he walked, as though trying to release grief back into the air. Nadya moved with quiet certainty, her steady gaze giving the rest of us something to anchor to. Cassian stayed near the rear, always watching the scroll as if daring anything unseen to try and take it.

We didn't talk much. What had happened in the village felt too heavy to break apart with conversation. The farther we walked, the clearer it became that each of us carried a different piece of what we'd seen, and those pieces didn't fit cleanly together.

Near midday we came over a low ridge. The path dipped into a shallow valley, the grass moving in long ribbons with the wind. At the center stood a stone altar—cracked, leaning, worn down by years of weather and hands. All around it were remnants half-swallowed by moss: a twist of iron, a charred beam, splinters of wood that looked like they had once held shape. A place touched by fire, but not claimed by it.

The wind crossed the valley and didn't quite finish its breath.

The valley held a different kind of quiet than the village—one you didn't have to perform for. It felt like a place where grief had been allowed to sit down.

"This isn't a destination," I said without planning to. "Just something the scroll insists we witness."

Gillie slowed beside me. "A place it remembers?"

The scroll shifted—not a pulse, not a warning, just a small incline against my spine that felt like acknowledgment.

We went down the ridge together. The air thickened as we descended, not with dread but with a kind of reverence that didn't need ceremony to prove itself. Even Rowan fell quiet. The grass brushed against our legs with a soft hiss, the sound of people lowering their voices out of respect.

Up close, the altar looked older than the village by decades, maybe centuries. Ash had settled into every crack in its surface—a gray so deep it looked part of the stone rather than something laid on it. Gillie crouched and sifted a small pinch between her fingers. It clung instead of smearing. When she lifted her hand, the ash drifted back down in a slow fall, like it had always belonged here.

"This isn't like the village," she said. "They wore ash like a badge. Here, ash is just… what's left."

Miriam's parchment trembled in her hands. "The fire still speaks," she whispered—one of the old lines, but softer now, as though she wasn't sure what answer she expected. A faint warmth pulsed beneath the surface of the stone, like an ember buried deep under years of cooling.

I placed my palm on the altar. The stone felt cold at first, then warm beneath—one slow beat, steady and patient. The scroll warmed in answer, a small pulse beneath the straps at my chest.

"Not every flame destroys," I said. "Some survive."

The scroll shifted again, pressing slightly forward—as if agreeing.

Gillie wiped the ash off her fingers, but the stain only set darker across her palms. She stared at the mark with a puzzled frown, like she wasn't sure whether it was choosing her or reminding her of something.

We stayed there longer than I intended. Pilgrims came in small numbers, one or two at a time—faces lined, hands empty or carrying small burdens. None of them chanted. None preached. They simply knelt, left what they had brought, and walked away.

A woman placed a piece of a bell on the altar and let her fingers linger before letting go. A man set down a coin and retreated as though the ground beneath him had shifted. A child folded a strip of cloth and smoothed it with three neat strokes. Others brought things that had clearly mattered: a cracked vessel bound with twine, a worn plow handle, a single feather black at the tip.

Gillie leaned toward me. "This isn't like the square," she said quietly. "These people aren't trying to lift anything up. They're just trying to remember."

The scroll answered with a low pulse, steady and attentive. It recognized this place, and the sorrow held there. With each offering, the weight on my back felt more certain—heavier, yes, but in a way that felt right, as though it were settling into place.

As the sun sank, the valley dimmed but didn't lose its clarity. The sounds grew softer—grass shifting, stone settling—but the place still held the kind of presence you didn't argue with. The scroll pulsed once, a brief hum under its bindings, then went quiet again.

"It's heavier now," Gillie said, touching the clasp.

"Because it recognizes what happened here," I answered. "What was written. What wasn't."

A shadow crossed her face—not fear exactly, but recognition. "Then it still carries him."

"Yes," I said. "And it carries us."

The valley darkened, but none of us felt rushed to leave. We slept near the stone. The earth was hard, but no one complained. Once in the night I woke to a faint hum from the altar—steady, rhythmic, almost like a heartbeat. The scroll pulsed once in answer before going still. I lay awake a long time wondering which had spoken first.

At dawn the valley shimmered with dew. Every offering caught the light—coin, cloth, feather, vessel, plow, bell fragment—as if refusing to disappear. The plow handle leaned slightly, ready for work. The feather quivered with a faint breeze. Even the coin seemed to hold a dim glow at its center.

"It remains," Gillie said quietly.

"Memory isn't weakness," I told her. "It's witness."

She nodded. "Then we keep moving. Grief stays here. We don't put it on our backs."

By the time we stepped onto the ridge again, the scroll felt different—still heavy, but carrying something more than sorrow. The ash didn't cling to us as we left. It stayed where it belonged, in a valley that had learned how to hold what others tried to forget.

We walked north, and the scroll settled into its familiar place.

Not only mourning.

Holding.

The road ahead felt open in a new way, not cleansed but clear.

The scroll remains.

A Voice in the Crowd

By late afternoon the valley was well behind us. The road widened onto a plain where several worn paths crossed. A small market sat at the center of the intersection, no bigger than a handful of stalls around a hard, packed square. Most of the awnings were patched with old sailcloth. The wind moved through the ropes until they gave off a low hum. The air held the smell of baked bread, onions, sweat, and warm metal.

Our boots scuffed across loose gravel, and the noise seemed louder than it had any right to be. Snatches of conversation reached us in pieces—prices called out, the thump of crates, the scrape of a cartwheel hitting a rut. Nothing hostile. Just a place that noticed strangers and decided to watch before deciding anything else.

One stall displayed a row of newly made bells. When the wind brushed them they gave off thin, fragile chimes, the kind that sounded like they wouldn't survive a real storm. The smith behind the stall kept adjusting the hooks as if the bells needed convincing just to stay where they were.

We slowed without talking about it. The scroll stayed firm against my back—quiet, neither tightening nor relaxing. Gillie touched the clasp once, a small check, then let her hand fall. The Seven closed in around us out of habit: Miriam counting her breaths, Cassian scanning the crowd, Sera humming under her breath, Rowan too quiet in the way that meant his head was busy, Tomas taking everything in with wide, unsettled eyes.

The ground beneath the stalls had been stamped flat by years of feet, but dust still rose at each step. A few people wore faint gray smudges on their brows or along their sleeves—old ash, not fresh. I'd seen marks like that in other places, usually from people who couldn't quite explain why they touched ash before they prayed. Just that "it's what we do" and "we've done it since the bell fell," as if that explained anything.

Children darted between crates and barrels. They paused when they saw the scroll, then pretended they hadn't paused at all. Two older men sat on an overturned trough in the shade, watching us with the flat, measuring look of people who have lived long enough to know the difference between pilgrims and trouble and aren't sure which we were yet.

A group had gathered near the center of the square. Not festival-thick—just people standing close because they expected something. Some held loaves of bread, coils of rope, jars of oil. Many held nothing. All eyes were fixed on the old stone well. Someone had dragged a trader's cart beside it and turned it into a platform.

A man stood on top of the cart. His sash had once been white; now it had settled into a permanent gray. A small shard of bell metal hung from a cord around his wrist. He lifted it slightly when he spoke, like he'd practiced the motion in front of a wall until it felt right.

"Light has returned," he called out, voice smooth and used to being heard. "The toll was obedience. The name is refuge."

At his feet sat a basket of glass vials. Each one held a little oil and a pinch of ash settled on the bottom.

"Keepings," he said. "For your doors, your fields, your children. Ash to remember. Oil to bless. A gift for any who give toward the altar on the hill."

Another breeze slid across the square. It brought more than smell. You could feel a quiet tension in how people shifted their weight, in how fingers tightened around what they held. Some leaned forward a little, wanting to believe this would make them safer. Others stood back, as if waiting to see who moved first.

A woman near us brushed her hair forward, trying to cover a forehead that didn't bear an ash mark yet. "We missed the dawn blessing," she murmured.

Sera's hum wobbled off-key. Rowan muttered something about reeds and wind. No one asked him to repeat it.

Gillie gave a small nod. "Stay close," she said. Not scared. Just braced.

The man on the cart lifted the bell shard again. It tapped against the cord with a dull click instead of a clear ring. His mouth tightened for a heartbeat before he smoothed it over.

He began in a rhythm that sounded older than he was, older than this square.

"Ash remembers," he said. "Ash keeps. When the bell fell, ash marked the faithful. When the bell cracked, ash marked the doors. When the world shook, ash stayed."

A few people near the front mouthed the words with him. This wasn't new to them. This was something they'd been taught long before Joshua's name reached their ears.

Then the seller shifted the words.

"Now ash remembers him," he said, voice rising. "Joshua bore the fire. Joshua stood in the toll. Joshua's name is our refuge."

The scroll pulsed once against my back. Not bright, not hot. Just a firm tightening, the way a body flinches at an old bruise being pressed. I felt—not in words, but close enough to them—this has happened before.

The crowd didn't hear that. They heard only the man.

"Joshua," he said again, tasting the name like it strengthened his own. "His silence was obedience. His fall was our lifting. His name keeps what the bell broke."

It was close enough to the truth to sound right. Close enough to break things if it settled in.

The man nudged the basket of vials with his boot. "Take and mark," he said. "We've done this since the bell fell. We know how to be kept."

He spoke as if the first bell and this broken shard were the same story—and Joshua fit wherever the story needed a name.

The scroll settled heavier. Gillie's jaw worked. She'd watched this happen once already, in a different swamp, with a different crowd. Back when Joshua was still alive and they'd nearly turned his voice into an altar.

The man on the cart drew breath to speak again.

"Joshua—"

The word never finished.

"Don't," a child said.

It wasn't loud. It didn't need to be. The square went still.

Heads turned. A boy stood at the edge of the crowd. Barefoot. Nine, maybe. Dirt on his knees from kneeling near stone. His hands hung open—damp, as if he'd just touched the well.

The seller tried an easy smile. "Careful, child. We're speaking hope today."

"Then use its name," the boy said.

There was no drama in his voice. Just the tone of someone who knows what he's saying and has finally decided to say it.

"What name is that?" the seller asked, turning to the crowd to draw them in. A few chuckles answered, quiet and uneasy.

The boy didn't smile. He looked over the faces, then toward the distant hill, then back to the well.

"Not his," he said. "Not again." He dipped his chin in the hill's direction. "You don't tie what you're doing to his name. You're doing it the way they did before, and it broke him once already."

The coin in my pocket warmed—one short pulse, then another. The timing was too clean to be accident.

Several people shifted. One woman hugged her loaf closer to her chest, as if uncertain whether it was still a blessing.

The seller spread his hands. "Names are how we hold truth," he said. "We've always named the one who keeps us. Since the bell fell, ash has marked the faithful. Now ash carries his story."

"Truth doesn't need to be held," the boy said. "It needs room to breathe."

Gillie's shoulders eased a fraction, like the boy had spoken something she'd been waiting to hear.

The seller picked up one of the vials and held it so the light caught the swirl of oil, the dark fleck of ash at the bottom. "Breath blesses," he said. "Ash keeps. A mark on the brow. A mark on the door. A simple vow. You know this. Your fathers knew this. Their fathers said the words when the first bell rang."

The boy shook his head. "Ash only remembers what fire did," he said. "It doesn't carry what light wants to do next. You don't bind breath to a man. That's how the first trouble started."

A low murmur moved through the crowd. Someone tightened their grip on a rope. Someone else traced a mark on their chest, then stopped halfway.

The seller's smile thinned. "Who sent you?" he asked. "Who taught you to talk like that?"

"No one sent me," the boy said. "The ground did the teaching."

He stepped forward. The people in front of him shifted aside as if the choice had been made before they realized they were moving. At the well he laid both palms on the stone lip and closed his eyes.

"Don't put ash in it," he said quietly. "Please."

A woman snorted. "It's a pinch. We've done it since the bell fell."

"Since the bell was taken," someone muttered, then stared down at their hands like they'd said too much.

The boy opened his eyes. He didn't look like a prophet—just tired in the way people get when they've watched others walk toward a cliff they already fell from.

"Watch the water," he said. "If you pour ash into it and bless his name over it, it'll start to taste like iron. Like nail. You'll drink, and it'll feel wrong in your mouth, but you'll tell yourselves it's strength."

He swallowed, like he hated knowing it.

A few heads turned toward the well.

"Watch noon," he added. "The light will pause. Shadows won't know where to stand."

"Enough," the seller snapped.

"Watch the bread," the boy said, not raising his voice. "It'll crumble. You'll eat and still feel empty." Hands tightened on loaves. One man shifted his grip as if checking the firmness.

"And watch the small," he finished. "We'll feel it first. We always do."

That last sentence landed heavier than anything else he'd said.

The seller's patience snapped. "Hold him."

Two men in light cloaks pushed through the crowd, ash smeared up their sleeves. Cassian shifted his weight, ready to move. Gillie lifted her hand a little. He stopped, like someone had placed a palm on his chest.

"Let him go," she said, level and calm. "You don't need a mark on him to know he spoke the truth."

One man slowed. The other reached. The boy stepped aside and the hand closed on air. The crowd made a small sound—surprise more than approval.

Tomas walked forward until he stood beside the boy. He didn't touch him or speak. He just stayed.

The seller swung the bell shard in frustration. It cut the air with a thin metallic crack, too slight to be a real toll. The coin in my pocket warmed against my thigh, remembering a different bell, a different day, when a man had stood in the wrong center of the story.

At the well, a woman hauled up a bucket. The rope creaked. The water shone clear. She dipped her fingers, tasted, frowned, tasted again.

"It's iron," she said. "Like sucking on a nail."

"Old pipes," the seller said quickly. "Heat. That's all."

A mason shook his head. "The well's cut stone." He didn't raise his voice. He didn't need to.

The boy looked at the seller one last time.

"If the bell tolled once," he said, "why are you trying to ring someone's name with the pieces?"

No one answered.

He walked east, out of the square. No flourish. No final look back. We didn't follow. Chasing him would have turned him into a sign we could use, and we'd already seen how that story ended for Joshua.

The seller called after us as we moved toward the edge of the market—an offer for the road, a blessing for the vow. His voice sounded thinner now. A few people still listened. Others watched the well.

At the last stall an older woman caught Gillie's sleeve. Ash coated her palms; her eyes were red.

"If the water really changes," she asked, "does that mean we've broken something? Will the bread change too?"

Gillie didn't reach for a riddle.

"If it does," she said, "it means you're tying the wrong name to the wrong thing. Stop doing that. Start asking the right One. You'll see what changes back."

The woman nodded and let go.

We stepped past the last stall. The wind shifted. Awnings hummed lower. The new bells chimed again—still thin, less sure. Some stalls closed early. People gathered in tighter circles, voices low, as if the boy's words had already crawled under their skin.

We took the northern road. None of us had to say it. The scroll settled that way, steady and firm, and we followed.

Rowan watched the sky. "Feels like noon's dragging its feet."

Halfway up the rise, the sunlight hesitated—just a breath—and the shadows blurred around our legs, as if they'd lost their line.

Tomas swallowed. "Is this the beginning of something?"

"Maybe," Gillie said. "Or maybe it's mercy giving people one more chance to listen."

We walked on. Behind us, the square broke into argument and uneasy quiet. Ahead, the land opened and waited.

The scroll rested against my back—silent, steady.

Not grieving.

Ready.

The Flicker and the Firebrand

The Ember Path

The scroll pushed us north before any of us were ready to move. It didn't jolt or flare; it just leaned—slow, deliberate—until staying put felt like holding our breath too long. So we followed. We always did. None of us pretended we understood its reasons anymore.

But the northern road didn't welcome us. It felt like a place trying to remember how to be a road and failing. Stones lay split and crooked, as if heat had once lifted sections of the path and then dropped them without care for where they landed. Dust rose with every step, fine enough to sting the throat, bitter as ash.

No one said much. After the market, silence felt safer than guessing out loud what any of it meant.

Gillie kept a few steps ahead, her stride even, her hand resting close to the scroll as if checking its weight without thinking. Every so often she glanced down the road—not searching, just making sure the next stretch was still holding together. Cassian walked a little to her right, eyes sweeping the ditches and the broken weeds. He didn't say a word, but the way his jaw worked told me he was preparing for anything he didn't want to see.

Sera tried to keep the quiet from sinking too deep. She hummed lightly, barely above the wind, as if matching her breath to something steadier than her nerves. Rowan walked with his gaze fixed on the stones, his lips moving the way they do when he's trying to turn a thought over without letting it escape too soon. Miriam held her charred scrap of parchment tight against her chest; her knuckles had gone pale, but she didn't loosen her grip.

Tomas hovered close—not pressed against any of us, just unwilling to let too much space open up. Eliah kept his palms half-open at his sides, the river ash still dark on his skin even after a dozen washings. Nadya stayed a little behind, her shoulders pulled in, steps quieter than usual.

None of it needed explaining. The road had a way of making everyone's habits show themselves.

The air carried a trace of heat even though the day was cooling. Not warmth—just the scent of places that burned long before we arrived. Soot clung to the cracks in the stones. Iron threaded the dust.

Then a firefly appeared.

It lifted out of the broken weeds like it had been hiding there for a lifetime, its glow small and trembling. For a second I thought my eyes were playing tricks on me. I hadn't seen a firefly since I was a kid—back when summers still felt whole and the nights didn't press so hard around the edges.

Gillie stepped closer, watching it blink once before fading into the dusk.

"I haven't seen one in years," I said.

She let out a quiet breath. "Me neither. I almost forgot they existed."

Another light rose ahead of us, slow and unsure, as if testing whether the world would take it back.

The tiny light hesitated in the air. It drifted across the path, faded, and vanished into the dusk.

Another rose a few yards ahead. Then two more. Then a thin scattering of them, scattered like someone had shaken a bag of old sparks across the road. Their lights didn't pulse with the quick, easy rhythm we remembered—they blinked slow and uneven, as if following a breath the rest of us couldn't hear.

Gillie slowed until she was beside me. She didn't reach for the scroll this time. She just watched the lights weave in and out of the weeds.

"Not normal," she said quietly.

"No," I said. "Not even close."

She didn't argue. Neither did I. Some things didn't need naming to feel wrong. They felt like a warning taking shape.

A firefly brushed my cheek. For a breath its light shifted—gold to white—and I saw Joshua. Not the broken version at the end. Younger. Standing knee-deep in swamp water, both hands on the scroll, his face split by light and shadow. The image snapped away so fast it felt stolen.

Gillie watched me carefully. "You saw something."

"Yeah."

She nodded once—not surprised, not shaken—just confirming what she already suspected.

More lights drifted toward the Seven.

Eliah dropped to his knees, breath catching. "I heard her," he whispered. "My sister. Before the river took her." He wiped at his eyes with the back of his hand. "She called my name."

Sera stopped walking. A firefly hovered at her ear, flickered, and her expression changed. "That's my mother's song," she whispered. "I haven't heard that since…" She didn't finish. Her hum shifted—broken at first, then steadying.

Rowan opened his eyes like he'd been holding his breath too long. "These flickers aren't new," he said. "They're leftover. That's all I'll say." He didn't look ready to say anything more.

Nadya caught one on her palm. The small glow lit the tears she hadn't meant to shed. "This feels like grief I never spent," she murmured. "Silence sits heavy, doesn't it?" She let the firefly go.

Cassian flinched when a light touched his sleeve, then turned sharply away from us. He spoke under his breath, almost too soft to catch: "Father."

Tomas stood still while three lights circled him. His whole body leaned forward like he was listening to voices none of us could hear. When the lights faded, he swallowed hard. "Not for me," he whispered. "For him." He didn't say who him was.

Miriam was pale. She didn't reach for the lights. She watched them the way people watch storms—trying to decide if they're coming closer.

"These aren't insects," she said.

"What, then?" Gillie asked.

Miriam shook her head. "Fragments of memory. Something refusing to stay buried."

We stood there a long moment—long enough for the last firefly to dim and drift away. The night seemed to fold itself back into place, but something in the air hadn't recovered. I felt it under my ribs, a kind of pressure that didn't match the open sky.

A thought flashed—old as the Withering: *memories don't come when you call them.*

I told myself it was just grief.

The air didn't believe me.

We walked on, slower now, into a field of flickering light. The path ahead wasn't bright or dark—just unsettled. Every pulse made the stones blink in and out of clarity. The fireflies hovered over the ground as though reading something we couldn't see.

Shapes appeared in the dust. Carvings worn down to ghosts—circles, intersecting lines, a faint outline of a bell cut into rock so old it was almost gone.

Miriam stumbled to her knees. Gillie caught her by the shoulder.

"What do you see?" Gillie asked.

Miriam pressed her parchment to the carvings, her breath tight. "These marks… they're older than the villages. Older than anything we've touched. They were burned in, not carved."

Her eyes widened. "A flame eating itself. A heat that warms no one." She swallowed hard. "It keeps whispering… 'the Firebrand.'"

The name landed heavily. Even the fireflies dimmed, their light thinning as if the word had pushed against them.

The scroll leaned heavier against my spine—not pulsing. Just sorrowed. The same way it had reacted when the seller in the square tied Joshua's name into the older rites.

Gillie drew her knife—not threatening anyone, just holding it out the way someone does when they're trying to steady their own thoughts. The blade sat uneven across her palm, the tip dipping the slightest bit, still carrying the same imbalance it had since the swamp.

A firefly drifted down and touched the metal.

For a second, the blade caught the glow—brighter than it should have, brighter than steel alone could explain—but the light didn't settle into it. It slid off, the way water slips from a surface not ready to hold it.

Gillie exhaled through her nose, not quite frustration, not quite fear.

"It's still not right," she murmured.

I didn't disagree. Even the little flash of firefly light had looked… borrowed. Like the blade wasn't rejecting the light, but wasn't ready for it either.

Gillie let out a small breath. "Grace taught me something once," she murmured. "A blade without purpose swings at shadows. A blade with purpose…" She didn't finish the sentence. She didn't have to.

Rowan finally spoke, voice steadier than before. "A firebrand doesn't start with a blaze," he said. "It starts small. An ember in a corner. It waits until the air leans the wrong way. Then it burns what it touches—slow at first, then too fast to pull back." He rubbed his eyes. "Someone like that doesn't strike loud. They strike patient."

The fireflies flared once—bright, quick—and then scattered into the grass. Darkness returned in the space they left.

We stood in it for a while. The world felt thinner, like the path ahead was being decided for us instead of by us.

The scroll shifted—firm, anchored. Not resisting. Choosing.

Gillie slid her knife back into place.

"Looks like we're on the Ember Path," she said. Not an announcement—just naming what the road had already told us. "So we watch our steps. And we don't walk blind."

I nodded. The fireflies had thinned, but the air still felt charged, like someone had walked ahead of us carrying a lantern we couldn't see.

Then—deep under the stones, or right beneath our boots—we heard a single, low toll.

Not a bell ringing.

A bell remembering.

Asking for an answer.

None of us spoke. Even Rowan didn't try to turn it into a riddle. The sound faded slowly, settling into the ground like it had been waiting there for years.

We kept walking.

The fireflies drifted off into the weeds. The road rose a little, then curved north. The quiet stretched out—not heavy, just long. Enough time for nerves to settle and questions to stack themselves where we couldn't avoid them later.

By the time the sun dropped behind a line of twisted trees, the land opened again, and the shape of a building came into view—leaning, half-forgotten, the way old places do when too many travelers pass by without stopping.

A Stranger Named Shim'on

The waystation sat where three roads used to meet.

Only one still looked anything like a road. The other two had given up, swallowed by weeds and runoff until they were little more than shallow ruts disappearing into brush. The land carried the memory of their paths, but not their purpose.

The building itself leaned slightly, as if one of its corners was tired of holding weight. A roof beam ran split straight through, forcing the whole structure to sag. Another beam bowed inward, like it had been carrying storms alone for too many seasons.

Whitewash flaked off the walls in curled patches. Up close, it looked less like peeling paint and more like skin shedding after a burn—thin, fragile, lifting at the edges.

A broken bell hung from a splintered crossbeam above the entrance. Its clapper was gone. Rust coated the rim in thick reds and browns. The empty mouth faced the road like it wanted to speak but had forgotten how.

Wind pushed through the gaps in the wood with a thin whistle. The sound wasn't eerie—just tired. A place worn down by weather and waiting.

Soot stained the stones around the doorway, as if someone had tried lighting a fire out front more than once and given up each time. A rope hung from a bent hook near the entrance, frayed and stiff with age.

I caught a faint smell of dust, old rope oil, and something damp coming from inside—like spilled water that never fully dried.

Gillie slowed, scanning the dark gaps in the walls. "Doesn't look abandoned," she said quietly. "Just… neglected."

Cassian didn't answer. He was already shifting his stance, eyes tracing every shadow.

We didn't walk straight in. None of us did that anymore. Out here, the rule was simple: announce yourself, wait, and hope the person inside preferred company to surprise.

Gillie looked at me, then at the scroll on my back. It didn't push or pull—just settled into stillness, the way it did when it recognized a threshold worth paying attention to. Not warning. Not urging forward. Just aware.

"That's as close to permission as we're getting," she murmured.

I raised my voice enough to carry through the doorway. "Travelers approaching. We mean no trouble and won't stay long if the place is spoken for."

Silence answered first. Not tense—just tired.

Then a voice: "Door's open. If you need rest, take it."

Plain. Steady. Not hiding anything.

Gillie nodded once and stepped through.

Inside, dust floated in the slanted light from a tear in the roof. A capped well sat in the corner, covered with a board weighted by stone.

Three tables leaned on bricks like they were held together more by habit than strength. Iron hooks hung over a blackened hearth, empty of kettles that had been gone for years. The air smelled of old soot, rope oil, and damp that hadn't finished drying.

A man sat with his back to a half-wall, mending river cord with a bone needle. He didn't startle. He didn't stand. He just looked up at us with eyes rimmed red—the kind of red that comes from broken sleep or waking too early too often.

His tunic was plain and worn. His hands were thick, knuckles scarred from work that didn't forgive mistakes. When he finally rose, I saw the limp—left knee stiff, foot set wide, the practiced gait of someone who had learned to move alongside pain instead of through it.

"Another group on the run," he said. His voice was low and rough. "Or on a calling. Hard to tell the difference these days."

He didn't say it unkindly. More like a man stating the weather.

Cassian shifted his weight. "Shadows wear faces too."

The man didn't bother answering that. A faint curl of ash lifted from the cold hearth as if stirred by his breath alone. Miriam's parchment trembled in her grip.

Gillie stepped forward. "What's your name?"

He finished tying off the cord before answering, like he wanted the knot right before giving us anything else.

"Shim'on."

Rowan studied him, not the name. "That's not a name you give lightly," he said. Not judgment—just the kind of observation Rowan makes when he senses weight behind something.

Shim'on huffed a quiet breath. Not a laugh—more like someone acknowledging a truth they carry around whether they want to or not.

"Names outlast the men who wear them. Some days mine fits. Some days it doesn't."

He glanced toward the torn section of roof where the light came through. "If light ever found me, it wasn't because I was looking for it. And if I walked near it at all, it was by accident more than anything else."

"You talk like you've been close to it," Gillie said.

"Close enough to know I didn't deserve the nearness," he said, rubbing his knee as if the memory lived there. "I trip over myself more than I follow anything. But it keeps showing up. I don't know why."

The scroll shifted slightly against its strap—not warm, not cold. Just focused. The way it reacts when it recognizes something before I do.

Cassian watched him closely. "Men who speak too easily about light either practiced lying, or lived enough truth to get careless."

Shim'on didn't take offense. He shut his eyes, breathed once, and opened them again. "I'm not asking you to believe me."

His gaze dropped to Miriam's scrap of parchment. "Fire never asks if the wood is ready," he said quietly. "It burns. Then you're left to decide what the ash means."

Her parchment crackled in her hands, the edge flaking off. She looked shaken by how brittle it had become.

Gillie softened her tone slightly. "Why are you here?"

"Because I can't seem to stay away," he said. "Even when staying away would be wiser."

Rowan tilted his head. "You sound like someone carrying something."

"I am," Shim'on admitted. "But not fire. Not pain. Something in between."

Gillie looked toward the scroll on my back. "Say something," she murmured—not to Shim'on, but to it.

The scroll didn't pulse. It tightened—like someone inhaling sharply through a closed mouth.

The coin warmed in my pocket—one slow beat—then held.

Shim'on flinched. His eyes flicked to the scroll and then away, like looking straight at it would make it decide.

"If it remembers me," he said, "that's its mistake."

The scroll disagreed. Quietly. Completely.

Nadya crossed her arms. "Or it remembers you to test us."

Shim'on opened his hands. Old scars lined his palms. "I'm not a prophet. I'm not Redeemed. I break more vows than I keep." He looked at Gillie, then at the scroll, then down. "If I called the Word 'Lord,' it would be habit, not honesty. I'm a sinful man."

Nothing about him felt dramatic. Just painfully true.

He leaned against the wall. "I left nets once—not river nets. Other ones. I heard 'follow,' and I thought it was meant for me." His voice wavered only once. "I didn't follow well."

Gillie's eyes softened. "None of us did."

Shim'on nodded once. "When the bell tolled, I ran," he said. "I saw braver men step toward the fire. I stepped back. A child asked me for bread. All I had was ash. I gave it anyway and called it a blessing." His voice thinned. "He tried to bless me."

No one spoke.

He took a breath like it cost him something. "Ever since, something pulls me. Heat that wants feeding. And another pull—cool as wind—asking me to open my mouth and stop lying to myself." He shrugged. "I don't always know which one is right."

Cassian pointed at the capped well. "When it's your turn to keep something, what do you pour?"

Shim'on moved with a slight hitch in his step. He lifted the stone slab covering the well and lowered a bucket with practiced ease. When he hauled it up, the water was clear.

"I don't pour anything," he said. "I'm not fit to anoint." He set the bucket down where everyone could see. "I keep watch instead. Sometimes that's the only thing I can trust myself to do."

Eliah breathed out slowly, relief loosening his shoulders.

Gillie stood straighter. The scroll shifted with her. "Do you want to walk with us?"

Shim'on hesitated—not long, just honestly. His left foot moved first, like it had made the choice before the rest of him did. Then the right followed.

"'Want' isn't the word," he said. "But I'm pulled, and I don't know what that says about me."

"Being afraid isn't failure," Nadya said.

He breathed out a small laugh. "It sits close beside it."

"Then come," Gillie said. "Walk until you decide otherwise."

"I can't promise anything," he warned. "I break promises faster than I make them. If I leave, it won't be because of anything you did."

The scroll tightened slightly against my back—not alarm, not welcome. Just caution.

We shared food in the open air—bread, a little cheese, dried fruit. Nobody suggested staying inside the waystation. The place had a hollow feeling to it, like a shell that once had purpose but didn't anymore. One gust of wind made the rafters groan, and Cassian shot it a look that said everything: *No roof over our heads tonight.*

Shim'on waited until three of us had eaten before taking his portion. He tore off a piece just big enough not to seem ashamed, chewed it slowly, eyes lowered.

Night settled in. The waystation sat behind us like something that wanted to be left alone. We made camp just beyond it in a thin stand of trees, where the air felt less trapped. Shim'on kept to the edge, back against a twisted trunk. No one assigned watches; the night decided who woke and who didn't.

Sometime near the darkest hour, I stirred and saw Shim'on crouched beside the bucket of water. His hands hovered above it—not blessing, not touching. Just paying attention.

He realized I was awake.

"If I hold onto this," he said quietly, "I remember not to cling to anything else."

"What is it you're holding?"

He thought a moment. "Hunger," he said. "The quiet kind. The kind that gets men in trouble."

He slept afterward, breathing like a man bracing for whatever waited in his dreams.

Dawn came soft. Cloaks folded. Bread broken. Water that tasted clean. The scroll felt heavier that morning—not warning us. Preparing us.

When we set out, Shim'on walked behind us—not too close, not too far. The distance of someone keeping escape and faith at the same arm's length.

Gillie looked back once—not at him, but past him. Like she was measuring the space a person needs when they're deciding what kind of man they want to be next.

We turned north. The road shifted under our boots like it was still deciding what story it wanted to tell. By midmorning, smoke thinned into the sky ahead. A roofline showed between the trees, and the wind carried the faint scent of cedar and old burn.

Shim'on followed.

The scroll approved—barely—but it was enough.

The Firebrand's Speech

We followed the road until it bent toward a small settlement—just a handful of leaning roofs behind a low fence, the kind of place that kept going mostly out of habit. A brazier burned near the middle of the square, cedar smoke drifting in thin curls with something sharper underneath. People stood around it in loose shapes, each giving the fire a respectful bit of space.

A shard of a bell hung from a leather strap at the gate. Now and then the wind tapped it—soft, tired. A woman rubbed a coin between her fingers like she needed her hands busy more than her mind.

That's when I saw him.

He stood on a blackened paving stone, long coat weather-scored, jaw streaked with soot where someone had tried to strike him. He didn't look like a leader or a keeper. Just a man who'd been through something and somehow kept his feet.

When he spoke, his voice was steady, not loud.

"You who keep quiet and call it peace," he said. "You who hide your knives and call it mercy. You who teach your hands to stay still—listen a moment."

Gillie stopped short of the crowd. The scroll settled lightly against my back, alert but not uneasy. Shim'on stood beside us, jaw tight, as if bracing for something only he expected.

A whisper slipped across the people near us: "The Firebrand."

Rowan tilted his head toward a nearby old man. "Why that name?" he asked quietly.

The old man didn't look away from the speaker. "He walked through a burning shrine last winter. Three others didn't. He came out scorched but standing. Folks said if fire couldn't keep him, nothing would."

He hesitated before adding, even lower, "And there's talk he once walked side by side with a man who broke the Law of Faith and Love—walked with him through the fire he made… and came out unburnt."

Gillie heard that. So did Cassian. None of us turned.

The scroll shifted on my back, the way an animal might lift its head at something familiar.

Then the Firebrand's voice cut clean through the square.

"The bell tolled," he said, "loud enough to wake the dead and embarrass the living. But hearing a sound isn't the same as carrying its meaning. That's the choice—marked by it, or moved by it."

His tone was plain. No prophecy in it.

"Light came back," he said. "You called it a flood. It wasn't. It was a lamp."

He let the word settle.

"Lamps don't erase the dark," he went on. "They show you how to walk through it. They leave the rest untouched. Waiting."

A few people shifted.

"There are lights that guide," he said, "and lights that replace. Don't confuse the two. One helps you move. The other changes what is."

He glanced toward the brazier, then away.

"If the dark remains where the light claims to stand, you're not being healed. You're being managed."

"The fields hum," he said. "The trees hold their breath. Some wounds healed too fast. You're calling that a blessing because the real truth scares you."

Sera's hum surfaced—steady, quiet. He didn't turn toward her, but something in his posture recognized it.

"You want mercy that doesn't move," he said. "Peace that doesn't ask anything of you. And ash—"

His gaze touched the woman with the coin.

"—you polish it because it's familiar. But it's still ash."

The scroll nudged between my shoulders—just a gentle weight. The coin warmed in my pocket. Shim'on widened his stance.

"I'm not a keeper," the Firebrand said. "I don't sell jars of comfort. I'm here to speak to the part of you that remembers who you were before fear started naming everything for you."

He took in the crowd with a slow breath.

"When water tastes like iron and you still hand it to your children… when noon lands in the wrong place… when bread fills your stomach but empties your eyes… when the fields hum on too long—those are the moments when you'll be tempted."

He let the last word hang.

"Tempted to rename things. To call ash mercy. To call flame a friend. You do that long enough, and the names start owning you."

Rowan murmured, "Smoke blinds."

The Firebrand nodded. "It does. And it spreads. You get used to it, and pretty soon you think clean air is the strange thing."

Eliah lifted his palms, unsure of why—only that something in him pulled toward the man's words.

The Firebrand stepped down from the stone and walked among the people. They gave him space without meaning to.

Up close, he carried the scents of cedar smoke, river silt, and rope pulled too hard for too long.

"I'll keep it simple," he said. "The bell tolled. Now you have to carry what it meant. Know which name belongs to flame and which belongs to breath. Flame praises whatever feeds it. Breath doesn't flatter you—even when you listen."

He paced, quiet and unhurried.

"You won't choose in front of a crowd," he said. "You'll choose when you're alone. When a lantern lifts at the wrong hour. When someone you love asks a question you don't want to answer. When silence seems easier than truth."

Then he spoke what he'd seen—not predictions, but the shape of drift:

"Water turning bitter. Light wandering where it shouldn't. Bread breaking in hands that meant it kind. Harvest refusing the hungry. Air carrying songs no one taught. Words stretched until they mean nothing. Markets blessing false weights. Doors opening to no one. Wounds treated like decoration. Houses lit every night but never morning."

Every one of us felt one of those land.

"You want a charm," he said. "A shortcut. A sentence to fix your life. I won't give that. Keepers get rich by convincing you not to look at what's already in front of you."

"So here's what I will give," he said, hand hovering over the brazier. "When the Light asks for your breath—give it. When the Word asks for your name—give it the one you carried before you hid behind smaller ones. And if flame asks for your children—tell it no."

The heat shimmered under his palm.

He added, almost like he hadn't meant to say it aloud, "And when balance stands in front of you—strike true, even if everything in you says to wait."

The words hit Gillie like they'd been meant only for her.

The scroll pressed lightly against my back, recognizing something I didn't. A soft, pained laugh escaped someone in the crowd and died in their throat.

He glanced at Shim'on—just once—then away.

A boy bumped the bell-shard. It rang, high and bright.

The Firebrand's eyes sharpened.

"Sweet isn't a sign," he said. "Sweet is just sweet."

Nadya asked, "Then how do we tell the difference?"

"You hold it," he said. "You hold it long enough to see whether it tries to own you. Only one thing in this world breaks you to make you whole."

Silence took the square.

"I don't want your coin," he said. "I want your mouth open to the right name. The name that doesn't punish you for not knowing it yet. The name that won't flatter your fear."

He stepped back onto the stone and let the quiet finish his work.

People drifted off. The woman hid her coin. A mother pulled her child from the brazier's heat. Sera's hum faded. Shim'on pressed the center of his chest like something there ached.

The Firebrand turned to leave. Smoke followed him like an old promise.

"Wait," Gillie said.

He stopped.

"You said we have to know which name to answer," she said. "What if the name we know… isn't the one we want?"

He looked at her with a gentleness that didn't soften anything—only made it clearer.

"Then you're at the beginning," he said. "Beginnings are honest. Painful, but honest. Listen—flame will forgive you today and punish you tomorrow for the same thing. Breath won't."

"I walked with a man who broke the Law of Faith and Love," he said, voice low now, no longer meant for everyone. "The fire didn't take me."

His eyes shifted to mine.

"It only takes those who refuse to step between it and what it wants. Walking beside a breaker won't."

A pause.

"Staying silent when the fire asks for blood does."

His gaze touched the scroll—recognition, not surprise.

"The Word doesn't need steady hands," he said. "Flame does."

He turned slightly, then paused again—voice lowered to something only the nearest few could catch.

"And keep this with you: balance is never far. When it nears, you'll know—not because it comforts you, but because it doesn't."

Gillie inhaled sharply.

He finished quietly: "Anyone can turn back toward the light. Anyone can be redeemed… or walk with the Redeemed."

He said it like it wasn't meant for any one person—yet it hit Gillie square in the chest.

He nodded and walked toward a road none of us would take.

We stood a moment longer.

"The choice is the same," Rowan murmured. "The hour isn't."

"Then keep the hour," Nadya said.

Cassian exhaled hard.. "We're moving."

We left the square. The bell-shard clicked behind us—two dry notes.

Shim'on kept to the edge of the group, same distance as always, but the air around him felt different.

A firefly drifted near Eliah's shoulder. Then another. Then a third. They hovered as if waiting for his answer.

One brushed Gillie's wrist. It flared gold—and for a heartbeat she remembered a knife placed in her palm by a man who walked through another kind of fire.

She blinked. The firefly drifted on.

We said nothing.

The scroll rested against my back—steady, sure.

We didn't make decisions that day.

The decisions had already made us.

We walked until the square was nothing but a thinning glow behind us. No one spoke at first; it felt wrong to break the air after a man like that had used it.

Rowan finally said, "He wasn't guessing. He knew exactly where to aim."

Gillie didn't answer. She reached toward the scroll's strap where it crossed my shoulder, her thumb brushing the worn ridge like she was checking for a heartbeat.

Sera's hum faltered, then steadied again—comfort, not call. She swallowed and spoke without lifting her eyes. "Those lines… they didn't land like warnings. They landed like confession. Mine, anyway."

"What part?" Nadya asked gently.

Sera's fingers curled into the edge of her sleeve. "Bread filling the stomach but emptying the eyes." A small, rueful breath escaped her. "I've fed people quiet when they needed truth. Told myself it was kindness. Told myself they were already too tired."

No one answered her. They didn't need to.

Rowan exhaled through his nose, then glanced toward Tomas.

Tomas rolled the coin once across his knuckles, then stilled it in his palm. "Noon landing in the wrong place," he said.

He tipped his head back, looking up at the sky as if measuring it. "I've stood under daylight that felt like ash. Knew something was wrong and called it weather. Let the day pass anyway."

"Iron water," Nadya said softly. "I handed someone a lie because the truth would have cut deeper. It tasted like iron even as I spoke it."

Shim'on walked a step behind us, jaw clenched. He didn't speak.

Eliah rubbed his palms together, restless, as if warming them against something unseen. "For me it was mercy," he said quietly.

He hesitated, then forced the words out. "I withheld truth because I didn't want to wound someone already bleeding. I called it grace. But it was fear wearing a gentler face."

His voice cracked, embarrassed. "It felt like he was pulling me back toward the moment I chose comfort over honesty."

The fireflies drifted ahead of him, rising and falling like small lanterns caught in someone else's memory.

Gillie said nothing. She hadn't looked away from the road since he'd told her to strike true when balance stood before her.

The scroll warmed faintly against my back—the way it had when the Redeemed first placed a knife in her palm in Joshua's Withering.

Gillie swallowed hard.

"He spoke to all of us," I said. "But it felt… not general. Not broad truth. More like he knew the shape of each of our failures."

Rowan nodded. "And the shape of what's coming."

Shim'on finally spoke. His voice was thin around the edges. "When he looked at me… it wasn't judgment. It was… like he'd seen the place I almost turned back. The place I still might."

None of us responded.

The fireflies drifted higher, circling once above our heads before scattering down the road like they meant to lead instead of follow.

Gillie watched them go. “He knew,” she whispered. “He knew things we haven’t said aloud.”

“Prophets know,” Rowan said gently.

Gillie shook her head. “He wasn’t guessing. He wasn’t warning. He was… remembering.”

No one argued. He didn’t speak like a man telling the future. He spoke like a man who’d already watched us fail… and survive it.

We continued north. The lanterns of the settlement faded behind us. The road grew quiet again—quiet in the way rafters learn after fire.

The scroll steadied on my back.

Whatever waited next already knew we were coming.

Echoes in the Ember

The town released us in shifts, as though each door had to consider us before closing. The brazier behind us snapped in small, brittle sounds—like the remnants of a fire not quite ready to admit it was dying. Smoke clung under the eaves and refused to rise. No one spoke. The Firebrand’s voice still hung in the air, tugging on anything that wasn’t nailed down inside us.

The coin tapped my leg every third step. Not loud. Just enough to remind me it wasn’t finished with me.

A post appeared where a lantern once hung. Only the iron hook remained, leather loop still clinging to it. Ash ringed the wood like someone had tried to keep a light alive and failed.

“You hear that?” Rowan asked softly.

“Hear what?” Cassian said.

Sera’s hum dipped, then steadied. Gillie breathed once through her nose—agreement, maybe prayer.

Rowan didn't answer. He just kept walking, listening like the road had started speaking in a language only he half remembered.

At the edge of the hamlet, a soot-dark lantern sat in a small iron shrine. A barefoot boy stood guard with the solemnity only children and old soldiers seem born knowing.

"Does it belong to you?" he asked.

"No," Gillie said. "Nothing that needs keeping is ours."

The boy's eyes slid past her toward Shim'on.

"You with them?"

Shim'on paused—half a breath too long.

"Just passing," he said.

The words landed before he could catch them. His shoulders flinched, as if struck by something he hadn't meant to throw.

The boy wet the wick and left the bell-shard untouched, like he'd decided the metal didn't deserve to speak today.

Rowan murmured, "When the bell is heard, carry." He didn't look at Shim'on when he said it.

Fields reclaimed the road. The hum in the stalks wasn't louder, only close enough now to deny ignoring. Grass brushed our ankles. Somewhere, a rooster called at the wrong hour. The coin nudged again.

"You're counting," Nadya said.

"Probably."

"Steps?"

"That," I said. "And ways out. Ways back."

She waited.

"And?"

"And names," I said. "The ones we'll answer to. The ones we'll pretend weren't ours."

She didn't push. That was her gentlest kind of agreement.

The lane tightened into sheds and lean-tos. Light spilled from a wide doorway where lanterns crowded a workbench—iron, brass, blue-glass, bottle-green, cloudy-clear. A man with soot across his jaw lowered a fresh pane.

"Not for sale," he said by habit. Then he saw us. "There's a Vigil tonight. Lantern House. You're carrying something that wants to be seen."

He didn't glance at the scroll. He didn't need to.

"No coin," he added quickly. "Keepers charge for things they shouldn't. We don't."

"Who runs it?" Gillie asked.

"My sister. She used to keep. Got tired of selling fire to men who didn't need it."

Rowan murmured, "Breath keeps better."

"Breath keeps badly," the man said. "That's how you know it's worth something."

"What happens at the Vigil?" Cassian asked.

"Three lanterns," the man said. "Three words."

Nadya tilted her head. "You write any of it down?"

He shook his head. "Memory holds what matters. Whether we want it to or not."

His gaze drifted and stuck on Shim'on for a heartbeat too long.

"Men like you come because they want to want what's right," he said.

Shim'on didn't bristle. "I came because I couldn't stay away."

He sounded like he wished the words had chosen someone else to speak them.

We left him to his glass and his unspoken thoughts.

None of us said we were going, but no one turned away either. Sometimes that's how choices happen—small steps that don't feel like choosing until you're standing inside the doorway.

The Lantern House was long, narrow—benches polished by years of sitting with things heavier than hands could carry. Niches lined the walls. A wide table held three lanterns: a plain iron one, a brass one too eager to shine, and a thin-framed one that looked like breath held in metal.

A woman stood behind them. Rope scars crossed her wrists. Her hair was knotted back with cloth. She looked at us like she'd already heard the excuses we hadn't spoken aloud.

"You're early," she said. "Good. Small groups remember their own."

"We didn't say we were coming," Cassian said.

"You came," she answered. That ended it.

People drifted in: a farmer, a girl with a cut lip, two brothers touching knees to stay anchored, an older woman whose stubbornness could be mistaken for faith. Sera hummed a soft chord and everyone adjusted to it without thinking.

The sister didn't ask for names.

"Three lights," she said. "Three truths. One keeps. One praises. One smokes."

She looked at us—really looked—like she knew we weren't locals and wasn't about to let us guess our way through something that mattered.

"The iron keeps," she said. "That one takes a straight word and holds it the way it was given. No shine. No shadow. Just the truth you offer."

She tapped the brass with one finger. "This one praises. If you speak to be seen, or to be comforted, it'll flare for you. Doesn't mean the word's wrong. Just means you want something from it."

Then her hand hovered over the thin lantern. The frame shivered in the draft. "And this one smokes," she said quietly. "Not to punish. To show the parts you're fighting with—the shame, the hiding, the half of the truth you don't want to say out loud."

She straightened. "Pick the one that fits your word. Not the one you wish did."

The farmer spoke first. The iron lantern took his word cleanly.

The girl chose the brass. It flared bright enough to flatter her into smiling. The thin lantern trembled, unsure whether to shame her.

The pattern continued—breaths measured by flame.

Then the sister looked at Shim'on.

"You," she said.

He froze.

"I'm only—" he began.

"Passing," she finished. "I heard."

This time the words didn't fall away. They stayed in the room like smoke that refuses to lift.

Shim'on stared at the bench, not avoiding her gaze—avoiding ours. The wood dipped under his weight, as if trying to hold up a man who wouldn't let himself be held.

He looked like someone who'd betrayed a truth he hadn't finished believing in.

Gillie kept her hand on the scroll. Not guarding—anchoring.

"Later," Shim'on whispered.

"Later's still a promise," Nadya murmured.

The sister nodded once. "We don't count. Remembering does."

Dusk soaked into the corners. The thin lantern smoked for some and spared others. The brass flared for anyone hungry for praise. The iron stayed honest—never flinching.

When it ended, the sister trimmed wicks, placed each lantern where it belonged, and shook the thin one's smoke into the lane like dust from a cloak.

"If you fed that one," she said, "wash your hands before you touch your children."

No one argued.

She wiped her palms on her apron, then lifted her eyes—not to all of us, just enough for the room to feel smaller.

"The ritual isn't about what people say," she said. "It's about what they can't."

Her gaze slid toward Shim'on. Not long. Just long enough for him to feel it.

"Words come easy," she added. "Silence doesn't."

She stepped aside to let us pass, as though nothing more needed saying.

We left the Lantern House in smaller knots. The glassworker rested a hand on his sister's shoulder. She didn't turn—just nodded. Enough.

Night stretched across the settlement. Lamps flickered in windows. Two restless roosters muttered at the false daylight. Wind nudged them, then moved on.

Later, footsteps passed near the outer wall.

A woman whispered, "He can't say yes. Not yet."

A man answered, "Then he'll say yes later—when it costs him more."

A hinge creaked. Silence swallowed it.

I didn't sleep. Too much counting—steps, truths, guilt. The coin warmed once, then cooled. A rooster challenged its own dream again.

Before dawn, two soft taps brushed the courtyard door. Gillie rose before the second.

The sister stood with an unlit lantern.

"I sleep poorly when I leave something unfinished," she said. "At first bell we lift a lantern. Naming in the open. You're welcome. Not required. But if your friend comes"—she didn't look at Shim'on—"men hear truth differently in the morning."

"We'll be there," Gillie said.

Promises tightened the courtyard like rope around beams.

Shim'on stared at the cold ash in the bowl where we'd kept a coal.

"I'll keep watch," he said, not meeting our eyes.

No one challenged him. Some truths can't be shared by force.

Dawn pulled the yard from gray toward clarity. We washed, packed, and followed the lanterns hung straight along the lane.

A tall post waited in the square with a single lantern at its top, panes wiped clean. People gathered in the half-curious way crowds do when they hope not to be noticed.

The sister raised the lantern.

She glanced over our group—quick, practiced, like someone who'd spent half her life watching travelers try to hide the truth behind their faces.

"You'll be heading north," she said quietly, as if stating something she'd already confirmed. "Road splits up there. One path avoids the outpost. The other doesn't."

Her gaze moved from face to face, lingering a moment on Shim'on.

"If you're carrying truth, you'll end up at the outpost anyway. Don't mistake that for being ready."

She said it plain, the way someone speaks a fact people ignore until it finally stands in their road.

Gillie checked the scroll's strap on my shoulder. Cassian scanned the edges. Sera felt the air for hums. Rowan almost spoke, then swallowed it. Eliah knotted his fingers. Nadya listened to the unasked questions.

Shim'on stood apart—close enough for truth to reach him, far enough to pretend it wasn't speaking his name.

The sister struck a match, and the lantern caught with a clean, honest note.

The barefoot boy from the shrine spotted Shim'on and spoke before anyone could redirect him.

"You were with them," he said.

The space before Shim'on's reply tightened. He opened his mouth, found nothing, closed it, swallowed, and tried again.

"I keep watch nearby," he said at last, his voice thin as wick smoke.

He didn't look at us or the boy, only at the flame, as if it might burn away the words he'd just spoken.

Somewhere behind the wall, a raven shifted and gave a low, scraping call—wrong sound for morning, close enough to sting.

Then a single firefly drifted out from behind a post, its light thin and testing. Another rose from the dust near Shim'on's boot, then another, until they hovered around him—not accusing, not comforting—just waiting, like memories that had been holding their breath for the right moment to speak.

The morning hadn't arrived, but the truth had.

We stood in that half-light while the lantern learned our faces and the fireflies circled his.

As we turned to leave, the scroll shifted against my back, barely, like a hand adjusting its grip. Not a push. Not a warning. Just a weight leaning north, the way a person leans toward a thought already chosen.

I didn't say anything, but Gillie felt it too; her breath caught for the smallest second.

North—toward the outpost the sister had named, toward whatever waited for us there.

The day hadn't started, but it was already counting.

We took the ember with us and moved on.

The Lantern's Voice

Arrival at the Outpost

We reached the ridge at last light, when the sky hadn't decided if it was done for the day or not. Colors washed out. Edges blurred. The outpost came into view where two roads met and leaned on each other like two tired men. It wasn't a grand fort. It was a collection of stubborn decisions: rough palisade, patched roofs, smoke stains on wood that had already seen more fire than it wanted to remember.

Split timbers stood in a tight ring, tops shaved flat. Rope soaked with pitch had hardened along the posts and gate in dark veins. Someone had cared enough to seal every gap wind or trouble might find. From where we stood, we couldn't see much inside—just the shadows thrown by travel-lanterns hung from crossbeams. They clicked in the cooling air, metal speaking to itself in the cooling air.

A rooster coughed somewhere beyond the wall and tried again, like it had swallowed smoke and wasn't sure if it should be calling anyone to anything anymore.

The gate didn't open because we arrived. It opened to a pattern.

Three sharp snaps.

A quiet stretch of air.

Two more snaps.

I couldn't see the man's hand, but the sound was practiced. A code. No shouted passwords. The lantern over the gate brightened and dragged a bar of light across us. It lingered a heartbeat longer when it passed over the scroll on my back, as if the glass knew how to hesitate.

"Names," a voice called from behind the gate. The tone wasn't curious. It weighed.

"No names," Gillie answered, calm and clear. "Travelers. Bearing the Word where it still needs hearing."

Something shifted behind the wood. Not an opening—just listening.

A second voice spoke, closer to the gate. Short, clipped. "Captain. River road."

Boots thudded across the overhead slats. The lantern swung again and threw a bright seam of light through the gaps in the gate, illuminating just enough dirt inside to suggest movement. Pitch smoke rolled off the wood, sharp and bitter, catching under my tongue.

A familiar feeling rose in my chest—the same one from the swamp. That sense that you could stand upright and still feel like the ground was tilting toward drowning.

It came from the stillness on the other side—something waiting in the dark, unseen but undeniable, like the air itself didn't trust what shared space with it.

The gate bar scraped.

The doors pulled back.

Only then did the yard reveal itself—hooves and boots had pressed the dirt flat, lantern light spilled across hardened rope, and a still patch in the far corner held its breath as if watching us arrive.

And he stepped out of that stillness like he'd been waiting for this exact moment.

Marcus.

The name hit like a slap inside my skull. Gillie stiffened beside me. She didn't breathe for a beat. Every one of the Seven shifted in their own way—Nadya's jaw set, Rowan's hand closed, Miriam's fingers went straight for her charred scrap, Eliah's shoulders hunched like he'd taken a blow.

We had watched Marcus split apart in the Withering—watched light tear through him in a thousand beams, dragging him into itself until nothing human remained. Judgment didn't just take him; it erased him. That should have been the last time we saw him.

But there he stood.

His hair had more gray threaded through it now. A clean scar traced along his jaw, thin and pale, like a line signed by something that meant it. His coat wasn't the old performance piece we'd seen before. This one was worn and practical—patched at the elbows, stained with oil, the cut of someone who expected to work in it. His eyes were still wrong: iron that assumed it would be obeyed, even when the rules changed.

The yard went quiet. No formal call, no shouted command. People just moved out of his way a fraction, like their bodies remembered what their heads wanted to forget. You could tell he wasn't the declared commander anymore, but you could also tell the outpost still bent itself around him.

His gaze dropped to the scroll on my back.

The shift in his expression wasn't big: the faint recoil of someone seeing a wound they thought they'd buried. Then the disgust rose—plain, unhidden. He didn't bother to mask it.

"Drop that," he said. Not shouted—dismissed. "It's a rotted scrap of memory. A corpse stitched in leather. You want to live, you cut loose the dead weight. That thing's just rot strapped to your spine."

Heat shot up my throat. I wanted to spit back that he was the rot. That if anything deserved dropping, it was him.

"Figures," Marcus added, eye cutting over us. "You lot always did prefer dragging a story on your backs instead of facing what's in front of you. Easier to blame paper than your own choices."

The scroll moved first.

Gillie reached toward my back before I could answer, her fingers finding the strap. Not to shield it—just to touch it. The leather warmed under her hand.

The scroll reacted.

Not heavy.

Not pushing.

It lifted.

Just enough for my spine to lengthen, for breath to move clean through my ribs. The anger didn't vanish, but it lost its edge. The opposite of weight. Like someone bracing your shoulders from behind, not to restrain you but to keep you from charging the wrong way.

Gillie felt it too. A small breath caught in her throat, almost surprised. Her stance eased—not toward Marcus, but toward me, toward us, toward something steadier. One heartbeat earlier she'd looked ready to launch straight at him. Now she still burned, but she was held.

Marcus's lip curled—not the usual disdain, something tighter. His stance shifted without meaning to. The lanternlight above him pressed harder across his shoulders.

He noticed.

He hated that he noticed.

"You weren't just taken," Gillie said. Her voice didn't rise, but every word came like it had teeth. "We watched the light tear you apart. Not once. Not clean. Over and over. A thousand beams through bone and shadow. It pulled you into itself until there was nothing left to fall."

For a heartbeat, something like memory flickered in Marcus's eyes. Then he wiped it away with contempt.

"Light scatters," he said. "Fire burns. When they're done, they leave. That's all."

His gaze flicked past us, quick and involuntary, to the high lantern above. He dipped his head a fraction, like somebody being reminded of a line.

Then he looked back. "I don't."

"I saw you die," I said. I heard the edge in my own voice and didn't soften it. "All the way. There wasn't anything left to stand back up."

"You think too small," he said, soft and cold. "You can't kill what's already dead. You just rearrange it."

Gillie's blade came clear of its sheath. Steel never sounded louder than when everything else was quiet. She kept it level, the point angled at his chest, as if years of weight balanced on that line again.

"You broke Joshua," she said. "You dragged him. You tore him away."

"That blade stinks of life," Marcus said, eyes on the steel. "You hold it like you want to make the world right with one good stab." His mouth twisted. “You hate me enough, you'll turn to stone before the metal ever reaches me. Go on. Swing if your arm needs the lie.”

“You don't get to talk about lies,” I snapped. “You built a whole ruin on them.”

The scroll pressed hard between my shoulders, not painful but firm—like a hand pushing me back from the edge. My next words caught and died behind my teeth.

I wanted to add more—call him butcher, coward, whatever else my throat could find—but the pressure at my back held steady, like the scroll had decided we'd hit the limit of what anger was allowed to say.

Gillie's knuckles whitened on the hilt. “You ripped Joshua apart,” she said again, lower, more dangerous. “You call that judgment?”

Marcus's eyes brightened just a hair, like metal catching wet light. “I showed him himself,” he said. “That's all judgment is. Men follow what feeds them. Your friend liked what he saw, right up until he didn't.”

Rowan opened his mouth, eyes burning with something I rarely saw in him—raw hate. Whatever proverb he'd reached for, he let it go. He swallowed and left only one word.

“He even thought he was choosing,” Marcus went on lightly. “That's the part people never forgive.”

“Enough.”

“Lie,” Nadya said. Just that. No extra. Her stare made the word land like a stone.

The scroll steadied at my back. A reminder instead of a command: Don't become him.

Gillie's arm lowered a fraction. Her grip eased from steel to strap. She kept the knife out, but the scroll guided her posture more than Marcus's taunts did.

"No other road," Marcus murmured, almost to himself but loud enough for us to hear. The tone said he didn't like that fact any more than we did.

"No other road," Nadya echoed, unflinching. "You made half of it hell."

Eliah's eyes stayed half-closed, listening. "The river's still running the way it should," he said quietly, like he was checking whether that was still true.

Marcus watched us for a breath, then raised his hand. The yard pulled tight. Men froze mid-motion. Even the horse seemed to hold its breath.

"No one leaves until—"

He stopped. Every muscle in his jaw locked. His eyes snapped to the high lantern overhead. Something passed over his face—obedience he didn't choose, like a hand tightening on the back of his neck.

His lips formed a word without sound. A bow. Shallow. Forced.

"—until first bell," he finished flatly. "After that, dismiss by rows."

His men moved because the words told them to, not because Marcus had.

Gillie kept her knife up. He still didn't ask her to lower it. Something like satisfaction flickered across his face, and something sick twisted in my gut at the sight—like he enjoyed being hated as long as it meant we were still watching him.

Marcus's gaze slid past us to the gap in the wall, then back again.

"Inside," he said to the gate crew, not taking his eyes off us. "If they're staying, they stay where I can see them."

No one touched the bar. It was already up. The men at the posts stepped back a pace, opening just enough space for us to cross the threshold without pretending it was welcome.

The yard waited behind him—torchlight, lantern glow, shadows stretching out like they knew his shape and were used to making room for it.

The scroll pressed again between my shoulders—not heavy. Never heavy. More like a hand steadying the middle of my back, urging me to step, not dragging me.

We walked in.

The yard swallowed us and rearranged itself.

A farrier held a hoof between his knees, rasping the edge flat. He glanced up at Marcus every few seconds, eyes measuring how much of the day still belonged to him. Two boys wrestled a coil of thick rope across the yard, shoulders already telling the story their backs would learn later. A woman polished a glass lantern globe until it showed her face. She wiped the cloth over her cheek with the same motion, a habit that might have started as prayer and turned into something tighter.

Marcus stepped into the center of the yard, knowing exactly where the lanternlight would slice across his shoulder. He'd already told us once to drop the scroll—told us it was dead weight, useless, a relic that only slowed us down. Now he let his eyes drag over it again, heavier, nastier this time.

"Why would you still want to carry that carcass of leather and lies?" Marcus said. "What are you hoping for—that it'll cough up Joshua if you hug it hard enough?"

He didn't wait for a reaction.

"Or maybe that's the point," he added, voice dropping. "Maybe you like the drag. Gives you something holy to blame when you sink."

A dry sound escaped him—half scoff, half disgust.

"I told you before—dead weight. It'll pull you under long before it saves you."

Marcus's eyes passed over us again, sharp and cold.

Something caught inside him.

A string pulled too tight.

"You think carrying that thing makes you better than me?" His voice rose, cracked with heat. "You think you've got truth strapped to your back? You think that forgives—"

He took one step too close.

"Say his name," Marcus demanded—then stopped.

The high lantern clicked once.

The rage drained from his face like hot oil cooling too fast.

"Dawn," he said instead. "You pass at dawn."

Marcus straightened slowly. Rage came back in pieces. Confidence did not.

His eyes didn't meet ours. Marcus wasn't ruling anything. Marcus was being ruled.

I stepped forward without meaning to, ready to drive something sharp into the truth of him, but the scroll pressed hard against my back and stopped me cold. Gillie didn't flinch. She reached back and touched the strap at my shoulder, steady and grounding, anchoring me where I stood.

"It carries us," she said. "You'd know that if you hadn't tried to kill what it was asking you to be."

Marcus's jaw ticked, an involuntary twitch he couldn't hide. The lantern above him flickered once—not from wind, but pressure—and he shifted his stance as if the ground had just reminded him it owed him nothing. His eyes lifted to the lantern again, quick and automatic, checking whether the correction was over. Then he faced us, the mask reassembled but not convincing.

Eliah stood with his palms open to the air, reading what it was doing. Cassian tracked the exits with his eyes. Sera hummed a thin note that steadied the men nearest us without them realizing it. Miriam rolled her charred scrap between her fingers like a coin she wished she'd never spent.

"You're not the first to bring breath into this yard and call it judgment," Marcus said. "But you're the first to do it since I died."

"Didn't take," Rowan muttered.

"We're not here for you," I said. "We're not here to fix what you broke."

Gillie didn't lower her knife. "We won't lodge," she said. "We pass through."

"Passing is what men do when they're afraid of finding out where they belong," Marcus replied. "Run if you want. We'll see if it's passing or hiding."

He turned to his men. "Keep the East—" He flinched again, barely, his eyes jerking up to the lantern. A whisper escaped him, raw and soft.

"Forgive—"

He swallowed it down, corrected himself like he was reading from a script only he could hear. "Keep the west walk. South gate stays shut. Rotate by two."

The orders were normal. The obedience wasn't. It was like watching a man corrected mid-sentence. Fear moved under the yard like water under floorboards—quiet, but present.

We found a strip of wall and put our backs to it. No one sat fully at first. Every time Marcus turned, someone's hand brushed a weapon, until the scroll eased the tension. Food came—thin stew in chipped bowls. We ate it anyway. Better to chew something than chew rage. Every time I thought about throwing the bowl at Marcus's skull, the scroll warmed against my back until the impulse burned out.

Nadya watched faces. Rowan tasted the mood. Miriam stained her fingers darker with char. Eliah cried quietly and called it work. The scroll steadied me like a hand between my shoulders saying: This far. No further.

A boy crossed the yard carrying a lantern pole. He paused, studied Shim'on, and said stiffly, "You. Lantern House. My aunt says your kind don't come when there's counting."

Shim'on froze—not from fear of the boy, but from something deeper. "I keep watch nearby," he said evenly. "You're mistaken."

The boy nodded, relieved, and left.

The lantern above us clicked—two short knocks, one long. The flame didn't change. But it had been listening.

The quiet that followed wasn't rest. It was waiting.

A girl arrived with a water bucket, slowed when she saw Shim'on, and said, "You were at the Vigil. On the bench. You didn't speak when she asked for words." Her eyes narrowed. "You're standing now."

Shim'on's fingers whitened on his bowl.

"Wrong man," he said. "Lots of men limp."

"Lots do," she agreed. She didn't argue. She just nodded once and went on with her water, the way water does—forward, down, into whatever cracks it could find.

Near the farrier's stall, a hammer struck a nail. The sound rang out sharp and honest. The horse shifted and settled. The yard dropped into a rhythm that always forms in places where people are forced to wait: small tasks, half conversations, eyes keeping one part of themselves on whoever holds the next order.

Marcus approached again. He didn't rush. He walked like a man absolutely sure the ground belonged to him—and like he'd enjoy proving it if anyone said otherwise.

"You," Marcus said, fixing his eyes on Shim'on. "We had a report from the ford last winter. Fog rolled in, and somebody was out there trying to speak two truth-words they could barely get out. Looked like the kind of words a man says only when he's tired of lying to himself." His gaze sharpened. "That you?"

Shim'on opened his mouth. The brave answer didn't make it out.

"I don't know what you're talking about," he said. The sentence came too smooth, too fast. Men who've rehearsed a line sometimes forget to let it sound human.

Overhead, the high lantern clicked again.

The lantern answered first—a thin, broken rhythm, wrong for the hour, learned too well to be accidental. It wasn't the right time for it. That's what made it land.

Marcus's mouth twitched, not into amusement, but into something he might have used as a smile if he'd remembered how. "Men like that either become hinges in a place like this," he said, "or splinters."

Shim'on flinched as if the word had weight. He stood up so quickly the bench scraped and nearly tipped. His hand shot out to catch the table. The stew in his bowl sloshed, a small wave trying to get away.

Then he turned and ran.

Not like a thief escaping with stolen goods. More like a man whose legs had spent years learning how to carry him away from the exact kind of question he'd just been asked.

His limp gave him a lopsided rhythm, but it didn't slow him much. He cut along the wall, slipped through a gap in torchlight, and disappeared between a stack of crates and the far corner of the palisade.

Eliah half-rose, ready to follow. Gillie's hand touched his sleeve, two fingers on worn cloth.

"Let him be," she whispered.

The quiet listened. I could feel the scroll's steady weight against my back again, holding us in place when everything in me wanted to run after Shim'on and drag Marcus to the ground in the same motion.

Marcus watched Shim'on's retreat the way a man watches a cart roll downhill—not surprised, not pleased, not entirely sorry either. Then, again, his gaze flicked to the high lantern. It burned with the same steady brightness, giving him nothing and giving us everything we needed to see.

"We all answer to something at the gate," he said, not quite to us, not quite to himself. "Light tells on a man."

Gillie watched him like she could burn a hole straight through his chest by will alone. The scroll at her back didn't change, but I could feel its steadiness in the way she didn't move from hatred into attack.

Marcus lifted his hand. The yard tightened again.

"First row, break—" he started, and then the word snagged in his throat. His eyes tugged upward. "No," he breathed, and the sound was so soft it almost vanished between his teeth. "—hold," he said louder, correcting himself. "We move on bell."

His gaze drifted, ended on the tip of Gillie's blade.

"You leave at dawn," Marcus said. "Before that, you stay put."

"We're leaving now," Gillie said. Even her breath sounded like it was ready to fight him.

Marcus's jaw worked once, tight. For a second I thought he might spit something vicious. Instead, the muscles in his face pulled like reins yanked from outside. "Doesn't matter what you want," he said. "Dawn's the only time you get."

He didn't sound like he believed in the rule—he sounded like a man repeating something he'd been forced to say, and hating every second of it.

The scroll pressed into my back again. Not a shove. Just enough pressure to tell me that pushing this fight now would mean fighting more than Marcus.

We didn't lie down because he told us to. We settled in because the scroll didn't press us to leave. The boards at our backs were rough and carried the memory of older winters. Men shifted. Somewhere, a bucket tipped and clattered; someone cursed quietly and set it upright again. The smell of stew, sweat, and old smoke settled over everything like a thin blanket.

I slept in pieces. When my eyes closed, I saw Marcus breaking apart again in the Withering, and then standing whole under this lantern. When they opened, I saw him only a few yards away, head bent slightly like he was listening to something above him. Each time I started to plan what I'd say, what I'd shout, the scroll warmed along my spine just enough to cool the words.

Dawn came in slow, gray streaks along the top of the wall. The high lantern had burned itself low, its flame soft, barely clinging to the wick. The rooster finally hit something like the right hour and called it out with more confidence, as if the world had finally given it permission.

Marcus waited at the trough with two tin cups in his hands. He hadn't filled them yet. Water sloshed in the bucket beside him, reflecting a ragged stripe of sky.

"He'll come back," Marcus said, eyes on the water. "Or he'll find somewhere softer that lets him stay broken. Men like that don't vanish. They just rot slower."

Anger rose again. I wanted to tell him he didn't get to talk about anyone's fear after what he'd done.

The scroll pressed against my back—firm, steady—like a hand warning me off the next sentence.

Marcus dipped the cups into the bucket, filled both, and handed one to me.

"He said he was passing through," I said.

Marcus made a low sound in his throat, halfway between a scoff and something more tired. "Men say that when they're afraid they might have to stay," he answered. "Roads remember the ones who pretend they're only guests. Sometimes they collect."

The water tasted of tin and earth and something older. I swallowed it anyway.

We gathered our things. No one rushed, but no one dragged their feet either. Gillie tightened the scroll's straps and checked the edge on her blade. Sera tied her hair back with the same knot she used on hard days. Rowan tested the morning's air with two fingers, like he was checking the direction of a wind the rest of us couldn't feel. Miriam rubbed the last of the char dust from her hands into her skirt, leaving new, dark lines in the fabric. Eliah opened his hands to the light. Nadya counted us with her eyes, then counted again, as if she still expected Shim'on to step out from behind some post and swear he hadn't gone far.

At the gate, Marcus laid his hand on the bar and didn't lift it right away. He made us stand there and feel the wait.

"North," he said when he finally moved it. "River that's tried to change its mind more than once this year. Fields that carry a low hum when pride gets loud. Men thanking weights that lie to them because the lies feel better in their hands than the truth."

He looked at me, then past me at the scroll.

"You'll be asked what your mouth is for," he said. "The next stretch doesn't let that stay an easy question."

"Breath," Rowan answered. It sounded like the only word he trusted.

"Heat," Marcus said. "Or truth. Most men pick heat. Easier to burn a thing than confess it."

He lifted the bar. The gate complained the way old wood always does, with a mix of pain and duty.

He didn't step fully aside. He left just enough space, so each of us had to choose whether to brush close to him or give him the widest berth we could.

Gillie walked past at a distance that wasn't afraid but wasn't friendly either. She gave him a short nod.

Not thanks.

Not respect.

Acknowledgment—like you'd give a wall you were choosing to walk around instead of through. The scroll seemed to rise a little at her back, steadying her choice not to spit in his face.

He accepted it like wages he knew belonged to another man.

We stepped out into a morning that hadn't decided what it would be yet. The air was cooler, but the promise of heat lingered under it. Behind us, the outpost resumed its movements. Boots scraped. Hinges groaned. A horse shook its head. Ropes creaked on posts. The high lantern's flame finally gave out, a soft sigh of smoke disappearing into the brighter light.

I didn't look down the narrow run where Shim'on had fled. Looking can be a kind of invitation, and I wasn't sure yet what we'd be inviting.

Instead, I felt his absence the way you feel a missing tooth with your tongue—compulsively, aware of the gap even when you're trying not to think about it.

At the bend in the road, where the outpost's walls fell out of sight and the lantern's reach stopped, the fields before us rustled in a low, steady tone. Not words. Not warning. Just a sound that said the world still moved forward, with or without us.

The scroll rested at my back.

"Walk," Nadya said.

"Through," Rowan added. No riddle. Just that.

We obeyed. Not because we understood everything that had just happened in that yard, but because obedience was the only thing that didn't feel like selling something—or becoming him.

Behind us, the outpost settled into its day. Somewhere, the rooster called again, just to make sure the hour knew it had been named.

And just as the gate bar dropped back into its cradle, I heard Marcus's voice carry out after us. It was softer now, unwilling, shaped by something he hadn't chosen but couldn't ignore.

"The Lantern approaches," he said.

The wind thinned it out. The road took it. We kept walking.

Sermon of Power

By the time the outpost dropped behind us, the sky had climbed past gray into a flat, tired blue. The road leveled. Fields thinned. Fences returned—short runs of stone, a few posts leaning like they'd quit arguing with the wind.

Ahead, the road widened into something like a square.

They'd built a stage where the road forgot it was meant for passing.

Canvas stretched over a frame patched too many times with old slogans and market cloth. Poles lashed together. Two braziers at the front corners coughed pitch smoke that clung low to the boards. Lanterns hung at different heights so the light climbed in steps instead of falling clean. Between two posts, broken bell-shards hung on wire, each piece tied off with a different thread. Bowls waited at the foot of the platform for coin—

set just far enough away that you had to walk toward the light to reach them.

We arrived while the town was practicing not looking.

Water-sellers rested their poles but didn't set them down. Merchants covered their scales. Children edged forward through the press, testing how close they could get before an adult hand found their shoulder.

Gillie kept the scroll close and quiet. The strap dug deeper into her shoulder the way promises do when the road gums up instead of clearing. Nadya counted faces. Cassian's eyes walked the alleys and doorways, counting exits. Miriam tucked her char scrap to her breastbone. Eliah stood with his palms open at his sides. Sera let a low hum slip into the boards under our boots; what came back was thin but willing.

Rowan muttered, half under his breath, "Feed a lantern long enough, it'll make any lie look warm."

Near the edge of the square, just inside the crowd, I saw her.

The cut on her lip had healed into a thin pale line, but it still tugged the corner of her mouth. She held a dented tin cup in both hands, fingers wrapped high on the metal like she didn't trust the handle. Her gray dress looked made for someone taller. A bit of twine at her throat held a small locket—the kind of thing that knows too much for how small it is.

I couldn't have named her, but I knew her.

Not from her face. From the way she stood—feet set, shoulders squared, braced for a question that hadn't been asked yet. From the way her eyes flinched at three lantern frames stacked near the back of the platform: iron, brass, and a thin one that looked like it might rattle itself apart if you breathed wrong.

Her gaze slid past us, caught on the scroll, then jerked away. She lifted the tin cup as if to drink, but didn't. The locket tapped once against the rim—small, nervous sound.

Somewhere near the front, a man murmured, "The Lantern approaches."

Not loud. Not ceremonial. Just the kind of warning people give each other when they've learned what comes next.

A hush pulled through the square.

Then he stepped onto the platform.

No crown. No sash. Just a man who knew where to stand so the light would claim him. When he took his place, the lanterns above brightened a notch without flaring, as if the wicks had been waiting.

"Neighbors," he said.

The word dropped into the square like bread into a room where people had forgotten they were hungry. Heads lifted. Feet shifted closer.

"We meet under the kindness of order," he went on. "Your children sleep. Your doors hold. The river stays in its banks. Why?"

He let the question hang, smiling like a teacher who already knows nobody's going to risk the wrong answer.

"Because we govern the small lights that build a town," he said. "Flame is faithful—when you speak to it with care."

Behind the canvas, bellows hissed. The braziers swelled, then steadied. The crowd made the sound fear makes when someone puts clean words around it.

The girl with the cut lip drew a breath like she might speak. Shoulders rose. Her mouth opened just enough for air to become the start of a word.

One of the braziers spat a brighter tongue of flame and the crowd leaned toward it.

Her jaw snapped shut. She stared down at her cup, cheeks flushing like she'd done something wrong by almost saying anything.

"We're past the old days," the Lantern said, "when bells tolled and men ran wild with words. Breath belongs first in here." He tapped his chest. "On the tongue, it turns to storm."

His gaze slid across the front of the crowd. It skated over the scroll and refused to land.

"Keepers," he called.

Three men and a woman moved among the people with trays. On each tray, rows of tiny vials—thumb-long glass capped with brass, holding a little oil. Each had a narrow cord tied to it, ready for a wrist.

The Lantern uncorked one and held it up for everyone to see.

"There is talk," he said, "of travelers who carry parchment and call it breath. They'll ask you to open your mouths to nothing and pretend nothing will hold you."

He smiled with practiced pity.

"Here is light you can see."

He touched the vial's lip to a short wick, struck a spark, and let the flame catch.

It rose the wrong color—a soft, sick green. The breeze crossing the square should have worried it. It didn't. It burned steady, pleased.

"It sings off-key," Sera said quietly.

"It sings bought," Nadya answered.

The girl with the cup winced. Her fingers crept to the base of her throat, feeling for something that didn't belong there. The locket tapped against the tin again—one, two.

The Lantern held the small strange flame higher.

"Here is heat that answers your hand," he said. "Order you can weigh."

"Weights next," Cassian muttered.

Right on cue, someone rolled out a small platform scale. The pans shone like they'd been polished for a vow. The Lantern dropped a leather bag into one side; a stamped weight into the other. The scale dipped, seesawed, then settled—almost even, just a hair off if you knew how to look.

He frowned, not with anger, but with a sadness that admired itself.

"We bless fair measure," he said. "We curse cheats—not the man, the harm. We will not tolerate those who bottle drought and sell it as salvation."

People nodded. It was close enough to something they already believed to feel safe.

The scroll didn't.

It tightened colder against Gillie's back. Not crushing—just firm enough to say: watch.

"We don't preach," the Lantern said. "We provide."

The keepers moved faster, tying cords around wrists. The vials swung and clicked, catching green in the glass. The Lantern turned the flame so its color crawled across their hands.

"Hang this by your door," he went on. "When old songs wake in your children, when fields hum with strange voices, don't open your houses to breath that calls itself holy. Light what is given. Flame is faithful when it's fed."

The girl's keeper reached her. He didn't look at her face—only her arm.

She lifted her hand like she meant to offer him her wrist. At the last second she twisted, letting the cord drop over her locket instead. The vial knocked against it and hung there, trapped against what she actually wanted to keep.

The keeper didn't notice. Busy hands miss quiet rebellions.

“You travelers,” the Lantern said, turning his attention our way without quite meeting our eyes, “rest under our watch. Speak if you must—our lanterns are generous. But let your breath keep house here.”

He tapped his chest again.

A few people laughed. The laughter went sharp at the edges, then smoothed itself out.

“To show this is not just talk,” the Lantern said, “a small demonstration.”

A boy was brought forward—ten, maybe older. A healed cut along his eyebrow. A nervous way of swallowing, like he was waiting to find out if this counted as trouble. He kept glancing at the girl with the tin cup. She kept her eyes on the ground, but her shoulders leaned his way.

Three lanterns were rolled to the front edge of the platform. Iron. Brass. The thin trembling frame.

Under my ribs, another night answered—another three.

The Lantern smiled down at the boy.

“Simple lesson,” he said. “Some frames protect. Some flatter. Some just smoke.”

He nodded to the iron first.

The boy lit it with a taper. The flame rose steady and plain, giving just enough light to do the job.

He moved to the brass.

As soon as the wick caught, the lantern flared. The metal grabbed the light and threw it out in showy ripples. The boy flinched, then smiled, embarrassed. The crowd chuckled. Everybody likes the bright one.

When he reached for the thin frame, the Lantern’s hand snapped out and caught his wrist.

"We don't feed that one here," he said—soft enough to sound gentle, loud enough to be the only thing anyone remembered. "Smoke doesn't get a say."

The crowd murmured approval. The thin lantern sat there, empty.

The girl with the cut lip stared at it like someone had covered her mouth with a hand.

Her chest lifted. A word wanted out.

Her lips parted—

A keeper brushed past her and said, "Careful with that cup, little one," without looking.

She swallowed what she'd almost said.

"By morning," the Lantern promised, "there'll be a lamp at every post. Stamps on every weight. Names listed by household at the hall."

He spread his empty hands.

"So if you need help, we can find you quickly. No more slipping through cracks. No more going missing without anyone knowing."

The scroll turned colder against Gillie's spine. Sera rubbed at her arms as if a draft had found her.

"For each house—a vial," the Lantern said. "For those who stand watch—two. Not because coin buys safety. Because men on the wall shouldn't freeze."

A keeper drifted close and held a cord out toward me. The vial swung, green catching in the glass. It looked ordinary. Easy.

For a heartbeat, I wanted it—wanted what it promised: hang this by the door and call it enough.

The scroll steadied once, firm and final.

The wanting went out like a candle sealed in a jar.

The keeper moved on.

Movement at the edge of the square caught my eye.

Marcus.

He didn't stride in. He slipped along the side of the crowd and stopped near the steps—close enough to be seen, far enough that people could pretend he was only part of the wall. He looked thinner than at the outpost. The scar along his jaw caught lantern glare. His eyes didn't leave the Lantern.

The Lantern looked down at him once.

No words. Just a look—like a hand set lightly at the back of a neck.

Marcus flinched—barely. A swallow. A small dip of the head. He turned and adjusted his men along the edge of the square. To anyone else, it looked like routine.

To us, it looked like a lead.

"You've been through enough," the Lantern told the town. "Drought. Unfair hands. Promises that filled the air and left your tables empty. Still—you kept your children close. You held your doors. You learned your neighbors' names."

He opened his palms again.

"I'm proud of you," he said.

People straightened. Backs came up, shoulders rolled as if someone had finally told them surviving wasn't failure.

Even my chest wanted to lift with them.

The scroll wouldn't allow it. Cold bled into my spine, stealing the warmth from the sentence before it could settle in me.

"Tonight is simple," the Lantern said. "We don't let the dark decide for us. We mark our doors, we tend our lamps, we keep what's ours."

Coins began to ring in the bowls at the foot of the platform.

A keeper passed close and brushed a vial cord against Gillie's sleeve, almost an accident.

She didn't move away. She didn't take it.

Rowan's hands closed, fingers pressing into his palms. "He's writing a key," he muttered, "and selling it as safety."

"Keys keep doors," Nadya said. "And lock them."

The Lantern's eyes swept the crowd again, almost resting on the scroll before choosing the nearest green flame instead.

"We don't silence," he said. "We tune." He pointed to the lamps overhead. "A town that hums one song keeps thieves from thinking they belong."

The crowd liked that. People want to belong even more than they want to be safe. He'd offered both and made the cost sound small.

The girl with the cut lip edged closer without meaning to. One foot found the thin strip where two lanterns' light didn't quite meet. Her locket and vial cord pressed into her skin. Her free hand hovered near her throat again. Every time he praised the cords on their wrists, she flinched as if the words were fingers.

"Some will try to scare you," the Lantern said. "They'll breathe on your children's dreams and call it holy."

His voice didn't harden. It softened—pity, patient warning.

"Don't hate them," he said. "Pity their mistake. Feed your lamps. Hold your doors."

His gaze slid to Marcus again. A look. A flick of the chin.

Marcus shifted three of his men without being told out loud. The town saw competence and relaxed into it.

"Neighbors," the Lantern said, letting his hands fall. "Rest. Speak kindly. If strangers must speak, our lanterns are generous—but let their words come out cooled. Tomorrow we finish the stamps and post the names by household. No one will vanish without being noticed."

Gillie kept the scroll where it was. She didn't lift it. She didn't hide it. Her closed mouth did more work than any argument would have.

When the Lantern's eyes finally brushed her, there was no anger in them—only a note, filed away for later.

He lifted his hands in a blessing that belonged to no one but himself. People bowed their heads. Some made gestures out of habit—forehead, chest, shoulder—without thinking where the habit began.

We didn't crowd the platform when it broke up. You don't wrestle an army of habits with one loud objection. The Seven—and both of us—found a place where we could see the square and the road out at the same time. The scroll stayed steady. Waiting.

Marcus moved toward the steps as the Lantern stepped back under the canvas.

For a moment, they stood in the same slice of light.

Marcus started, "Hold the north—" then blinked and swallowed. His head dipped a fraction toward nothing we could see.

"West," he corrected. "Hold the west walk. Rotate by two. South lane stays shut."

The men answered like they'd heard a clean, confident order.

The town relaxed. Somebody laughed. Someone called a thanks for "keeping the posts manned."

The Lantern stepped forward one last time and let the square settle on him again.

"Strangers," he said. For the first time his gaze nearly touched the scroll before turning aside. "Our road belongs to those who carry good work. The lanes are clear. The posts are watched. If your errand pulls you onward, don't let our hospitality tie down what purpose has already set loose."

He smiled like a man refusing to keep guests longer than is polite.

"Go as you came," he said. "Under care."

He didn't say whose.

Marcus's jaw worked. For a second it looked like he wanted to speak. Then whatever held him gave a small tug.

He faced us without facing the scroll.

"You heard," he said. "Make your road now."

The words cost him. You could hear it.

We left as people began the art of being grateful out loud. Lanterns along the lane flickered and steadied—pleased to be the new thing everyone trusted. Vials swung at wrists. Coins clinked in bowls. Laughter tried to sound relaxed and almost made it.

The road out of town was lined with posts. Some already had cords nailed to them, waiting for lamps. Others stood bare.

Gillie slowed half a step. The scroll shifted against her back—not a shove, not a pull. Just a quiet change.

Notice.

"Their lamps will ask flame to keep out breath," Rowan said, watching the new glass go up.

"And breath won't pretend to like it," Sera said.

"Breath never has," Gillie answered. She hitched the strap higher on her shoulder—an instinctive, steadying move, the kind people make when they're carrying something on purpose.

Behind us, the square glowed brighter as more vials were lit. The light looked clean if you didn't know how to look at it. If you did, you could see green hiding in the corners.

Above the roofs, the real stars kept their distance.

In the thin strip where two hanging lanterns couldn't agree on how far their light should reach, the girl stood. One hand gripped her locket and the vial cord together. The other hovered at her throat.

She watched the stage, mouth a tight line over the healed cut.

Her eyes said what her tongue didn't risk:

Not this.

Not this way.

The Ashmaker's Prayer

We left the square and followed the road until the roofs thinned and the dark felt more like field than town. None of us talked about sleep. The Lantern's voice hadn't left our ears yet. It clung the way pitch clings—soft enough to spread, hard enough to stay.

Behind us, the lamps hummed like they were pleased with themselves.

We reached the next cluster of houses before dawn—still the same town, just its outer edge, where streets narrowed and jobs started early. Windows were trying to remember their shapes in the half-light. The air still held last night's heat.

A cart waited in the square with its tongue down. Someone had bolted a brazier-box onto the bed. A drift of gray ash sat heaped beside it—too much to be from one night. Buckets nested inside each other. A row of sieves hung from nails. The whole thing smelled like pitch, old bread, and corners nobody sweeps.

From a lane's shade, a man's voice—thin, careful—floated just far enough away to pretend it wasn't speaking to anyone.

"First light," he said. "Ashmakers. They'll stripe the doorframes. Say it keeps breath from eating the wood."

Rowan scratched his jaw. "Some men build fences against wind," he said. "Others figure out where to stand."

Nadya brushed her fingers over a bell-shard nailed to a post. A carved loop-and-bar symbol sat in the metal—someone's idea of discipline.

She jerked her hand back like she'd touched something that didn't like being remembered.

Then I saw her—the girl from the sermon.

Same gray dress, too much hope for its size. Same locket on twine tapping her collarbone. The healing cut on her lip looked fresh in morning light. She held a tin cup like she'd forgotten it belonged to her.

When the brazier breathed, she lifted her fingers halfway to her throat and stopped. The locket tapped again—one, two, three. A rhythm she didn't choose, but kept anyway.

They came in pairs: two ashmakers in gray aprons, hands already dusted from past mornings. One pushed the cart. Another carried a long pole with a cup fixed at the end. Behind them walked a third—bare-armed, steady—with a tally book on a cord around her neck. A bell-shard badge hung neat at her collar.

At the first door, a woman scrubbed the beam above the jamb with a clean rag. Cleaning made the ritual feel honest, even if it wasn't. The ashmaker dipped the pole's cup, shook it once, and held it under the wood like he was reenacting a gesture taught by tired fathers.

Gray sifted down: a line, a cross-stroke, a binding curve. The woman bowed—not believing, not really—just going along the way people do when everyone around them has decided fear looks like good manners.

The tally-keeper watched the man's mouth and wrote down the shape of the sound he made instead of the word itself. Instructions mattered more than meaning.

Sera's hum flattened, thin at the edges.

Gillie murmured, "Listen."

The ashmaker began the prayer, his voice worn flat by use, stripped of warmth until it sounded less like belief and more like a rule being enforced. Ash fell from the cup in a thin gray stream as he spoke, dusting the threshold as though the house itself were being taught to bow.

He called ash back to ash and commanded the night to stop at their doors. The people answered in a single, low murmur, not lifting their heads, asking that the dark forget their names as if anonymity were the only mercy still available to them. He spoke of ember returned for ash taken, of burning as a bargain that guaranteed silence. They repeated that what was burned would not betray, that breath must remain outside, that seams must hold whether they wished to or not.

The words gathered weight as they went, layering one fear atop another. Hinges were told to brace. Wood was told to remember. Even the ash itself was begged to keep count of those who had submitted to it. When he warned that the fields might hum and old songs might wake in children, the response sharpened into something close to panic: do not open, do not answer, do not let it in. When he spoke of drifting weights and water tasting of iron, they insisted it was not sickness but proof — proof that danger had been driven away, proof that obedience was working.

He lifted the cup again, letting the last gray powder sift down like a thin, lifeless snow.

Flame, he said, was faithful when fed.

The crowd answered at once, too quickly, promising to feed it, to keep feeding it, to give it whatever it required so long as it kept them from being chosen for something worse.

No one raised their voice. The prayer did not need volume. Fear had already done the work of shaping their breath, flattening it into the shallow, synchronized rhythm of people who had learned that safety came from sounding like everyone else.

Gillie didn't move. The scroll rested cold against her back—cold the way metal gets before it's used for something true. A correction without threat.

Miriam whispered, “Not curse. Imitation.”

Like she couldn’t stop the truth from finding her mouth.

We walked with the ashmakers without being noticed. People looked forward, not sideways.

Door to door. Beam to beam. Gray drifting like an obedient season. The tally book filled quickly; full pages made a small, triumphant sound that didn’t match anything we were seeing.

At the fifth house, the tally-keeper finally looked at us. Her face was young, but her eyes had the washed-out look of someone taught to obey before she learned to question.

“You’re not from here,” she said—not suspicion, just sorting the world into columns. “You carry quiet like it owes you.”

“We carry what owes itself,” Gillie said. She didn’t lift the scroll. She let its presence say what it needed to.

The woman nodded once. “We used to mark our brows with soot,” she said. “When the bell fell. Just for a day. Washed it off at dusk. Ate supper. Went on.” Her fingers brushed the gray cross forming on the doorframe. “Now they tell us to mark the wood instead. How high. How thick. Who pays.”

“Does it help anyone?” Nadya asked.

“It keeps our hands busy,” the woman said. “Busy feels like safe.”

A little boy tried to reach for the ash. His mother caught his wrist. “Don’t smear it,” she whispered, as if that one action might undo the whole keeping.

Eliah bent close to the drifting gray and sniffed. “Salt,” he murmured. “Fat. A touch of lye. Something sweet so it tastes like you should trust it.” His eyes watered. That part always made him honest.

The girl followed us from house to house. She didn’t join the line. She didn’t get in the way. She kept the exact distance of someone who wants to witness something without being caught doing it. Each time the ash fell, she took a small breath and pressed her palm to her chest, then dropped it before any watching mother could correct her.

The third time we passed, her lips moved—toward no one, shaped for no ear.

“Nine shall walk the broken path,” she whispered, so softly it might’ve been breath mistaking itself for words.

We turned a corner and found the cistern—half-buried in earth, stone lip worn smooth by years of hands. Someone had set up a small altar beside it: three bell-shards, a brass weight polished too often, a strip of gray cloth tied between two pegs. People queued with jugs, patient and quiet.

The ashmaker sprinkled a pinch across a plank laid over the opening. His voice took on practiced solemnity:

“To the water that forgets—”

“Remember sweetness.”

“To the weight that wanders—”

“Sit where we set you.”

He lifted the plank, dipped a cup, sipped, and didn’t flinch. Keeper’s tonic hid the taste. The crowd relaxed.

I tasted iron in memory and kept my hands off the jug.

“May I?” Nadya asked, holding out a square of cloth. The tally-keeper nodded like refusing a healer might be a sin.

Nadya dipped, lifted. The water darkened too fast. She touched the cloth to her palm. The ash clung and made a paste.

“It will cake in the throat,” she said.

“We say it binds what wanders,” the woman answered.

“It binds breath,” Nadya said. Not accusing—just naming.

Gillie asked, “Who taught you the prayer?”

"The hall," the ashmaker said. "Keepers came. Said the old words made us weak. These ones keep a town steady."

"And before that?" Rowan asked, gentle.

"We marked our brows with soot when the bell tolled," he said. "Ash was sorrow you wore for a day so you didn't wear it for a life." His eyes caught on the gray cross forming on another door. "Doors last longer than faces," he muttered. He didn't sound proud.

The girl slipped the cord she'd taken last night off her locket and closed her fist around it. A small act. But it was hers.

At the next door, an older woman held a bowl like she was ready to argue with it.

"Not the cross," she said firmly. "Just the top beam."

"The mark is the mark," the ashmaker replied.

"Above only," she repeated. "My son coughs at night. I'm not choking him with something pretending to be love."

The tally-keeper opened her mouth to correct her, then closed it again—like the words didn't taste right anymore.

Gillie stepped up. She didn't show the scroll. She pressed her palm flat to the door instead, as if checking its heartbeat.

"Ash is for grief," she said quietly. "It's not a door. Breath is the door."

"Breath lets in plague," someone muttered.

"Breath lets in morning," Gillie said.

The ashmaker hesitated, then sifted a single stripe along the top beam. No cross. No bind. The old woman nodded, satisfied. She pressed a handful of beans into the tally-keeper's palm. Payment turning into blessing where no one pushed it.

"You'll be reported," the ashmaker warned.

"I'll write 'rot in the lintel,'" the tally-keeper said, voice flat.

We stayed until the line thinned.

The coin in my pocket—Cephas's—warmed and cooled in its own rhythm. The scroll stayed steady on Gillie's back, patient as a slow breath.

The voice from the shade drifted out again, softer now. "They turned ash into a sacrament," he said. "Feels like obedience. Tastes like safety. Right weight for fear."

"What do we do?" Cassian asked. Anger suited him too easily.

"Teach them to be hungry without ash," Nadya said.

"And to breathe without asking," Rowan added.

Gillie loosened the strap one notch—not enough to show the scroll, just enough to let the Word breathe where the town had been taught not to.

The tally-keeper slowed as she passed us. Her voice stayed low.

"There's a boy with a cut lip on Mill Lane," she said. "Knows how to light lamps too well for a place like this. If you pass him—tell him not to tie the cord yet."

It was all the rebellion she could afford.

Mill Lane.

The name slid through me like a draft through an unlatched door—cold, familiar in a way I didn't have the history to explain. My lower lip tightened on its own. Old scar. Old ache. I touched it without thinking, then dropped my hand.

Back at the cart, the bell-shard badge had a new loop tied in three neat knots—waiting for a wrist that hadn't claimed it. The eave where the girl had stood earlier was empty. If she'd gone to warn the boy, she'd gone fast and quiet.

At the last corner, a figure stepped out from a post and let himself be seen.

Shim'on.

He kept his eyes on the ground. "I heard them bless proof," he said. "Didn't think I'd live long enough for that."

"They're blessing fear," Gillie said.

He nodded, small—like a wound figuring out its edges. "Breath will make a liar of me again. It always does. It'll ask, and I'll answer wrong."

"Then it'll ask again," Nadya told him.

Shim'on almost smiled at the cruelty of hope. "There's a line they don't print," he said. "Old man whispered it when they marked his door."

He swallowed. "Ash forgets the hand that scattered it."

He didn't wait for us to answer. Limped down a side street. Not running. Saving that for later.

We took the river road out of town. Behind us, doors held their fresh marks like they believed in them. Ahead, the fields hummed on a single note—lower than the day before. The wind carried iron and a sweetness I didn't trust.

Somewhere behind my ribs, that half-memory scratched again—Mill Lane.

Like a place where something important had happened.

To someone small. Quiet.

At the bend where houses gave up and became hedges, I looked back. The eave was just shadow again. The shard still hung with its three knots. If the girl had gone to Mill Lane, she'd chosen her moment well.

We set our feet to the path and did the only work a vow knows:

We didn't call fear mercy.

We didn't teach our lungs to hide.

The scroll rested steady against Gillie's back, like a reminder that ash remembers endings—

but breath remembers beginnings.

The Whispered Name

We turned off Mill Lane where the houses thinned and the river started braiding around old storage sheds and woodpiles. Out here the banks forgot which town they belonged to. The fields on the far side kept that low hum we'd first heard at the hall—same note, but dropped half a step overnight.

Lanterns hung along the lane, neat as stitches. Their light burned with the tidy, wrong confidence we'd seen in the square.

The tally-keeper had said: a boy with a cut lip on Mill Lane.

We found him where the road pinched tight to let a millstone through. Small shoulders. Bare feet. A brass-mouth lamp tucked under one arm like he was trying to stop it from doing anything foolish. He stood in a doorway with no door, the wall behind him smoked black where winter steam had escaped.

When he saw the scroll on Gillie's back, he flinched—as if some rule he didn't write had tapped him.

"You came," he said, like he half expected he'd imagined us.

"We're passing through," Gillie said. Gentle, but not soft enough to be mistaken for *we came just for you.*

He jerked his chin toward the black gap behind him. "Not inside. It hangs on to smoke. Hard to breathe."

He stepped into the lane. The brass lamp bumped a bucket and rang a small, embarrassed note.

"She told me to wait," he added, eyes low.

"The tally-keeper?" Nadya asked.

He nodded once.

"What's your name?" she said.

His fingers brushed the small, half-healed cut on his lip.

And before I could stop it, mine did too—an old scar tugging on its own, like a memory reaching up through skin without asking permission.

"People call me Boy," he said. Not offended. Just accurate.

"What do you call yourself?" Rowan asked.

The boy stared at the dirt between his toes like he'd buried something there. "Names are for saying," he whispered. "If I say mine, they'll write it down and keep me in the house. I don't want the house."

A little wind moved through the lane. Sera's hum followed it without thinking.

"You lit for the hall," Cassian said. Not accusing. Just setting facts down.

"They asked," the boy said, like that answered everything. "They made the brass one sing." He lifted the lamp a little and lowered it again. "Said the thin-frame one was wrong. Told me to leave it." His eyes flicked toward the scroll and away. "It's my favorite," he whispered.

"Mine too," Sera murmured.

He looked at her like something small inside him lined up.

Gillie crouched a little. "Do you know why we came?"

He thought the way careful people think. "Because the wrong light makes people sleep standing up," he said. "And then they forget they're standing."

Gillie's mouth twitched. "Will you walk with us?"

"Only as far as where the reeds say things," he bargained. "Past that, my father notices."

We walked. Houses peeled away until only lean-tos clung to the lane. The path sagged toward the river. The ground was packed and dusty, thin grass trying to be brave in the cracks. The air smelled of damp wood, old flour, and a faint iron note creeping into the water.

The river widened here, pretending to be still while it slid past. Reeds stood in clumps, their tips catching the thin gray of first light. Pale insects drifted over the surface, sluggish, not sure morning was worth it.

The boy set the brass lamp on a flat stone, turning its mouth away from the water like he didn't want to interrupt it. The flame shrank, offended.

He crouched—elbows on knees, eyes on the place where bank met current.

"When my father sleeps," he said, "the fields sing in my room and the walls sing back. I can't tell if it's outside or in my chest." He swallowed. "Sometimes it sings here too. It says a word without saying it."

"What word?" Nadya asked.

"I can't make my mouth do it," he said. No shame. Just fact. "But the air can, if I don't try too hard."

Gillie shifted; the scroll settled higher like it was choosing a better ear.

"Show us," she said.

He nodded. Scooted closer. Set his hands before his mouth—neither cupped nor folded in prayer. A narrow gate.

He breathed out.

At first, nothing. Just a thin exhale.

Then the nearest reeds leaned the wrong way—toward him, not the wind. A ripple walked through them in a ring.

Sera's hum slid to match whatever note had crossed the water.

He breathed again—longer.

This time the movement had shape. The reeds came forward, paused, and slipped back in a pattern—curved twice, then a short straight catch. Like air trying to write.

A small whirl formed on the water. Took two steps without going anywhere. Then let go.

The air pressed close for a heartbeat, bright and tight, like a word tried to form and changed its mind.

Something in my jaw tingled. My scar burned, faint as a match that didn't quite catch.

Gillie straightened. The scroll lifted lightly against her spine—like someone standing up in a crowd because they recognized something.

Cephas's coin warmed against my leg. It stayed warm.

Rowan exhaled. "Some names don't like ink," he said. "They'd rather live in air."

Before I could answer, the river shifted. The iron smell thinned, washed clean, then crept back—stubborn as habit.

"What do the reeds say?" Gillie asked.

"They say *don't* a lot," he said. "Don't tie cords too tight. Don't shut what you don't own. Don't put ash where breathing goes."

He frowned. "They say a *do* too. I don't know it yet."

"You will," Nadya said.

He breathed again—three small gusts.

The reeds answered: one clean lean, one full and heavy, one that snapped back sharp. The hum in the fields shifted—bright, then rough.

The scroll tightened once, like it filed something away.

Behind us, boot steps tried to be quiet and weren't.

"Time," Cassian murmured.

A voice carried down the lane, pleasant as a salve. "Neighbors. Don't trouble the river after hours. Hall's open if you've got the night in you."

Another voice, flatter: "Names for the list."

The boy brushed my cloak—not clutching, just checking I hadn't vanished—then snatched up the brass lamp and led us between two sheds. Boards sweated old moisture. A beetle worried its way along a crack like it had nowhere better to be.

The sheds opened into a small slipway where boats were dragged out for patching. One skiff lay half on land, ribs bare. The boy ducked under it and we followed, stooping.

He laid his cheek to the dark wood. The boat creaked once, like recognizing an old story.

He didn't hum aloud, but something in his throat worked, and the ribs took it up. A faint vibration traveled the keel and the air changed—tight, then open.

Three pulses slid through the space: one sharp and bright, coin-light; one low and full, like held breath; one rough, like metal bending against its own will.

Above us, the reeds echoed the same shape—stronger now. The pattern bent toward us—no, toward *me*—and the ache behind my teeth deepened, like a memory trying to stand.

Gillie knelt with her hand on the keel, the scroll steady on her back, listening hard. Sera touched the plank, eyes far away. Nadya counted the boy's breath like tracking steps in a pattern. Miriam held her bit of char as if she'd been assigned homework. Eliah didn't bother to hide the tears.

Light swelled at the mouth of the slip. Keepers. Lantern glow pressed forward, then hesitated—like even wrong fire knew better than to step under this hull.

"Neighbors," the pleasant voice called. "Come to the hall if you've got energy. We'll put it to record."

A pause.

"Those who leave their names, we can help."

They didn't come closer. The light retreated.

The sound under the boat settled. The boy lifted his cheek from the wood.

"Did you hear it?" he asked, braced for disappointment.

"I did," Gillie said softly, her eyes shining—not from fear, but relief.

"What's it called?"

"It calls," she said. "That's enough."

He nodded, grateful.

"Someone else heard," Rowan murmured.

A shadow shifted at the lane's edge, one leg dragging. Shim'on. He didn't come closer. He stared at the boards like they'd said something he'd heard once before and hoped never to hear again.

"I heard the hall teach fear to sound like sense," Shim'on rasped.

"They bless fear," Gillie said.

Shim'on nodded. "Breath will come back. Ask me something. I'll answer wrong again."

"Then it'll ask again," Nadya told him.

His mouth twitched—almost a smile.

"Old man said something when they marked his door," Shim'on added, voice rough. "Didn't write it down."

Rowan waited.

"Ash forgets who threw it."

Shim'on turned away, limping back into the dim.

The boy watched him go. "Will the fields stop? When it hums like that?"

"No," Nadya said gently. "But you'll know what you're hearing."

Something bright crossed his face—sudden understanding. "Do I say it? The word?"

"Sometimes," Gillie said. "Sometimes you hold it. It's a window, not a charm."

"My father says windows are where thieves come in."

"And mornings," Rowan said.

Eliah wiped his face. "We can't keep the river from tasting iron. But we don't have to call iron sweet."

The brass lamp sat quiet on the stone, its flame smaller now—humbled.

"Do you want to keep it?" Gillie asked.

He shook his head fast. "It likes hearing itself. I don't sleep right."

He held the lamp out to me. "Give it to someone who believes in it. They'll like it more."

It was heavier than it should've been.

"Tomorrow," Sera said, "tell anyone who asks you were listening for board-rot. Men trust jobs."

He grinned, uneven teeth showing. "I can tell the truth and keep my teeth."

Then, sobering: "They like lists."

"Then don't stand still long enough for them to finish writing," Rowan said.

He nodded like he was making a deal with his own legs.

We walked him back to the doorway with no door. He slipped inside. No lamp. Just quiet steps choosing the fear he could live with.

At the bend, the reeds tried the almost-word again—softer now, like a tongue practicing a new sound. The scroll leaned with Gillie. Cephas's coin pressed warm. A memory I didn't have a right to stirred behind my ribs—aching to be known.

Far behind us, someone spoke a wrong prayer onto a door beam. I heard its shape and didn't answer.

We turned toward the north road. Shim'on fell in beside us—quiet, limping a little, but not peeling away this time. He kept half a step behind Gillie, watching the edges of the lane like a man who knows shadows by their first intentions.

"Will you say it?" I asked Gillie when the path widened enough for kindness.

"Not here," she said. She brushed the scroll's binding. "Not yet. We don't spend what children saved for us just to hear ourselves sound brave."

The fields hummed. The river glinted—clean in places, spoiled in others. Lanterns bragged behind us. Above everything, the sky kept quiet.

Shim'on walked with us, shoulders hunched, eyes scanning hedges like he expected the dark to argue back. He didn't speak again, but his presence steadied the lane in a way his absence never could.

We walked, and the almost-name walked with us—not on our tongues, but in the small clear room just behind them, where breath keeps its truest words until the world is quiet enough to bear them.

The Burden of Truth

A Circle of Doubt

Morning tried to stand where noon belongs and didn't make it.

We felt it first in the feet—truth always gets there before it bothers with the eyes. Shade leaned the wrong direction; our shadows dragged for a breath, then hurried ahead as if the hour had slipped out of its frame. The light was bright enough to trust and crooked enough to make you blink twice.

Fences looked taller by an inch. Memory felt shorter by the same.

A faint river-iron taste rode the breeze—metal on the tongue before the mind agreed. We broke bread because hands remember what mouths forget. The crust cracked clean. The inside tasted like home if home were a word you hadn't spoken in a long time. It filled my mouth. It didn't feed me.

Gillie watched the road, then my jaw, then the scroll strap crossing my shoulder. She tightened it once. Not fear—habit. Vows ride better snug.

"Proof," Rowan said, walking backward so he could read the sky off our faces. "Or plague, depending on who nails up the notice."

"Ink or rope," Cassian muttered, thumb resting near old reflex.

Nadya sifted the light with her fingers. "Noon pretending," she said. "Good enough to fool a baker. Not a widow."

I felt the lie settle in my molars. Familiar in the way a scar is familiar.

"Gillie," I said quietly. "The hour won't hold."

Her breath hitched—barely, but enough. She didn't answer, which meant: say it so she doesn't have to.

"We thought we'd come back to the Bearing," I said—and the word tasted wrong the moment it left my mouth. "But the light slips. Bread won't feed. Time can't stand upright. If this isn't the Bearing…"

She turned her head a fraction—like she wanted to interrupt me and couldn't quite manage it.

I swallowed, because the next part didn't want to be spoken.

"…then whatever this is, it isn't out there."

I let the last piece fall. "It's us."

Gillie's shoulders tightened. A flicker of panic passed through her posture like a muscle remembering pain—the same flicker I'd seen when the lantern tried to speak, when Marcus stepped out of a place he shouldn't have survived.

She'd been holding this fear longer than she wanted to admit.

The scroll pressed once against my back—steady and aware. Not accusing. Not correcting. Just agreeing.

Gillie's jaw worked—first in rejection, then in surrender to the truth she already knew.

"So the swamp was his sin," she said, voice low and tight.

"And this part," I said, "is ours. What we broke in faith and love."

She breathed through her nose—hard. A breath you take when you're fighting the urge to look back at something that hurt you. A breath that chooses before the mouth consents.

"Then we walk it right," she said. "All the way this time."

I looked to the Seven. Expected panic. Expected argument. Got neither.

Rowan shrugged one shoulder, but the motion was tighter than usual, like he was rolling a weight he couldn't name off his back. "Seven's enough," he said. "Roads mind numbers more than names."

Cassian let his hand fall from his belt. The fingers didn't relax—they hovered, adjusting to the fact that no blade was going to solve whatever this was. "If it's ours, then we carry it. That's the trade."

Tomas spat dust, wiped his mouth with the back of his hand, and rolled his shoulders as if bracing for a load he'd carried before. "Ground's crooked. Sky's late. Still a road." He kicked a stone forward and watched it stop too soon. "We've walked worse."

Nadya studied the strange light, narrowing her eyes the way she does at a lie dressed as certainty. "Wrong is reason enough to walk forward."

Shim'on scanned the treeline, jaw clenched, breath slow and deliberate to hide the tremor in it. "I'll keep watch." This time it landed heavier, like he knew watching wouldn't be enough.

Sera tried a hum. The note stuttered halfway through, broke in the center like something fragile remembering it used to be whole. Her hand went to her throat—lightly, almost apologizing. "Later," she whispered. "It'll stand later."

Eliah tilted his head, listening to something none of us could trace. "The river hasn't turned," he said. "When it does, I'll tell you."

Miriam touched the pocket where her bit of char warmed faintly, the way someone checks a heartbeat to make sure it's still there. "Ash remembers," she murmured. "Keep walking. Memory will catch up."

The circle closed around us without ceremony. Their steadiness hit harder than fear would have.

Gillie met my eyes. "They know."

"And they still walk," I said.

But the thought that followed wouldn't leave me alone.

What else did they know?

The fields kept their low one-note hum—half a pitch under what it had been. Birds argued over berries instead of the sun. Somewhere in a hedge, a rooster shouted the wrong hour and went quiet like someone corrected him behind the beak.

Eldholme didn't rise ahead—it revealed itself the way old truths do: by habit, not grandeur.

"Holme," Sera said softly. "An island for old things."

"Eld—" Rowan traced the sound into his palm. "Breath that burns."

"Measures," Cassian said, eyeing the road. "Warden brings things here to make them true. Pins them to the wall if he has to."

"Pins are honest," Nadya said. "Until you ask them to hold two lies at once."

Dust gave way to stone. The river forked around a mound that looked less like a hill and more like a decision. Two bridges crossed it. We took the east—fewer men with lists.

A sentry in a coat that used to be wool glanced at the scroll and then studiously away. That's how men keep their day simple.

Eldholme's square rose ahead like a rule proud to be obeyed. The Measure House faced the sun with an arched doorway that made you step smaller without being told. A brass sundial blinked the wrong hour without apology. Above the lintel, a plumb bob hung from honey-dark cord—still, precise.

Opposite it, a kiln leaned against the sky—throat black, mouth wide. A sign read:

HALL OF MEASURES—ALL WEIGHTS TESTED BY LAW

Underneath, neat ink: WATCHLISTS POSTED AT SEXT.

Shops leaned in around the square—yard-wands over doorframes, scales in windows, stamped weights arranged like schoolchildren. Two lanterns burned extra daylight in the far corner. Their light was straight. Too straight.

Children played at the sundial's shadow—walk the chalk line without stepping off, ring the bell if you win. But the shadow was wrong, so the chalk was wrong, so the winning turned into laughter that hid a bruise.

"The hour's off," Eliah said. Small sentence. Not a small truth.

The plumb bob creaked once, swung the width of a breath, and tapped the lintel with the quiet knock of a tool doing its job. The sound ran up my spine and warmed Cephas's coin where it sat against my ribs.

Gillie pressed her palm—first to the scroll strap, then to the sundial's stone, then to the air. Three touches. Three ways of listening. The scroll didn't pulse. It paid attention.

We crossed the square without disturbing it. Cassian took the right line, Rowan drifted left, Nadya paced Gillie, Sera adjusted her breath to something steady, Miriam kept her char still in her pocket, and Eliah watched every dry place for the promise of water.

A ledger-boy hurried past with board and nails, seriousness borrowed from men twice his height. He hammered a notice to the kiln—blank spaces for names. They always start blank.

"Think our names are there?" Cassian asked.

"They've got everyone's," Rowan said. "They just don't know the spelling."

"Then don't teach them," Cassian muttered.

A yard-wand over a shop door bowed a fraction when the plumb swung. Not corruption—just a day with bad posture.

"Smell that?" Nadya asked.

"Pitch?" Rowan guessed.

"Ambition," she said. "With sugar on top."

On the kiln's ledge, a brass rod waited across iron hooks—four rings cut along its length: the Standard.

"Rod today," Cassian murmured. "Plumb every day. Scales for decoration."

"What's it prove?" Sera asked.

"Who can be taught to carry weight they didn't choose," he said. "And who applauds."

A watchman stepped forward. His smile was washed clean of personality. He watched the plumb more than the people.

"Neighbors," he called, using the Warden's favorite leash-word. "Sext will bring the posting. Till then—trade fair, witness fair, keep the Hall's law in your mouths."

A child tugged on his mother's shawl. "What is my mouth for?"

She shushed him with a kiss.

The watchman answered for her. "For speaking when spoken to."

The crowd rewarded him with a laugh polite enough to pass as agreement.

Something brushed past me—no face, just the contour of it. A small head tilt, like catching a word that wasn't said aloud. It felt like a reed remembering wind.

Gillie's knuckles touched mine. Not comfort. Alignment.

"We don't speak first," she said.

"No," I answered. "We witness."

"That's speaking," Rowan murmured.

The sun climbed wherever it thought climbing meant. The sundial refused the compliment. The plumb tapped the lintel again. A breath not ours moved under stone.

Eldholme inhaled.

We did not.

We let it arrange its lesson: law on a string, honesty measured in metal, crowds leaning in to applaud precision while hunger waited in another unit of measure.

Gillie tightened the scroll strap on my shoulder—not bravado, not dread. Just readiness.

And the scroll made the smallest sound it can make:

Not warmth.

Not warning.

Just listening.

Rejection and Reverence

Doubt didn't break or lift; it just settled lower, like mist sinking into the low parts of a field.

By midmorning the square had shaken off its tension and gone back to its routine. Men weighed grain with the scales they trusted. Women leaned on familiar doorframes. Whatever we carried moved through the town the way a river learns its bank—brushing past, leaving small changes behind it.

"We can keep walking," Cassian said, scanning alleys the way he always did.

"Truer things know when to stop," Gillie said.

A breath later, the scroll pressed against my shoulder—gentle, but not uncertain.

We turned into a narrow lane where the roofs leaned toward each other, tired of holding their own weight. At the third house—a narrow frame, plank soft at the base, one thin ash line above the lintel—we stopped.

An old woman stood in the doorway holding a bowl close to her ribs. Not offering it. Holding it the way people do when they're trying to keep their hands steady. Her son coughed in the back room—a thin, practiced sound.

Her eyes moved over each of us, and something in her face loosened when she saw Gillie didn't bow.

"You were at the hall," the woman said. "You didn't bend. And you didn't let them mark the child when everyone else was watching."

The cough came again, harsher this time. She flinched at the sound.

"My boy hasn't breathed right since the cold months," she said. "The ash didn't help him. Fear made it worse. And the hall's 'prudence'..." She shook her head once. "It only takes. It doesn't give."

She searched our faces—checking for judgment, checking for danger. When she didn't find either, she stepped back enough to open the doorway the rest of the way.

"Come in," she said. "If what you carry can help him breathe, I need to know. And if it can't..." Her mouth tightened. "At least someone honest will tell me."

Inside, the room was plain and careful. A scrubbed table. A mended stool. A red thread hanging from a nail. The boy lay under a thin blanket, cheeks pale, chest rising too shallowly. Sera hummed a low greeting—just enough for the wood to answer with a soft creak.

The ash line across the beam looked harmless.

That was the danger.

"May I?" Gillie asked, nodding toward the lintel. She lifted her hand, warming the air near it without touching. The scroll leaned lightly into my shoulder, listening without showing itself.

Eliah crouched beside the boy. "May I move the air a bit?"

"You may move what's yours to carry," the mother said, stepping aside.

Eliah lifted his hands. Nothing in the room stirred, but something shifted anyway. The boy's next cough had a little more space behind it. Even the ash above the lintel looked unsettled, like it understood it wasn't welcome.

From outside, a neighbor's voice snapped, "You'll bring the Warden if you keep that door open."

Rowan didn't look toward the sound. "We'll bring daylight," he said, and the lane went quiet.

The mother set her bowl on the table and lifted a cloth. She hesitated once, then said, "If ash belongs to grief, then I'll put it where grief actually lives."

She wiped the beam clean, gathering the gray carefully. She marked her own brow, then her son's—no crossing mark, nothing binding—then folded the cloth into the bowl like she was putting away a tool.

Outside, people gathered the way they do when a street senses a story forming. A patient-faced man wandered up first. Then a sharp-eyed woman. Then several more until they stood shoulder to shoulder at the threshold, pretending they hadn't come to watch.

"Don't leave it open," someone muttered—habit wearing a human mouth.

"Open isn't the danger," Nadya said. "It's what you let in."

The ashmaker rounded the corner with his pole. The ledger-woman followed. They stopped at the edge of the doorway—close enough to see in, not close enough to cross.

The ledger-woman took in the room in two fast glances—the wiped beam, the bowl, the boy's breathing. She pushed her quill into her hair, like she didn't trust her hand yet.

"Who changed the mark?" the ashmaker asked, boots planted on the stoop.

"I did," the mother said. "Because I know what helps and what doesn't."

The ashmaker's shoulders eased for half a heartbeat, then he remembered the Hall and lifted his sieve.

Sera's hum dipped, thin as a warning.

"Not over this door," Gillie said. "Not today."

"Truth," the ashmaker said, chewing the word like it might break a tooth. "The hall calls this prudence."

"The hall sells it," Cassian said—flat, not angry.

He nodded down the lane. "Two watchers. One writing. One pretending not to."

The boy coughed again. The crowd stiffened, the way people do when a body reminds them they can't argue their way out of hunger.

The ledger-woman stepped forward—just enough to count as courage. "Custom allows a change for rot," she said. "Or damp. Or a lintel that's splitting." She met Gillie's eyes. "Sometimes for breath."

The ashmaker lowered the sieve.

"The hall will want a page," he said.

"You'll give them one," the ledger-woman replied. "We'll give the door what it asked for."

Down the street, a lantern flickered green. It licked at an awning, then calmed like it remembered it had rules.

A man stepped forward, face tight with worry. "Before you judge us," he said, "tell me what feeds my child when breath brings plague."

"Bread," Rowan said. "And a door that doesn't lie."

The man's hand jerked out—fast, defensive—and smeared ash onto Gillie's sleeve, careful not to touch the scroll strap on my shoulder. "You bring chaos," he said.

"I bring a question," Gillie answered. She touched the smear, then the doorframe, as if setting both back where they belonged. "Same as you."

"Then answer mine."

"When the boy can breathe."

Eliah lifted the blanket a finger's width. New air reached the boy. Sera's hum brightened, then steadied. When Eliah lowered the cloth again, the room smelled less of iron and more of morning.

The boy slept deeper.

The man who'd spoken stared at his own hands like they'd betrayed him, then stepped back into the crowd and let somebody else hold his fear.

A girl with freshly braided hair stepped up to the doorway. She rested her palm on the frame and lowered her head—not to us, but to the house. She whispered something—thanks, or hope—then moved aside.

Miriam knelt at the threshold and drew a small open circle near the step. No closing line. Just a mark that said the door was still meant for breathing people, not fear. The ledger-woman saw it and didn't object. She brushed her heel across it lightly—enough to make it look like accident to anyone who came later.

Cassian leaned in from the lane. "We need to move. Someone's gone to get a bell."

"Noise can help," Rowan said.

"It can also drown everything out," Cassian replied.

Gillie looked to the mother. "Do you want to keep the ash or wash it?"

"Either works," the woman said. "I'll wash it at dusk. Feed him first." She brushed the ash smear from Gillie's sleeve with a simple, steady gesture. "Go on. We're all right here."

Gillie nodded. She stepped back. I stepped with her. The others followed until the whole group was outside again.

The mother didn't close the door right away. She watched us long enough to know we weren't abandoning her, then pulled the door in gently and slipped the latch.

The lane held its crowd. People adjusted their faces the way people do when they want to pretend they weren't watching. A few looked away too quickly. A few stared too long. A few stood still—not afraid, just paying attention in a way that mattered.

The ledger-woman lifted her wrist for half a second. A pale cord-scar showed, then vanished again. Not confession. Just the only way she could say she understood.

Shim'on stood near the second post, close enough to hear everything, far enough to pretend he wasn't part of it. When a bell clanged somewhere deeper in the town, he flinched and leaned his shoulder into the wall as if steadying himself—but he didn't step back.

We started walking. Some of the crowd shifted aside. Some slipped back into their homes. Sera kept a low hum under her breath. Eliah wiped his palms on his coat. Cassian read every side street. Nadya held the cloth the mother had used, annoyed at it for pretending it had ever helped anyone.

At the corner, a boy with a cut lip—one who wasn't ours—stood beneath a fresh ash cross on a new-marked door. He stared at it like he didn't trust the meaning. He raised his hand and traced a faint, invisible line just above it, like correcting a mistake on a board. Then he dropped his hand before his father turned.

Something in the way he studied the mark felt familiar.

"Does truth always do this?" Cassian asked once the street gave us a little room. "Split a town this fast?"

"Truth only breaks what was already cracked," Gillie said.

"And what are we?" Cassian asked.

Gillie reached up and adjusted the scroll strap where it crossed my shoulder. "We're the seam," she said. "If we do this right, both sides might hold."

Cassian moved ahead toward the sound of the bell. Miriam walked beside me, her thumb still smudged with char.

"The fire's talking again," she said softly.

"What's it saying now?"

"It wants to know whether we understand the difference between exposure and shame." She glanced back toward the house. "We're about to find out."

Where the lane narrowed into the path toward the fields, dust showed a few footprints crossing Miriam's open circle. Some blurred it. Some avoided it altogether. One small bare foot stepped squarely inside the mark and pivoted sharply to leave—a quick motion, like choosing a direction.

"Signs," Rowan murmured.

Nadya shrugged once. "Dust tells the truth better than most people."

We didn't read them yet. Behind us, a watcher miscounted our number—fear always makes the hand shake. Ahead, the fields kept their low, steady hum. The scroll settled against my back again. Not warning. Not reassurance. Just weight. Purpose.

Rejection and reverence had taken turns at the same doorstep. The house still stood. The boy was breathing easier. By nightfall, the town would decide what story it wanted to tell about all of it.

We kept walking.

Signs in the Dust

The town let us go without ceremony. Nobody stopped us. Nobody called after us. We followed the street until the cobblestones thinned and the dirt road started—lighter underfoot, like it remembered travelers better than the people who lived there.

Miriam walked beside me, rubbing ash off her thumb. Rowan kept quiet, which usually meant he was thinking too hard. Sera hummed under her breath. Cassian counted alleys again—his nervous habit, the one he pretended was prayer.

Gillie looked back once at the house we'd left, then kept walking.

At the last bend, dust shifted around our boots. A low wind carried iron and something faintly sweet. The fields ahead made that soft, unsettled sound we'd heard earlier.

"Hold up," Miriam said.

The road ahead was marked. Not with paint—dragged by a small branch. Circles, half-circles, three short lines inside one of the shapes. Heel marks that doubled back, like whoever made them changed their mind twice. And near the edge, someone had copied Miriam's open circle—first clean, then sloppy, then honest. A child's heel print turned inside one.

"Don't step in the circle," a voice said from the right.

We all turned.

A man stood near the drainage ditch. Not hiding, not announcing himself—just there, like he'd been waiting for the dust to finish saying what it needed to say. Dust clung to his clothes. A hemp cord wrapped his wrist. A plumb-bob and folding rod hung from his belt. His face held that steady look that makes rushed people feel foolish.

"You've been reading us," Rowan said.

"I've been reading the ground," the man replied. He stepped closer—not toward us exactly, but toward the space between us and the markings. "Name's Micah. I measure where things sit. And where they don't."

"What do you measure exactly?" Nadya asked.

Micah lifted the plumb. It swung once, then settled—too neat to be luck, too slow to be performance.

"Weight that won't settle," he said. "Ground that remembers. Wind that can't agree with itself."

His eyes touched the scroll on my back and moved on, as if staring would count as a kind of theft.

"You're carrying something the road notices," he added. "Doesn't mean it objects."

"The ground speaks without us," Gillie said.

Micah smiled—not correcting her, not agreeing. "Sure. But sometimes it waits for a witness before it decides how loud to be."

He pointed at the heel mark. "Small foot. Carrying something she didn't want—rope, most likely. Came from the square. Stopped once. Turned back. Tried again. Cut across this way."

He knelt beside Miriam's open circle, careful not to disturb it. His fingers hovered near the child's heel print, close enough to feel the dust shift, never pressing down.

"She watched you yesterday. Watched again this morning." A pause. "She's trying to say something her house won't let her."

"The girl," I said.

Micah nodded. "She's practicing refusal where it won't be punished yet." His voice flattened. "It doesn't stay that way."

Gillie hesitated, then said, "Would you walk with us? Just for a while."

Micah lifted one hand, palm outward—not refusal. Measuring. "I'm not a guide. Guides point. I just check whether the ground agrees with what people are already doing."

He tapped the plumb lightly against his belt. "I go where things lean."

"Who taught you?" Miriam asked.

Micah shrugged. "Couldn't afford anyone worth learning from. So I watched longer than most people do."

He drew a long, curved line in the dirt—smooth, practiced. "Veins. Old ones. Ground holds steadier along them. If you're trying to leave quietly, you don't fight the veins—you let them carry you where they already want to go."

The scroll shifted against my back. Not warm. Not resisting. Just there—listening past what was being said.

Micah noticed and nodded once, like that settled something.

"Reed-stand ditch first," he said mildly. "Then the barley path that looks wrong until you walk it."

He handed the rod to Nadya. "Set it where the shadow holds two breaths."

She did. The shadow settled—clean, obedient.

Micah glanced at the sun. "See? Long way's kinder."

"Why help us?" Cassian asked.

Micah answered without pause. "Because the town would want someone to carry blame before nightfall. Because the door you came from will be fined for something it didn't do. Because that girl will be asked about her rope, and I'd rather she be late."

His gaze brushed the scroll again—lighter this time. "And because whatever you're carrying hasn't told me not to."

The scroll pressed once. Not assent. Not warning. Presence.

We walked.

Micah stayed left, near the reeds. His plumb tapped his leg in an easy rhythm. When he paused, it wasn't to doubt the way—only to confirm it.

He adjusted our line by a few degrees, set the rod down, and the shadow settled as if it had been waiting for the choice.

"You like circles," he said to Miriam.

"Open ones," she said.

"Good," he replied. "Closed things forget how to breathe."

We passed behind a mill wheel turning on less water than it deserved. Barley brushed our sleeves. Micah pushed it back with the casual care of someone who knew what it took to grow something—and when to leave it alone.

At the reed ditch, he slid down first, steadying the bank with his heel. The bell at the watch-post beyond sat silent, undecided.

"Stone warmed again," Miriam said.

"This line's older than the trouble," Micah replied. "Ground outlasts excuses."

Gillie moved closer to me. The scroll pressed harder—not warning, not approval. Weight.

"You don't have to carry all of it," she murmured.

"I will," I said.

She nodded, satisfied. “Just don’t carry it alone.”

At the fork—trees or river—Micah crouched and let dust slip through his fingers.

“Two sets passed,” he said. “One light. One dragging something they don’t want to name.”

“Which way?” Gillie asked.

Micah didn’t look at the river. “Trees. River carries sound too clean. People who want to follow you prefer echoes.”

No one argued.

Roots clacked underfoot. Sera hummed, and a jay answered louder than necessary, covering us. On the far side, Micah drew a straight line with his boot and let the wind soften it.

“Wind’s honest,” he said. “Hands less so.”

“Will you teach the girl?” Miriam asked.

Micah’s gaze lingered on Gillie’s hands—only a moment. “If she asks. And if she wants to learn where being seen won’t cost her yet.”

He straightened. “I’ll walk with you long enough to understand how you carry what you carry.”

“And then?” Rowan asked.

Micah smiled—pleasant, unreadable. “Then I’ll see if the ground still listens when I stop talking to it.”

We stepped onto a road that hadn’t settled on a shape. The last houses leaned away from us.

“You belong to a hall?” Cassian asked.

Micah shook his head. “I belong to things that sit right.”

We headed north.

Micah walked beside me, plumb tapping softly. Behind us, the town bells tried to guess our names and failed. Ahead, sunlight warmed the dirt—and something deeper that remembered being warm first.

Miriam glanced back at the markings. "Signs."

"Notes," Nadya said.

"Breath," Sera added.

Micah drew one final line beside our footprints—open at the top. The wind softened it, but didn't erase it. Enough for someone careful to find.

We walked on.

The road widened, narrowed, and widened again—the way roads do when they're willing to be convinced.

Something in me shifted with it.

The Girl Returns

The first hint came before the wind changed.

A flash—barely a thought—an image that didn't belong to the road in front of me.

A woman on the edge of a narrow bed. Hands in her lap. Shoulders shaking. A blanket folded too neatly beside her. The quiet, awful way she rocked as if something small had been in her arms and wasn't.

I didn't know the room.

I didn't know the season.

I didn't know the reason.

But the grief was familiar in a way I hated.

Before I could name it, the vision slipped away—clean and fast, like a hand wiping fog off glass.

The wind pushed us out of Eldholme and into open country. We let Micah's rod set our line and trusted the ground more than the last town we'd walked through.

Houses thinned, then stopped. Fences fell away. Even the faint lantern-hum we'd grown used to finally gave up. Fields broke into scrub, then into bare earth streaked with pale stone. The sun felt cleaner out here, like it didn't have to shine through anyone's lies first. Dust tasted sharp, with old salt at the back of the throat.

Under all of it was that sound we'd been pretending we didn't notice. Not a real bell—more the memory of one, low and steady somewhere under our ribs. Easy to call it nerves. Harder when it kept coming back.

Micah kept to the right-hand edge, where the wind still remembered yesterday. His plumb bumped his leg in a slow rhythm. Sometimes he stopped, checked a shadow, and gave a small nod. When he did, we moved. When he didn't, we waited.

The land flattened until it almost stopped being a place and turned into a surface. Low rises. Wind-cut stretches. Nothing tall enough to hide in. Iron came and went in the air like a rumor that couldn't decide whether to stay. A hawk turned slow circles overhead, tracing the same open shape Miriam liked to draw in dirt.

"Listen," Sera said quietly.

The hum in our bones thickened. Still not a proper note, but it had weight now—enough my shoulders felt it, not just my ears.

The ground ended.

One step we were on level stone. The next we were on the rim of a long red cut in the earth. The canyon dropped away—narrow, deep—its walls folded tight like frozen fire. Wind moved through it in steady drafts. Not wild. Trained.

We stopped at the edge. Heat rose from inside. Cool air slid past our faces, smelling of rock and something faintly metallic. Light pooled in the shadowed walls in a way that made time hard to trust.

Gillie set her hand on my shoulder where the scroll strap crossed. The weight on my back answered with a small, steady pressure, like it had been waiting for this place.

Micah squinted along the far side. "No path," he said. "Not unless you plan on walking on air."

"That's not what it's for," Gillie said under her breath.

Her gaze shifted—not down, but across. I followed it.

She stood on the far side of the canyon where no one should have been able to stand.

The girl.

Barefoot on a rock ledge barely wider than her stance. Same clothes as before, but they sat differently on her, like she'd grown into them overnight. Wind tugged at her hair but never quite turned it to a mess.

She held her right hand out where we could see it.

A spiral was etched into her palm. Not ink. Not a simple scar. Shallow grooves that caught the light when the air shifted. When the next gust rose through the canyon, the lines darkened for a heartbeat—as if the wind was tracing them from the inside.

The pattern matched the marks in the dust.

It also matched something in my chest that didn't have a name yet.

The scroll leaned forward against my back—no flare, no heat—just a quiet tilt toward her, as if it recognized her shape.

She didn't shout. She didn't need to. The canyon carried her voice clean.

"I heard the bell," she called. "I saw the lights over the hall. You're not the only ones who remember."

Micah set his plumb and watched it. The line swung out over the drop, then pulled back tight, settling faster than it should have. "There's an updraft," he said. "Strong one. Feels like steps you can't see."

He raised his voice. "Where did you come from?"

"From before the ash," she answered.

Gillie's breath hitched—the same small catch I'd heard when Marcus stepped back into a world he shouldn't have survived. Her fingers curled around the edge of my strap, like she needed to know exactly where the scroll sat in that moment.

"Then something new has started," I said before I could stop myself.

The canyon swallowed the words and kept them. That felt about right.

The girl lowered her hand and stepped off the ledge.

She didn't fall.

She moved—careful, certain—using narrow ridges and shallow shelves in the rock, pausing when a gust rose, letting the updraft hold her the way a hand would. For a breath, the wind made her light.

When she turned, the air revealed faded cord-burns on her forearm—scars that lingered despite healing.

She reached our side, stepped onto stone that should have belonged only to goats and mistakes, and finally exhaled. The spiral on her palm dimmed, leaving faint grooves in the light.

Gillie's voice came softer than usual. "What should we call you?"

"Kaela," she said.

No hesitation. Like she'd earned that name and wasn't letting anyone rename her again.

For a heartbeat, Gillie's breath caught—not surprise. Recognition. Not Kaela herself, but the way she stood. The set of her shoulders. The way she held her hands when she thought no one was watching.

Then it passed. She was only the girl again—steady, unafraid.

Up close, she still looked like a child and not like one. Dust clung to her ankles. Dried red sat at the edge of her lower lip, a half-healed split that echoed the boys we kept seeing. Her eyes moved over all of us in turn. When they reached me, they lingered a heartbeat too long.

Something in my chest nudged back—then went still, like a memory turning over in its sleep.

Kaela didn't make introductions. She didn't ask for ours. She turned and started walking along the canyon rim, steady and sure, as if there were lines drawn there only she could see.

We followed. Micah took the outside edge, watching for bad ground. His plumb tapped his hip. The bell-sound in our bones stayed with us, a little louder now that we had less between us and the depths.

"The line's tighter here," Miriam said, her thumb brushing the bit of char in her pocket without her thinking about it.

The canyon drew in. Walls pulled closer. Red stone darkened toward iron, streaked black in places as though it had known fire once and never cooled all the way. The echo of the hidden bell stopped feeling like imagination and started feeling like a thing we were walking inside.

Gillie moved nearer to Kaela. "Why bring us this way?"

"Because something that's been locked is going to give," Kaela said. Flat. Not dramatic. "When it does, the bell won't sound like it did in the town. It will sound like it does under your ribs."

She glanced back, eyes steady.

"That will be the last toll."

"And the nine shall walk the broken path," Rowan murmured—like the words had been waiting in him for the right air.

Micah glanced up at the sky, then back to the seam of the canyon. "What lock?" he asked. "Whose?"

Kaela lifted her palm again. The spiral looked ordinary until the wind shifted and the grooves gathered shadow enough to stand out.

"The one people made when they decided fear was safer than trust," she said. "They named it wisdom. They nailed it over doorways. They called it proof. They let it choose who could breathe and who had to earn it. They've been feeding that choice a long time."

Her mouth tightened.

"It thinks it deserves to live."

Nadya's jaw set. "You're talking about the ash marks."

"I'm talking about anything that pretends to protect and only chokes," Kaela said. "The ash is just today's version."

"Plagues, then," Rowan said quietly. "Consequences with teeth."

"Names," Kaela replied. "Water knows when it's been carrying iron too long. Fields know when breath has been strangled. Weights know when they've been forced to lean. Lanterns remember they were made to push darkness back—not own it."

Eliah's voice dropped almost to nothing. "The bell rang once in Joshua's swamp. You're saying it rings again?"

"Once for the whole world," she said. "Once for a single man. Some people think they dodged it the first time." Her eyes stayed steady. "They didn't. They're just late."

We reached a narrow place where the canyon walls nearly touched—a tight passage shouldered in stone. The wind slowed there and the sound changed, picking up a strand of grief—quiet but steady.

"Is this where you wanted us?" Cassian asked. He always sounded calmest when he didn't trust a place.

"It's where you can hear clearly," Kaela said.

Micah touched a line in the rock that looked like a crack and wasn't. "Step over this," he warned. "Looks solid, but it isn't."

We stepped. Dust kicked up in small spirals. Miriam scuffed a shallow open circle with her heel. The breeze passed through it and didn't wipe it away.

Kaela stopped in front of a tall red spur of stone and pressed her palm flat against it. The spiral darkened again, just a little—as if the stone was sending something back through her.

"This is a door," she said.

Cassian studied the rock. It looked the same as it had a moment before. "To what?"

"To a memory," she said. "Not just yours. Not just this town's. Bigger than that."

She took her hand away. The stone didn't move, but the air did. A new smell threaded in around dust and heat—damp earth, old smoke, and a faint sweetness that reminded me of oil used when people prayed over the sick.

"From where?" Micah asked, careful now.

"From before the ash," Kaela said. "From when people still knew what breath was for—and how wrong they were capable of being."

We stood together long enough for the moment to settle. The bell-sound quieted but didn't leave. The scroll on my back stayed still, like a person bracing just before lifting something heavy.

Cephas's coin warmed against my leg, then cooled again. Metal remembering metal.

"Come with us," Gillie said at last.

"I'll walk ahead," Kaela answered.

Gillie frowned. "Not with us?"

"Some choices have to be made with nobody else in the room," Kaela said. She looked down the pass, then back. "A man is going to deny what loves him before the day is done. Better for him if he doesn't mistake me for a second chance he can waste."

No one argued. There are lines you don't cross with more words.

Kaela walked along the rim, then paused and looked back. Wind tugged her hair and cloak. The spiral on her palm had faded until it was almost nothing.

"When the seal breaks," she said, "choose breath, even if it feels like starving. Don't call ash mercy just because it's familiar." She held our eyes a beat. "And when you hear the bell toll for a man, not a town…"

Her voice dropped low enough that the canyon kept the rest.

"Listen."

She stepped around the red spur and vanished.

Micah took half a step as if to follow, then stopped himself, jaw tight. Whatever path she was on, it wasn't ours to walk.

We waited until the echo of her footsteps—if that was what we'd heard—faded out. The bell-sound sank deeper again, back to the level where it hummed inside bone and thought.

"Messenger?" Cassian asked quietly.

"Feels like someone who remembers what this story started as," Gillie said. She tightened the strap a little. The scroll adjusted against my back, settling into the place it uses when grief and hope sit side by side.

Micah pressed his palm to the seam in the rock as if testing it. "There's weight behind this," he said. "Not the kind you can measure. The kind that tells you whether your measurements ever mattered."

"Will you keep walking with us?" I asked.

"I will," he said. He checked his rod once more, watched the shadow, and let out a slow breath when it lined up. "But we'll take the long way down. I'd rather not be the example in someone else's cautionary tale."

He led us into the narrow section of the pass, choosing each step like it counted. The walls rose higher, tightening the sky into a strip, and the wind changed tone—lower, more focused, as if it had stopped chatting and started working.

On my back, the scroll didn't push or burn or drag.

It simply waited—heavy and patient—the way vows do when they know the thing that will test them is already on its way.

Seeds of Doubt

The Listening Few

By noon the canyon's cool breath had finally settled into our bones.

We walked until the red stone slipped behind us and the ground remembered how to be brown again—ordinary brown, the kind you could farm or sit on or trust. Far off, barley fields rippled like someone smoothing out a blanket. The wind eased into the honest language of weather.

But the bell's weight stayed with us.

Quiet.

Stubborn.

A question that didn't care whether we were ready to answer.

Micah kept checking his rod as we walked. He did it the way a man keeps poking a bruise just to see if it has changed its mind. The plumb warmed in the sun and cooled in the next breath of shade. It behaved like something that half-remembered faith but didn't know if it wanted to taste it again.

"Where now?" Cassian asked.

He sounded like someone asking for the next step after a confession.

Nadya shaded her eyes and nodded toward a dip in the land where three hedges leaned together. "Somewhere people listen before they talk," she said.

She wasn't trying to be clever.

She meant it.

Shim'on was already looking that way. Not at the hedges—at the spaces between them. The places a man could stand without being seen. The places a watcher would choose if he wanted to hear without being counted.

Micah led us down into the dip.

Past the hedges sat a granary with its door pressed halfway inward by sacks, like someone had opened it with a hip and forgotten to fix it. A loft window watched the lane, the kind of window that never truly slept. Empty lantern hooks lined the eaves.

If you squinted, you could imagine what used to hang there.

If you didn't, you could imagine why they stopped.

We knocked the way Sera taught us—soft breath against the wood. A small tone hummed back, like the door was choosing to trust us. A deeper tone answered from inside. Then someone drew the latch.

Five people waited in the dim between bins.

Not gathered like a crowd.

Placed like parts.

The lantern-maker's sister, hands clean in a way that meant she'd scrubbed them too often. The ledger-woman from the ash cart, her mouth set like she'd bitten down on a truth and kept it there. A boy with a cut lip healing into a thin scar, eyes moving too fast for his small face. A flour-dusted older man whose hands had weighed grain long enough to start weighing people. And a rope-lullaby woman—arms strong, voice tired, eyes worn in a familiar way: exhaustion braided to endurance.

Each of them held a different splinter of it, tucked where the Hall couldn't see.

"We weren't followed," Cassian said quietly from the shadow between the bins.

I still didn't know how he beat us inside.

That's how regret works—it shows up before anyone names it.

Shim'on didn't contradict him. He only shifted his stance so his shoulder faced the door at an angle—ready for it to open fast, ready for it to stay shut. A man who'd been caught before learns what his body believes.

"We don't keep names here," the sister said. "Just ears."

The room smelled of grain and rope fibers and the slow patience of people who fix things instead of talking about them.

Sera brushed her fingertips along a crossbeam and hummed softly; the wood hummed back with steady trust.

Eliah poured a little water into a shallow bowl. The light on its surface didn't distort. No wrong shimmer. No quiet green.

Miriam drew an open circle in the chaff by the threshold and left the top unfinished. A draft slipped through, but the circle held.

Micah leaned his rod near the door where its shadow could betray any hour that tried to move wrong again.

Gillie kept the scroll tucked close. She didn't lift it.

It lifted when it wanted.

"You saw the mark," the ledger-woman said.

She didn't say Kaela's name. She didn't have to.

Gillie nodded.

The ledger-woman's shoulders dropped—one inch, like she'd been holding her breath since sunrise and had forgotten it was allowed to leave.

"We call ourselves the Listening Few," the flour man said, rubbing his thumb along his palm. "Keeps the watchmen from accusing us of building a church we don't want."

"Church is what happens when people stop listening," Rowan said.

He wasn't correcting anyone.

He was just naming a thing he'd learned the long way.

The boy pushed his hair back from his forehead. "So… what are we listening for?"

Nadya didn't answer like a teacher.

She answered like a knife laid on a table.

"Three things," she said. "What the town calls proof. What fear pretends is mercy. And what breath knows is the truth."

The sister set a plain iron lamp on the floor and stepped back from it. Its panes were spotless. She didn't light it.

"We only burn this if we understand why," she said. "Sometimes a lamp helps you see. Sometimes it announces you. Today we don't need either."

"Plain sight's enough," Rowan murmured.

Nobody preached.

We just talked.

It felt like trading sacks—lifting each one long enough to see what was inside, then passing it on before it could tear your shoulder.

"They changed the prayer again," the ledger-woman said. "Ash on the doorframe now, not the brow."

"My mother's lullaby bends when I sing it near the Warden's flame," the rope-lullaby woman said. "The baby wakes up scared every time."

"My weights test right in the Hall," the flour man said, "but lean here." He tapped his knuckle against the granary floor. "Like the ground's tired of pretending."

"When I whisper the word the reeds know," the boy said, "the lantern shutters snap like they're angry I remembered it."

Micah set the plumb against a post.

It swung once.

Settled.

Then slid sideways the smallest fraction—like it had decided to finally be honest.

"We stopped hanging lamps at dusk," the sister said. "Except one for sickness or midwives. Stars can handle the rest."

"Good," Gillie said. "Lamp-light gets proud."

Shim'on's eyes flicked up at the rafters—at the empty hooks. A quick check, like he was counting how many places a town used to put trust. Then his gaze fell back to the doorway.

Always the doorway.

Cassian leaned a shoulder against the wall. "What do you want us to do?"

Micah didn't puff it up.

"Small things," he said. "The kind that stay true when no one's watching. Keep the hour steady. Make weights sit right. Leave gaps where marks want to lock down."

"That sounds like chores," the boy said, almost disappointed.

"It is chores," Nadya answered. "The kind that matter more than speeches."

Silence settled.

A good kind.

Not heavy.

Just honest.

The scroll pressed once against Gillie's ribs.

Not a flare. Not heat.

A small, certain yes.

"Gillie," the sister said. "Say it."

Gillie didn't raise the scroll.

She didn't need to.

"When the seal breaks, choose breath," she said. "Even when it feels thin. Don't call ash mercy. And if a bell tolls for someone—don't make him pay to hope again."

No one argued.

The lamp stayed unlit.

Footsteps approached outside—quiet ones, the kind taught to be quiet on purpose. They paused at the hedges.

The ledger-woman set a yoke across two sacks like she'd been doing it all day. Cassian pressed deeper into shadow. The boy slid under the table and held still.

Shim'on didn't hide.

He moved.

One step to the side of the door. Not blocking it—just becoming the kind of shape a man's eyes register before his mind chooses what to do. A reminder placed where it mattered: you can enter, but you won't enter clean.

"Neighbors," the first man called.

"Grain check," the second said, holding a slate too clean to be honest.

"The Hall does checks," the sister called back, cheerful as weather. "We're doing chores."

A lantern outside flickered green before it remembered obedience.

"Curfew at Sext," the second voice warned. "Lamps visible."

"We like stars," the sister said. "They don't bill us."

They didn't come in.

Men who rely on borrowed light don't trust rooms with their own.

Micah let out a slow breath. "Seeds," he said.

"What kind?" the boy whispered.

"Listening," Micah said.

"Like bones," Nadya added.

We left them small work—quiet work:

An unlit lamp near the door.

Proof-cups rinsed in clean water.

The top of the circle left open.

Truths spoken only where they wouldn't be bent into currency.

"What if they come with ledgers?" the flour man asked.

"Give them a page," the ledger-woman said. "Keep the story."

At the threshold, Miriam's open circle held its gap like a promise that refused to close.

Shim'on stopped there.

He looked down at the open line.

Then he set his boot beside it—not on it.

A choice so small no watcher would ever write it down.

But the room saw.

"I'll stay near," he said, not to us alone—also to them. A vow you can live with. A vow that doesn't get you killed the first night you speak it.

"Near counts," Gillie said.

We left like people who'd done something ordinary and important.

Outside, Micah checked the rod's shadow. "The hour stayed steady," he said.

"Maybe it listened," Sera replied.

We turned north.

Behind us, the granary settled back into its chores.

Ahead, the wind carried a faint bell tone—thin, unpretending.

The scroll stayed still.

It listened.

And behind shuttered windows, hands we'd never see chose stars instead.

A Mother's Question

Dusk softened the sharp edges of the hedged lanes until everything around us felt half-remembered.

We were turning north when a woman stepped out from a narrow yard, a bundle propped on her shoulder and a baby on her hip. Her hands looked like they'd spent years tying rope and soothing children—strong in the ways work makes you strong, gentle in the ways worry makes you gentle. The baby breathed in that quick, shallow way common to rooms lit with the wrong kind of flame.

A girl peered out from behind the doorway—older by several years—then slipped back inside when her mother shifted her weight. The woman didn't call her out. She only settled the baby higher and tightened the bundle on her shoulder.

"Wait," she said. Not pleading. Not demanding. Just tired weather.

Shim'on had been a step behind us, keeping to the lane's edge like he belonged there. He stopped first—not because the woman spoke, but because the hedges went too still. His eyes traveled the line of posts, the places a lantern would hang, the angles a watcher would favor. Then he looked at Gillie and gave the smallest shake of his head.

Not here in the open.

Gillie stopped anyway, but she stopped the way you stop when you're willing to be seen for the right reason. The scroll stayed tucked against her ribs, quiet in the way it listens.

The woman drew a small breath and lifted her chin, like she needed us to stand inside the courage she'd gathered. "When the fields start humming at night, my child wakes up terrified," she said. "And I don't know what to trust anymore. Do I light one of the Hall's lanterns like they tell us, or do I open the window and let real air in?"

She looked down at the baby. "I need to know which one actually helps him breathe."

For a heartbeat none of us spoke. It wasn't fear—it was the weight of a mother asking the right question in a world that kept handing her the wrong answers.

Sera stepped forward first. She always did when someone asked something with their whole body. She let a soft tone slip from her throat, barely there. The baby's chest eased a little—not fixed, but loosening, like a fist deciding it didn't want to stay closed forever.

"May we come to your door?" Gillie asked.

The woman nodded and led us beneath a lintel missing its cross-line. Only the upper ash-stroke remained—a single sober mark above the doorway.

Shim'on waited a half-step outside, shoulder angled toward the lane as if he were only resting. But his attention never left the hedges. He wasn't guarding us. He was guarding her—so she wouldn't have to.

Inside, the room was simple: rope coiled neatly in the corner, a scrubbed table, a plain iron lamp waiting unlit on a shelf. A red thread hung from a nail—an old practice no one explains, just keeps. A bowl of water sat beneath it, as if waiting to be asked what it remembered.

"I'm not looking for a sermon," the mother said, rocking the baby without noticing she was doing it. "I just want to know what to do when it's midnight and the lanterns outside make the air feel clean in a way that isn't honest."

"Chores," Nadya said, and it didn't sound like dismissal. It sounded like mercy you could hold. "The kind that keep you from leaning when everything else tries to."

The woman's mouth twitched, like the word surprised her by fitting. "Which ones?"

Eliah knelt beside the bowl. "Start simple," he said. He dipped a cloth, wrung it carefully, and pressed it to the baby's brow. The child exhaled deeper—still shaky, but freer.

"Sing the song your mother taught you," Sera said. "The old one. Quiet. In the key that fits your voice."

The mother nodded slowly, as if retrieving the memory from a place she'd stopped visiting.

"And the lamp?" she asked, gaze sliding toward the unlit iron, then toward the lane where the Warden's lantern-hooks liked obedience.

"Keep it near the window," Gillie said. "Unlit, unless you need to see your child's face." Her hand hovered near the lamp without touching it. "Light should help you. Not judge you."

The baby took a fuller breath. The mother's shoulders dropped an inch—not relief, not yet. Just more air.

"And when the fields hum so loud the walls shake?" she asked. "When the corners of the room feel like they're pressing in?"

Rowan stepped forward from where he'd been leaning, nearly invisible. "Hold him near something open," he said. "An open window. Your own open breath. You don't have to shout to tell the wrong things no."

"I don't know the right names," she whispered.

From the doorway, Shim'on spoke without turning his head, eyes still on the lane. "Then don't give them yours," he said, voice low. "If a man comes asking what you heard, tell him: wind in the hedge. It's a true sentence. It's also a useless one. Useless keeps teeth in your mouth."

The mother stared at him a moment—surprised by the plainness of it—then nodded like she'd been handed a tool.

Cassian, standing just inside the threshold, added, "Borrow the morning for names. They sound different in daylight."

The woman swallowed. "There's a word the reeds carry," she said softly. "Do I teach it to my daughter?"

"Not as a spell," Gillie said. "Words like that are windows. She'll know when she can stand in the draft." Her gaze flicked once toward the inner room where the older girl had vanished. "Until then—teach her to breathe without asking permission."

The woman nodded. It wasn't confidence. It was resolve.

"And the ash?" she asked, touching her brow where grief tends to sit. "If it's for sorrow and not for doorways… may I wear it here?"

Miriam hesitated, then nodded. "Yes. For sorrow." She wiped a small thumbprint of gray onto the woman's brow. The mark looked real—not like proof, but like truth.

The baby fussed again. Sera matched his breath on the second try and steadied him. Eliah cracked the window a hand's width. Night entered quietly, taking only what it could carry. Outside, somewhere down the lane, a Warden lantern snapped its shutter in irritation and drifted on.

"And if I fail?" the mother asked.

"Then fail toward breath," Gillie said. "Fall forward, not inward."

The mother closed her eyes—not to hide, but to choose where to place her tears. She kissed her child's hair and did the quiet work we'd named: cloth to brow, lamp to window, old song begun in a key that belonged to her. The room seemed to settle, like it remembered itself.

Shim'on eased his weight off the doorframe and stepped back into the dusk, keeping his watch where it would look like loitering to anyone who didn't understand.

Micah appeared at the yard's edge like he'd been part of the fence all along. He planted his rod once in the dirt and watched the shadow sit where it should. "The hour will try to move while you're sleeping," he told her.

"Then I'll do the chores again," the mother said. There was no drama in it. Just courage.

We left her standing at the window, humming the old tune, the plain lamp beside her, stars doing the work only stars can do. Outside, the Warden lanterns clacked and postured for each other. The breeze shifted; the iron taste thinned until it was only memory.

At the corner, the mother called after us. "What do I tell the watchers if they ask what you gave me?"

"Bread," Rowan said.

"Listening," Micah added.

"Nothing to sell," Rowan finished.

Gillie didn't speak. The scroll rested against her side like a vow that remembered why it swore.

We turned north, and the hedged lanes thinned into scrub and stone. The last roofline slipped behind us. Red rock began to reappear in the distance, narrowing the horizon the way a throat narrows before a word. The wind lost its wander and started folding back on itself, and the canyon was already closing around our steps.

Behind us, a mother's voice braided itself with a child's breath until the house chose a better hour. And in the dust between us, three things kept their shape: an open window, an unlit lamp meant for truth instead of display, and a gray mark worn where sorrow belongs—on the inside, not the threshold.

The Whispering Canyon

The pass tightened around us until the red walls seemed to breathe along with our steps. The wind dropped to a hush—the kind that feels like it's waiting to see what you'll do. The weight in my pack felt heavier, as if the canyon had finally given it permission to matter.

Micah planted his rod and watched the shadow it cast. He always watched shadows the way other men watched faces.

"Edge stays honest," he said. "Middle doesn't."

None of us argued. Micah took the outer line, where the drop below was the kind you don't get a second chance from. It wasn't bravado. It was practice—like he'd learned long ago that if someone has to stand nearest the consequence, it should be him.

We followed, careful and slow. Dust took our prints like it meant to keep them. The rock held its lines tight and close, like pages someone had folded shut and forgotten.

At the next bend, a dark seam along the wall let out a thin breath. Not quite a word—more like a thought trying to remember the shape of one. Rowan's mouth opened before he realized it; he closed it again fast, like someone catching a door that shouldn't blow open.

Gillie murmured, "Hold your breath in your own house."

The seam breathed again and chose a voice.

"Child."

The word wasn't the one you hear in markets. It was older—the one mothers used when the world was smaller and the rules were simple enough to pretend at.

No one answered. The scroll answered instead—quiet weight settling along Gillie's spine. No heat, no shiver. Just the firmest kind of no: *Not that way.*

The seam eased back, disappointed in the way a liar gets when you don't even dignify him with a flinch.

Sera let out a thin, steady tone. Soft enough to miss if you weren't listening for it. The wind shifted—like it was trying on a calmer key.

A shallow shelf opened on our right, stone worn smooth by floods and by people who'd trusted their feet more than their luck. Small stone bell-shards lay there in a row, shaped and broken on purpose. Miriam brushed one with her thumb, then drew an open circle in the dust beside it, leaving the top unclosed. The dust held the mark without argument.

Micah squinted down the canyon. "Vein crossing," he said. "Two hollows arguing over who gets the echo."

"Who wins?" Cassian asked.

"Neither," Micah said. "Echoes don't keep score. They just get louder."

We climbed down into a stretch where the right wall leaned toward us like a tired guard. The whisper followed, sharpening its edge. It tried names the way a merchant tests coin—bright, practiced, meant to make you feel chosen.

"Keeper."

"Warden."

The voice was steady, convincing—the kind that always sounds helpful until you see the hook in the offer.

Shim'on's shoulder brushed the wall as we passed. He went still—not stopping us, just *noting*. His eyes slid to the seam, then to Gillie, then to the gap ahead as if he'd already decided where danger would step from.

"Not ours," Nadya said quietly, setting her breath like a blade laid flat.

Sera matched her rhythm. Eliah matched the canyon's.

The seam listened to our refusal and tried a softer angle. A smaller word. A truer one—weaponized.

"Fisher."

I saw it hit him. A softness crossed his face—wrong softness, the kind that comes from remembering something you didn't want help remembering. His mouth started to open, not with consent but with old habit: answer the call, take the bait, prove you're still human.

Gillie didn't touch him. She steadied the air near his jaw, like she could hold the hinge without closing the door. The scroll pressed lightly against her palm—a quiet yes.

Shim'on shut his mouth.

It cost him. You could see it in the way he blinked—like he'd spent something he didn't want to admit he needed.

"Not that name," he said finally, barely audible. Not a confession. A refusal.

The canyon widened enough for the wind to act like itself again. It tried new bait, dressed in clean syllables.

"Mercy."

"Order."

Cassian's jaw tightened, but he didn't rise to it. His hands stayed open at his sides, like he was teaching himself he didn't need a weapon to be real.

We reached a rise where the ground looked solid but felt like skin stretched over a story we didn't want to step on. Micah tossed his plumb-line. It swung twice and stopped on nothing.

"Step where I step," he said. "And don't answer anything that sounds like it's doing you a favor."

We followed single file: Cassian first, Sera second, Gillie third. I went after, and Shim'on brought up the back—where he always put himself when something might come from behind.

Halfway across, the whisper changed tactics.

It stopped offering titles and started offering *details.* Quiet, intimate failures. The kind nobody else could prove. The kind that make you want to speak just to stop the feeling of being seen.

It named the places we'd almost quit. The sentences we rehearsed. The small cowardices we called wisdom.

That's when whispers turn dangerous—when they stop trying to tempt you and start trying to *own you.*

"Tomas," it offered, soft as a bargain.

Tomas closed his eyes and nodded once—like a man refusing a drink he'd begged for in a weaker hour—and kept moving.

Behind me, Shim'on reached out and put two fingers briefly on the back of my pack—not gripping, not pulling. Just contact.

Still here.

Still walking.

The ground held. We made it across.

A fallen wall waited ahead, humbled by time. Three stones still stood on narrow ends, old cords strung between them—uneven knots frayed by wind.

"Markers," Micah said. "Witnesses."

Rowan smiled a little. "Small's a size truth likes."

From a patch of blackened stone came a quieter reminder, as if the canyon had decided to speak plain.

"Ash."

Miriam breathed out slowly. She wore ash on her brow like other people wore rings, and the canyon seemed to recognize it—not as proof, but as grief told honestly.

We found a crease wide enough to rest in. No one lit a flame. Gillie passed bread. Eliah lifted water in his palm but didn't drink. The scroll rested against the stone, quiet and steady, like it knew this wasn't the part where you perform.

"Listen," Sera whispered.

The canyon listened back. A hawk cried—one call, one pause, one echo. The wind moved in four slow strides, then one quick. Our breathing followed without asking permission.

"The hour's off," Rowan said.

"Not off," Micah said. "Just honest about who's holding it."

"The ground," Nadya said.

"And what's under it," Micah added. "A bell that isn't bronze. A hollow that remembers a promise."

Up ahead, the rock shaped itself into the hint of a mouth. Nearby, a seam had been filled—resin mixed with ash, spread smooth by someone who didn't want fingerprints. The fill was cracking. Breathing does that to lies.

"This is where they sealed it," Micah said. "Sweet on the surface. Bitter underneath."

"Will it break today?" Cassian asked.

"No," Gillie said. The canyon confirmed it with a quiet that didn't need an echo.

Shim'on stared at the seam like he'd seen a man's life sealed the same way. "If not today," he asked softly, "what do we do with the hours between?"

"Keep them from learning the wrong name," Nadya said.

The coin in my pocket tapped once against my leg—small, insistent. Not warmth. Not magic. Just weight reminding me it existed.

We set our watches without saying it.

Night came without ceremony. Stars took their places. The wind reset its pace.

Then the seam tested us.

"Who holds your mouth?"

We didn't answer. We breathed.

"Which name do you refuse?"

"The one that pays today and starves tomorrow," Gillie said.

Shim'on didn't add a name. He only said, very softly, like he was practicing for a day he wasn't allowed yet:

"The one that makes me smaller."

The seam accepted that. Acceptance is not agreement.

Near midnight, the canyon tried one last thing. It offered the name we each heard under the first bell—the one that held doom and hope in the same breath.

No one took it.

I held the almost-name and didn't spend it.

Deep below us, the bell-that-is-a-hole gave a half-sound—like it owed us the rest tomorrow.

We slept in turns. No fire. Just honest work: water shared, bread broken, a lamp set by the open, unlit, so the stars wouldn't feel replaced.

Toward dawn a rooster cried from far above—late, but trying.

"Soon," Micah said.

Light came thin, touching the seam, the resin, the red tooth Kaela named. It didn't fix anything. It told the truth.

Gillie stood. The scroll settled. It asked.

We answered by rising.

As we shouldered our packs, the canyon whispered once more. Not a name.

A verb.

"Carry."

Micah smiled, tired and steady. "The long way."

We walked on—the seam breathing behind us, the seal waiting ahead, the bell below counting without sound. Dust kept our footprints open at the top, leaving room for evening to decide what belongs.

The Mocking Chorus

The canyon let us go the way a throat clears—one long breath, then quiet. The walls opened into flats marked with thistle and wind-worn stone.

Far ahead, a temporary settlement sprawled across a shallow basin: poles, canvas, lanterns strung too neatly, a cart with a brazier lifted higher than any fire deserved. It looked like a stage that hadn't decided what story it wanted to tell yet.

Micah set his rod in the dirt. The shadow stayed where it should.

"They picked hard ground," he said. "Sound carries farther when the earth refuses to help."

We kept walking. The road ran straight into the gathering, and avoiding it would have only invited more attention. Places like this don't let you slip past unnoticed.

The first voices reached us as fragments—boys practicing the timing of their shouting, the way children rehearse games they don't yet understand. Then the whole crowd found its rhythm.

A man lifted a tin cone to his mouth, and the metal made his voice larger than his body.

"Neighbors!"

"Neighbors!" the crowd returned, obedient as breath.

"Order keeps!"

"Order keeps!"

"Breath deceives!"

"Breath deceives!"

Lanterns climbed a tall scaffold in a neat staircase, shutters snapping in time with the chant. Bell-shards were strung on ropes; they made a pretty sound until you realized they were meant to impress.

Painted boards leaned against the cart, letters fat and confident:

PROOFS. MEASURES. MERCY WITH RECEIPT.

Gillie didn't slow. The scroll sat against her ribs like it always did in rooms where fear was for sale.

Nadya counted exits without moving her head. Cassian kept his hands loose and open. Sera held a tone in her throat in case the air needed somewhere to rest. Micah stayed on the outer edge, watching how the ground refused to lift any part of the spectacle.

Shim'on walked half a step behind Gillie, where shadows tend to choose a person first. His eyes moved over the scaffold, the cart, the ropes—like he'd seen this kind of "care" before, dressed up and traveling.

We were noticed.

A keeper in a polished coat held up a glass vial between two fingers like it could save the world.

"Travelers!" he shouted. "Carriers of air! Come see our gifts—flame that won't betray you, scales that don't lie!"

The crowd answered like a tune they'd been waiting all day to sing:

"Feed and be kept!

Bless and be weighed!

Close when you're told—

Be less afraid!"

Children sang it brightest. They always do, before anyone teaches them what obedience is supposed to mean.

A boy with a small drum jogged alongside us, tapping a marching pattern meant to shape our steps. We ignored it. He faltered, then drifted back toward his mother, blaming himself for the crowd's failure to move us.

Near the cart, a ledger-woman—different from the one who'd found courage earlier—pretended to tally coin. She kept her eyes down. That was her whole rebellion: not seeing.

"We welcome breath," the Cone-voice announced, "in its proper place."

"Lungs," the crowd chimed.

"And out of which place?" Rowan asked lightly.

"Tongue," the chorus answered itself, missing the point entirely.

The cone lifted a fraction, as if pleased with how cleanly the crowd could be steered.

Then the show shifted—friendly to sharp without ever admitting the change.

The Cone-voice motioned, and three lamps were brought forward: plain iron, polished brass, and a thin frame barely holding its shape.

A quiet ache moved through our circle. Rooms remember lamps like those.

"To show," the Cone-voice purred, "that false smoke will not be fed here."

The crowd laughed—eager laughter, relieved to be given permission to be cruel.

"Ask your parchment to speak!"

"Blow on us, carriers!"

"Teach the wind to pay tax!"

They made a game of us, tossing names like stones to see which one hit bone.

"Fisher."

"Sister."

"Keeper."

The word *Fisher* flew truest. It wasn't an insult—worse. It was an invitation to become small and useful in a way the crowd understood.

Shim'on's jaw tightened. For a heartbeat his mouth softened, almost answering out of old reflex—prove you belong, prove you're harmless, prove you're the kind of man they can file away.

Then he swallowed.

He let the word die in his throat the way you let a hook slide past without taking your tongue with it.

It cost him, but he paid it.

On the edge of the table, the thin-framed lamp began to smoke though no one had lit it. The smoke rose uncertain, like it wanted to tell the truth about the room.

A child noticed. His frown was honest—the kind you only get once.

His mother turned him aside. Love learns bad habits under pressure.

Micah tapped his plumb twice. "Hear that?" he murmured. "The line won't move. They built their show on ground where truth has nothing to bounce off."

Sera let out a small, steady note. "Here," she breathed—not to oppose them. Just to give the air somewhere it could rest without joining the chant.

The Cone-voice produced a cheap mockery: a blank scroll rolled on flimsy rods, tied with bright ribbon. He unrolled it with flourish.

Nothing inside.

Laughter covered the emptiness the way paint covers rot—bright, quick, desperate.

"Words doing soldier's work," Cassian muttered.

"Only if we let them recruit us," Nadya said.

The Cone-voice lifted his tin again and feigned generosity.

"Speak," he said, pretending fairness. "Tell us how air behaves."

Gillie didn't step forward. She didn't raise her hand.

Her voice didn't climb, either.

"Mercy isn't louder just because someone charges for it."

A break ran through the crowd—not silence. More like an argument losing balance.

Two lanterns high on the scaffold stuttered. Embarrassment has a sound.

"Mercy is measurable," the Cone-voice insisted, tapping his ledger as if paper could sanctify anything.

"Measured where?" Rowan asked. "In heat? Or in breath carried into a house with no coin?"

"Mercy keeps lists!" the chorus answered. "Mercy knows names!"

"Breath knows names," Sera said softly.

It traveled farther than the tin cone ever could.

Beside the cart, the thin frame's smoke drifted into a seam on the table and shaped a letter—half-formed, then clearer, then gone. A girl near the rope saw it. She placed her palm over the smoke, not trapping it—making room for it to pass.

A watchman laughed the way trouble laughs when it knows the crowd will back it.

"Neighbors," he said, adjusting tone, "these travelers mean well. They ask questions. But we bring answers that hold."

Micah angled his rod toward the man's boots. "Your hold leans."

"Prove it."

"I can," Micah said. "But you won't like what you built it on."

The chorus shifted to a new rhyme—clever, empty, practiced for this moment:

"Ask and be shamed!

Name and be weighed!

Quiet is kindness—

Speak and be frayed!"

Crowds tire. Arms drop. Chants blur. Truth needs attention; spectacle needs stamina.

Gillie touched the strap of the scroll.

Then she did something small and impossible in a place like this.

She let it rest on the ground beside her.

The air changed—not dramatically. Just accurately. Like a room going still when someone finally stops lying in it.

The Cone-voice rushed to fill the gap.

"At Sext," he promised, louder now, "lists will be posted. Names in order. Cords to wrists. Lamps at lintels. Proofs!"

"Proof tastes like iron," Eliah said quietly.

Shim'on drew a breath as if to speak—then let it go.

Not fear. Discipline.

The coin at my pocket tapped once against my leg like a knuckle on wood.

Near the platform, the boy with the healing cut lip made a small opening with his fingers near his throat—the same quiet gate we'd seen before. One woman noticed. She matched it for three seconds so he wouldn't be alone.

A watcher turned his head.

Shim'on shifted—one step, nothing theatrical—just enough to put his body between that watcher's line of sight and the boy's hands.

A simple block. A small mercy that didn't announce itself.

The thin-framed lamp went out on its own.

No hiss. No smoke.

Just refusal.

Something in the air told us to move.

We moved—not fleeing. Passing through.

The chorus tried to follow with mock blessings but tangled its rhyme. A drum lost the beat. A ledger page lifted and slapped the Cone-voice across the face. He laughed so the crowd would know how to treat embarrassment.

At the last rope, a woman lifted a wrist marked with an old bell-scar—high enough to be seen by anyone looking for truth, low enough to avoid those writing lists.

The ledger-woman saw.

She didn't write it down.

We stepped back into the flats. The song behind us shrank into its echo.

"What do we call that?" Cassian asked.

"A rehearsal," Micah said. "They'll sing it again when the seal breaks."

"And us?" Sera asked.

Gillie picked up the scroll and set it back against her ribs like returning a blade to its sheath.

"We keep the hour," she said.

The scroll settled against her side—not dramatic. Just certain.

We turned toward the long road. Behind us, the scaffold lanterns remembered how to be ordinary light.

Ahead, the earth steadied.

A hawk drew a single open circle overhead.

Dust kept our footprints open at the top—just enough room for truth to follow later.

The Vein's Shadow

The Vein Stirs

The flats didn't last. Before long, the road began to tilt and the red walls crept back in on either side. The canyon tightened until the path stopped pretending to be a road and agreed to be only a ribbon carved out of stone.

The ledge liked small feet and people who understood there was always a price for moving. On our left, the wall leaned close enough to borrow a shoulder. On our right, the drop opened its mouth and kept its thoughts to itself.

What lay below wasn't water anyone thirsty would trust. The surface looked like black ink with the lid screwed on—light sliding off it instead of staying. Far beneath that black, faint strands of white, then pale blue, rose and fell in a slow rhythm. Veins inside a Vein. Looking down felt like touching the inside of a wrist and realizing the pulse under your fingers didn't belong to you.

The air knew iron and ash and refused to forget. Not rot—ritual. Every breath left a coin-taste at the back of the tongue, like the last sigh of a long-cooled forge. Mist clung around our ankles and stayed there, as if the ground had drawn a line and didn't intend to move it.

We didn't announce ourselves. The place had already done that.

Rowan lowered his head and moved his lips, words too small for anyone but stone to hear. Sera tested a tone, then pulled it back into her chest before the canyon could take it. Cassian counted edges—that's how his watchfulness prays when steel has been told to stay home. Miriam rubbed the char into her thumb, searching for where the room kept its honesty. Eliah listened for water we couldn't see and refused to call sorrow permission just because it was loud. Nadya moved the least; when she goes still, places start telling on themselves. Kaela walked barefoot, and the stone tried to remember her—half-prints near her toes, then nothing.

Micah kept to the outside, where the earlier wind still visited. His plumb tapped his thigh with each step, a patient metronome. When he snapped the line out toward the drop, it steadied faster than gravity alone should manage, like the stone wanted to be believed.

Gillie carried the scroll a little higher than usual. The strap dug into her shoulder—the kind a vow leaves when it isn't putting on a show. The Word didn't glow. It simply felt heavier. Endurance has its own language.

We rounded a rock shoulder, and the ledge tightened again. The black below rose closer, level with our knees, like a story drawing up alongside you and hoping you won't notice you're in it. Under the dark surface, the pale filaments rose and fell with the steady calm of something older than weather. The first pressure hit the ribs—the sense that something else wanted to set the rhythm of your heartbeat.

Nadya lifted her hand—not to push anything away, just to mark the moment.

"It's listening differently here," she said. "Not like stone. Like blood."

Her words went down and didn't echo. A hush shifted under our boots. A tremor touched the bones—not sound, just weight.

Shim'on had stopped two posts behind us and refused to come farther. He stood like a man keeping watch and asking the ground to lie and tell him he was only passing through. When Rowan glanced back, Shim'on looked away—the way denials rehearse before their real performance. We let him stay where he was. Some journeys choose their witnesses a step late.

We crossed a seam where the ledge lied about how thick it was. Micah brushed his knuckles through the air above it, the way a baker taps a loaf to be sure the center remembers the heat.

"Over," he said quietly. "This part likes to introduce men to certainty."

We stepped long. Dust rose in shy spirals and dropped into half-shapes—open circles with the tops left unfinished. Kaela's mouth tilted. She pressed her toe into one circle and closed it lightly. The mist refused to erase the mark.

"Smell that?" Eliah asked.

"Iron," I said.

"And oil sweetened so you'll trust it," Nadya added.

"Resin," Miriam said. "The ledger kind."

The Vein answered—not with ripples but with memory. A line of ash where grief should have been allowed to rest. Lamps humming the proud tune of tools praised too often. Doors practicing safety more than welcome. Far past the red stone, fields holding a note lower than yesterday—as if people had been teaching the ground a song and never asked if it liked it.

"Don't stare," Rowan murmured. "Pictures grow when you feed them."

Sera tucked her breath deeper into her chest. Cassian found a piece of rock he trusted and let his heel test it. Miriam let the char sit in her palm and stopped offering it to rooms that hadn't earned it. Kaela drew another simple sign—open, incomplete—and left it that way. Micah reset his line and gave the ground a tiny apology only stone and plumb would understand.

The hum thickened, pressing at the edges of thought. Overhead, the strip of sky narrowed. Cephas's coin warmed once against my leg and cooled again, like metal remembering where it belonged.

We came to a broader cut in the ledge—a place made for stopping without admitting it. Stone on three sides, the black below in front like a mouth deciding which word to use. The beat that had been nudging us along stopped pushing and waited instead.

Micah stepped to the lip and let his plumb hang. The line shivered once, then steadied.

"Stitching," he said. "Old. Tight."

"The seam," Sera whispered.

"The seal," Miriam said.

We didn't kneel. We didn't run.

"Breathe," Rowan said.

"We are," I told him.

"Do it anyway."

We moved on. The ledge thinned to something that felt like the back of a blade, then widened into a hallway of red stone trying to be useful after a long season of being dangerous. The hum slid aside to let us pass, then picked up behind us again. Below, the pale strands brightened and dimmed in a rhythm that felt almost patient and almost hungry.

Mist lifted, wound into a single column, then settled again. A half-phrase moved through it—not quite song, not quite speech.

Nadya raised two fingers. "There. Under the hum."

"The river?" Eliah guessed.

"No. A room behind this one, practicing its echo."

She closed her eyes gently. Sera matched her silence.

We rounded the next corner. The wall snagged a loose thread from Sera's sleeve and left us a line in return—drawn in dust without a visible hand. An open spiral. Unsealed.

Gillie's breath caught.

Micah didn't touch the mark. "We're close to what's pinned."

The scroll leaned into Gillie's back with quiet insistence.

"Hold," she said.

We did. Three shared breaths. Cassian traced invisible lines of approach. Miriam let the char dry into her skin. Kaela pressed one fingertip to the spiral and lifted it clean, leaving the curl open. Micah steadied his plumb. Nadya listened so closely the air seemed to fidget.

The black below didn't feel neutral anymore. It felt decided. Light fell into it and didn't return. The pale veins gathered that stolen light and rearranged it into shapes like an alphabet waiting for someone reckless enough to read it.

Wind braided itself into three thin threads and laid them on the dark surface as if setting out options. We didn't choose with our bodies. We still understood them.

"One keeps time kind," I said. "Like a hand on a child's back."

"The second's sweet," Nadya added. "Perfume that wants you to forget anything older than itself."

"The third's the clever one," Rowan said. "Turns whatever you see into proof that you're the problem."

"That's not our song," I said.

The hum paused. Then it pressed harder.

Gillie flattened her hand against her thigh. The blade at her hip felt it and stayed where it was. Steel stayed quiet. Restraint did the humming.

We followed the shelf as it bent along the Vein. Micah checked the shadow on his rod and gave a small nod. Rowan fell into a soft cadence—two steps, rest; two steps, rest.

The air ahead came cooler, threaded with wet clay and oil that wasn't cooking anything. Cephas's coin stayed cool against my leg.

"Steady," Gillie said.

We turned the last bend before the ledge narrowed into the kind of space the canyon saves for certain meetings. The hum pulled in close and waited.

A voice came out of the mist. Not raised. Not dramatic. Just sure.

"So," it said, "these are the ones."

The sound came from water and stone and a man's throat at the same time. He stepped into view where the ledge broadened by barely the width of a hand. No visible weapon. Work-colored coat. Hair that had stopped arguing with gray. A quiet scar at the mouth. A man at ease on ground that doesn't forgive.

Marcus.

He didn't feel like he'd arrived. He felt drawn forward, like a seam pulling tight. The pale strands below brightened when his boot found the rock. The hum shifted half a beat to meet his breathing.

His gaze moved along our line like a craftsman studying wood before the cut.

"Nine," he said. "And a measure."

No one rushed to fill the silence.

His eyes flicked toward the black below. "You're walking the seam. Good. It likes witnesses better than owners."

The filaments pulsed brighter at that.

The scroll pressed against my ribs with its steady insistence. It didn't speak back. It simply refused to be hurried.

Marcus turned his head slightly, listening to something behind the world we could see. The patient thread kept time. The sweet one rehearsed mercy. The sharp one waited.

He walked parallel to us now, matching our line without taking more space than the ledge allowed. The hum slid into step with him.

Rowan kept his cadence. The line held. Gillie didn't move her hand. Her blade stayed sheathed because her restraint did its work.

"That will do," Marcus said—to the water, to the stone, to the seam, and maybe to us.

The canyon held its breath.

We had come to the place where bargains pretend to be kindness.

We hadn't stepped inside that room yet.

The Bargain Maker

Marcus didn't take the center of the ledge. He walked beside us, matching our line without ever asking to lead it—close enough to be noticed, far enough not to own the path. His hands hung loose at his sides, empty but certain, as if he trusted the Vein itself to handle anything sharp on his behalf. The place seemed to agree; the pale strands below brightened by a shade, and the low hum under our ribs tucked itself under his breathing.

Rowan kept his cadence—two steps, rest; two steps, rest. A small rhythm, but steady enough to keep the moment from shaping us instead of the other way around. Gillie pressed her hand against her thigh, and the steel at her hip behaved. The blade always understood that signal.

"It's polite," Marcus said, glancing toward the black surface below. "It prefers bargains to blows."

Nadya didn't break stride. "Places don't prefer."

"They do when men teach them," he said. And disturbingly, the Vein seemed flattered.

He didn't start with threats. He used a bedside voice—the kind meant to convince you refusal is the hurtful choice.

"One name," he said to me, the look too familiar, like he'd been saving it. "Speak it here, speak it clean, and I'll turn back every shadow waiting ahead of you. They'll unmake themselves the moment the wind remembers where the door is."

Rowan lifted two fingers. "Three breaths. Nobody answers alone."

I took the breaths. Cephas's coin warmed once against my leg and cooled again, metal remembering what it was. The scroll gained weight at my ribs, slow and steady, reminding me that endurance has rules of its own.

Gillie didn't give him a smile. "A kind offer from your lips is a snare," she said. "Soft on the outside, meant to tighten."

Marcus's mouth curled—almost a smile, sharpened by her warning. He didn't argue. He let her words settle. The Vein listened too; its hum shifted, not in approval or retreat—just waiting to see what we'd do next.

Miriam's fingers stayed on Micah's sleeve, grounding him. Marcus's gaze moved along our line again, slow as someone searching for a foothold, a crack where one of his offers might take hold.

The air thickened—expectation braided with old memory. The bargain hovered there, ready to settle the moment anyone made room for it.

Marcus nodded, as if Gillie's warning was an opening rather than a refusal. "Kindness is a currency the Vein respects."

Miriam didn't flinch. "Kindness isn't currency," she said. "It's something you give without keeping the bill."

The hum tightened at the edges—offended, or hungry; hard to tell. Marcus let the moment slide off him.

He studied our line the way a craftsman studies grain—looking for where the cut could land without wasting the wood. His gaze paused on Micah's plumb a heartbeat longer than manners allowed.

"You keep measure," he said. "Good. I prefer men who know where the ground actually lies."

Micah didn't answer.

"You have a sister," Marcus went on, not as a question. "She waits by the river that learned to ignore the town."

Micah's jaw locked.

"I could bring her here," Marcus said. "No debt. No blood. And you'd stop waking with your hands reaching for air."

Miriam touched Micah's sleeve—a small anchor. "Hold," she said quietly.

The ground, strangely, did.

Mist stirred and lifted a thin hand out of the black. Too many small joints. Too precise. It hovered open, waiting to be named.

"Mercy has to choose a face," Marcus murmured. "Why not hers?"

"Mercy can wait," Micah said. The words sounded like they hurt coming out, but they were whole.

The hand collapsed. The surface smoothed. The Vein dimmed by a hair. Marcus's step caught for a second before he steadied it.

He walked on. "You carry your gifts like debts," he said. "No wonder this place hums. It smells interest."

He turned slightly, as if offering each of us a private kindness.

"Nadya—set the weight down for one watch. You'd be beautiful if you stopped carrying what isn't yours."

"Beauty keeps no one alive," she said.

"It keeps men from killing," he said, almost sincere—the strands below lifting toward his voice.

She didn't answer. Her silence did the work.

Marcus's gaze shifted, narrowing just enough to show he'd found a seam worth testing.

"Miriam—you draw eyes. They'll call that devotion." His tone softened, almost indulgent. "And you carry a steadiness others will turn into duty the moment you hesitate. I'd let it stay yours—call it whatever serves you."

Miriam exhaled once, steady. "I don't use devotion," she said. "And I don't keep steadiness. I just try to spend it where it belongs."

The hum tightened at the edges—not anger, not approval, just a place taking note of a line it couldn't bend.

"Sera—you ache to resolve what the air keeps undoing," Marcus said next, that soft persuasion returning like an old habit. "I could give you a note the wind can't bend."

Sera pressed her lips together. Silence answered for her.

"Cassian—I can tell you which of your nine will fail. You don't have to walk blind into knives."

"We don't walk into knives," Cassian said. "We carry them."

"Kaela—finish the sign. Close the top. Breath is a luxury when law needs structure."

Kaela drew a circle with her toe and left the top open. "Some doors should stay doors."

"Eliah—you could spend your sorrow where it counts. I can make grief efficient."

"No," Eliah said simply.

Marcus accepted it with a small nod, like weather acknowledging itself. And the trouble was—he still hadn't lied.

At last his attention shifted to Gillie. The Vein leaned toward her the way a clerk leans over the only page he thinks matters.

"You've been asking the wrong question," he said, warm as someone offering help he's already priced. "It was never can he be saved. It was always will you do what it takes."

Gillie didn't give him the courtesy of a pause. "Say his name."

Marcus's head tilted, almost a teacher's disappointment. "If I said it, you'd trust me even less."

Gillie let out a dry breath—not a laugh, just truth rubbed raw. "There isn't a 'less' left," she said. "You hit the bottom of that well a long time ago."

The line landed. Marcus's mouth twitched—too small to be called a smile, too sharp to pretend he hadn't felt it. The Vein listened too; its hum tightened around the edges, eager.

"Your blade knows it," Marcus said, recovering the tone he preferred. "Let the edge speak for us."

Steel gave a thin hum—glass under a cold breath. The Vein brightened, opening a narrow clean place for an edge to rest, hungry for someone to set it there.

"Set the blade down," Marcus murmured. "Take the offer up."

Gillie didn't move. Her hand stayed flat against her thigh—steady, unimpressed. The blade stayed in its quiet, held there by her refusal alone. Restraint made its own sound: small, human, stubborn.

The Vein didn't dim; being invited was enough to feed it.

"Three breaths," Rowan said.

We took them, the way people do who know hunger isn't the first thing that kills.

Marcus walked alongside us, patient. "Feel it brighten?" he asked. "Bargains feed it. A place like this respects choice. It doesn't care which one."

"That's a lie," Nadya said.

"It is," he agreed, cheerful. "But a useful one."

The surface below shifted—no ripple, just rearrangement. Ink sharpening itself into small private mirrors. Tomas's reflection wept. Miriam's wore a crown of light like a burden. Cassian's hands counted wounds that weren't yet made. Sera's mouth formed the shape of thunder. My own reflection smiled with a coin resting over one eye—a man enjoying the weight.

Gillie's reflection leaned toward the water. Her blade lifted above a faceless companion; the edge wanted to fall.

"That is not our Song," I said—too loud. The hum stuttered once, then pressed back harder.

"You keep saying that," Marcus said, not unkind. "Sing it, then."

Rowan shook his head slightly. Vows weren't for spending here.

A startled voice echoed from up the ledge—keeper's pitch forced through a throat not ready for it. "You—are you with them?"

Shim'on froze. He'd promised himself he was "only passing," and the lie bent his posture thin. "I keep watch nearby," he said. The words shrank him. Shame does that—it tugs a seam.

But his feet didn't move. He shifted instead—just enough to block the angle where the voice might see down the ledge, just enough to make himself a bad line of sight.

Rowan's eyes closed. Gillie didn't turn. Cephas's coin warmed and cooled again, deciding what was covenant and what was trade.

"You don't have to take all my offers," Marcus said, still companionable. "Just one. A dry blanket at dusk. A clear sky tomorrow. A true dream so you stop waking to the wrong face."

Miriam's breath caught. Rowan set his stance like a door braced in a frame.

"Or let me help another way," Marcus continued. "You won't save them all. I can tell you which ones you can. Imagine what that would do to your kindness—how precise it could become."

The strands adored that line. The black surface looked shallower, eager.

"Truth doesn't reduce to math," Micah said, barely more than a whisper.

"Everything reduces to math," Marcus answered, pleased with the shape of the argument. "The question is only whether you count early or late."

Then he looked at me again. Patient. Too patient.

"One name," he repeated. "The right one. No blood, no fire. Let the Vein carry you past the hour that wants to break you."

The word rose in my throat like honey poured over the wrong map. The scroll pressed against my ribs—steady, bright. It didn't bow. It didn't fight. It simply outlasted the pressure. My mouth closed before the sound learned it had a shape.

"I'm not your priest," Marcus said mildly. "I don't need confession. I'm a host offering bread in a house that respects guests who accept what's given."

"Bread feeds," Miriam said. "This asks to be paid back with the part of a person that shouldn't have a price."

His step faltered. The Vein sharpened his reflection—jaw clenched, mouth too wide, eyes catching someone else's shadow—then softened him again.

He made his final pitch to Gillie. "You don't have to carry that," he said, nodding at the strap-mark the scroll pressed into her shoulder. "Let it carry you. Set the blade down and take the offer up. I'll show you where mercy is hiding—if you're brave enough to be cruel at the right time."

The blade hummed once, hungry for the compliment. Gillie's hand stayed flat. The hum retreated to something like shame and then quiet. Balance chose her again. The Vein, denied its prize, was satisfied just being asked.

Rowan raised two fingers. "Three breaths."

We took them. Marcus didn't interfere.

"You think I'm your enemy," he said at last, sounding tired for the first time. "You'll meet worse than me—thunder, silk, laughter that wounds you in ways you admire. I'm only bringing this truth: choice can cost less pain than you're used to paying. Don't bleed on purpose to prove me right."

"Choice isn't for sale," Nadya said.

"Everything is," he answered easily. "You're simply particular about the currency."

He looked toward the water. Asked it a question without speaking. The surface smoothed—our reflections came back, unchanged, ours again.

He paced us for three more lengths, patient as someone willing to wait outside a door until the person inside gets tired of pretending not to hear the knock. The hum followed him. The strands brightened at every sentence that made choice sound like mercy. Even our refusals fed the light. That was the canyon's trick—appetite grows on the smell of bread alone.

"Hold for three," Rowan kept reminding whenever a word tried to jump. "No one answers alone."

We obeyed. The scroll stayed silent, heavy with its own courtesy.

Marcus's final look went to Gillie's blade—the one that hadn't moved. "You'll sleep better if you let it sing," he said softly.

"Sleep is for later," Gillie answered.

"Later," he agreed, stepping back a breath's width, offering the Vein to its own appetite.

Wind braided sweetness through the air. The black surface drew up a soft pitch—the kind that asks hands to unclench.

"That will do," Marcus said to the Vein.

And the Vein, pleased and brighter for the hunger he'd stirred, obeyed.

The Siren's Thread

Marcus didn't leave when he fell quiet. He eased to the side the way a man shifts in a crowded room—still present, still listening, still letting the Vein hum around him like a fire settling after being poked. The air held the remnants of him: warm, careful, a little too confident.

That was when she arrived. Not by footsteps. Not by sound. More like the mist remembered someone and decided to shape itself around the memory.

A thin sweetness threaded through the air—something Marcus had left hanging behind his last words—and she caught it, twisted it, made it hers. Pale hands hovered over the black surface; wherever her fingers passed, the Vein tightened and shivered, reacting the way skin reacts to cold.

She didn't sing. She hummed a tune that used to be a song—half-forgotten, still beautiful, but limping. Even the limp worked in her favor.

The strands below rose toward the sound. The hum in our ribs slipped away from us and joined her, as though it had only been waiting for the right throat.

Elana.

She didn't look at the scroll. She looked at us—at our mouths first, at the places where weariness hides. Seducers read lips before they read hearts. Her beauty didn't announce itself; it settled in quietly, making you aware of your breathing, your posture, your doubts. Her hair caught the faint Vein-light in flashes—pale gold one second, ash-gray the next, as if whatever made her lovely hadn't quite committed.

Rowan lifted two fingers. "Three," he said.

We breathed together. Shim'on did too—late by half a beat, like a man still learning how to arrive without apologizing for it.

Elana's hum warmed anyway, pleased to have an audience.

"It listens to me," she said—not bragging, not whispering, just stating what she believed the room already knew. The Vein rippled in agreement, eager to please.

The scroll answered in its own language.

Weight. Not heat.

Another slow ounce along Gillie's shoulder strap. Another small climb along my ribs. Not punishing—reminding. Gillie shifted the strap a fraction to settle it. My breath adjusted to the new pressure. Endurance isn't loud; it's steady.

Elana moved closer. She didn't touch anyone—she never touched. Seduction works better when it stops just short and lets the imagination finish the reach.

She found Nadya first.

"Nadya," she breathed, using that copper-and-honey voice she keeps for people who don't fall easily. "You'd be beautiful if you stopped carrying their grief."

The Vein flattened its surface beneath Nadya's reflection. It showed her lighter—shoulders unburdened, eyes bright, a mouth not clenched by duty.

Nadya's jaw clicked once. "Beauty keeps no one alive."

Elana's tone softened—not kindness, but memory. "It slows the knives," she said, and then she turned her eyes to Gillie and gave a small, knowing wink. "And it hides the thrust, when the blade remembers how to be used."

The strands below twitched upward, waiting to take her side. They didn't get permission.

She drifted sideways—no walking, just the room making space for her—and found Miriam. Miriam stood the way people stand when kindness has cost them sleep: tired, but unwilling to stop being kind.

Elana drew a breath that hovered between sigh and note. "You give more than anyone should. They'll drain you dry."

The Vein adored the sentence. Under Miriam's reflection, a pale crown shimmered—soft, bright, tempting.

Miriam lifted a char-scarred hand halfway, as if to bless or refuse. She lowered it. "Light isn't mine to keep."

Elana's hum slipped an inch out of tune. The Vein made a small, dissatisfied sound beneath the water—like a bell muffled before the strike.

Elana didn't press. She shifted again, this time toward Kaela.

Kaela's bare toes wrote their quiet grammar on the ledge—marks only God and the poor know how to read. She watched Elana with the stillness of someone who listens for the second movement of danger.

"Do you remember your first verse?" Elana asked, weaving her voice with an old rhythm as though she had every right to it. "I do."

Kaela's toe made an arc, then another—leaving the top open. "Wind taught me. And doors."

"I was there," Elana murmured, wearing modesty like jewelry. "Not in body. In echo. You thought it was yours. It was mine first."

The Vein pulsed, eager to agree.

Kaela's lips shaped a sound before remembering whose breath she'd be returning if she finished it. She shut her mouth with the gravity of someone who knows that even true notes can be stolen.

The scroll leaned harder against its straps. My breath thinned. Not from fear—just the work of resisting her cadence. Charm wears truth like a borrowed cloak. The Word doesn't like borrowed truth.

Elana turned her attention to Sera. Sera's chin lifted—instinct hunting danger the way a tuning fork hunts pitch.

Elana warmed her hum. "You want a note the wind won't ruin. Let me hold it steady."

Rowan's fingers rose again. "Three breaths."

Sera took them. She turned her mouth away from Elana's pitch the way people turn from mirrors that ask for something they shouldn't give. Elana let her go. It cost her nothing.

She drifted again—gentle, practiced. The Vein followed her hum like a housecat following sunlight. Even the cliff seemed to tilt, persuaded without realizing it.

She stopped beside Gillie.

Not touching. Close enough that a shift in breath would have made contact.

Her gaze moved from the strap to Gillie's shoulder, then to the stillness of her hand, and finally to the steel at her side.

"Some edges belong in the light," she said softly. "Let them see what you carry."

Her eyes lingered too long on the blade. Her hum wavered. Something like recognition moved through her face.

"I know that steel," she whispered. "It wasn't forged for you… but it follows you as if it remembers."

The blade gave a faint, embarrassed hum. The Vein brightened a thin path ahead, eager to guide an edge wherever she wanted it to fall.

Gillie opened her hand flat against her thigh—steady, grounded. The steel quieted beneath her restraint.

The Vein sulked like a refused child.

"Three," Rowan said.

We breathed. The urge in the steel loosened.

Elana smiled and slid on, the mist fraying slightly at her wrist where the Vein had snagged something in her. She smoothed the seam with a small, practiced shift in melody.

She found Cassian next.

"Cassian," she said warmly. "You guard too many windows alone. Give me one night. I'll show you which ones can stay open."

"I prefer drafts," Cassian said dryly.

Danger tells on itself when you let in air.

She granted him the courtesy of not arguing.

Then she turned toward Micah, catching the leftover heat Marcus had left hanging in the room.

"Micah," she coaxed, "set the plumb down for one song. You'll like how the world feels without measure."

Micah's grip tightened.

Silence worked better than refusal.

Elana counted the silence as interest.

She shifted toward Rowan.

"Riddles wear you out," she said gently. "Some doors want a key. Wouldn't you like to be answered once in your life?"

"Answers break faster than questions," Rowan said. "I don't buy fragile."

She loved the line. Hummed it. Pretended it belonged to her.

The scroll added another ounce. My shoulders negotiated with breath. The coin warmed once—cooled again, metal practicing a lesson it learned in a darker room.

"Let me help," Elana whispered—not to us, but to the tired part of each of us that wished saying no didn't hurt. "You're weary of restraint being mistaken for fear. Set the beautiful thing where the world can see it."

Gillie's fingers curled—then flattened again.

Restraint held. The blade honored her for it.

Elana's eyes flicked over me the way people look at open doors they're saving for later. She didn't stop long. She knew what she wanted first.

She returned to Nadya with gentler teeth.

"You carry grief like law," she murmured. "It bends your back. Ages you past your mother. Lay it down a day. You'd breathe again."

"I'm not a statue," Nadya said. "I don't work for pretty."

Elana's hum stuttered—just once. The Vein clicked its disapproval. She smoothed the stumble with a softer run of notes.

The ledge narrowed beneath us. The filaments thickened. Refusal requires balance, and she knew it.

Kaela drew another open spiral in the dust. Micah set his rod where the shadow held true for two breaths. Measure and mercy wrote themselves quietly into the air.

Elana hummed through all of it. Her pitch followed the room the way a thief follows a distracted guard.

"Three," Rowan said again, quieter.

Our bodies responded before our minds caught up—breathing on his cue even when he didn't raise his hand. Elana noticed and smiled—like a teacher amused by a child who brought a stick to a sword lesson.

She bent toward Miriam again, voice like a blessing offered through a cracked doorway.

"You pour everything out," she said softly. "Let someone pour back into you once. Let the light stay."

Miriam closed her eyes. "If I try to keep it," she said, "it goes out."

The Vein tried to crown her again and failed.

A tiny thread snapped near Elana's wrist—the place where a true song would have reached for mercy. Elana replaced the snap with grace, pretending it hadn't happened.

She angled back toward Gillie.

Repetition is rhythm; rhythm makes rules.

"Some edges belong in the light," she said again, almost tender. "Set it where mercy can see itself."

Gillie's eyes sharpened—not grief, not fear. A very specific anger women save for lies that come dressed like gifts.

"Mercy doesn't ask the knife to sing," Gillie said. "It asks it to keep the beat."

Her palm stayed flat. The steel steadied, relieved.

Elana's smile thinned but stayed. Her eyes slid to the water, checking if the Vein took offense.

It didn't. Not quite.

Places like this reward persistence, not truth.

She hummed again, and the room leaned with her—stone, water, air, all bending toward a promise none of it would ever receive.

The scroll grew nearly unbearable—one last ounce. My grip tightened around breath. The coin flickered with cold.

I thought, for a moment, of setting the scroll down. Not to be rid of it. Just to rest. The thought felt wrong enough to stop me.

"Three," Rowan said softly.

Gillie shifted her stance and took some of the weight with her shoulder without looking at me. The Word steadied.

Elana tilted her head, listening to something we couldn't hear. "You feel it?" she asked. "Music remembering what it was before men taught it to pay."

She lifted her hand.

The Vein rippled under her gesture—like a bow learning an old instrument.

"We don't pay," Miriam said.

"You do," Elana replied gently. "You just call it vows."

Nadya's mouth pulled tight. "We call it love."

Elana's hum lowered. Not sadness—calculation.

"Let me carry what you insist is yours," she said. "You'd be surprised how light it becomes."

The Vein rose to her generosity. Filaments stitched a delicate ladder under the surface—from our feet to hers.

My heel almost leaned toward it.

Micah's plumb kissed the air, then settled.

"No," he said—to me, to the room, to himself.

Elana's pitch wavered exactly where holiness should have landed. A thin line of light snapped under her wrist. She hid the falter well.

At last, she let her eyes settle on the scroll.

Not respectfully—strategically. The way a guest glances at a host just long enough to seem polite.

She let her gaze slip toward me—slow, knowing, deliberate.

"Unfinished one," Elana said, tasting the words like they were a secret I'd left on the table. Her voice curled around the title as if it already belonged to me, as if the name waiting for me were something she'd been allowed to overhear.

"Do you ache for a name that breathes when spoken?" she asked. "I can give you one that opens doors without pretending to choose."

The coin burned frost. The scroll pressed harder.

"A name is only beautiful," I said, "if it remembers who gave it."

"Then let me remember for you," she said, almost laughing. "I never forget."

Something—Joshua, or the canyon's seam, or the part of me that still feared false comfort—rose like a warning. It moved through me before I could name it.

Elana heard the rival melody and refused to show jealousy.

She returned to Gillie once more. Breath-soft.

"Some edges belong—"

"Don't," Gillie said quietly.

It was enough. The blade stayed loyal.

Elana's smile held, even with the tension around it. Her eyes flicked to the water, checking her standing with the Vein. It allowed her a sliver of approval—less than before, but enough to keep her trying.

She hummed again, lowering the room toward a pitch that wanted surrender.

The ledge leaned. Stone forgot to stand straight. Somewhere behind the red, a door remembered it used to be open.

Rowan lifted two fingers.

"Three."

We breathed as one.

Elana smiled like someone who believed breath belonged to her.

She might have continued.

The Vein shifted—a single ripple under the black, small as a cat jumping from a sill—announcing someone else.

Elana heard it. Annoyance flickered through her calm, like a host whose partner arrives early to steal the scene. She gave us a soft kindness meant to sting later, then let the mist fold around her.

Above us, from the crooked perch of the canyon wall, laughter gathered itself. Cold. Harmless on the surface. Practicing cruelty.

The siren thread loosened.

Another hand reached for the line.

The Trickster's Hand

He'd been there the whole time. We just hadn't let ourselves notice.

Where the canyon wall hooked out over the Vein, a crooked limb of stone jutted into the air like a finger pointing at our narrow path. He sat on it as if the ledge had grown for him alone—bare feet swinging over the black, back against the rock, at home in a place that didn't forgive. In his palm, a pale pebble turned from knuckle to thumb and back again, like a story deciding whether to be told or swallowed.

Raven grinned down at us—the grin boys wear when they've found a window left unlatched and can't wait to prove it.

The first pebble dropped.

Soft splash. Hard shatter. The black surface buckled and stretched our reflections out of shape—mouths pulled too wide, eyes hollowed, like masks left too long over real faces. The pale strands below jumped toward the sound, bright as delight until you remembered delight doesn't usually laugh at ruin.

"Micah," Raven called, sing-song, as though names were stones he could skip across us. The canyon didn't echo him. It swallowed the sound and threw it back louder, twisted. "She's already traded your name, you know. Gillie. You just haven't bled for it yet."

Micah's hand went to the strap across his chest before he could stop it. In the Vein, the water drew a scene: a pale sketch of Gillie standing over a kneeling figure—no features, just shoulders we all recognized. Steel angled down, not wild, not cruel—just precise. Obedience dressed up as mercy.

Gillie didn't move. Her real hand stayed flat on her thigh. The blade at her hip hummed once under her stillness, bracing against a lie it wanted to answer.

A second pebble spun between Raven's fingers and fell.

"Gillie," he said this time, using her tone, her cadence, and putting it where tenderness was supposed to live. "You know what he's done." His voice went soft enough to pass for concern. "You just won't say it."

The Vein listened too well. The black opened into a corridor I knew in my bones—the door I'd left speaking to itself, the coin hot in my palm while I waited too long to choose, mercy turning sour because I'd held it past its hour. Not invention. A truth shard, shaved sharp.

Gillie's jaw tightened. She still didn't reach for steel. The hum under her palm deepened, like the metal had decided it could take the blow for her and resented being told not to.

Raven cocked his head, that half-curious, half-cruel tilt he wore like a second face. The pebble box in his hand clicked. "Edges choose their wielders," he said, almost musing, eyes on the knife at Gillie's side. "Mercy chooses everything. That blade was given 'not for death, but for life.' It remembers the hand that turned it once to killing… and the hand that holds it now for healing." His gaze narrowed. "So which edge are you, Gillie? The one that protects, or the one that punishes?"

The steel trembled—recognition, not hunger. Gillie's palm pressed harder. The hum went still. Not absence. Restraint.

Raven flipped himself upside down on the stone limb as if gravity were just another audience. Hair dropped into the mist. Ankles hooked careless around the rock. His smile split—one side bright as mischief, the other almost pained—then the brightness won.

"Rowan," he chirped, head hanging, voice too light for the words he chose, "when your God goes quiet, whose mouth speaks for him? Yours… or ours?"

Rowan didn't look up. "Three," he said to us instead, fingers rising. We took the breaths together. Shared air left less room for Raven's.

The third pebble fell.

"Our voice was the first Kaela learned," Raven sang, sweeter now. "She'll finish in our key."

Kaela's bare toes went still. The open circles she'd drawn along the ledge blurred at the edges, then firmed again, like the stone had been asked to betray her and thought better of it.

Raven rolled back up into a crouch, spine curved like a question mark. His laugh scattered the mist into little ribbons that tried to knot around our ankles. The Vein loved the sound; the black churned like a crowd deciding it must have whatever the seller had brought.

The fourth pebble skipped from his fingers. More followed. The Vein learned to mimic faster than it remembered truth. What we'd whispered in kindness came back as accusation. What we'd confessed as weakness replayed as verdict.

Sera's hum rose under it all—thin but steady—not cutting his lies, just proving the air still had a pitch that wasn't for sale.

"Micah," Raven crooned next, slipping into a keeper's voice from a town three cities behind us. "Do you really think she's keeping that vow for you?" In the water, Gillie's reflection tipped the blade toward a smaller throat. "She keeps it for the knife."

Micah's lips parted around a name and closed again—his sister's, not the steel's. The plumb at his side steadied, as if the stone itself refused to join the gossip.

"To you, Gillie," Raven went on, changing masks mid-sentence, wearing my mother's gentlest whisper like a stolen scarf. "Remember the door he left? Remember the boy who watched him go?" He smiled like he was returning something dropped. "He'll leave you too."

Copper burned the back of my tongue. Cephas's coin warmed hard against my thigh and cooled in the next heartbeat, like a confession deciding not to be spoken.

Raven flashed me a look that tried for pity and landed closer to fond cruelty. "And you," he said, light as if we were sharing a joke. "Kaela's lines open what you think you're closing. You haven't seen it because you want the map to be yours."

The Vein obliged him. The black arranged an almost-convincing picture: Kaela's spirals finishing our enemies' work, her open signs turned into doorways for what had no permission to enter.

Rowan didn't look up. "He twists what he sees," he said—plain, steady, naming the cruelty without offering it respect.

Raven went still. Stiller than was natural for anything pretending to be a boy.

His head tilted, the grin thinning as if something inside him had been jostled.

"Say we," Raven whispered—not playful now, but offended at the root. "When you speak of us—" Another voice slipped beneath the first, quieter, too honest, a boy under the mask: "…of me." Raven smothered the intrusion with a brighter sharpness, a smile pulled too tight. "Say we. They. Them." His eyes gleamed with a knowledge he thought we should have already known. "You're all pieces of the same broken thing—you just pretend you aren't. Poor manners to reduce a choir to a solo."

"We see a man," Rowan said quietly, lifting two fingers again, the steadiness of the gesture a counterweight to the fissure Raven tried to widen.

"They," Raven hissed—the pronoun cracking between his teeth like something bitten too hard. The Vein bucked beneath us, reflections doubling and blurring until the surface looked like arguments snarling under glass.

"Stop feeding it," Nadya said—not a command, a plea. "Don't give the river your grammar."

Raven laughed in thirds—one note high, one low, one somewhere sidelong. Voices we couldn't see seemed to borrow his throat. "You think we lie. That's the game," he said, almost cheerful. "Games only cheat the people who won't listen."

Pebbles fell faster. So did the scenes.

Gillie's reflection raised the blade higher. Her eyes in the water turned hollow—not empty of courage, just empty of grief, as if the cost had been taken out of the picture on purpose. Nadya's reflection opened her mouth and ash poured out in a steady stream. Eliah's shadow knelt to pray while off-beat laughter crawled under his ribs. Sera's "amen" formed, and the Vein tried to keep the word for itself.

"Don't look," Rowan said.

Which, of course, is when looking gets easier.

A not-quite-pebble dropped—a heavier thing. No splash. Just a small, sick satisfaction. The Vein showed Micah a hand—almost his sister's, but not quite—reaching up from water that wasn't water. The palm opened empty, waiting for his name.

"No," Miriam said into Micah's sleeve. Not argument. Vow.

Micah shifted his weight a finger's breadth. The picture lost its appetite and broke apart, like bad glass under the heel.

"You hear well," Raven told Miriam, and tossed a stone toward her kindness. The Vein crowned her in pale light, the way it loved to, and then darkened the crown toward something that wanted to be a shackle.

"I borrow light," she said, jaw set.

The crown thinned, then ran off her like unminted coin.

"Enough," Cassian said—not to Raven, to his own hands. His fingers had started counting: pebbles, breaths, glances that were almost betrayals. A plague of numbers crouched behind the tally, patient.

"Count this," Raven purred, dropping a pebble to where Cassian's pulse beat.

The water listened. It lifted a ledger of stains—every mark we'd taken and forgiven—then traced them again, darker, as if forgiveness had been pretend and the Vein preferred ink that didn't wash.

"Three," Rowan breathed. We answered with our lungs. The chalk-writing rinsed itself, like a slate caught in unexpected rain.

The stone limb above us creaked. Raven cocked his head at the sound and used it, tuning the canyon like someone tightening strings he meant to break. "We could do this until you admit you like the music," he said, then spoke with my own voice from his mouth—my tone, my timing—asking whether Kaela had ever told me who taught her first line.

"Stop," Sera said. It was the hardest word she'd thrown at anything in days.

"Say they," Raven hissed again. We didn't.

His rage shook the pronoun. "We" rattled into teeth. The black frothed, ink stabbed with an invisible quill. His laughter came back to him cracked in the stone—turned inward, punishing its own throat. The Vein charged him for it. You could feel the price.

The ledge seemed to shrink. The canyon closed its fingers a little tighter around us. We were one stone away from coming apart along Raven's favorite line—turning interpretation into law.

Kaela moved.

She stepped from rock to black as if the surface were only a darker road. The Vein should have swallowed her. It didn't. The pale filaments rose and twined around her shins like minnows around a leg in shallow water, writing thin lines of light along her bones. Her toes drew a path and the surface bowed, as if truth itself owed her foot a courtesy.

Raven's laugh hiccuped. He reached for another stone and found his hand empty.

Kaela didn't look at him. She looked at us. Her eyes held the same simple promise fields hold when harvest is a vow, not a mood. When she spoke, the canyon had a pocket of silence ready for her, as if it had been saving the space.

"Nine shall walk the broken path," Kaela said. Her voice was not loud. It didn't need to be. "One with flame. One with silence. One with song. One with sorrow. One with truth. One with riddles. One who watches. One who shields. One who bears the light. When all have spoken, and the ninth has not, the scroll will open—not in words, but in wounds."

The sentences landed like a bell with no metal in it—only pressure, choosing how stone would remember.

The Vein did not like being told its future by bare feet and dust.

It liked it enough to obey.

Elana's hum died at the edge of a resolve she'd been reaching toward. Somewhere along the seam, Marcus's mouth probably tilted—craft recognizing craft. On the bent limb above us, Raven thinned. His outline wavered like a grin drawn in steam, bright for a breath, then smudged into the mist as if the Vein were tired of holding him together.

The canyon let out a breath we hadn't realized it was holding and then waited for us to teach it the next one.

We weren't relieved. Relief is a trade. We were steadying ourselves.

Gillie's palm stayed flat. The balanced blade at her hip hummed again—soft this time, like a plumb-line set where shadow finally behaves.

Raven couldn't fully help himself. He pulled together on the limb—thinner now, a sketch of a man drawn in malice and smoke—and flicked one last stone.

The Vein showed a patient image: Gillie, blade raised over a fallen ally. Not faceless anymore, just blurred enough that hating the right person would come too soon. The black loved the picture. It held it long enough for our ribs to recognize the shape.

Kaela's words still rang under the water like iron cooling at its proper time. When all have spoken, and the ninth has not… Raven's false picture pressed itself against that promise, testing for gaps. It wanted to be prophecy too. It quivered beside her words like a shadow trying to pass for stone.

"No," Gillie said.

Not to Raven. Not to the river. To the future that thought it could write itself without witness.

Her hand stayed at her side. The blade refused to move. The picture didn't vanish—true or twisted, visions rarely do—but it lost its nerve. It thinned and slid downstream, sulking.

The place went quiet. Not peace. The after-sound in the bones when a hammer has finally stopped hitting the same spot.

"Are you with the scroll?" someone hissed from the red above—a watcher's voice, wearing a Warden's question like a borrowed coat.

"I… I keep watch nearby," Shim'on answered. The old dodge. Not yes. Not the only honest no. His shadow stayed outside where no one could count it properly.

Cephas's coin warmed and cooled against my thigh in a rhythm that refused pattern. Gillie rolled her shoulder, accepting another ounce of the scroll's insistence. She didn't complain.

We didn't feel united. We chose to be. That's the only kind of unity the Withering can't put a price on.

"Hold for three," Rowan said, one more time.

We did.

The mist forgot Raven's grin. Elana's melody thinned into ordinary weather. If Marcus still watched, he had the decency to pretend he wasn't.

"Walk," Gillie said.

We obeyed the vow we'd brought with us, not the feelings the river had offered for free. The Vein sulked and wrote possible futures in its black, each one hungry for our attention. The blade kept quiet. The coin practiced remembering who it belonged to. Our feet chose, again, to be nine.

Behind us, the water rehearsed Gillie's raised steel until even the picture grew bored and broke apart into scum. Ahead, the ledge narrowed toward the kind of tight place where prophecy likes to test whether numbers hold.

We didn't trust the quiet.

We trusted the count.

The Masters of the Vein

The Commands

The hum had gone on so long it stopped belonging to sound and became a condition of the world. It wound itself into stone and marrow, into the shallow cracks along the canyon walls, into the place just beneath the ribs where breath begins. Hours, maybe days—we had lost the thread of time somewhere inside its unbroken drone.

The sun kept rising and falling, but only in theory. We no longer marked it. Our thoughts smoothed along its single, stubborn line until even fear was worn thin, just a film on the skin. It wasn't music. It wasn't warning. It was presence—unyielding and vast, neither hostile nor merciful, simply there, like gravity.

Then it faltered.

Not into quiet. Quiet would have been kindness. The note thinned instead, stretched too far, fraying at the edges. The canyon shivered as if its pulse had missed a beat. For a moment—one dangerous heartbeat—I thought it was mercy. I almost welcomed it. Almost believed the slackening could be release.

But silence here was not mercy. Silence was unveiling.

The hum split.

It cracked like a whip striking bone. Air recoiled in sharp, brittle shards. The sound didn't stop—it splintered. Needles of it pierced the ear and scored the lungs. Dust shook loose from every ledge, drifting like ash from an unseen fire. The air tasted metallic—copper, old blood, a wound reopened.

Each of us felt the break as something personal.

Gillie jerked sideways as if an invisible palm had cracked across her cheek. The surprise stole her breath; she caught it with a sharp inhale and whispered, "That wasn't… from outside."

A tremor ran through Miriam. She folded her hands hard against her sternum, knuckles whitening. "It's in the bone," she managed. "Not the ears—the bone."

Micah doubled over next. His hands clamped over his ears by instinct, even though it did nothing, even though the noise lived entirely within. "I can't— it's inside me," he gasped, voice shaking like wet stone.

Grinding teeth were the only warning before Nadya's patience gave way. Her jaw locked so tight the muscle jumped along her cheek. "It's cutting through thoughts," she muttered. "Feels like it's trying to take one."

Stone scraped under Rowan's knee when he dropped, fingers splayed wide to anchor himself. Dust rolled under his palm—his one proof that down still existed. "Stay with the ground," he whispered. "Just stay with the ground."

Sera pressed a fist to her mouth, swallowing a sound that wanted to break free. Her ribs fluttered with it. "It's too loud to hear," she said, barely audible. "How is that possible?"

Tomas stood rigid, jaw locked, shoulders pulled tight by old training. His hand hovered near the empty place where a weapon used to be. "Hold steady," he murmured, though the words shook. "Don't let it take more ground."

Only Kaela leaned in. Her head tilted, eyes half-lidded as though she were listening not to the sound, but to the seam beneath it. "This isn't noise," she breathed. "It's… speaking."

And the scroll—its weight slammed harder against my ribs, grinding breath into a tight, painful measure. I clenched my jaw, tasting copper. "It's choosing," I said—or maybe warning. "Trying to choose for us."

The canyon buckled in the next heartbeat.

A collective stagger rippled through us before the true break came—sharp enough to split the air, sharp enough to make even the Vein forget its own pitch.

Something shifted in the mist—not arrival, not footfall—just presence remembering it still owned them.

A thin ripple unstitched the air to our left, and three shapes bled into view as though the canyon had been holding them behind its own ribs and finally exhaled.

They looked wrong.

Marcus appeared first, knees bent, hands braced on stone that wasn't supporting him so much as holding him upright against his will. His eyes weren't fixed on us—they were fixed on the ground, as if something beneath the ledge was speaking and he was the only one forced to hear it. His shadow dragged behind him a heartbeat late, like a prisoner being marched.

Elana stood several paces back, arms wrapped around her ribs in a mimicry of self-embrace, but her fingers were digging in, not holding. Her face glistened as though she'd been crying in silence long enough to accept it. Her lips trembled with the ghost of a hum she wasn't choosing to swallow—she simply couldn't find her own note anymore.

Raven came last. Perched low on a slanted stone. Smiling too wide. But his body did not match the smile. His hands trembled in small, frantic pulses, like he was trying to stay inside his own skin while something else tried to climb out. His shadow writhed at his feet, not behind him, as if positioning itself for a blow.

None of them spoke. None of them tried.

Gillie whispered, voice tight: "They weren't hiding."

Kaela's breath hitched, the closest she came to fear. "They were being kept."

And the hum we'd all been enduring tightened around them like a leash yanked short.

Marcus's spine bowed. Elana's breath stuttered. Raven's grin twitched as though sewn into place.

We didn't need to ask what had done it. They were already half-bent. Half-wrecked. Half-claimed.

The canyon buckled.

And then—shadows reacted before bodies.

Marcus's outline tore upward from him first—jagged and wrong—like his shadow had been yanked by a puppeteer pulling too hard on tangled strings. His body followed after, lagging, convulsing, forced to obey its own silhouette. Elana's shimmer cracked, splitting into prisms—her shape fractured into too many reflections of herself, as if someone had struck glass without shattering it. Raven's form twisted between halves that no longer agreed they were one—his wings rupturing into east and west while his own frame hung suspended between the pull.

We drew together without discussion. We had seen Marcus snarl, Elana unravel truth with honeyed syllables, Raven laugh with teeth meant for wounding—but this wasn't power they wielded. This was the revelation of something that wielded them.

"They're not fighting us," Gillie said, voice steady in a way her eyes weren't.

"Then who holds them?" Miriam asked, fingers pressed so tightly against her breastbone the knuckles paled.

"Not masters," Kaela said softly. "Threads."

The word rang like iron tapped against glass—precise, too final. Not sovereigns. Not weavers. Threads.

The scroll pressed deeper into my chest, weight the same but somehow unbearable. I longed for blaze—for the light that had once scattered every shadow in Joshua's Withering—but it denied the impulse. No fire. No spectacle. Witness, not weapon.

Marcus's chest heaved as though drowning in air too thick to swallow, yet his jaw stayed clenched. The shadow beneath him grinned with a mouth that wasn't his, syllables forming against his will. Elana's cheeks streamed while her lips poured out doctrine in a cadence that belonged to some other will. Raven's cry doubled—one note shrill, one guttural—two voices trying to occupy one throat.

A fissure spidered across the far wall. Dust fell in soft sheets. The hum hadn't died. It had been claimed.

"If Marcus trembles," Micah whispered, shaking, "what are we?"

The scroll pulsed once—against bone, against breath. Not comfort. Reminder.

"It was never them," Nadya said. "All this fear—it's borrowed."

Rowan pressed his palm flat to the ground, eyes closed, as if trying to steady the canyon itself. Sera's tears gathered but did not fall. Tomas steadied her shoulder. Kaela dug her toes into dust, redrawing an invisible line.

"Close ranks," Gillie said. "No one stands at the ledge alone."

We moved inward, shoulders meeting shoulders.

"One line spoken," she said. "Three breaths silent."

We obeyed. One line of breath—covenant. Three silences—armor.

The torment deepened. Marcus convulsed again, and his shadow bared teeth he wouldn't. Elana sagged while silk kept spilling from her lips. Raven's divided voices raked each other raw in his throat. The canyon no longer echoed their strength—it echoed their chains.

"Threads fray when pulled too far," Kaela murmured.

The scroll pulsed harder. My hands trembled with the instinct to fling it open, to scatter whatever held them—but its silence was a wall. Use me wrongly and miss what has come to reveal itself.

Dust thickened. Breath grew tight.

Raven shrieked—two notes clashing, a dissonance that made the stone itself tense. Elana's hymn broke and reformed in the same breath. Marcus's gums bled.

"If even they are chained," Micah groaned, "what chance have we?"

"They chose shadows," Gillie said. "We must not."

My pouch tapped wood—Cephas's coin knocking once, as though asking to be remembered.

Then the hum vanished.

Not in relief. In rupture.

Silence dropped heavy as stone, thick as fog that refused to breathe. The canyon held its air, as though something waited to step through the torn seam.

Presence seeped in—weight without form, shape without outline. It slid through shadow, through stone, through the trembling bodies of the Bound. It did not speak. And we heard it.

Elana's silk-song faltered. Her eyes widened—not in terror, but in recognition. Marcus choked and dropped to his knees. His shadow stood. Raven's wings folded inward like paper crushed in a fist.

"It was never about power," Kaela said softly. "It was about permission."

"Then we revoke it," Gillie breathed.

The scroll stirred—not opening, not demanding. Inviting. My hand went to its clasp.

And then the first command struck.

A word, if it could be called a word, tore through the canyon—not sound, but force, a single intent hammered into bone.

BOW!

The word struck before meaning caught up. Pain snapped through spine and ribs, as if every joint had been told to twist the wrong direction at once. Mist recoiled inward into a shape like a fresh wound. Shadows lurched, startled—animals flinching at lightning they hadn't seen.

Marcus folded first—not to the knee, but at the waist. His body snapped forward in a brutal hinge, hands braced on his thighs, teeth clamped so tightly a thread of blood slid from the corner of his mouth. His shadow obeyed more completely than his flesh—bowed low, forehead pressed to dust, submission acting faster than breath.

Elana cried out. Her hum died in her throat. She clawed at her neck as if something unseen had gripped the back of her skull and forced her down, her upper body folding despite her legs trying to hold her upright. Words spilled from her lips—lush, reverent, wrong. Praise twisted into obedience.

Raven held out the longest—arms out, chest lifted, refusing to dip. But his shadow bent first. It folded sharply, hooked itself to the ground like something dragged by chains. His body followed with a violent jerk, spine folding midline. His scream fractured into too many voices.

All three mouths moved in terrible unison—their voices not their own: Make it stop. We bow… We obey… the masters.

We did not move—not from obedience, but from the shock of watching them undone.

And in the same breath, Shim'on—who had stayed a half-step back for hours, like a man afraid his shadow counted too much—went very still. His hands came up, not in surrender, but to cover his mouth, as if he didn't trust what the command might drag out of him. His eyes found Gillie's flat hand on her thigh and held there like it was instruction.

"We are many," Raven gasped, voice splitting. "We are not bowed. We are not—"

The canyon answered for him.

BEND!

The force struck inward this time—marrow to muscle to skin. It was not a push. It was a collapse issuing from inside the bone.

Marcus dropped immediately. His knees slammed into dust with such force the stone groaned. His spine bowed deeper still. His fingers dug trenches into the ground, hands shaking with the effort to resist the posture—not rising, barely holding.

Elana toppled sideways as her legs buckled. Her knees hit stone. Hair fell like a curtain across her face. Her lips kept shaping borrowed liturgy—its beauty marred, cracked, stolen. Tears rolled unchecked.

Raven's defiance tore mid-breath. His knees hit stone hard. His arms flailed as if he could fight gravity itself, but the unseen hooks dragged him lower, folding him at the waist and knee both.

Again, obedience poured out: We kneel. We kneel. We serve.

The Vein brightened—hungry, thrilled.

"If not by them," Miriam whispered, voice barely holding, "then by what?"

Cassian's jaw tightened into a locked hinge. Micah's fingers dug into the strap as if reaching for a vanished hand. Rowan's prayers tripped into one another. Nadya held her palm out to hush something unseen. Kaela carved thin lines in dust with the point of her toe—ritual, map, refusal.

"Not masters," she said. "Threads."

Truth struck clean. Cold.

Then the third word arrived.

BREAK!

It didn't shout. It didn't need to. It fell like stone surrendering its last grip on a cliff.

Marcus convulsed. His arms buckled completely. His chest hit dust. His shadow collapsed beside him—shuddering like a banner ripped down in disgrace. His back bent so far it nearly folded him in half.

Elana's song snapped mid-syllable. Her knees, hips, shoulders followed a downward pull she could not resist. Her lips froze in a smile that wasn't hers while her body wept. Her shadow tore itself free and struck the ground with its own cry.

Raven shattered. His scream broke into a dozen contradictory tones—mockery, grief, laughter, fear—spilling out at once. His shadow split in two: one half reaching out, one dragged backward. Both collapsed into ash. His whole frame spasmed, fighting to hold together.

The Vein flared white-blue—no warmth, only appetite.

The scroll pressed against my ribs, heavier, insisting, refusing spectacle. It did not open. It bore witness.

"Even they," Miriam said, voice breaking, "even they can break."

"Then we won't," Gillie said. Her fingers hovered near the blade but did not draw. The restraint itself was a vow.

"Threads," Kaela whispered again. "Not masters. Never masters."

Dust hung in the air, suspended, as if the canyon itself was holding its breath.

Their voices rose once more—raw, ragged, nearly unhuman: We break… We are… yours— The last word tore apart mid-sound.

We stared—not in triumph. In dread. We had not defeated them. They had been claimed.

The scroll remained closed.

Gillie took a step forward. The canyon groaned—not in anger, but in recognition. "We are not threads," she said.

Kaela rose. Nadya beside her. Miriam lifted her head. Micah's fingers stilled. Rowan's eyes opened. Sera breathed once, steady.

I stepped last. The scroll's weight cracked pain across my ribs. A voice from a buried memory whispered: You were never meant to carry this. Still—the scroll did not bow. It did not bend. It did not break.

We stood because it did.

Presence thickened—three distinct strands braiding themselves into the fracture. Weight arrived without bodies. Mist tightened around us like a fist. Dust lifted in a clean, straight line—as though an invisible blade traced the ledge.

Another presence hummed sweetly—almost holy, deliberately wrong. A third announced itself with a small, brutal pop by the ear.

We did not bow. We did not bend. We did not break.

At the lip of that terrible silence—just before the unseen Masters stepped into view—we stood counted and counting, the scroll cold against my chest, refusing spectacle, insisting on witness.

The Masters Step In

Wind rose where the canyon had been absolutely still. Not a breeze—something removed, as though the air was being pulled out through a slit in the world. A thin seam ripped straight across the ledge, slicing mist apart like cloth under a needle. Dust didn't swirl; it lifted in a dead-straight line, suspended, as if gravity had forgotten which direction to choose.

Heat followed—dry, sulfurous, acrid. The kind of heat that doesn't touch skin first but nerves. It rolled over us, metallic at the edges, stinging the back of the throat. "Iron," I whispered, tasting hot rust. "And… something burnt." A yellow haze bled into the canyon, drifting low, never dispersing.

Micah turned away, eyes watering, but there was nothing to look away from.

A second presence braided into the first. A hymn floated in—soft, sweet, almost light-bearing—until it bent flat, like honey left too long in the sun. Beauty swelled and soured in the same breath. Shadows nearby stretched toward the sound, wan and hungry, as if the pitch were gravity. Miriam lifted a hand to bless—then froze mid-sign. Her breath stalled. "Wrong mercy," she said. Not fearfully. Accurately.

The third didn't enter. It snapped open.

A single brutal pop beside the ear—like a bone forced back into its socket. Mist tightened so sharply it pulled our hair upright. The canyon dimmed without losing light; the shadows bent first, dragging toward something not yet shaped. Shim'on flinched at the pop like it had found his name. His hands rose, not in surrender, but to cover his mouth—holding his breath in, as if the canyon might steal it and speak for him.

Then everything went silent.

And then, they were simply there. Not appearing. Not arriving. As if the canyon had only now remembered it had occupants.

Ash drifted upward in a lazy spiral—rising where it should have fallen. The stone beneath our feet webbed with new cracks, fine as spider silk, radiating outward from where nothing yet stood. Insects—what few dared live in the canyon—fell still. Even the Vein's black pulse seemed to hesitate.

The first figure came into focus by absence: a narrow man of angles—thin as wire pulled too tight. His silhouette sharpened before his body did, a shadow stepping forward half a beat early. Every movement shaved air into slivers; tiny seams hissed around him, slicing the mist like paper. The smell of burnt iron thickened near his feet. The ground blistered where he passed—not aflame, just already burned.

The second arrived inside his own light. Colors brightened around him at first—gold, rose, dawn-soft hues—and then curdled at the edges. His gentleness looked immaculate, his closed mouth shaped like a blessing. But his smile made roots draw back into the soil, made the yellow haze deepen. He was kindness designed in a place that had never known consequence.

The third flickered between states—too young and too old at once—blurred, then crisp, then blurred again. Every time her head tilted, the air popped like a knuckle forced backward. Obsidian dust glittered around her ankles. Stone bowed inward beneath her feet, dimpling as if her weight were not weight at all, but pressure.

Marcus jerked his head up. His mouth opened on instinct, a name fighting for release. "Lu—" The rest strangled into a wet choke. Blood filled his mouth. His spine bent tighter. At last, broken and surrendering, he exhaled: "Lucien… the master of fear…"

Elana's lips parted as if to sing, but no voice came—only breath shaped by someone standing within her skin. Her eyes were blank, shining with someone else's reflection.

A pop snapped near Raven's skull. The mist cinched around him like a closing fist. He pressed his forehead to stone, trembling between halves that no longer agreed.

None of the three Masters raised a hand. They never needed to.

Lucien stepped first—if stepping was the right word. The ground cracked beneath each movement, a delicate fissure radiating outward. Shadows angled toward him like iron filings toward a magnet. He stopped before Marcus.

"You thought fear belonged to you," Lucien said softly, almost lovingly. "No. Fear belongs to me."

Marcus tried to grin. It tore his lip open.

Lucien didn't touch him—air did the work. A seam of wind sliced Marcus's cheek with surgical precision. Red welled. Marcus swallowed blood and spat a darker thread of it.

"You wore fear like a crown," Lucien mused. "But crowns have thorns. And you forgot which side faces out."

A second seam sliced beneath Marcus's eye. A blood tear fell. His scream sounded shockingly young.

The gentle one did not walk. He simply leaned closer without moving, the world bending him forward. His reflection appeared in the Vein, then rippled outward into Elana's skin, as if she were hollow and he was the liquid filling her.

Elana choked on a breath that wasn't hers. "Julian…" she whispered—not calling to him, not pleading—naming the presence already inside her. Her voice trembled on the syllables, as if the name itself pressed down on her throat.

"Beloved," Julian murmured through her mouth, warm as honey. "Why cut yourself into wounds, when you were meant to be a song?"

Tears spilled down her cheeks. Her lips curved in a smile shaped by someone else's mercy.

Julian turned toward us without turning his head—his regard unfolding like silk. "Do you see them?" he asked softly. "Souls who mistake stubbornness for virtue. They will call her traitor. They only fear what beauty demands."

"Beauty is obedience to the better truth," Elana said—his doctrine shaping her jaw.

"Lies," Miriam whispered, trembling.

"Mercy makes no demands," Julian crooned, drifting through her breath. "Mercy blesses what already is."

His hymn bent flat again. Rowan's prayer stumbled; he gasped and caught it by habit.

"Would you refuse such mercy?" Julian asked, tilting Elana's face toward Miriam. "Why burn, child, when you could sing yourself quiet?"

Before Miriam could speak, the third presence crouched beside Raven.

Pop. Pop.

Each one a click inside his skull, joints forced back into place. Raven's eyes rolled upward, unfocused. "K—Kali…" he choked—not a warning, not an introduction—a name dragged out of him by the thing already perched inside his shadow.

Kali answered as if he'd merely forgotten his manners. "Little mirror," she said, almost tender. "Tell them who we are."

Raven's jaw moved without consent. "I am— We are— I— we—" Another pop split the thought like a crack in glass. His shadow ripped wider down the center. Both halves shuddered—one reaching forward, desperate for an anchor, the other dragging backward into a silence that wanted to swallow everything.

"You don't need one name," Kali purred. "You need six. You need none. You need to be whatever the room rewards."

Laughing cracked into sobbing. Sobbing snapped into giggles. Both spilled uncontrolled until his shadow tore entirely into two figures—one shrieking, one whispering a frantic, breathless chant: "we / we / we…"

Raven's voice splintered as the halves tugged him apart. "The… mistress of silence…" he gasped, his words fracturing like shattered mirrors.

Tomas clutched his chest, sweat slickening his brow. Micah throttled his strap, knuckles white. Miriam raked her fingers through her hair, breath ragged. Rowan's prayer sank to a single syllable. Nadya raised her palm to hush the collapsing air. Kaela scraped desperate lines into dust—grammar against chaos.

The scroll crushed against my ribs, weight doubling.

Lucien flicked a single finger. Air sliced Marcus again. He collapsed fully, choking. "Fear belongs to me," Lucien said.

Julian smiled broader through Elana's trembling mouth. "Mercy makes you beautiful," he said. "Beautiful things obey."

Kali tilted her head, admiring Raven's ruined halves. "Silence severs," she said. "Silence teaches."

Gillie's voice trembled, but her blade stayed sheathed. "They chose shadows," she whispered. "We must not."

"We," I said, holding the scroll tighter, "could do nothing but witness."

The canyon held its breath around us—and for the first time in our journey, I feared the scroll might not open quickly enough to save us.

Dread of the Nine

Marcus lay where the commands had left him, one cheek in the dust, breath dragging through iron. Every exhale tasted like metal even from where we stood. His hands still twitched, fingers clawing at grooves he'd already carved into the stone, as if his body hadn't caught up to the fact that the command had stopped.

Elana knelt a little off to his left, spine bowed in a posture that might once have meant worship. Tears streaked her face in clean lines. Her mouth, though, still held that soft, borrowed smile—gentle, merciful, not hers at all. Whenever her lips tightened at the corners, the muscles around her eyes flinched like they were being forced to agree.

Raven stayed somewhere between. On his knees, shoulders hunched, hands hovering uselessly over his lap. His shadow had split and collapsed in two uneven shapes on the stone—one huddled forward, one pulled back. Neither aligned with his body. When he breathed, both shadows shivered, unsure which one belonged to him.

The canyon didn't echo any of it. It didn't send their broken noises back to us the way it had played with our words before. It just took them in and kept them, like a grave swallowing the last clink of dirt and then closing its throat around the sound.

Then Marcus made a sound. Not rising, not calling—just a soft, broken "please—" dragged out of him like a stone across bone. His fingers curled toward Elana's ankle, as if he meant to anchor himself to something human. His hand didn't make it. A tremor cut through him so hard his wrist slammed back into the dust.

Lucien chuckled. Quiet. Satisfied. The sound a man makes when a fire catches on the first try.

"Still begging," he said. "After all this time."

Marcus's breath hitched. His cheek pressed deeper into the ground. "I did as you asked," he whispered. "I— I did everything—"

Kali popped the air beside his ear, sharp and neat. Marcus flinched so violently his boots skidded an inch. The Vein's white-blue pulse dimmed under him, then brightened like the canyon recoiled and thought better of it.

"You obeyed poorly," Kali said. "You always do. That's why you break so beautifully."

Raven made a small, strangled sound. One shadow reached toward Marcus; the other recoiled. His whole body wrenched between them.

Elana lifted both hands to cover her ears, but Julian pressed through her, forcing them down into blessing again. Her shoulders jerked once in protest. He used her mouth to sigh.

"Marcus, beloved," Julian crooned. "You have failed us before. You will fail them now. All your stories end the same."

Elana sobbed harder, her tears dripping like her face was leaking grief she didn't consent to feel.

Behind us, dust crawled a few inches along the ground without any wind. A scatter of pale insects fled from a crack in the stone—only to freeze mid-movement and die as though some invisible heat had touched them.

Raven saw it and whispered, "No… not again. Don't—"

"Again," Lucien echoed. "He remembers."

Kali stepped lightly through Raven's two shadows. She didn't look at him. She didn't have to. His spine bowed toward her presence like a plant reaching for warped sunlight.

"You fall apart so easily," she murmured. "You never learned the lesson."

Raven's breath stuttered. "I tried," he whispered. "Last time— I tried—"

"Last time," Julian said with a soft laugh. "Oh, Raven. Must we relive your failures every time you lose your footing?"

Marcus reached toward us again—a blind, desperate drag of fingertips. "Don't leave me," he rasped. "Please—please don't let them—"

Lucien stepped on his hand. Not hard. Just enough to pin it.

"Mercy," he said lightly, "is for those who grow stronger from it. You, Marcus, only grow obedient."

Marcus whimpered. A sound grown men look away from.

We didn't look away. We couldn't.

Mist pressed closer, slow and deliberate, settling around our necks like a hand deciding which throat to close first. The Vein under our boots kept pulsing white-blue, a faint, stubborn beat trying to match a heart not our own. The air cooled, warmed, cooled again, as though the canyon were adjusting itself, choosing the temperature that made us flinch most.

None of us moved.

Marcus was still shaking. Elana kept wiping tears she didn't choose. Raven sat folded between two shadows that didn't match him. That alone held us quiet.

Micah finally broke it. "If Marcus trembles," he said, voice cracking, "what does that make us?"

The question hit harder than he meant it to. Gillie's jaw tightened. Miriam rubbed her sleeves like she was trying to warm her hands. Tomas pressed his palm to his chest again, checking whether his heartbeat was still his.

The scroll hummed once against me. Barely a sound. Just a reminder that it was there and we were not done.

Cephas's coin clicked in my pouch. One small knock. Ordinary, almost embarrassing for how normal it sounded compared to everything else.

Nadya snapped next. Not loud—sharp.

"Why are we still standing here?" she said. "If this place does that to them"—she jerked her chin at Marcus, Elana, Raven—"what do you think it wants from us? Hope? A miracle? It's not giving either one."

Rowan flinched. "Don't—" He swallowed. "Just don't say it like that."

But Nadya didn't stop. She stepped closer to the edge. Dust slid under her heel. The Vein glowed brighter like it was paying attention.

"We should move," she said. "Not into them. Not back. Sideways. Standing still feels like giving them permission."

"The canyon bends," Miriam whispered. "There is no sideways."

"Then we make one."

She turned fully toward us, shoulders set. Even the mist seemed to lean in.

"Either they write the rules," Nadya said, "or we decide we're done following them."

Gillie didn't wait.

"They chose shadows," she said. Calm. Not raised. "We must not."

That landed. Clean. Even simple. And somehow the mist drew back an inch as if the air didn't like hearing it.

Nadya's voice dropped. "Saying we 'must not' isn't enough. Tell me it means something."

"It does," Gillie said. "It means we don't bargain with something that uses its own people like this." Her eyes flicked over Marcus before she looked away. "We don't accept the songs they offer. We don't call their control 'mercy.' And we don't let fear decide which way we go."

The scroll hummed again. A small answer: I heard you.

Kaela knelt down. Drew a line. A second. A circle.

"'Nine shall walk the broken path,'" she said.

Sera stared at the circle like it might start falling away beneath us. "Nine," she whispered. "Nine."

Micah shook his head. "It felt solid when we all knew who we were. Now it feels… thin."

"Truth doesn't thin," Tomas said. "We do."

Before anyone could answer, Kali flicked her fingers beside Raven's head. A small pop. Raven jerked like he'd been slapped. His shadows snapped in opposite ways.

Julian didn't even pretend to look at us. He kept Elana's hands in that forced blessing.

Lucien traced a line in the dust with the toe of his boot—straight, casual, too sharp for comfort.

Micah lifted his head again. "If Marcus trembles, what are we?"

"No," Gillie said. "We're not living in that question."

Miriam wiped her face with both wrists. "Say the unity again."

"Close ranks," Gillie said.

We did. Shoulders bumped. Clothing brushed. It didn't feel brave—just necessary.

Marcus's shadow stretched toward us but couldn't reach. Raven's halves leaned in and out like they couldn't find a center. Julian's smile on Elana flickered.

"No one stands at the ledge alone," Gillie said.

"We're not theirs," we repeated. Quiet. Steady.

Rowan whispered one word: "Help." Honest. Raw. No performance.

The canyon didn't twist it this time. It just held still.

Julian forced Elana's hands up again. "Rest is love," he murmured. "Rest is obedience."

"Rest does not ask you to lie," Miriam said. "If it does, it isn't rest."

Lucien drifted closer in tone if not steps. "Standing still isn't weakness if fear isn't the reason."

"I don't take counsel from hands that cut," Gillie replied.

"You already do," he said. "You're carrying a book that cuts deeper than mine."

The scroll hummed again. Not offended. Just clarifying something none of us understood yet.

Micah spoke up again. "Why show us this? What do you want besides fear?"

Julian answered gently, almost sweet. "Continuance. Yours or ours. Both require surrender."

"Fear balances the accounts," Lucien added.

"Silence tidies the edges," Kali murmured.

Gillie didn't blink. "We will not."

Silence landed heavy.

Kaela drew another circle. "If we stay standing, the canyon has to choose—stage or court."

"We're the witnesses," she added. "Not the performance."

"I can do witness," Miriam said. "I just don't want to be their entertainment."

"We're the ones who don't mistake chains for crowns," Gillie said.

Another hum. Warmer this time. The coin tapped.

Nadya turned to me. "Name what we're doing."

I swallowed. "We endure. Here. We let them keep their chains. We refuse ours. We don't bow. We don't bend. We don't break."

"Not because we're strong," Rowan added, "but because grace doesn't need a show."

"One line," Gillie said. "Three breaths."

"We are not theirs."

The canyon did not argue.

A stone clattered somewhere deep. Long fall. No echo.

Micah breathed out. "I can pray in this. Not well, but I can."

"Enough is enough," Miriam said.

Nadya rolled her shoulders. "I still want out. But I can stand here for the right reason."

"Good," Gillie said.

Rowan tried a small, broken hum. It wasn't pretty. It wasn't meant to be.

Kali watched like she was waiting for someone to crack. Julian held Elana like a puppet. Lucien dragged another line that stopped short of our feet.

"Cephas," I murmured, touching the coin.

"Threshold," Kaela said. "It becomes a door when someone names it."

Tomas nodded. "Then it's named."

Micah looked at the three shadows of the people we'd once feared and then looked away. "We have to carry this with us so we don't forget. Even the cruel bow to something older."

"That isn't comfort," Miriam said.

"No," Micah said. "It's truth."

Gillie eased her hand off her blade. "We move when the way opens."

"And if it doesn't?" Nadya asked.

"Then we die standing in our own names," Gillie said. "Not theirs."

Raven's two shadows whispered "we" one last time. Then went still.

Marcus didn't lift his head. Elana cried through someone else's smile.

The masters watched like nothing in the world could surprise them.

We were not brave.

We were not many.

And we were still standing.

The Threshold of Plagues

The canyon didn't know dawn. Its walls never softened to morning; they barely tolerated light at all. So when the mist thinned and a pale glow pushed through it, none of us believed it was real. It looked like daylight trying to remember how to work—a weak sheen sliding along the Vein, more sickly pearl than gold. The air cooled beneath it, enough to make us squint as if the sun might be rising, even though the sky stayed empty.

Gillie didn't move her feet, but her shoulders locked.

"That's not day," she said. "Not ours."

Still, the light pressed against our faces like it expected recognition.

Then a voice came out of it.

"You are with them."

It wasn't Lucien. Not Julian. Not Kali. The tone was wrong for any of them—smaller, familiar in the way an old wound is familiar. It sounded like someone we'd trusted once: a keeper who'd soothed hunger, a voice you'd lean toward in the dark.

The words struck Shim'on first. His breath stuttered, ribs lifting too fast, like he'd been punched. The false dawn caught his eyes and lit them from the inside, and for a heartbeat he looked young again—like someone who still believed he could answer cleanly.

"You are with them," the voice said again.

Shim'on shook his head hard.

"I am not."

No dodge. No half-answer. Just the truth he wanted to be true.

Then the sound came—not a rooster's crow, but the shape of one. Three sharp calls, a pause, then two more. The exact lantern rhythm we'd heard before, twisted thin and hollow by the canyon, striking something deep he couldn't defend.

Shim'on staggered back. His hands scraped at the air like he was trying to find a wall. Shame hit him fast and hard, washing over his face and leaving nothing behind to hide it.

He dropped to his knees, pushed himself back up, and looked at us.

His face said everything.

I didn't mean it.

I didn't want it.

I don't know how to undo it.

Then he ran.

Straight into the false light—arms tight to his sides, steps uneven, heart louder than breath. The mist swallowed him whole and folded behind him.

No scream. No cry—only the sense of a door closing somewhere you couldn't reach.

Miriam did not look at the light. She watched the mist where Shim'on had vanished, measuring the space it left behind. Rowan started forward, but Gillie caught his shoulder.

"Let him go," she said quietly. "The silence will say what we can't."

Miriam made a thin sound, too small to be prayer. Tomas pressed both hands to his chest, like he could steady something slipping inside him.

Nadya looked away, jaw clenched; she could not afford to feel this all the way through.

The false dawn flickered, then drained out of the air—pearl to gray, gray to nothing. Whatever had pretended at morning let itself die, and the canyon took its night back without comment.

But the masters weren't finished.

Someone shifted in our line—a pilgrim who had been with us since the swamp. He hadn't spoken much on the road. He carried his pack without complaint, took his turns at watch, shared water when it was asked of him. The kind of presence you only notice when it moves.

He stepped forward now, not hurried, not afraid, as if something gentle had finally reached him and he had chosen to answer it. His hands lifted, palms open, empty.

"Mercy," he said.

To them.

Julian—still wearing Elana's body—smiled wider. Lucien's eyes flicked toward the traveler, assessing him like another number in a ledger. Kali tilted her head, and the air popped sharply beside her ear.

The mist split open. He walked into it—one step, then another—and was gone. No cry, no shadow left behind. The canyon took him so cleanly it felt like the world swallowed between beats.

We froze. A breach by consent was worse than any attack. Fear we could fight; willingness left no footing.

"No more," Nadya said. Not loud. Just final.

"Close ranks," Gillie said.

We moved instantly. Shoulders met shoulders. Breath matched breath. The line wasn't strong, but it held.

"No one stands at the ledge alone," Gillie said.

We spoke it back.

"No one stands at the ledge alone."

The scroll hummed—a low, steady sound. Not promising rescue, just reminding us that presence counted. Cephas's coin tapped once in my pouch.

Threshold.

The covenant still held—but it had narrowed. Not everyone who entered would leave the same way.

The mist pulled back farther than before. The Vein showed itself fully—dark, swollen, listening. Shadows on the far side bent wider, folding around a point we couldn't see.

Then they parted.

A man stepped forward with his head bowed, hands folded like he was about to pray with us instead of against us. The air around him brightened the way metal does just before it's hammered.

Before he spoke, a voice came from our side of the line.

"Master," said a pilgrim who had joined us in the village—one who had helped us find our way when the road split, who had spoken when we hesitated, who had known when to press on and when to wait. "I have done what was asked."

The man in the light turned his head just enough to see him. He smiled—not approval, not kindness, but recognition.

I knew him then—not by name spoken aloud, but by the way the light bent to him, by how the air seemed willing to listen.

The Lantern.

He faced us again.

"I am no master," he said, his voice soft, almost careful. "I only bear the light they give me."

Behind him, without seeming to move, stood Lucien, Julian, and Kali, their presence arranging itself into something like a throne.

The pilgrim lowered his gaze and stepped back into the line. He did not look surprised.

The Lantern lifted two fingers, a gesture small enough to miss if the Vein hadn't pulsed with it.

"Step forward, Herald," he said.

Something shifted behind him. A figure peeled out of the shadows as if released from them—shoulders hunched, clothes still marked by swamp-water memory. When he raised his head, an ember flickered behind his eyes, wrong in a way that made the light feel colder.

Gillie gasped.

"Joshua."

Joshua didn't look at her. He looked at the ground.

"You don't know what you're carrying," he said. His voice wasn't loud. It didn't need to be.

Joshua did not step closer, but his shadow did. It stretched across the stones until it brushed our feet, thin and wavering.

When he spoke again, the edge was gone.

"I didn't fall all at once," he said. "I broke."

He looked down at his hands.

"That's what happens when something hard meets light it can't bear. It doesn't bend. It fractures." He lifted his head, eyes dulled like embers starved of air. "Strong souls split clean and pretend they're whole."

His gaze moved across us—not counting, not measuring. Recognizing.

"Everything that split learned how to walk without me," Joshua said. "I watched it happen."

The river shifted behind him, thick and listening.

"The Vein doesn't want you," he went on. "It wants what I left in you."

Silence pressed in.

"If you survive what's coming," Joshua said, quieter now, "you won't leave empty-handed. Some of you won't leave at all."

The scroll hummed—not louder, not brighter—but longer.

Miriam's breath caught.

Joshua's mouth tightened.

"Either way," he said, "I don't stay broken."

Behind him, the false light stirred. The Lantern's fingers twitched once. The glow dimmed a fraction, then smoothed itself back into place.

"Enough," the Lantern said.

Not to us.

To Joshua.

Joshua stiffened. His jaw worked, then stilled.

The Lantern turned toward us, his voice gentle again.

"You hear fracture," he said. "I hear refinement."

His eyes never left Joshua.

"The river will answer what was asked of it."

A beat passed.

Then Joshua spoke again, clear.

"You don't have to go through this. Not like this."

He looked at the Lantern, then back at us.

"There is a way to stand where the pain doesn't reach," Joshua said. "A way to bend without breaking."

His gaze lingered on the scroll at my chest.

"I chose not to bend once," he said. "I let go instead."

The words landed heavier than any threat.

"You're being offered a choice," Joshua said. "Kneel to the light that will carry you through. Walk with them. Spare yourselves what's coming."

He swallowed.

"Choose wisely."

Gillie didn't hesitate.

"We choose true light," she said.

"Not light that demands a knee," I added, steady, "and not light that trades truth for quiet."

"We will not join a false flame," Gillie finished. "Not now. Not ever."

For a moment, no one spoke.

Cephas's coin tapped once in my pouch—not loud, but final.

The Vein answered beneath our feet, pulsing once, deep and slow.

And the ground held its breath.

Blood in the Veins

The River Answers

The ground kept holding its breath. Too long. Long enough that the silence began to hurt—pressure without sound, weight without movement. The insects along the ridge went still, caught mid-whine. Even the Vein seemed to draw inward, as if the world itself had forgotten how to exhale.

Then the ground convulsed once—hammer-hard, a blow we felt in bone before sound—and the breath broke.

The Vein answered.

Shim'on made a small sound like a swallowed prayer. His shoulders tightened, then he forced them down again—control by habit, not peace.

Water surged upward and frothed red. The first breath of iron hit our noses like a slap. The stream didn't flow; it writhed, swelling and thickening as we watched, dragging itself across stone like muscle trying to remember how to move. The surface buckled in slow waves that never settled.

The humming trees along the ridge groaned.

Then they screamed.

Bark split down the trunks with sharp, cracking reports. Dark red sap pushed through the seams and spilled out, smoking when it hit the air. Every drop that touched rock hissed and raised a welt, blistering stone like skin held too close to flame. The smell was wrong—sweet and metallic at once—and it coated the back of the tongue until breathing felt like swallowing coins.

Blood found our ankles.

It clung. Sticky. Warm.

"No—" Micah swore, kicking hard. The stuff climbed anyway, ropey as ivy, tightening with every new pulse. It burned—not a clean burn. First the sharp sting of salt in a cut, then a slow, mean heat that curled under the skin and stayed.

Nadya slapped at her calves. Red peeled away in strings, then seeped straight back out of her pores in darker streaks, as if the liquid outside was only the symptom.

Tomas hauled Miriam upright by the elbows. Stains streaked her robe top to hem. The cloth seemed to learn as it drank—the marks deepened, black-red, like shame setting in. Where he touched her, his own sleeves darkened too, spreading outward as if the fabric had decided for him.

A dozen small noses bled at once—Rowan's, Sera's, Shim'on's mine. Thin lines, sharp and sudden, tasting of pennies. Our tongues split along the center line. Not enough to ruin speech, just enough to make every breath taste of iron and salt. The blood in the Vein heard us tasting and throbbed in answer.

The insects that had been whining along the ridge stopped mid-buzz.

The silence they left behind felt like a floor dropping.

"The river remembers the hand that bled it," Joshua called across the bank.

His voice was steady now. Bitter. To most of us, it sounded like accusation—like a lesson learned the wrong way and repeated until it hardened.

The canyon agreed. Blood rose higher. Sap wept harder. Iron crowded our lungs until even standing still felt like effort.

"You said once the river remembers every kindness," Gillie said.

She didn't shout. She didn't argue. She remembered out loud. Her voice snagged on his name, but she didn't look away.

Blood hissed louder. Drops landed and didn't echo; they were swallowed. Even our own footsteps came back doubled, as if the canyon were rehearsing agreement with every fearful thought before we could stop it.

Lucien never moved his hands, but every flicker of suspicion along our line made the sting sharper. Julian's cadence hummed under Elana's tears, smoothing our doubts until they sounded almost reasonable. Kali laughed softly, a sound like a spark snapping—one chuckle out, a murmur back, as if a crowd we couldn't see had nodded along.

Cassian stiffened beside me.

Our watchman. Counter of grain. Noticer of loose ledges and weak beams. The man who kept records so others could sleep.

But now his gaze slid off rock and onto skin.

He scanned the line.

Micah's calves bright, the red climbing. Nadya's robe spotted twice, then three times. Miriam's trembling hands freckled red though she'd never touched the current. Cassian's lips moved without sound, shaping numbers: stain, flinch, hesitation.

The plague had turned people into ledgers. Every drop of red looked like a debt.

Shim'on stood a step behind Cassian, jaw clenched hard enough to ache, breathing in the measured lantern-rhythm he used when panic tried to write first. He didn't speak. He just kept his hands open—empty, visible—as if proof mattered.

Miriam noticed something then—not the pain, but the pattern. The blood thickened fastest where words went untested, where agreement formed without truth to anchor it. She didn't say it. She held it, the way you hold a thought you're not ready to name.

"Don't let it mark you—wash it!" Gillie barked.

She tore a strip from her sleeve, dropped to her knees, and grabbed Miriam's wrist. She scrubbed hard. The blood spat back at her, thinned, then crept in darker, as if it had stepped back only to gather itself.

Elana's mouth moved around a sob that wasn't hers. Julian pushed words through it.

"You see?" she said. "Suspicion is not sin. Suspicion is wisdom. Would you rather be betrayed by blindness?"

Cassian's head snapped up.

For a heartbeat I saw the guard on the wall.

Then something shifted.

A different kind of watcher stood in his place. The tally marks behind his eyes sharpened. He looked like a man deciding which sheep to cull so the flock might live.

The scroll shook against my chest and hummed once.

Reminder, not rescue.

Cephas's coin tapped my pouch again. A knock from an old parable: pay in love or pay in fear.

Across the blood-bright channel, Joshua stood very still.

"The river remembers," he said again.

Flatter this time. Heavier.

Gillie's cloth froze mid-swipe. Her eyes did not. Her face shifted, lines rearranging around something that looked stubbornly like mercy.

The blood escalated.

It thickened around our shins, trying to set. Clots spun up and drifted, dull as old embers. They stuck to skin like burrs and refused to be brushed off.

Wherever two of us agreed in the same suspicion—a whispered *she shouldn't lead*, a muttered *he'll break us*—the blood heard it. Two voices sharing the same doubt, and the red swarmed. It twisted itself into braided vines around their calves.

Nadya hissed as it climbed her and Sera together. Each had breathed, *Tomas will slow us*, thinking the thought was private. Now both wore matching ropes of red up to the knee.

"Stop," Gillie said.

Her voice went low and sharp.

"Break the word. Now."

"I never said—" Sera started.

"You thought it," Nadya spat. Pain sharpened her. It wasn't fair, but it was true.

"Say truth," Kaela warned, eyes fixed on their legs. "Or it drinks deeper."

"Tomas," Sera gasped, "I was afraid. Not sure. I'm sorry."

"I meant the risk, not you," Nadya forced out. Her jaw trembled with the effort to separate the man from the fear.

The vines loosened a finger's width.

Not mercy. Mechanics.

The canyon took language seriously.

On the far bank, Marcus twitched as if he meant to step down and help a pilgrim whose legs had locked. Lucien snapped him back from inside like a rope yanked tight. Marcus convulsed, teeth flashing pink.

Elana reached toward a child whose wrist was splashed red. Julian steered her hand mid-motion and turned the reach into a blessing for the plague instead. She sobbed as her fingers betrayed her.

Raven's shadow flinched toward a woman who had dropped to her knees. Kali clicked her tongue. The sound split his voice.

"We—we—we," was all that came out now, running together until the word sounded like a saw.

They punished their own in front of us.

Not for drama.

For policy.

The trees wailed. Sap slid down their trunks in noisy ropes and smoked where it pooled. Micah wiped his split tongue with the back of his hand, flinching when salt hit the fresh seam. Tomas's nose bled a clean line to his lip. He sniffed it back, ashamed of the instinct—as if swallowing red might count as agreement.

Gillie moved again.

She went to Nadya and Sera together, not one before the other. She dipped the torn cloth into a pocket where the red had gone more sludge than water.

"Wash and witness," she said. "Two hands. One truth."

Shim'on dropped with them without being asked. He tore a strip from his own sleeve, grimacing as the cloth stuck to blood, and pressed it into Miriam's hands like offering mattered more than speech.

She reached back without looking and caught my wrist, pulling my hand down to help. We scrubbed at Sera's ankles first. The blood fought us, rope-tight. Every drag of the cloth felt like rubbing against teeth.

Then a shadow fell over our hands.

Joshua's.

For one breath, the sting went out like a snuffed candle.

The blood let go, slack as dead nettle. Sera's skin came back to itself, pale and shaking.

The shadow moved away.

Pain came rushing back as if it had been held at the door and finally shoved through.

"Did you feel that?" Micah whispered.

"Mercy is not a bedtime story," Gillie said. "It's physics here."

"Or theater," Cassian muttered. "Look up and you'll see the puppeteer."

I looked.

Joshua hadn't moved more than that one lean. His face stayed tight. If his shadow gave relief, it wasn't because he'd decided to be kind. It was because something older than him liked the shape of what we were doing and forced the rules to pause.

"The river remembers every kindness," Gillie said over the hiss.

Half to him. Half to the canyon.

"Kindness won't carry you out," Joshua said. "It didn't carry me."

Cassian's breath went ragged. His fingers twitched at his belt—not for steel, for a ledger that wasn't there. He was counting more than stains now. Micah looking away when the blood hissed. Nadya flinching when Tomas steadied her wrist. Miriam's raw, helpless sobs—as if surrender had already happened in her chest and waited for her mouth to sign.

The plague wasn't just in the river.

It was in his math.

"Cassian," Gillie said, without standing.

"I'm watching," he answered too fast.

"You're calculating," she said. "There's a difference."

"Only if we live long enough to be poetic about it," he snapped.

The scroll pulsed against me, harder than before.

Not warning.

Grief.

My knuckles whitened around the leather. It didn't blaze. It didn't open. It hummed—low and stubborn—like a heartbeat behind rock.

Gillie shifted to Miriam. She ran the cloth along a wrist veined thin and bright with pain. The blood sizzled and withdrew half a thumb's width.

"You are not what clings to you," Gillie said.

Julian's cadence slipped. Elana's mouth faltered. For a heartbeat, a stitch missed. The doctrine stuttered. The canyon sounded almost like itself.

Kali laughed. The sound bounced off bark, then came back doubled, then tripled until even the trees seemed to copy it. The doctrine caught again.

Cassian lifted his hand.

Not to strike.

To divide.

His fingers twitched in small, sharp points—Micah, Miriam, Nadya. His lips shaped silent verdicts. I could almost see the numbers he was scribbling: one-against-eight… two-against-seven.

The Vein pulsed harder, as if the land enjoyed watching love curdle into audit.

"Stop," I said.

"I'm trying to keep us alive," Cassian shot back.

"You're trying to own us," Gillie said, getting to her feet. The cloth hung heavy and red from her hand. "Those are not the same thing."

"You can't wash this away," Cassian said. "You can count it or drown. Those are the options."

"I'm not trying to wash it away," Gillie said. "I'm trying to remember."

"Remember what?"

"That we were kind," Gillie said. "Even when it cost."

"Kindness is rot," Cassian said, but there was a knot under the anger now, a doubt he didn't know where to put.

"No," Gillie answered. "Kindness is resistance."

The Vein surged.

One long, ugly pulse rose to mid-shin. Bark split fresh seams. A skin-blister smell lifted off the stone. The canyon groaned like it hated the sound of itself but couldn't stop making it.

Joshua took half a step forward. Wrong light caught wet at the corner of his eyes.

He looked at Gillie. At Cassian. At me.

"You think mercy will save you?" he asked. "It didn't save me."

"Maybe it did," Gillie said softly. "Maybe you forgot."

Joshua's mouth opened, then closed.

For one stretched breath, everything held—blood, sap, even the echoes.

Julian moved first.

He leaned very slightly closer to the Lantern, as if sharing a quiet joke. Elana's lips shaped a whisper that scraped down my spine.

"Helar," he breathed.

Elana flinched like the syllables burned her tongue. A sharp line of blood slid from the corner of her mouth. Lucien's head snapped sideways—a quick, sharp look that said *enough.* Kali's eyes narrowed, just a fraction, as if a child had said a word from a room he shouldn't know exists.

I didn't understand the name.

The canyon did.

The air went tight, as if the world itself had clenched its jaw and then forced it relaxed again.

Lucien smoothed his expression and cut across the moment.

"Mercy is weakness," he told us, calm as a man balancing a ledger. "It delays judgment. It softens truth."

"Mercy is blindness," Julian added through Elana's lips, wiping the blood away with the back of her hand. "It forgives what should be named."

"Mercy," Kali said, popping the air near Raven's head, "is a lie you tell yourself so you can sleep."

Gillie didn't argue.

She turned back to us.

"One line spoken," she said. "Three breaths silent."

We obeyed.

The line wasn't a spell.

It was somewhere to put our feet.

The first breath tasted of iron. The second, ash. The third tasted like nothing at all—like air scraped clean—and we took it anyway.

The red tugged at our legs but did not climb higher.

Cassian's hand lowered. The numbers in his eyes didn't vanish, but they flickered—like a column of figures someone had just been told might not be the whole story.

The scroll pulsed again. This time the note felt different. Less like grief. More like a muscle remembering work.

The river still bled. Bark still wailed. Echoes still lied about consensus. But the line held.

For the first time, the canyon did not echo the masters.

It echoed us.

And the river listened.

The Bargain Returned

The river did not run out of red. It just… changed.

After a while the surface stopped fighting. The violent writhing eased into a slow, glassy slide, like the Vein had learned how to hold still without becoming harmless. But under that calm, darker clots gathered and rose in lazy drifts. They were small—each one about the size of a fingernail—dull at first, then slowly brightening until they carried a sick, inner glow.

They lifted out of the red like fireflies that had forgotten the sky.

When the wind moved through the canyon, the flecks came with it. They floated to shore, brushed hair and sleeves and cheeks, and stuck. They didn't burn the way the blood had burned. They itched instead—the kind of itch that digs straight for the oldest wound.

Micah flicked one off his sleeve. It clung to his palm like wet ash. Then it pulsed—once, hard—and his eyes went unfocused.

He sucked in air through his teeth, like something had jabbed behind his eyes.

Gillie snapped, "Don't touch them by yourself."

Micah swallowed. "I didn't— I just—"

"I know," she said. Her voice wasn't angry. It was sharp because it had to be. "Two hands. Same as the vines."

Kaela watched another fleck settle on her wrist like a bright seed. She didn't flinch, but her jaw tightened. "So they're not just blood," she said. "They're... memory."

Memory—like the fireflies on the Ember Path, I thought. Those had carried what we hadn't said yet. These carried what we wished we could deny.

"Or guilt," Rowan muttered.

Gillie nodded once. "And if it's either one, it lies. Or it keeps score."

Kaela's mouth twitched in something like humor that didn't reach her eyes. "Then it's both."

We tried it the only way we'd learned anything in the Vein: together.

Sera steadied Nadya's elbow while I pressed a cloth against Nadya's wrist. Gillie spoke in a low, practical voice—what happened, what we meant, what we actually said, not what fear wanted to rewrite—and the fleck flickered between our fingers like it was deciding which story to live in. Then, slowly, it dimmed. It didn't vanish. It turned to ash and fell.

Where we got impatient—where someone slapped one away with the back of a hand—it split in the air, like a thing that enjoyed being struck. Three flecks drifted down in its place, brighter than the first. Heavier.

Across the blood-bright channel, Marcus watched like a man watching a market open.

He wiped his mouth with the back of his hand and left a crimson smear on his skin like paint. When the glowing flecks drifted onto his boots, he didn't brush them away. He smiled at them.

Then he looked up at us and spoke like we were all standing around the same cookfire.

"Does it sting?" he called. "It doesn't have to."

We didn't answer him.

Marcus spread his hands, easy. "You won't save them all," he said, like he was reporting a simple fact. "But I can tell you which ones you can."

Shim'on's fingers twitched once at his side—an old reflex, like reaching for a lantern cord that wasn't there—then stilled.

No one moved.

That was new, for us. Earlier, a line like that would've pulled somebody forward, even if it was only to argue. Now we'd learned what a bargain costs before it asks for payment.

Marcus's gaze slid and landed on Micah again, like he'd been waiting.

"Micah," he said, slow, tasting the name. "Your sister waits. Say her name, and she lives."

Micah went very still.

The fleck on his palm brightened, as if it had been waiting for that exact syllable. His lips parted without him deciding to. A sound came out—half-formed, not even a full name yet—and the fleck snapped upward, quick as a moth.

It landed on his tongue.

Micah jerked like it burned, but it didn't burn. It pulsed, once, deep. His eyes watered. His throat worked. He didn't spit.

Rowan stepped in and put a hand on Micah's shoulder—not yanking him back, not making a scene. Just anchoring him.

"Hey," Rowan said, low. "Don't."

I put my hand over Rowan's wrist. Two hands. Same rule. We weren't washing blood now. We were holding a person in place while the Vein tried to rewrite him.

"Your sister isn't currency," Rowan said to Micah, but he kept his eyes on Marcus when he said it. "Love isn't a lever."

Micah's jaw trembled. The glow on his tongue flickered, like it was listening.

Marcus tipped his head, amused. "Do you know what fear can do with love?" he asked. "Anything it wants."

His smile twitched.

Not a normal twitch. A sharp, wrong pull at the corner of his mouth, like a wire had been jerked. His shoulders hitched. For one second he looked like he was choking on his own words.

The air around the far bank smoothed, the way it had smoothed when the Lantern stepped into view earlier—like the canyon itself was being told, quietly, to behave.

Marcus swallowed hard. When he spoke again, his voice had a second edge in it—another voice riding underneath his, impatient and tight.

"Say it," Marcus rasped. "Say it, boy. Say her name so the pain knows where to go."

Micah's whole body shook as if doors were slamming inside him. The canyon leaned in for it. It wanted proof that love could be spent.

Micah's lips parted again. The fleck on his tongue flared brighter.

And Miriam moved.

She didn't grab Micah like she was saving him. She reached like she was keeping him from stepping off a ledge he didn't realize he'd reached. Both hands closed around his wrist—steady, careful.

"Micah," she said, quiet enough that he had to lean toward her to hear it. "Test the voice."

His eyes darted to her.

"If it needs your pain to make a promise," she said, "it's not the One we follow."

Micah's mouth closed slowly, like he was forcing the hinge shut.

He looked at Marcus again. This time he didn't look away.

"I'm not doing it," Micah said.

The words came out simple. Human. Not a speech.

And they cost him anyway. Blood rose in his nose and he swallowed it back. The taste of iron hit his breath.

The fleck died against his teeth and went dull.

Marcus let out a laugh that sounded like a canteen turned upside down and found empty. "All right," he said, and for a moment the cheer sounded real again. "Not yours."

His eyes slid past Micah and landed on me.

"But you," Marcus called, and his smile widened like he was offering help. "Keeper. Your book wants a bargain worse than I do. Open it. End this."

The scroll didn't flare. It didn't answer like a weapon.

It got heavier.

Not in a dramatic way—worse than that. In the slow, grief-heavy way that makes your shoulders burn. Like the book was reminding me it could be used wrong. Like it was warning me: don't.

Cephas's coin tapped in my pouch—once, then again—patient as a habit.

Gillie's voice cut through, firm. "We're not for sale."

Marcus's eyes flicked to Cassian. "Not even him?" he asked, nodding like Cassian was a piece of equipment, not a man. "He's already counting the cost. He only needs a market."

Cassian didn't flinch, and that's what made it land. He didn't deny it, either, and that was worse. His gaze stayed fixed on Gillie's back like it was the only straight line left in the canyon.

A fleck drifted down and settled on Tomas's cheekbone.

He swatted at it out of reflex—and it burst, not into ash.

Into an image.

Tomas froze. His pupils widened, then narrowed, trying to focus on something that wasn't really in front of him.

Nadya stepped in. "What did you see?"

Tomas blinked hard. "Nothing."

Miriam didn't look at Tomas's cheek.

She watched Tomas's face instead—the pause where certainty should've been, the way his throat worked, like he was swallowing something that wasn't food.

And then—quietly, like she was measuring a wound by the space it left—she said, "Say what it left out."

Kaela's voice came right behind it, calm and flat. "Truth."

Tomas exhaled like he'd been holding his breath too long. "I saw Micah take the water ration," he said, and his voice cracked with how much he hated repeating it. "Out of my pack. Drink it alone."

Micah's head snapped up. "I didn't."

"I know," Tomas said fast. "I know you didn't. But it looked like… like remembering."

Micah's mouth tightened. Then he did the most dangerous thing a person can do in the Vein.

He told the truth that makes you look guilty.

"I didn't take it," he said. "But I thought about it."

The fleck on Tomas's cheek still glowed, hungry for a cleaner story.

Rowan stepped in and cupped the ugly light between thumb and forefinger like he was pinching out a coal. "Wash and witness," Rowan said.

Nadya put her hand over Rowan's. Two hands. "Truth out loud," she added.

Tomas swallowed. "I love my rations more when I'm afraid," he said.

The fleck sputtered.

Rowan's voice came steady. "And I love you more than my memory."

The fleck dimmed, collapsed into ash, and fell.

Across the bank, Elana's face—Elana's mouth—smiled.

Julian's warmth slid through her like perfume over rot. "Beloved," he called, gentle as a lullaby, "if truth and doubt both ease the sting… why not take the sweeter story and call it faith? Let memory heal you by changing."

Two pilgrims behind us nodded without thinking—same rhythm, same agreement.

The blood at their ankles reacted like it had been waiting. It tightened into vines, fast and hard, lacing their calves. They yelped and grabbed at each other.

Gillie was already moving. "Together," she said. "Now."

We dropped in twos. Cloth. Hands. Breath. Words that were plain enough to feel embarrassing.

"I doubted because I'm small."

"I accused because I was scared."

"I believed the picture because it was easier than the promise."

The vines loosened, sulking back into the red like they'd lost a game.

Raven's voice scraped out beside Kali, breaking the way it always did now. "They're teaching you how to pray to yourselves," he rasped. "Go on, then. Sing your little songs."

Kali popped the air near his ear like a fingertip snapping. Raven flinched and swallowed the rest.

More flecks rose.

Dozens. Then scores. Then hundreds.

The Vein turned into a field of dim stars, and every leaf overhead caught them. The branches looked constellated with guilt.

A child we didn't recognize reached up for one like it was pretty.

It bit.

She sucked in air and screamed—not a cry, a sentence.

"You left me!"

The woman beside her—mother, aunt, someone—reeled like she'd been struck. Her hand flew to her throat. "I never—" she began, and stopped. Her eyes flooded. "I wanted to," she whispered. "Once."

The fleck on the child's wrist brightened into something awful—like a tiny sun that wanted witnesses.

Miriam moved first.

Not running. Not dramatic. Just fast enough to matter.

She gathered the mother's hands and placed the child's palms on top, like she was building a small table strong enough to hold truth. Her voice stayed steady.

"Say the help," Miriam told Kaela softly. "Not the hurt."

The child sobbed, breath hitching. "Help me want to forgive."

The fleck dimmed mid-bite.

It hesitated—confused, like it had lost the script.

Then it fell to ash on the child's wrist.

"False memory cuts deeper than truth," a voice said behind us.

Joshua's shadow had slid closer without his body following it. The shadow reached us first, long and cold, brushing across the stones at Cassian's feet before the man himself had moved.

Most of us heard the sentence as rot. If memory could lie, then everything could.

Gillie didn't turn right away. Her chin lifted in that old way—the way she carried a word inward, not toward an argument but toward weight. Toward the scroll. She didn't nod. She didn't reject it.

She tested it.

"Say it again," she told Joshua, blunt as a hammer.

Joshua's jaw tightened. For a moment he looked like a man who hadn't expected to be asked twice.

"False memory cuts deeper than truth," he repeated, flatter this time. Cleaner.

I felt the canyon lean in again, eager for how we would hear it.

"To most," I said, finishing the thought that rode behind his words, "that means everything is corrupt." I swallowed, tasting iron still clinging to the back of my tongue. "To us, it means test the memory against the Word."

Joshua looked at me like a man hearing his own voice echo off a hill he used to live on. Something softened in his eyes. It didn't last. He hardened it again, almost angry at himself for the pause.

Across the channel, Lucien watched us the way a butcher watches a family discuss prices over meat already paid for. His fingers lifted—two of them, barely—and the air tightened, smoothing again.

Marcus jerked like a man yanked back on a leash.

"Back to the bargains," Lucien murmured, not loud enough for us to hear cleanly, but enough for the canyon to catch it.

Marcus obligingly brightened.

"You," he called to Rowan, cheer settling back over his face like a mask. "Your prayers would sound truer if they hurt more. I could give you a word that draws blood every time you say it—if pain is the proof you need."

Rowan didn't answer.

Marcus's smile slid sideways toward Sera. "And you," he said lightly. "You want to be brave? I can take fear off your hands. Remove the part of you that remembers your name."

Sera flinched despite herself.

A fleck landed at the hollow of her throat and began to glow.

Nadya was already there. Her palm came up—not striking, not frantic—just steady, covering the light like soil over a seed.

"We keep our names," Nadya said.

The fleck guttered, offended, and went dull.

Marcus's gaze shifted to me again. "Keeper," he said, almost kindly. "You could open the book for a heartbeat and cauterize this whole mess. It would only eat who it needs."

The scroll answered before I could.

It didn't blaze. It didn't open.

It weighed.

The kind of weight that makes your knees lock if you don't respect it. Grief-weight. Responsibility-weight. The kind that reminds you what happens when fire is used to choose instead of to refine.

Cephas's coin knocked once in my pouch.

I didn't look down.

"Not for sale," I said, and the words scraped going out.

Cassian's jaw worked. He wasn't moved by poetry. He never had been. He was moved by numbers, by angles, by what failed first when pressure came on.

The flecks hovering above us seemed to sense that. They drifted closer to him than anyone else, arranging themselves like a crooked halo. They whispered in a cadence that felt almost reasonable.

She will slow you.

He will fail you.

This one will bargain.

That one will break.

Julian sweetened the whispers until they sounded like consensus. Kali doubled them, sent them bouncing off stone and bark until the canyon itself seemed to agree.

Cassian's mouth tightened.

"Say what you're thinking," Gillie told him without turning. She refused to let words rot into power by staying unspoken.

Cassian drew a breath that made every fleck lean closer.

"If I were on a wall," he said slowly, choosing each word like it might fall apart in his mouth, "I would move the weakest where a breach would cost least."

Micah stiffened. Sera flushed. Miriam went very still—which is a kind of flinch, if you know what to watch for.

The blood at our ankles quivered, ivy ready to climb again.

Gillie turned then. "And if you were a shepherd?"

Cassian stared at the river. The red reflected in his eyes made him look older.

"I would carry the weakest on my shoulders," he said finally, "and make the strong walk angry."

"Then be a shepherd," Gillie said.

She didn't argue it. She placed it.

Something in Cassian clicked—quiet, internal—like a latch that had rusted in place and just remembered how to swing. The flecks above his head lost interest and drifted back toward the far bank, where Marcus accepted them with open hands.

Kali sighed, bored.

Raven's mouth opened on *we* and came out with *I*—only it wasn't his. A woman in the far cluster jerked as if she'd been struck. Raven spoke in her husband's voice, cadence perfect, tenderness sharpened to a weapon.

"I only wanted you safe."

The woman gasped. A memory-that-wasn't jammed itself into her ribs—hands that held too tightly, words that wrapped instead of guarded. Flecks swarmed her shoulders, trying to dress her in a past she had not lived.

Miriam reached her first.

Miriam's fingers closed around the charred scrap at her waist—not to look at it, not to show it. Just to feel the edge where fire had stopped.

She had learned something from things that burn and stay burned.

They don't rewrite themselves to survive.

She let it go and took the woman's hand.

"Test it," she said, steady as a handrail on a moving cart. "Against the Word. Not your fear."

"What word?" the woman choked.

"That love protects," Miriam said, "and without protection it is possession. Possession isn't love."

She didn't raise her voice. She didn't soften it either.

The flecks trembled. Sagged. Fell to ash down the woman's back.

Julian frowned for the first time—a thin line at the corner of Elana's eyes.

"Beloved," he murmured, doctrine sliding smooth and fragrant, "protection feels like holding. Why refuse what holds you?"

"Because hands can be prisons," Nadya said. "And gates swing both ways."

The flecks near her withdrew as if the ground had gone bad.

Marcus clapped once, amused. "Oh, well played. Liturgy against liturgy. You might last the day at this rate."

His smile jerked again.

Lucien had tired of humor.

"Offer them the choice," Lucien said, voice tightening Marcus's throat from the inside. "Choice is the sharpest hook."

Marcus nodded, obliging.

"You won't save them all," he said. "But I can tell you which ones you can. Give me three, and the river loosens for the rest."

"Three what?" Tomas asked, though he already knew.

"Three names," Marcus said, eyes shining with borrowed light. "Say them now. The others walk dry."

"No," Gillie said immediately.

Marcus blinked. "You don't decide this."

"Mercy isn't a butcher's scale," Gillie replied.

"It is when fear runs the market," Marcus said pleasantly.

A fleck landed on Cassian's wrist—bright, sharp, pulsing. It showed him a picture: Gillie saying three names—Micah, Sera, Miriam—and dry ground opening under the rest.

Cassian almost believed it.

Joshua's shadow slid across his hand.

"False memory cuts deeper than truth," Joshua said again, very low.

Gillie didn't flinch. She passed the blade.

"Test it," she told Cassian. "Against the Word."

"What word?" Cassian asked, raw now.

"That a shepherd lays down his life for the sheep," Gillie said. "Not names. Not numbers."

Cassian stared at the fleck until it dimmed—not from shame, but from hunger unmet.

Marcus sighed, like a merchant whose customer had refused a bargain that should have been obvious.

"Suit yourself," he said. "The river remembers. It can keep this scene. It improves with retelling."

"Not if we keep telling it true," Rowan said. His voice shook, but it held.

The flecks answered that sentence like iron answering a magnet. They surged toward Rowan's head in a loose crown, then faltered—hesitated—as if the air around him wouldn't carry them. They drifted back, confused, scattering.

Words make weather in the canyon. We had forgotten that. We remembered.

"Count," Kaela said, stepping forward and drawing a spiral in the dust with her heel. She cut it clean through with a straight line. "Not names. Costs. The bargain always comes back because it believes it will find you softer the next time. It will wear voices you trust. It will wear your memories like clothes. Test. Wash. Witness. Refuse math that asks for blood to buy quiet."

"Say the move," Sera whispered. Her hands needed something to do.

"Wash and witness," Gillie said.

We began again.

Two at a time. No rush. Receiving each fleck instead of swatting it. Saying the truth the lie had tried to decorate and letting the ash fall where the canyon could see it die. The work was slow. The work hurt. The itch dug deep, searching for wounds we hadn't named yet. But where Joshua's shadow crossed our hands—even by accident—the sting stopped for one clean breath, and the red couldn't argue with that.

Marcus tried new offers when boredom set in. Lucien pulled him back into shape when the offers strayed off-script. Julian tuned Elana's smile until sweetness curdled. Kali doubled whispers until the canyon said them back.

We learned to watch hands, not mouths.

Cassian stood between Gillie and me and did the thing he had always been made to do: he watched. Not to own. To protect. When a fleck drifted toward Miriam's face, his palm rose like a roof over her eyes. When a bright dot hovered near Micah's mouth, Cassian closed his jaw gently until the light drifted away to someone easier.

"Your gift isn't a cage," Gillie told him once, without stopping her work. "It's a gate."

Cassian didn't answer. He didn't need to. Gates speak by holding.

By dusk the fireflies of guilt had thinned to a minor constellation. The river still ran red. The trees still wept. But our ankles were free of ivy, our tongues didn't split again, and our noses bled only when we lied—and we had stopped lying.

Across the channel, the masters recalculated with the boredom of kings realizing the city would not burn fast enough to entertain them before supper.

"We'll be back," Marcus said, voice already leaning toward someone else's throat. "Plague by plague. Wound by wound."

"We know," Gillie replied. She didn't sound sentenced. She sounded resolved.

Joshua looked at her across the water. He didn't nod. He didn't vanish. He faded by degrees, like a shadow remembering the shape of the man that cast it and being ashamed of how clear it still was.

The Lantern had not moved.

That was the worst of it.

He hadn't argued. He hadn't corrected Marcus or restrained Lucien. He hadn't reached for the river or the flecks or the blood. He had only watched—measuring what held, what bent, what refused. Light around him stayed smooth, untouched by the struggle, as if refinement were happening somewhere else and we were only ore.

When the masters withdrew, he remained a moment longer, gaze resting on Miriam—not possessive, not curious. Appraising. As if noting a fracture that hadn't happened.

Then the false brightness dimmed, and the canyon took its night back.

We made camp in a way that wasn't camp. No fires. No tents. Just a circle of backs and a bowl of water we kept clean by stubborn miracle. When a fleck drifted near, we didn't swat. We received it. We named it. We let it fall to ash in the open.

Before sleep, Miriam spoke.

"Say the line," she asked, because sleep in a place like this is a border you shouldn't cross alone.

"We are not theirs," we said.

"Breathe," Gillie said.

We breathed. One. Two. Three.

The river kept its red. Our hope kept its honesty. The bargain returned—and we returned it unopened.

And somewhere beneath it all, the Vein listened, waiting for the next question to be asked.

The Silk Between Words

Night didn't come as relief. It seeped into the canyon the way infection spreads—slow, stubborn, everywhere at once. The stars were there, but dimmed, filmed over by a red haze rising off the river. The blood still moved, though it had lost its urgency. It folded in on itself now, clotted and heavy, catching on rock like muscle that had forgotten how to flex. The smell hung low and thick—iron and something spoiled underneath it—and every breath scraped the throat raw.

Near the banks, the ground stayed tacky. Boots didn't lift clean. Footprints clung as if the land wanted a record.

The masters hadn't gone anywhere.

They lingered across the channel, still as cut stone, letting the plague do its talking for them. No gestures. No commands. Just waiting to see what would give. We sat close—shoulder to shoulder—but our eyes didn't always meet. Unity held, but it held under strain.

The scroll pressed against my chest like a weight that refused to shift. It didn't burn. It didn't open. It didn't even hum. It simply bore down, steady as a millstone, as if to say: *This is what holding feels like.*

For the first time, I wished it would blaze—anything to cut through the thick, suffocating half-light.

It didn't.

Then Elana lifted her head.

Tears still tracked down her face, carving clean lines through the ash that coated her skin. Her eyes were red, glassy—but when she spoke, the cadence wasn't hers. The words came smooth, sure, threaded with something soft enough to trust.

"Doubt isn't failure."

Her gaze settled on Gillie and stayed there.

"Doubt is truth."

The sentence slid through the canyon like incense—sweet, close, clinging. It found gaps between ribs and settled there. Miriam flinched, lips moving in a prayer that stayed plain and unfinished. Micah shook his head once, sharp, like he was clearing water from his ears. Cassian didn't react outwardly at all. He watched. Measured how far that idea could travel if no one stopped it.

Gillie pressed her palm hard against her thigh. Muscle tight. She'd stood against shouted commands before. This wasn't that. This was suggestion—quiet, careful—trying to bend her own memory back on itself.

"You've carried too much," Elana went on, voice steadying as if grief itself had found a spine. "Every misstep. Every wound. Every doubt they've had—you've taken it all and kept going." Her mouth softened. "And what has it earned you? More cracks. More damage."

Gillie didn't answer.

"You say you guard them," Elana said. "But guarding can become neglect. Restraint can become refusal."

Kaela had dropped to her knees in the dust. Her finger traced a spiral—smooth, precise. Then another. Then another. The shapes widened, overlapping, perfect in a way no tired hand should manage. The pattern spread like a net laid quietly at our feet.

"Kaela," Nadya said, low and close. "That's not yours. Don't let them use your hand."

Kaela didn't look up. Her eyes had gone half-lidded, breath caught in a rhythm that wasn't her own. The spirals kept coming.

"I restrain because mercy demands it," Gillie said at last. Her voice stayed level. "Mercy isn't neglect."

Elana's smile turned calm in a way that didn't fit the tears still slipping down her chin. "Mercy that starves the strong becomes cruelty. Mercy that hesitates becomes betrayal. Mercy that doubts is just death waiting for permission."

The canyon leaned toward her. Roots along the ridge cracked. Old blood seeped from the bark again, slow and dark. Where our hands braced against stone, stains reappeared—thin threads of red sinking into lifelines and nailbeds.

"It doesn't come off," Miriam whispered, scrubbing her palms until fresh blood welled. "It wants to stay."

"Be counted," Rowan said quietly, staring at his own hands.

Cassian's gaze fixed on Gillie. The sentinel had become an auditor. The stains on her skin looked different under that light—less like shared burden, more like evidence.

"She's marked worse than the rest," he said. Not accusing. Assessing. "If stewardship spreads the plague, she's the breach."

Gillie snapped toward him. "I will not be accused for carrying what you wouldn't."

For a heartbeat, the silk wavered.

Elana slid into the gap without raising her voice. "Anger is confession," she said gently. "Guilt always speaks loudest when it knows it's guilty."

Shim'on flinched at that—quick, almost private—like the word *guilt* had landed closer to him than she intended.

Gillie didn't recoil—but something flickered behind her eyes. A real question, sharp and unwelcome: *Had restraint become refusal?*

At her thigh, the balanced blade answered with the faintest hum—steel responding to strain.

"She doubts," Cassian said, leaning forward. "That's proof."

Joshua's shadow rippled along the ground. His broken laugh caught in the silk like grit. "Doubt bends the blade before the hand."

Cassian heard confirmation.

Gillie heard instruction.

The scroll pressed heavier—still no light, no voice—just that deep, bone-level thrum: covenant, not accusation.

Kaela's spirals reached Gillie's boots. Gillie looked down, then planted her heel and ground one circle through. The pattern snapped like a string pulled too tight. Kaela gasped and pitched forward, hands shaking.

"They almost wrote me out," she said hoarsely, staring at her stained fingers. Her eyes cleared. "Almost quieted me."

Gillie turned fully to Cassian. "Doubt isn't truth," she said. "It's the crack where truth gets tested. I won't hand us to them because I trembled."

Cassian opened his mouth—and then closed it. The stains on all our hands pulsed together. Not proof of one guilt. Testimony that none of us stood clean. The arithmetic in his eyes faltered. He looked away.

Elana tried again, softer. "The clean must guard the stained. The strong must bind the weak. If you refuse to count, you'll fall together."

The scroll pulsed once. Heavy. Certain.

Gillie lifted her marked palm. The wound the river had burned into her skin shone wet in the dim light. "We won't count each other as rot," she said. "We'll carry each other as covenant."

The canyon echoed her.

Not the silk.

A sob broke from Elana—this one hers. Real. Unborrowed.

Behind her smile, something hissed. Laughter cracked across the river, multiplying where it landed. Cold pressed in from the banks like a hand testing a door.

But for that heartbeat, the silk tore.

And in the tear, truth breathed.

The Severed Edge

The Vein slowed.

What had been a rushing, violent surge of blood thickened into something reluctant, as if the river had grown tired of its own hunger. The sound changed first—no longer a roar, but a wet, dragging pull, each draw against stone coming back heavier than the last. The air sharpened with it. Copper and rot. The smell of old wounds forced open again.

We watched the surface knit itself together. Strings of red drew tight across the current, binding ripple to ripple until even movement carried weight.

"Sluggish," Nadya muttered. "Like it doesn't want to go."

It wasn't just the water.

The light itself had thickened. Every reflection we caught—on the river, on our hands, in each other's eyes—came back wrong. Doubled. One face where there should be one, and another just behind it, waiting its turn.

Micah saw it first.

He jerked back from the Vein, one hand clawing for the strap across his chest as if to hold himself together. In the red, his reflection split—one mouth moving in prayer, the other curling into something meaner.

"I can't—" He swallowed. "I don't know which one's mine."

"Neither of them," Rowan said, steady but strained. His own reflection trembled beside him—one side murmuring, the other silent. "That second face isn't you. It's what they're offering."

The canyon didn't answer. It only breathed heavier, as if waiting to see who would accept the split.

Raven laughed.

Not the jagged, broken sound from before, and not the doubled shriek either. This laugh carried voices inside it—voices we knew. Familiar. Intimate. They slid through his throat like silk pulled too tight.

Nadya froze when her mother's voice came out of him—flat, precise, unmistakable.

"You left me to die."

"That's not her," Nadya said, teeth clenched.

Miriam gasped as her brother's voice followed, sharp with accusation.

"You prayed while I drowned. Your silence killed me."

Tears spilled before she could stop them.

Micah flinched as another voice cut through—young, raw.

"You wanted me gone. You never came back."

Each sentence landed like memory, shaped perfectly to fit the fear it named.

Behind Raven, Kali crouched and tilted her head. The air popped softly each time she moved.

"Little mirror," she said, pleased. "Why speak with one face? Give them all of them. Show them what they already suspect."

Raven shuddered.

His shadow tore.

Feathers split in midair, each quill severed clean down the spine. They struck the stone and twitched—Kali's mark written plain: divide, fracture, separate.

Nadya grabbed a stone and hurled it across the Vein. It passed straight through Raven's body and struck his shadow instead. The halves writhed, then settled. The laughter sharpened.

Feathers littered the far bank, each one split in two.

"Shadow only," Kaela said quietly. "Not flesh. He's hers already."

Gillie's blade hummed at her thigh—low, furious, a vibration that carried up through my ribs. Her hand hovered near the hilt.

Kali leaned closer, eyes narrowing. "Edges choose their wielders," she whispered. Stone cracks echoed her words. "Which edge are you?"

The hum sharpened in reply.

Gillie's fingers stayed suspended between silence and steel. She had sworn restraint—no drawing unless mercy itself demanded it. But the edge wanted blood.

"Every edge drinks," Kali said, smiling. "Better it be yours."

The scroll pressed down like a coffin lid. Not blade-hunger—grief. A mourning weight for every cut that had ever been made to sever instead of heal. My knees bent under it.

Cassian's breathing turned rough. His eyes flicked from Gillie's hand to the doubled reflections, to Raven's shredded shadow, to the stains still dark on our palms.

"She'll cut us," he whispered. "She'll cut us apart and call it mercy."

Gillie snapped her head toward him. She didn't speak. The blade answered, humming louder.

Raven's borrowed voices piled on—Tomas heard his wife's grief, Sera a lover's betrayal. Different names. Different memories. The same wound turned slightly, like light breaking through uneven glass. Each echo pressed until even our own faces felt unfamiliar.

Cassian's fingers twitched for a ledger that wasn't there. His lips moved without sound—counting: one failing, two faltering, three fractured. He was close now. Not to violence—but to betrayal by arithmetic.

Joshua flickered on the ridge.

He didn't step forward. He existed between reflections, bent between shadow and substance. His laugh came cracked—half mockery, half mourning.

"Edges don't choose," he said. "Mercy does."

The sentence cut the canyon clean.

Most of us heard scorn and shrank from it. Cassian's mouth twisted, ready to take it as proof that Gillie had already failed.

Gillie heard something else.

Her chin lifted. The blade's hum softened—not gone, but steadied. An edge waiting, not demanding.

"If mercy chooses," she said, raising her stained palm, "then mercy chooses us still. I won't sever."

The blade quieted. Fury resolved into resonance, like a bell waiting for its hour.

Cassian stared at her. The judgment in his eyes shook, then loosened. Slowly—as a soldier lowers a spear—his breath evened. Numbers fell away. He stepped forward, not to accuse, but to stand between us and the river.

At the margin, Miriam moved.

She didn't rush Raven. She didn't shout him down. She went to the child whose palm still glowed faintly, caught between faces.

Miriam knelt and covered the child's hand with her own.

"Look at me," she said softly. "Not the picture. The space it leaves."

The child's breath hitched.

"You are not what clings to you."

The glow wavered.

It did not vanish all at once. It thinned—lost its grip—slid away from the child's palm as if it no longer recognized where it belonged. What remained broke its own outline and fell as ash between their hands.

Gillie felt it then.

Not in the blade. Not in her fingers.

In her chest.

A pressure she had carried without naming it—years of it, quiet and constant—shifted and loosened, like blood finally finding a passage that had been closed too long. Her breath caught.

For an instant she was somewhere else: a small kitchen, late light pooling on the counter, an old woman's voice steady and unremarkable, spoken as if it were nothing more than good sense.

You are shaped by the One who made you, Olivia had said, not looking up. *Not by what tries to hold you.*

Gillie's fingers trembled. She looked at the child again and understood—not clearly, not fully—but enough. Blood recognizing blood. A line unbroken, even when bent.

Miriam didn't lift her voice. She didn't look at Joshua.

"I learned it the moment something else claimed him—and he let it."

The words landed crooked in the air, like a stone striking glass that didn't shatter but rang all the same.

Joshua's jaw tightened. Not in anger. In dismissal.

He didn't look at Miriam. He didn't look at the child. His gaze fixed instead on the Vein, on the place where the blood had thinned, as if whatever truth had crossed the ground had already passed him by.

"Careful," he said lightly. "You mistake survival for surrender."

But the shadow at his feet shifted—just a fraction too late to be coincidence.

Gillie swallowed.

"I didn't know how to stop it," she said, the words leaving her before she decided to speak. Her voice thinned. "I thought surviving was the same thing."

Behind them, Joshua did not move.

But the shadow cast from him did.

It recoiled—not backward, but sideways, folding wrong, tearing along its own edges as true light crossed it from an angle the body itself had not felt. Joshua's shoulders eased—not in release, but in surprise, as if something had been lifted that he had never known how to set down.

For a breath—only a breath—the false shadow thinned.

Not gone.

Not forgiven.

Just exposed.

The canyon breathed.

The Vein shuddered—not in hunger, but in surrender. The red that had thickened the current loosened, then thinned, then cleared. What had been blood was suddenly water again—cold, transparent, moving without weight.

Miriam smoothed the scrap of blackened cloth between her fingers and tucked it away again.

The fire had not lied to it.

And neither had she.

Along the banks, stains faded where they clung. Sleeves darkened by the plague lightened beneath our eyes. Palms scrubbed raw by red came clean without washing. Even the copper taste in the air thinned, leaving only stone and damp wind behind.

The scroll pulsed once. Heavy. Witnessing.

Raven's laughter cracked and fell silent. His shadows twitched, then stilled. Kali's eyes narrowed. Lucien's wind sliced sharp with irritation. Julian's cadence slipped, half a note off.

We stood marked and exhausted—but whole.

Shim'on stood a step back from the line, as he always did. When the red thinned to water, his shoulders loosened—but only for a breath. His gaze flicked to the banks, as if waiting for the stain to climb again.

We did not break.

We did not sever.

And the Vein—no longer blooded, still wounded—moved forward again.

Joshua laughed again—once, under his breath. Not sharp this time. Worn. The sound of a man who had learned which truths cost the most to say aloud.

"You think it's over," he said. "Because the river stopped accusing you."

He lifted his head, and the light caught his face wrong—not doubled now, but hollowed, as if something had been scraped clean and left exposed beneath. His eyes found each of us in turn, lingering just long enough to bruise.

"But blood was never the hardest thing to carry."

The canyon seemed to lean toward him.

"There are sins that bleed," Joshua went on, voice steadying as if rehearsed. "And there are sins that dry. Ones you survive by swallowing. Ones you learn to live with. Ones that teach you how to keep walking without ever asking where you're going."

Kali smiled, thin and knowing. Lucien's wind stilled, attentive. Julian's cadence found its footing again.

Joshua looked past them—past all of us—to the pale stretch ahead where the stone lost its color.

"You've learned how to endure," he said. "That's why this will hurt more."

His gaze flicked—just once—to Miriam, still kneeling, ash dusting her hands. Something unreadable passed across his face, too fast for the dark to seize.

"Grief doesn't drown you anymore," he said. "Not like it used to. You've learned how to keep it moving. How to carry it forward. How to let it settle."

The Lantern's glow sharpened, pleased.

Joshua swallowed.

"But what you never named," he finished quietly, "will feed on you instead."

The wind shifted.

Ahead, where the canyon widened, the air dulled—not darkened, not red—but paled, as if color itself were being starved out of the world.

Joshua turned away first.

"Don't ask to be spared," he said, already walking. "That won't help you now."

He did not say what would.

He did not look back.

Behind him, the stone exhaled.

And where the Vein's red had cleared, something finer began to fall—soft, soundless, weightless—

Ash, not from fire, but from everything that had burned long ago and never been mourned.

Ashes to Ashes

The Strangers in the Grove

The canyon tightened until it felt less like a place and more like a passage someone had abandoned halfway through building.

Micah slowed without being told. Tomas caught it immediately and passed the signal down the line with a small lift of his hand. After the river, none of us trusted narrowing ground—or quiet that arrived too neatly.

The Vein's red banks were gone. So were the dark cliffs that had hemmed us in like jaws. Everything here had been leeched pale. Trunks rose smooth and white, bone-colored, as if wind and ash had spent years sanding them down. Their branches crossed overhead in a loose lattice that felt almost protective—almost—like ribs closing around a chest that no longer needed breath. Light slipped through in thin bands, unsure whether it wanted to stay.

"Don't relax," Nadya muttered. "This is where it changes shape."

The ground looked solid until we stepped on it. Then it sighed and gave way—not collapsing, just yielding—like walking on old hearth-ash sifted too many times. Kaela tested each step before committing her weight. Even that felt like permission granted too easily.

The silence pressed harder than any hum we'd heard before. Not empty—resistant. Our footsteps made the soft sound of pages turning after the story was finished. Breathing scratched. The air tasted faintly burned, and each inhale stung the back of my throat.

Tomas coughed—once, sharp enough to snap attention. He pressed his sleeve to his mouth and pulled it away too fast. The fabric smoked faintly where it touched his lips. When he lowered it, a thin red line traced the corner of his mouth, bright against the gray. For a moment it looked too familiar—like a stain from a different fire he'd once breathed through.

"Don't swallow it," he said quietly. "It burns if you take it in whole."

Micah coughed too. The sound dragged. He swallowed, winced, and shook his head.

Micah shifted the strap across his chest. "Why is it so still?"

Kaela crouched and traced a spiral in the ash with her toe. "It's listening."

Shim'on shifted behind us, just far enough back that the ash blurred his outline. His eyes kept scanning the pale trunks, as if expecting something to answer when no one else did.

The line slipped as she drew it, blurred—and then corrected itself. The curve tightened into a clean coil that wasn't quite hers. Her jaw set. She pressed harder. The spiral held, but gray feathered outward from it, like the ash had a pulse of its own.

"Still wrong," she said.

We closed ranks without deciding to. Even with room enough to spread, our shoulders brushed. The flat light drained our faces. Nadya glanced at a pale film of water pooled at a root and swore under her breath.

"I look like I died on my feet."

Tomas fell back a half-step, letting Miriam move ahead of him, his hand hovering near her elbow.

Where the ash thinned at our wrists and throats, the skin beneath looked smoke-worn, like flesh after a danger has passed but never really left.

For a breath, I smelled the river again—copper and panic—and my chest remembered what happens when a plague decides you've learned enough to be punished. The Withering didn't invent new lessons. It repeated them.

Ahead, three figures waited.

They sat on low stones in a rough triangle, heads bowed, hands folded. Pale robes. Skin too smooth—wax-smooth, like faces warmed in a room where no one lived. When the middle one lifted his head, my stomach dropped.

His eyes were wrong. Gray and flat, like ash packed into hollows. No laugh-lines. No grief. Just a surface shaped to resemble peace.

"Strangers," Nadya breathed.

The middle figure raised a loaf.

It was white—unnaturally so—with a thin, dry crust. He broke it. The sound cracked like chalk.

"Eat," he said gently.

The others tore pieces and chewed. Their jaws moved in a rhythm too even to be alive. When they swallowed, their lips curved upward. Not relief—performance. The smile never reached their eyes.

"Shared bread is shared truth," the middle said.

"Shared truth is safety," said the one on his left.

"Safety is joy," finished the one on the right.

They held the loaf out again.

Shim'on didn't look at the bread. He watched the hands that held it.

My stomach clenched, sudden and sharp, like it had been empty too long. The feeling didn't fade when I swallowed. It was the kind of hunger that meant continuing, not living. It widened—an ache that promised nothing would satisfy it.

Around me, others shifted—hands to ribs, weight redistributed—the quiet signs of bodies realizing they were running out of something they hadn't spent.

Nadya spat into the ash. "That's ash," she said. "No fire burned here."

Rowan glanced back toward the canyon, where residue still clung to us—in our clothes, our breath. The plague hadn't changed. It had just learned new words.

Micah shook his head. "No. Bread without salt is a curse." His voice cracked on the last word.

The scroll pressed hard against my ribs. It didn't open. It didn't burn. It watched.

Eliah stepped forward.

Grief lived close to the surface in him, but it had never been small or self-serving. He carried sorrow the way others carried tools—carefully. Ash dusted his lashes and webbed the creases of his palms. He raised his hands.

"Bread without reverence isn't a covenant," he said softly.

The middle stranger smiled wider, and the light in the grove dimmed a shade.

"Then take reverence with it," he said. He tore a thin slice and laid it flat on his open palm. "If you carry sorrow, eat. Your grief will rest."

Eliah swayed—just a breath toward him. The ache in him wanted quiet. Ash flaked from his hands.

Tomas brushed ash forward instead of away.

"Grief stops killing you," he said under his breath, "when you let it walk."

Gillie tensed—not at the man, but at the ease of it. Relief offered without weight.

Her blade hummed—low, bone-deep. She set her hand over the hilt, steadying it.

"Not for death," she said. "For life."

The blade's note shifted, settling into something steadier.

The middle stranger leaned closer. "If not for death," he echoed, "then for life. What life is greater than joy without sorrow?"

"Joy without sorrow is fake," Gillie said. Her fingers trembled. She didn't draw.

Their gray eyes reflected us doubled—each face twice, one full, one hollowed.

The grove moved.

No step. No sound. We blinked and stood again at the entrance—the same pale corridor, the same ribs of branch overhead. My heart slammed. Behind us, the ash was untouched except for our fresh prints.

No one remembered turning.

"A flicker," Kaela said. She bent to redraw her spiral. The ash corrected it too cleanly—then erased it, guiding her toe back to the start. "The Withering runs us backward."

"Then distance means nothing," Tomas muttered. He steadied Miriam by the elbow. She coughed into her hand. The phlegm was gray. When she wiped it on her skirt, it left a sharp-edged print that didn't fade.

The ash coated our sleeves, our hair, our breath. It made us look older. Emptied.

Covering isn't the same as becoming.

We edged forward again.

The three figures hadn't moved.

"Eat," said the middle.

"Eat," echoed the left.

"Eat," finished the right.

A voice came from behind us—close enough that no one jumped.

"Lost already?" Raven said lightly. "Or did the bread sit like joy in your throat?"

He stood on the ash path, hands loose at his sides. His smile widened, then slipped.

"We were hoping you'd take it," he added, one hand pressing briefly to his sternum.

Miriam flinched as her brother's voice slid out of Raven's mouth.

You prayed while I drowned.

She clapped her hands over her ears.

Then Nadya's mother—precise, clipped.

You left me.

Micah staggered when his sister's voice followed.

You wanted me gone.

Each line landed exactly where we'd begged God it wouldn't.

Shim'on flinched—not at the words, but at the space after them, like he was waiting for a name that hadn't been spoken yet.

The ash thickened.

"Relief," Kali murmured through Raven's smile. "Lay it down. Nothing hurts."

Eliah folded over his hands. Tears cut gray lines down his face and stayed.

At the grove's edge, Joshua flickered. Ash-marked. Silent.

Was he grieving—or showing us how to grieve wrong? I couldn't tell.

"Shared bread is shared truth," the middle sang.

"Shared truth is safety."

"Safety is joy."

"Joy without truth is poison," Rowan said—not to argue. To remind.

"Say it," Sera whispered.

"We are not theirs," we said.

Ash drifted like snow that never melted. It burned only when you tasted it.

"Breathe shallow," Tomas warned. "It scalds if you pull too deep."

The middle stood, loaf cradled like an infant. "If sorrow slows you, eat. We live light. We don't need hope. We don't weep."

Eliah didn't lift his head. "Hope isn't a stone. You can't trade it for speed."

"Then trade sorrow," offered the left.

Gillie's blade thrummed again. Her hand closed on the hilt.

"Not for death," she said. "For life."

The branches flinched. The strangers glanced at one another—just enough to break rhythm.

"Life without sorrow," said the right, almost pleading, "is pure."

"No," Miriam rasped. "It's cheap."

Rowan whispered, "The Lord is near the brokenhearted." It didn't clear the ash. It made room.

The grove blinked us backward again.

"It wants repetition," Kaela said. "Numbness is easier."

Raven tilted his head. "Tell it faster. You'll forget the heavy parts."

Eliah stepped toward the bread—not to take it. To refuse it.

"Don't," Nadya said. "They'll hear consent."

Eliah stopped. "I will carry sorrow," he said. "It honors what was lost."

The middle blinked. "We can teach you honor without pain."

"That isn't honor."

Behind us, a traveler tore a piece and ate. His lips numbed. He smiled empty. "It's light," he said—and coughed.

The scroll pressed—not command. Witness.

"Name and breathe," Gillie said. "Name a real grief."

Eliah closed his eyes. "We lost the man who kept watch in the swamp."

"Answer with joy," Gillie said.

Rowan spoke. "He came back. He washed a stain. And stayed."

The memory held.

We breathed together.

We didn't eat.

We didn't forget.

And Gillie's blade hummed—soft, steady—as she kept the vow that held us there:

"Not for death,

but for life."

Questions Without Breath

The three pale Seekers did not tire.

They watched us the way a dry well watches a thirsty town—without hurry, without doubt, certain the turn would come. The bone-white grove held its breath with them. Ash lifted and settled in slow tides, flakes so fine they found the wet of the eye and the seam of the lip and stayed. It didn't fall straight. It wandered, choosing where to land. Where it touched skin, it left a dull warmth—not heat, but the echo of it, the way a room remembers fire after the hearth has gone dark.

Tomas turned his head away before anyone else thought to and covered his mouth with his sleeve. When he lowered it, he didn't look at the cloth. He folded the fabric inward instead, careful, like something could still burn.

We tried to move past.

They didn't step into our way. They didn't need to. The ground softened, the light slipped, and somehow we were again before them—the same rough triangle of stone at their feet, the same ash untouched except for our prints.

The middle one tilted his head. "Why is the scroll hidden?"

Shim'on's jaw tightened. He didn't answer. He had learned what questions did when you stepped toward them too quickly.

The figure on his left followed without pause. "If you trust one another, why does the blade rest with her?" His chin tipped toward Gillie's hip.

A white branch overhead creaked, though no wind moved. Fine dust sifted down the bark's grooves like powder shaken from an old book. Our shoulders rose together, then eased—too late.

The one on the right smiled as if we had already agreed. "If you trust the blade," he said gently, "why does it never sing?"

Julian's cadence threaded their speech. Each sentence landed a beat short—an amen withheld—like our answer would complete a song already poisoned.

Gillie didn't answer right away. The scroll pressed hard against my ribs—no heat, no flare, just weight, like an oath laid over bone. Miriam kept glancing at me as if a look might pry the latch. It couldn't. We had paid enough to learn the lesson: witness, not weapon.

The middle Seeker softened. "Why is the scroll hidden?"

"Because we are not its masters," Gillie said. "Because it is not a torch for us to wave at what we hate."

The grove caught her words and looped them back wrong—not its masters… not a torch…—shaving truth into slogan.

The Seeker on the left pressed, still pleasant. "If you trust one another, why does the blade rest with her?"

"Because it was given to me," Gillie said.

The steel at her thigh answered with a thin hum—agreement you could feel through your teeth.

The right-hand Seeker leaned in, voice almost tender. "Given for what? To give life—or to keep it from others?"

"Not for death," Gillie said, palm steady on the hilt. "For life."

The blade's hum answered like a vow. The grove leaned forward, waiting for spectacle. None came.

"Then let us speed life," the middle suggested, turning his smile toward Eliah. "Open what is hidden. Share what is hoarded. End this grief."

He let grief hang unfinished. Eliah's breath caught in the gap.

Ash thickened. Tomas coughed into his sleeve again, sharper this time.

"You can ask questions without reverence," he muttered, like he was talking to himself. "That's how they get in."

The ash clung to his sleeve when he moved, reluctant to let go, as if it had found a warmth it remembered.

Shim'on took one step forward, then stopped himself. Intervening had never gone the way he hoped it would.

Then it punished him. His throat closed first, then his chest, like a door pulled shut from the inside. He doubled, breath scraping out of him in strips, and for a second the world narrowed to metal and dust.

Kaela touched Gillie's elbow. "Change the rhythm," she whispered. "Don't land where they want."

Gillie nodded and shifted the cadence. "The scroll is hidden because a thing can be true and still not be ours to say."

She let ours fall last. The grove stumbled, expecting say to be the end.

The left Seeker's blank smile widened. "And the blade? If you trust one another—"

Rowan stepped forward, voice rough from air that refused to be good. "We show trust by refusing to use each other's gifts to feed our fear."

The right made a small sound that felt like approval and mockery at once. "Then trust her to use it."

His gaze tugged at Gillie's thigh, like looking might draw steel.

Gillie didn't yield. The blade's note steadied into something like breath—ours, when unity remembered itself.

"Not for death," she said again—this time not for them, but for us. Her eyes flicked to Tomas. He didn't meet them. "For life."

Eliah swayed. Ash marked his palms; he pressed them together—not yet praying, just reminding his body how. Despair offered him a quicker liturgy: relief, resignation, numbness named peace.

The middle Seeker persisted, kinder still. "Why is the scroll hidden? If it is witness, let it witness. We would like to hear it."

"Flickers follow pattern," Kaela murmured, tracking the dust. "If they loop us, they'll pull us backward through our own answers."

Nadya frowned. "What if the loop is us talking?"

"Then stop finishing," Kaela said. "Or change the beat."

The middle asked again. "Why is the scroll hidden?"

"It hides itself," I said before I planned to speak. "Not because we are unworthy—because it will not be used."

The grove reached for used. I let it end on will. The trap slipped a step.

The Seeker on the left turned to the line of us, voice gentle as kneeling beside a child. "If you trust one another, why does the blade rest with her? If you trust her, why stand still when fear wants speed?"

Cassian's jaw worked. Ash at his nostrils darkened with the breath he refused to take full. Suspicion had rooted in him two plagues ago; we had only begun to tear it out.

"Because mercy chooses," he said, surprising himself. "And we won't make mercy serve our panic."

The right-hand Seeker turned to Eliah. "Then what is sorrow for, if not to be soothed? Pray, if you must. But you pray so long. Wouldn't kindness be to be done?"

Eliah's lips parted. Ash trembled in the web of his fingers. He almost quit.

Tomas stepped half a pace forward, then stopped himself. His hand flexed at his side like it wanted to reach for something that wasn't there.

"You don't have to say it out loud," he said too quickly. "I can carry it. Breathe. I've got it."

The ash thickened around his boots, darkening where his weight settled, like it preferred him still.

"Name," Sera whispered. "And breathe."

Eliah obeyed. "I am tired of being sad."

He said it without drama. Reverent. Honest.

The scroll pressed harder against my sternum. It did not speak, but its silence made grief holy instead of hollow.

Rowan answered with memory. "Your sadness made us gentle," he said. "When you begin to speak, we lower our voices."

We inhaled together—one, two, three—and the ash thinned a hair, like truth making weather.

A Flicker rode our breath. Water beaded on a pale root spilled upward instead of down, reset, then misbehaved again.

"Second flicker," Kaela whispered. She caught the wrong cadence and bit her lip hard enough to draw blood. The water corrected itself.

"Why is the scroll hidden?" the middle asked again, smiling like repetition could turn truth into etiquette.

"Because it is faithful," Gillie said. "And because we are not."

The left's tenderness edged toward cruelty. "If you trust one another, why does the blade rest with her?"

"Because it was given for life," Gillie answered. "Not for death."

The right leaned forward. "Then open life."

"Not yours," Gillie said. "Not in your rhythm."

The trap deepened. Questions came faster. Answers arrived late, growing tired of being weighed.

"Don't listen to them," came a voice from the rim.

Joshua stood half-hidden by a white trunk. Ash streaked his cheeks; his mouth looked raw, like truth had been scraped thin across it. He didn't step closer.

The light around him didn't behave. It bent sideways, pooling in the hollows at his collarbone and leaving the rest of him dull, as if the world could not decide which version of him to finish rendering.

"Don't listen to them," he called, like a man speaking from water. "They sink in. They teach you to keep walking so you never have to ask where you're bleeding."

Shim'on looked down at his hands.

Miriam flinched. "Do you hear?" she whispered. "He speaks their poison."

Gillie didn't flinch. The warning was old. She held it like a coal that still warmed if handled right.

"We test every voice," she said.

Joshua's eyes closed once. When they opened, there was unhidden pain in them—and the smallest nod he hoped no one saw.

The middle Seeker tried again. "Why is the scroll hidden?"

"Because it refuses theater," I said. "And we are not an audience. We are a people."

"People share," the left replied softly. "So why does the blade rest with her?"

Cassian flattened the old math under his heel. "I'm not moving the gate," he said. "I'm standing in it."

A hairline crack touched the right-hand Seeker's smile.

"You want spectacle," Gillie said.

"We want joy," the middle corrected. "Joy without sorrow."

Eliah made a sound—not a word. A sob caught and held.

"Name," Sera breathed.

"I fear my grief is carving hope out of my friends," Eliah said.

Miriam answered before the ash could seize the gap. "You taught me to lament without hating God."

We breathed together. The ash backed off a fraction.

Joshua leaned against the trunk. In the ash beside Eliah's knee, a clean palm-print appeared. Eliah nearly cut his prayer short in gratitude. He finished it instead. The print sealed crisp.

The edges were too sharp for chance. Lines cut through gray where the skin had pressed, each whorl intact, as if the ash remembered being touched and refused to forget.

"We will wait," the middle said at last. "You will tire of reverence."

"We do not tire of breathing," Gillie said.

The grove stumbled.

We did not open the scroll.

We did not draw the blade.

We did not quit the prayer.

Behind us, the Vein pulsed dull. Above us, the sky powdered ash. And Tomas stood a step apart now—not by choice, not yet—but because the ash had learned where to settle.

The Test of Laughter

By dusk the grove had gathered us the way ash gathers after a long burn—not all at once, not violently, but patiently, settling where breath slowed. Pale trunks ringed the clearing in a loose, uneven circle, their bark rubbed smooth and colorless, as if the world had practiced forgetting them. Someone—no one said who—had coaxed a small fire from damp branches. It smoked more than it burned. The flame held no warmth, only enough light to show where faces still were.

We sat close. Not for comfort. For counting.

Ash drifted constantly—fine enough to breathe in if you weren't careful, heavy enough to cling to lashes, sleeves, the backs of hands. It didn't fall like weather. It settled like consequence.

For a while, no one spoke.

Then Tomas cleared his throat.

The sound scraped, like it had to push past something it didn't want to disturb.

"I don't have a story that passes the time," he said. "But I have one people sometimes mistake for that."

No one laughed.

He leaned forward, elbows on his knees. He didn't look at the fire or the trees. He watched the ash collecting at his boots, as if he were measuring how much had fallen since we sat down.

"There was a child," he said. "Young enough that rules still sounded like promises. Old enough to know when something had gone wrong."

Ash slipped from a branch overhead and dusted his shoulders. He didn't brush it away.

"He wasn't supposed to be near the Veins," Tomas went on. "He didn't know what they were—only that the ground felt thin. Like a place the world hadn't finished deciding on."

The fire hissed softly as ash landed in it.

"He stepped where he shouldn't have—not out of rebellion. Out of curiosity. Or fear. Or because children don't know how to tell the difference yet."

A sound brushed the edge of hearing—not close, not far. A breath shaped like amusement.

Someone laughed.

Not among us.

Beyond the trees.

No one turned. We all heard it.

Shim'on went still. Not startled—recognizing.

"The ground gave way," Tomas said. "Not collapsing. Just… opening. And the child fell through a place that wasn't meant to be crossed alone."

Ash thickened—not falling faster, just accumulating as if the grove had decided we needed more weight.

"He wasn't alone when he landed," Tomas said quietly. "There were others there. Older. Stronger. They saw him."

The laughter came again—longer this time. Familiar in a way that tightened the chest before the mind could place it.

"They knew what he was," Tomas said. "They knew he didn't belong. They knew he wouldn't survive what was coming."

A few people shifted. Someone closer to the fire drew their knees in.

"They could have helped him," Tomas said. "They chose not to."

The ash answered. A pale veil settled over the clearing—thin, unmistakable.

"What came for the child meant him harm," Tomas said. "Not confusion. Not warning. Harm."

The laughter deepened. Enjoying itself now.

"They told themselves he wasn't their responsibility," Tomas said. "That stepping away wasn't the same as choosing."

The fire dimmed.

"The child ran," Tomas said. "And when he couldn't run anymore, he found something on the ground."

He swallowed.

"Something that could stop what was coming."

The laughter crested—not cruel, not sharp. Comfortable. The sound of agreement. Of course.

"He didn't understand laws," Tomas said. "He didn't understand breath. Or burden. Or what it means to decide who gets to keep breathing."

Ash slid from a trunk in a soft cascade. It coated the ground at Tomas's feet more thickly than anywhere else.

"He only understood that if he didn't act, he would die."

The laughter swelled again, pleased.

"So the child acted," Tomas said. "And lived."

A pause.

"And someone else didn't."

The laughter broke into layers—braided, distinct. Some bright. Some low. Some old enough to recognize without seeing.

Around the fire, a few people smiled despite themselves. Not because it was funny. Because laughter is contagious, and silence takes work.

Ash fell heavier.

"They told the story later," Tomas said, "as proof that survival was enough. That walking away clean was wisdom. That the child had no choice."

The laughter approved.

"They said," Tomas went on, voice thinning, "that it was better him than them."

Ash crept into folds, up boots, over hems—making us look older than we were.

"And the child," Tomas said, "never spoke again."

The laughter beyond the grove didn't stop.

It enjoyed the story very much.

The laughter didn't fade when Tomas stopped speaking.

It lingered, drifting between trunks like smoke that had learned to shape itself into breath. It came in waves now—some sharp and bright, some low and rolling—voices we knew well enough not to need faces.

A few travelers glanced toward the dark reflexively, then stopped themselves. No one wanted to see what they already recognized.

"That's it?" a voice called softly from beyond the trees. Amused. Curious. "That's the tragedy?"

Another laugh answered it, warmer, indulgent. "He lived."

Ash slid from a branch and dusted the fire. It hissed, then guttered lower.

Tomas didn't turn. His shoulders had gone tight, as if he were holding a door shut with his back.

"He was a child," Miriam said. The words came out hoarse, scraped raw by ash. "He didn't understand."

A ripple of laughter answered her—mocking, delighted.

"Exactly," a voice said. "He didn't understand. That's why it's forgivable."

Another voice overlapped it, silkier. "And useful."

The ash didn't fall faster. It chose more places to land.

"He was alone," Eliah said, palms open in his lap, gray already coating the lines. "He shouldn't have been there."

A chuckle—closer now. Near enough that breath warmed bark.

"And yet," the voice said, "there he was."

Someone on the far side of the circle laughed nervously, then clapped a hand over their mouth as if they'd been caught stealing.

"It wasn't murder," another voice said easily. "It was necessity."

Necessity carried weight. It pressed against the clearing like a thumb testing a bruise.

Tomas swallowed. He shifted where he sat, ash darkening beneath him as if it preferred his stillness.

"They said that too," he murmured. "Afterward."

The laughter loved that.

"Yes," came a familiar cadence, smooth and pleased. "Say it again."

"They said," Tomas continued, slower now, "that breath taken to preserve your own isn't stolen."

The fire dimmed another shade.

"They said the world makes those decisions every day," he went on, voice flattening—not louder, not softer, just… less his. "Floods. Wars. Hunger. Someone always breathes last."

Ash crept higher along his boots.

"Why should a child carry guilt for what the world demanded?" a voice asked kindly.

A few people nodded before they realized they had.

Gillie's fingers curled, then forced themselves open. Her blade hummed—uneasy.

"That isn't true," Nadya said. Her voice shook, but it held. "Survival doesn't erase choice."

A laugh snapped bright and pleased. "Listen to her," someone said. "She still believes that."

Another voice—low, patient. "You believe it too. You just don't want to say it out loud."

The ash thickened enough to mute sound when it hit the ground.

Tomas drew a breath and coughed hard, bending forward. When he straightened, the corner of his mouth was darkened with red again. He wiped it without looking.

"They said," he continued, and something in the way he spoke made my stomach turn, "that if you can walk away, you should."

The laughter surged—approval rippling like unseen hands clapping.

"That staying only multiplies the dead."

"That leaving keeps at least one alive."

"That grief is lighter when you don't carry it."

A voice laughed close enough that the sound grazed my ear. "You hear that, little one? Smart choice."

Miriam surged to her feet. "Stop," she said, hands clenched. "Stop laughing."

The laughter sharpened instead.

"Why so angry?" a voice asked, faux-concerned. "He survived."

Another chimed in, bright. "Would you rather he'd died too?"

Ash spilled suddenly, heavier than before, as if the grove itself had flinched.

Around the circle, faces tightened—not with humor, but with terror at finding agreement in their own chests.

I felt it: the pull. The terrible, reasonable thought.

What else could he have done?

The ash loved that thought. It settled warmly where it touched skin.

Tomas heard it too.

He laughed.

It startled us—short, breathless, wrong. It scraped out of him like it hadn't asked permission.

Shim'on's eyes snapped to him, sharp with something like fear—like a man watching a trap close where he'd once been caught.

The laughter beyond the trees answered instantly, delighted.

"There it is," a voice purred. "That's the sound."

Tomas froze, hand still half-lifted. His eyes went wide—not with humor, with horror at what had come out of him.

"They laughed when they told it," he said hoarsely. "Later. When the danger was past."

His breath hitched. Ash surged at his feet, climbing the leather of his boots.

"They laughed," he said again, words fighting him now, "because laughing made it lighter. Because if you laugh, you don't have to stay."

Joshua stirred at the edge of the clearing.

He had been sitting in shadow, half-seen, listening like a man overhearing his own name spoken in another room. At the sound of Tomas's laugh, his head snapped up.

For the first time, his face did not look empty.

It looked… remembered.

The laughter shifted, recognizing him.

"Yes," a voice said warmly. "You know this."

Joshua's hands curled, ash streaking his palms.

Tomas shook his head, breath shallow now. "No," he whispered. "No, it wasn't—"

The laughter rolled over him.

"Say it."

"Say what saved you."

"Say what saved the child."

Ash fell thick enough to blur outlines. Tomas pressed his palm to the ground as if to steady himself. When he pulled it back, the print stayed—sharp-edged, dark.

"He lived," Tomas said, voice breaking. "And they said that meant it was… enough."

The laughter erupted. Not cruel. Triumphant.

Around the fire, terror finally broke through—not fear of death, but fear of how easy it was to laugh at it. And somewhere in the dark, something waited to see who would laugh next.

The laughter wanted more. It pressed in now—no longer drifting, no longer patient—voices stacking, harmonizing, urging the story forward like hands at a back.

"Finish it."

"Tell them what it cost."

"Tell them why it was worth it."

Ash fell thick enough to soften edges. The fire was little more than a suggestion now—a dull pulse in gray, like a heart remembering heat. Tomas drew another breath and nearly failed to get it back. The air scraped going in. Coming out hurt worse.

"He lived," he said again, but the words snagged. "That's what they said. That living makes it… neutral." The ash around his knees darkened, soaking up the sentence like spilled wine. "That surviving cancels the rest."

A laugh—close enough now to feel against skin.

"Doesn't it?"

Another voice, sharper: "The dead don't complain."

Something twisted hard enough to show on Tomas's face.

"No," he said.

Small. Barely there.

The laughter paused—not stopped, curious.

Tomas pressed a hand to his chest as if checking whether breath was still allowed. When he spoke again, his voice shook—not with fear, with recognition.

"They told it like this," he said. "Later. When the blood was gone. When the place didn't look like death anymore." Ash slid from his shoulders as he straightened. "They laughed," he said, louder. "Because laughing made it sound like sense."

The laughter rose, eager.

"Yes."

"Yes."

"That's wisdom."

Tomas's mouth opened—and stopped.

Something cold moved through him then.

Not ash.

Memory.

"I laughed too," he said.

The sound hit the circle like a dropped bowl. Joshua's breath caught.

"I laughed," Tomas repeated, and the horror was unmistakable, "not because it was funny. Because laughing meant I didn't have to feel where the breath went when it left."

Ash surged in a sudden sheet—thick and choking. Coughs tore through the ring. Someone retched dry. Someone sank to their knees, gasping.

The laughter turned sharp.

"There it is."

"That's the truth."

Joshua stood—not fully into the light, not retreating. Standing like a man who recognizes his own handwriting in another's journal.

"No," Joshua said.

The word scraped out raw.

The laughter wavered—just a hair.

Tomas turned toward Joshua's voice. For a heartbeat their eyes met, and something passed between them that had nothing to do with the grove.

"I hear it now," Tomas said. Not stronger. Clearer. "How it bends."

He turned back to the fire, to the listening ash, to the unseen mouths waiting for him to finish the lie.

"They said," he continued, "that if the child lived, then the death didn't count." Ash pressed against his calves. "They said," Tomas went on, and now every word cost breath, "that taking a life to save your own is just the world doing what it does."

The laughter leaned in.

"Yes."

"Say it."

Tomas shook his head.

"No," he said again—stronger this time. "That's where it broke."

The laughter hissed.

"That's where it worked."

"No," Tomas said, forcing the word past burning air. "That's where breath was stolen."

The ash stopped falling.

Not lifting.

Holding.

"I lived," Tomas said, ragged now, "and they taught me to laugh so I wouldn't hear the sound of the breath that didn't."

Silence crept in at the edges—not absence. Pressure.

"I laughed," he said, and this time the confession didn't bend. "And laughing didn't make it lighter. It made it rot."

The laughter fractured. Some voices scoffed. Others went quiet.

Joshua staggered one step forward, ash slipping from his shoulders like a mantle he hadn't known he wore.

"That's…" he started, and stopped. His mouth worked, searching for ground that wouldn't give. "That's what I told myself."

The admission tore free of him before he could stop it.

The grove reacted—not violently. Gravely. Ash that had clung to sleeves loosened, drifting down like something released.

Tomas looked at Joshua—not accusing. Not forgiving. Witnessing.

"You walked away," Tomas said simply. "And I learned how."

Shim'on flinched as if the words had struck closer than intended.

The laughter tried to surge again.

"You survived."

"You're here."

"That proves—"

"No," Tomas said, cutting through it. He drew a breath that burned like fire through paper. "It proves nothing except that I learned to live with the wrong sound in my chest."

Ash climbed higher now—waist-deep, chest-deep—pressing, scalding, demanding agreement. Tomas sank to one knee. His hand shook as he pressed it to the ground.

"I won't laugh anymore," he said. "Not at this."

The laughter turned cruel.

"Then drown in it."

"Carry it forever."

"Be buried with it."

Tomas lifted his head.

"I won't carry what isn't mine," he said. "I won't let another breath disappear just because mine didn't."

He coughed hard—blood flecking ash.

Around the circle, people cried out, reaching.

"No," Tomas said—not to them, to the pressure. "I know what this costs."

Joshua moved without thinking.

"Don't," Gillie snapped.

Joshua froze. For once, he listened.

Tomas looked up and met Gillie's eyes—not pleading. Certain.

"This is where it ends," he said. "For him."

The ash surged violently, roaring without sound, trying to smother him into silence.

Tomas inhaled anyway. The breath tore through him like broken glass.

"I'm sorry," he said—not to the dead child, not to Joshua, not to the dark—but to the breath itself. "You were not meant to decide who breathed."

The words landed like a bell struck too hard.

The ash convulsed.

Tomas exhaled—and the grove lunged for the next breath before it could return.

His throat locked. His chest seized like a door slammed from the inside. For a heartbeat he was nothing but widening eyes and a hand clawing at the air as if air were something you had to earn. Ash surged up his shins, then his knees, climbing fast, hungry for surrender.

Rowan lurched forward. Gillie caught him by the wrist—hard. Not punishment. Containment. Two hands. The rule. Don't let panic write the ending.

"Tomas," Miriam rasped, already moving, palms up as if she could hold a breath in place. "Look at me. Stay here."

Tomas convulsed once—violent—then forced his mouth open against the choke. A thin, ugly gasp scraped in. Not clean. Not full. But real.

Air.

His shoulders jerked as it hit, as if his body didn't trust it yet. Another ragged pull followed, shallower, shaking, but his chest moved. He coughed—hard—doubling forward as gray dust burst from his lips in a sick plume. A red fleck followed, bright against the pale, and vanished into the ash like a swallowed ember.

The ash shuddered, thrown off balance. It had wanted silence. It got resistance.

Tomas braced a fist against the ground to keep from collapsing completely. His handprint sank dark and sharp in the powder. He dragged in another breath—still wrong, still burning, but unmistakably his.

The laughter beyond the trees flared, irritated. Then it shifted—testing—trying to turn his refusal into performance.

"Oh," a voice purred, close enough to warm bark. "So brave."

Another voice, amused: "So holy."

Tomas lifted his head. Tears cut tracks through the grime. His voice came out shredded, but it held.

"Don't make it pretty," he said. "I'm not doing this for you."

The laughter faltered—not stopped, just… checked.

The ash that had been climbing him lost its rhythm. It didn't retreat. Hell doesn't retreat. But it hesitated, as if it had met something that would not break cleanly.

Around the ring, people found their breath again in small, ugly pieces—one gasp here, one stifled sob there. The pressure didn't vanish. It changed shape, pulling back from Tomas's throat and spreading through the clearing instead, settling on shoulders, in hair, in the seams of eyelids. A new weight. A new way to choke.

Joshua dropped to his knees because he felt something beginning that no one else could. The lie had snapped, and the sound of it breaking hurt more than blood ever had.

Shim'on didn't move. His hands were clenched so tight the ash split around his fingers, fissures spidering outward like the ground itself was learning where a man refused to bend.

The laughter beyond the trees did not rise again.

It withdrew—slowly, resentful.

Not defeated.

Marked.

The Law of Breath had been named.

And the grove—denied its easy ending—kept us alive long enough to make sure we understood what it would ask for next.

The Quiet Departure

The laughter thinned—lost its sharpness—but it did not go away. It gathered instead, drawing in from the pale ribs of the grove the way smoke leans toward a lung. Not dispersing. Collecting. Waiting for the breath that would pull it deeper.

It came in familiar voices, half-heard, half-remembered. Mockery without bodies. Approval without faces. Not loud enough to challenge. Not soft enough to ignore. Exactly the volume of something that expects to be obeyed eventually.

Tomas breathed like a man borrowing each inhale.

Ashes to Ashes

Ash kept falling. Not fast. Not heavy. Just enough to coat the tongue when you forgot to guard your mouth. Just enough to remind us that the grove had decided we were not finished speaking about death.

Tomas rose slowly—too slowly—like standing might invite the laughter to step closer. Then he swayed where he stood.

His hands hung at his sides, fingers trembling in small, uneven bursts he did not seem to notice. Each breath came shallow and sharp, as if his lungs were still negotiating with the air. He had not looked at anyone while he spoke. Not once. Now he stared at the gray dust coating his palms as if it had arrived while he wasn't watching—as if the story itself had settled there and refused to brush off.

"That's the whole of it," he said quietly, voice scraped raw. "That's how the story goes when you tell it clean."

The laughter shifted—not louder, but closer. Somewhere beyond the trees, something laughed harder, pleased in a way that suggested the telling had not ended anything. It had prepared something.

As if the story were not confession.

As if it were an invitation.

I felt it then. Not memory. Not vision. Recognition—the sensation of a blade being drawn in the next room, the knowledge that sound would follow.

Tomas was not finished with us. But he was no longer steady.

"I saw it once," he said, just as quietly. "A long time ago. Before I understood what it meant to leave."

The ash answered—not falling faster, but settling nearer, clustering at his boots, his shoulders, the hollows at his collarbone. Listening the way predators listen: not for meaning, for weakness.

"There was a child," Tomas continued. "Too young to be standing where he was. Too small for the choice placed in his hands. He crossed somewhere he shouldn't have—fell through a place that didn't care how old he was."

My chest tightened—not with memory, but with the certainty that this story had not been told to be heard. It had been told to arrive somewhere.

"He was found," Tomas said. "By men who should have known better."

Joshua flinched.

"They didn't mean for it to go wrong," Tomas said, not excusing—naming. "That's what they told themselves. But when it did, they stepped back. Just enough. Long enough."

The words sat heavy.

"The child survived," Tomas said. "Barely. And because he survived, everyone decided that was enough."

My throat closed.

"But later," Tomas went on, voice roughening, "one of them came back."

The ash thinned around his feet.

"He didn't come with judgment. He didn't come to undo what couldn't be undone. He came because leaving wasn't the end of the story."

Tomas drew a slow breath.

"And he said this."

The grove went very still.

"You were not meant to decide who breathed."

The words struck me like something set carefully in place.

"That was not your burden to keep."

Pressure built behind my eyes—breath waiting for permission.

"You survived," Tomas said, softer now, "and that does not make you guilty."

The ash burned thinly at the back of my throat.

Tomas hesitated. Just a beat. And then—

"I'm sorry we left you there."

The words were not absolution. They were return.

My chest ached—not with grief, but with understanding. For years, silence had felt safer than speech. Endurance had felt like faith. Survival had carried a weight I never learned how to set down.

Some burdens aren't lifted by surviving them. They're lifted when someone finally comes back and names them.

Across the clearing, Joshua had gone very still. Half-lit. Half-erased. Ash streaked his hair and clung to his sleeves, but his face looked stripped. Not hardened. Exposed.

For the first time since I'd known him, he wasn't watching us. He was listening.

The laughter faltered. Not stopped—checked. Like a blade meeting bone.

Joshua's mouth opened once. Closed. He swallowed.

"That's not how I told it," he said.

Tomas looked up.

"No," he agreed. "It isn't."

The Lantern's glow sharpened. Light bent sideways around Joshua, pooling wrong at his shoulders. The air pressed tight, as if something were drawing a breath it didn't intend to give back.

Joshua flinched. Not away—from himself.

"I said he did what he had to do," Joshua murmured. "I said surviving was enough."

The laughter surged again—hungrier now.

Yes.

That's right.

Enough is enough.

Joshua's hands curled into fists.

"And it wasn't," he said.

The words fell straight down.

The Lantern reacted instantly. Light warped around Joshua, folding sideways, collapsing inward as if the world itself rejected the thought. He cried out—not a scream of terror, but of something being torn loose—and dropped to one knee. Ash burst upward around him, startled, then fell heavier, clinging to his shoulders like blame.

The grove recoiled.

Something in the ash changed. It no longer searched us. It reached for him.

Tomas stepped forward—not suddenly, not bravely. As if his body had already decided.

"Stop," Nadya snapped. "Tomas—"

He didn't turn.

"I won't tell it that way again," Tomas said. His voice wasn't loud. It simply refused. "Not like the walking-away didn't cost anything."

The laughter faltered—just a fraction.

The ash around his boots darkened. Clarified. This was not the ash that starved. Not the ash that numbed.

This ash remembered fire.

"It wants the story clean," Kaela whispered. "No weight. No names."

Tomas nodded once.

"That's the trap," he said. "That's how he learned to leave."

He glanced at Joshua—only once.

"And that's how the rest of us learned to call it wisdom."

Something shifted behind Joshua. Not the Lantern. Something older.

His shadow thinned. A pressure eased at his back, like breath returning to a lung that had learned not to trust air. The part of him that had stayed behind—the witness that had never agreed—pulled free.

Joshua gasped.

"I won't decide who deserves to breathe," Tomas said. "Not for you. Not for me."

The ash reached higher, climbing his calves, his knees—warm now.

"But I can give back what I took when I learned the wrong lesson."

The words settled. Heavy. Final.

"Tomas," Kaela said, already moving.

He shook his head—not in refusal, but in thanks.

"No," he said softly. "This part doesn't need saving."

He stepped into the open space between us.

"If I keep standing here, I'll laugh again."

He knelt. Not in prayer. Not in surrender.

The ash lifted around him—like something being released.

Tomas exhaled.

And did not draw another breath in.

For a heartbeat, nothing happened.

Then the ash moved.

It lifted from him in a fine column—silver-gray at the edges—nothing like the ash that had fallen before. It did not cling. It rose, thinned, and vanished into the pale canopy like breath returned.

The weight in my chest eased so suddenly it made me stagger.

Kaela reached him first. Fingers to his neck. Her hand stilled.

"No," Nadya said. "No—"

Shim'on moved before anyone else understood they were swaying. He did not kneel at once. He set his palm flat against the stone beside Tomas's body, as if testing whether the ground would hold.

"It will hold," he said—not loudly. Simply certain.

His voice did not rise above the ash. It settled into it.

"We do not scatter now."

Only then did he kneel.

He did not touch Tomas immediately. He let the space be what it was—terrible and sacred.

"Grief is not collapse," he said. "It is weight. And weight belongs on stone."

His hand closed gently over Nadya's wrist before she realized she was shaking.

"Stand," he told her. "We stand."

Tomas lay as he had knelt. Peaceful. Unclaimed.

He had not been taken. He had been restored—and in restoring, spent.

Joshua screamed. Not in pain. In fury. In grief.

The Lantern flared, enraged. Light snapped tight around Joshua, constricting. He staggered upright, dragged backward toward the periphery where the dark gathered.

He looked at Tomas as he was pulled away.

And this time—he didn't look away.

Marcus's voice carried from the shadows.

"Will you be next?" he asked lightly. "Will you turn to dust for them?"

Lucien's pressure rode the words.

"You've seen how it ends," Marcus continued. "One breath given. One life gone. All this grief—avoidable."

Thunder murmured somewhere beyond the grove. Still no rain.

"You can end it," Marcus said. "Right now. Agree that survival is enough. Agree that silence is wisdom."

The ash waited.

I stepped forward before fear could choose for me.

"No," I said. My voice shook—but it held. "We keep the breath."

Marcus smiled.

"And if it costs you?"

"We learned," I said, thinking of Tomas, of a child who had survived and paid for it twice, "that breath is not something you trade to feel clean."

Beside me, Nadya straightened.

"Truth doesn't make deals," she said. "It speaks. Even when it hurts."

Marcus laughed. Not kindly. Not fully.

Lucien's wind rose at his back.

"Then let's see how well you speak," Marcus said. "When the sky answers."

Thunder murmured beyond the grove.

Still no rain.

The ash fell once more—thin, reluctant—and stopped.

We stood together—whole, broken, grieving.

The plague was over—not because it had relented, but because it had finished teaching what it came to teach

And the next law was already gathering its voice.

Thunder Without Rain

The Song that Silences

We did not bury Tomas. We stood where he had knelt, and it felt like the world had erased the receipt of mercy.

There was no ground that felt willing to take him. No soil that didn't already feel claimed. The ash he had released was gone—not scattered, not lifted by wind, not settled into cracks or folds of earth. It had risen once, clean and luminous, and then vanished, as if breath itself had decided it had finished with this place. We stood where he had knelt, staring at ground that bore no mark, no shadow, no proof that a man had given himself back to the world and taken something with him when he went.

For a long moment, no one spoke.

Shim'on stood nearest the place Tomas had knelt, as if he'd taken a post without meaning to. His eyes kept moving—ground, trees, sky, back to the bare patch of ashless earth—like a man expecting the world to accuse him for still standing. When it didn't, he flinched anyway, jaw tightening as though he could feel the question in his bones.

Then the sky answered.

Thunder cracked directly overhead—too close, too sharp, too sudden to be mistaken for weather. The sound didn't roll so much as tear, splitting the air with a violence that made several of us flinch outright. My chest seized on instinct, breath locking halfway in. The noise passed, but the pressure stayed behind, pressing inward like something heavy leaning against the inside of my skull.

No rain followed.

Kaela swore quietly. Nadya didn't. She just closed her eyes for a beat and counted her breath under her tongue, the way she did when the world started asking her to lie.

"That's not a warning," Cassian said at last. "That's a demand."

Another rumble followed, lower this time, dragging itself across the sky like a weight pulled over stone. The sound didn't fade. It lingered, vibrating through bone and teeth, settling into the body as something that wanted a response.

Still no rain.

We moved because standing still felt like consent.

The ground sloped gently downward into a shallow basin, a wide bowl cupped by pale trunks and thin white branches that looked less like trees than bones that had learned to stand upright. The floor of the clearing was carpeted in small flowers—pale blue, almost translucent, five-petaled, their veins catching the light like ice under water. They swayed as we entered, bowing and lifting in a rhythm that suggested wind.

There was no wind.

The earth beneath them compressed under our weight, then eased back again, as if testing whether it meant to hold us. Each step sent a faint recoil through the bed of flowers, a collective shiver that moved too smoothly to be natural. My ears rang—not with sound, but with pressure, the way they do before a storm breaks when the air can't decide where to go.

Micah staggered and caught himself on a knee. "My head feels wrong," he muttered. "Like there's a drum behind the eye."

"It's not sound," Nadya said. She knelt beside him, steadying his shoulder, her voice careful and precise. "It's weight. Like the sky wants to fall and can't find the hinge."

That landed too close to true. My breath came out late, as if the air took a beat to agree that I had exhaled. When I tried to speak, my mouth opened before my thought finished forming, the word lagging behind intent just enough to feel dangerous.

"Don't talk yet," Nadya said sharply. "Test first."

Rowan frowned. "Test what?"

She tried a word under her breath—just one, barely sound—and grimaced when it came back wrong, arriving half a heartbeat after she had already moved past it. "That," she said. "Your voice doesn't belong to you right now. It's trailing."

Shim'on's shoulders drew up as if the word trailing had brushed an old bruise. He didn't speak, but his gaze flicked from mouth to mouth along the line, watching for who would be made to finish someone else's sentence.

Another thunderclap split the sky, louder than before, the sound punching down into the clearing with a force that made the flowers bow deeper. The pressure spiked. Several of us sucked in breath at the same time and had to force it back out, lungs resisting release as if even breathing needed permission.

No rain.

At the center of the basin stood Elana.

She wasn't elevated. She wasn't framed by light or shadow. She simply stood where the ground dipped lowest, hands folded loosely at her waist, posture relaxed in a way that would have read as humility if it hadn't felt so deliberate. Her dress was silver-gray, plain, unadorned. Her hair was bound neatly at the nape of her neck. Nothing about her demanded attention.

She was humming.

The sound was low, steady, almost kind. It didn't land cleanly. Each phrase fell just short of completion, like a sentence that ends before the final word and leaves the listener to supply it. My scalp prickled. My teeth buzzed faintly.

The flowers leaned toward her.

"Peace," Rowan whispered reflexively—and winced when the word returned to him wrong, echoing back half a beat late, thinner than when he'd sent it.

Elana opened her eyes.

They weren't wet. They weren't cold. They were simply attentive, watching us the way a physician watches a patient who has already told her everything important.

"You've had a hard night," she said. Her voice was warm, human, perfectly reasonable. "You're carrying a death you didn't get to grieve."

Kaela stiffened. I felt the words land in my own chest like a hand pressed flat over a bruise.

"That's not an accusation," Elana added gently. "It's an observation."

Thunder rolled again—closer now, heavier, like something pacing overhead.

"You don't have to keep carrying it," Elana continued. "You don't have to keep choosing."

Nadya shook her head once, sharp and controlled. "That's not peace."

Elana tilted her head slightly. "Isn't it? You're exhausted. Your bodies are asking to stop. I can give you a cadence that holds without effort."

The hum deepened. The flowers bowed further, stems bending without breaking, obedient.

Micah swallowed hard. "Feels like pressure behind the eyes."

"That will stop," Elana said kindly. "So will the ache in your hands. So will the urge to decide who's right and who's wrong."

Her gaze flicked—not lingering—toward Gillie's hip.

"If you agree," she said, "the steel will stop asking."

The blade hummed in response, low and tight, a sound that made my stomach twist.

Gillie didn't move. Her hand hovered near the hilt without touching it. "What's the cost?"

Elana's smile softened. "Nothing you weren't already losing."

Thunder cracked again, directly overhead this time, the sound so violent it rattled my teeth and drove several of us back a step. The pressure thickened, pressing inward, down, like the world was trying to compress us into agreement.

"Peace isn't quiet," Nadya said, her voice steady despite the way the air resisted it. "It's obedience."

Elana nodded, almost approving. "Yes. Exactly."

The flowers shuddered, pleased.

"Truth bends," Elana continued, her voice smoothing into something dangerously calm. "That's how it fits inside people."

Nadya laughed once—short, sharp, humorless. "That's a lie wearing manners."

The air tightened. My throat burned as if I'd inhaled smoke.

"Lies shout," Elana replied softly. "Truth persuades."

The pressure surged again. Words stacked up in my mouth, desperate to get out first. I clamped my jaw shut hard enough to ache.

"Don't answer," Nadya said quickly, not looking at me. "She wants agreement, not obedience."

"Agreement is obedience," Elana said immediately—too fast.

That was the tell.

Joshua stood at the rim of the basin. He looked wrong. Not cruel. Not triumphant. Hollowed, as if something essential had been scraped thin inside him. Thunderlight carved him into uneven pieces—face too bright, hands dim, shadow misaligned, lagging behind his body by a fraction that made my skin crawl.

His lips moved with the hum for one measure. Then missed it. Again. Again.

"He's breaking cadence," Sera whispered, her voice barely carrying.

"Or failing," Cassian muttered. "Hard to tell."

Joshua didn't look at us. He watched the flowers. He watched the ground. He missed another beat deliberately—subtle, almost lazy—like a musician striking the weak angle while pretending to follow the grain. The wrongness of it made my teeth ache. He missed again.

Elana's hum faltered. Just a fraction.

Her jaw tightened—not in anger, but in restraint, like someone holding a note past the point where breath wants to give out.

"Still," she said, and the word landed heavy, flattening the air. "Just stillness. No more deciding."

The thunder overhead answered immediately—no crack, no release, just a deeper gathering. The sound pressed downward, compressing the space between sky and bone.

Nadya stepped forward—one pace, no more. Her voice didn't rise.

"That's not peace," she said. "That's silence pretending to be mercy."

For a moment, Elana didn't respond. Her eyes flicked—not to Nadya, not to us—but somewhere inward, as if listening for permission that hadn't yet been given.

Then pain crossed her face. Not dramatic. Not loud. A sharp intake of breath. A twitch at the corner of her mouth. Her shoulders drew in a fraction, like a hand had pulled an invisible cord tight between her shoulder blades.

The hum surged back into alignment—stronger, heavier, unforgiving.

"You speak," Elana said, voice steady again, "like someone who still believes truth survives being spoken."

The words were clean. Too clean.

Nadya didn't blink.

"It does," she said. "Even when it hurts."

The pressure spiked so fast my knees nearly buckled. The flowers bowed almost flat, petals trembling under a weight they hadn't earned. My lungs resisted release—breath sticking halfway out, as if the air itself were being rationed.

Elana gasped. Just once.

Her hand twitched at her side, fingers curling and uncurling like they were being corrected by something only she could feel.

Behind the hum, another rhythm pressed in—colder, sharper. Not song. Measure. Control.

Julian.

Not named. Not seen. But present in the way a leash is present even when it isn't pulled.

Elana's hum widened—fuller now, relentless—and the sky answered with a roll of thunder so close it felt like it tore straight through my chest.

No rain.

"This is the plague," Kaela said quietly. Not fear. Recognition. "It doesn't drown us. It presses until we agree."

Another missed beat. Joshua again.

This time Elana cried out—a small, involuntary sound she swallowed too late. Her posture stiffened, spine locking as if something had yanked her upright from the inside.

"Enough," she said too quickly. The word cracked at the edge. She corrected it immediately. "Enough deciding."

The thunder hovered—angry now, restless, no longer patient. It didn't roll away. It waited.

I stood there with my breath half-kept, grief still lodged at the back of my throat where it hadn't been allowed to finish, and understood something too late to make it gentle.

What we had just survived wasn't about death. Death had already been paid for.

This was about what came after. This was about what we would say next.

The pressure didn't threaten us. It leaned close and waited—for explanation, for smoothing, for justification. For us to say that what had happened was unfortunate but necessary. That survival counted as innocence. That silence could be wisdom.

The flowers bowed again, deeper this time, as if the ground itself were listening for the right phrasing.

Shim'on's mouth tightened. He stared at the bent flowers like he could feel the shape of the sentence the sky wanted from us. When he finally spoke, it was barely above breath—plain, steady, not a sermon.

"Don't give it words," he said. "Give it weight. Stand."

Nadya's jaw tightened. She didn't look at the sky. She looked at us.

Thunder rolled once more—closer, sharper, no longer content to stay aloft.

No rain.

The sound wasn't warning anymore. It was expectation.

And whatever answer the sky was waiting for, I knew with a certainty that hollowed my stomach—

—it would not forgive us for choosing comfort over truth.

Truth Under Pressure

The thunder did not wait for us to choose.

It came down hard, sudden enough that there was no time to brace—no rise, no warning roll—just impact. The sound struck with a force that bent my knees and drove breath out of my chest in a sharp, involuntary gasp. Pain flared behind my eyes, hot and immediate, like pressure forced too quickly into a sealed space. I tasted iron. Somewhere to my left, someone cried out and then stopped, the sound cut short as if the air itself had closed around their throat.

The silence that followed rang high and thin inside my skull while the pressure stayed, pressing inward, refusing to disperse. My ears popped painfully. When I tried to inhale, my lungs hesitated, resisting the motion as if breath itself had become a decision the body was no longer certain it was allowed to make.

Micah stumbled and dropped to one knee, one hand slapping the ground hard enough to sting.

"No—no, no," he gasped. "Something's—wrong."

Kaela bent forward, retching air that wouldn't settle, fingers digging into her thighs like she was trying to keep herself from folding in half. "I can't—" she choked. "I can't get it all the way in."

Cassian swore under his breath and staggered sideways, bracing against a pale trunk. The tree shuddered faintly at the contact.

"Breathe," he snapped, whether to himself or us I couldn't tell. "Just—breathe."

The word landed wrong. None of us could make it obey.

Another thunderclap followed almost immediately.

Closer.

This one hit lower, heavier. The ground jumped. The flowers flattened outright, petals slapping against the soil as if struck by a physical hand. A shock ran up through my boots and into my calves, sharp enough that my legs buckled and I had to catch myself with both hands to keep from falling forward.

Fear sharpened then—not abstract, not moral, but immediate and physical. This was no longer a warning. The thunder was learning where we were weakest and returning there.

"This isn't weather," Nadya said. The words cost her. Her voice came out rough, breath shaved thin by pain. She was bent slightly at the waist now, one hand pressed flat against her ribs as if holding herself together by force. "It's containment."

The thunder answered the word with violence.

A concussive crack tore down so hard my vision went white at the edges. I felt it in my teeth, in the joints of my jaw. Sera cried out—high and sharp—and collapsed, hands clamped over her ears as if she could keep her head from splitting.

I dropped to one knee beside her, breath sawing uselessly in and out.

"Easy," someone said—maybe me, maybe Miriam—but the word came out wrong, flattened by the pressure before it reached her.

"It hurts when you talk," Sera gasped.

I shut my mouth immediately, nodding instead, even though the motion made the pressure flare.

Elana stood unmoving at the basin's center.

Her hum had not stopped, but it had changed—tightened, stripped of warmth. Each note landed cleanly now, precise, disciplined, as if forced back into alignment by an unseen hand. I saw it clearly: the way her breath corrected itself the instant it wavered.

She was no longer shaping the storm.

She was being kept in tune.

Another thunderclap tore down, so close it felt like the sound came from inside the bowl rather than above it. Kaela screamed and went down hard, palms scraping skin off her hands as she caught herself on the ground. Cassian lurched toward her, but the next wave of pressure hit before he could reach her, driving him back with a strangled grunt.

The storm was not responding to movement.

It was responding to restraint.

Every time someone held breath too long. Every time grief pressed up and was forced back down because now was not the time.

The thunder struck again—

Not overhead.

At Nadya.

The sound hit the ground just in front of her boots with surgical precision. The earth split in a jagged seam that raced outward and stopped short, heatless but violent. Flowers along the fissure collapsed into gray husks, veins darkening as if burned by sound alone.

Lucien had taken hold.

Elana gasped—a sharp, involuntary sound—and folded forward a fraction before snapping upright again, spine locking as if yanked by an invisible cord. Pain flickered across her face, quick and undeniable, before she smoothed it away.

"Please," she said, and this time the softness was strained thin. "You're hurting yourselves. The storm doesn't need answers like this."

Her eyes flicked inward for half a heartbeat.

Correction followed.

The hum deepened. Hardened.

Julian's hand was firm now.

Behind us, laughter flickered—bright, fractured, uncontained. Raven's voice rode it, easy and amused, chaos wearing charm like a borrowed coat.

"Well," he said lightly, "this escalated fast."

The thunder pulsed in approval—not louder, but tighter, like a lid being pressed down.

Nadya straightened with visible effort, forcing herself upright against the weight that seemed determined to fold her back down. Her face had gone pale, lips pressed tight, a thin line of blood darkening one nostril.

"No," she said, and the word scraped out of her like it cost something real. "This is what happens when truth is delayed long enough to be considered optional."

The storm answered immediately.

The pressure slammed down so hard Cassian collapsed fully, breath torn from him in a wet, choking sound.

"I—" He tried to speak and couldn't.

Miriam dropped beside him. "Cass—Cassian, look at me. Breathe. Just—just take it slow."

He clawed at the ground, a raw sound breaking out of him as air refused to come back clean.

"I can't," he rasped. "It won't—"

"I know," Miriam said, voice shaking. "I know. Stay with me."

Shim'on was there before I registered he'd moved. He didn't crowd Miriam. He didn't take her place. He simply set one hand down on the ground beside Cassian's shoulder—flat, steady—like he was giving the earth a job.

"Count with me," Shim'on said quietly to Cassian, voice unforced, the way you speak to someone in shock. "Not the thunder. Not her song. Your breath."

Cassian's eyes were wild.

"In," Shim'on said. "Even if it's small."

Cassian dragged in a ragged thread of air.

"Good," Shim'on said, like that thread mattered. "Again."

Elana cried out again—this time louder.

Not in sympathy.

In pain.

Her hand flew to her side as if something unseen had twisted there. Her posture jerked, then stilled, jaw clenching as Julian forced alignment back into place.

"You don't have to do this," she said through clenched calm. "Say less. Let it pass."

The offer again.

Stripped bare now.

Raven laughed softly. Kali shimmered through him, restless, delighted. "See? Nobody's asking you to lie. Just… not say everything."

The thunder leaned in.

It was not asking for falsehood.

It was asking for silence dressed as wisdom. Silence that let someone else carry the weight.

Nadya shook her head once. Small. Controlled. Blood dotted her lip now, dark against pale skin.

"That's how it survives," she said. "That's how it always survives."

The thunder struck her.

Not lightning.

Not flame.

Pressure.

Her body jerked as if hit by an invisible blow. She cried out and dropped to one knee, breath torn from her chest. Gillie moved instinctively—but Nadya lifted one shaking hand, stopping her.

"I'm still here," Nadya gasped. "Still speaking."

The sky screamed.

The sound tore through us, knocking Kaela flat, driving Sera to curl inward with a strangled cry. I collapsed forward, palms slamming into the ground, vision narrowing to white. The pressure was no longer testing—it was punishing.

And still, the sky refused release.

No rain.

Only compression.

I understood then—bodily, immediate—why the rain never came. Rain would have meant release. It would have meant the truth had somewhere to go.

This storm was designed to trap it inside us.

Nadya pushed herself upright again, trembling violently. Blood ran freely now from her nose, streaking her lip and chin. Her eyes burned—not with fury, but resolve stripped of ornament.

"This is what you do," she said—to the sky, to Elana, to Raven, to the unseen hands pulling the storm's strings. "You make truth expensive so people choose silence instead."

The thunder faltered.

Just a fraction.

Enough to be noticed.

Raven's smile twitched. Elana staggered, clutching her side as Julian fought to maintain control. Lucien pressed harder, but enforcement without coherence only multiplied the damage.

"Tomas died," Nadya said, voice breaking but unyielding, "because silence had already been practiced."

The thunder erupted—wild now, unfocused, striking without precision.

"For years," she continued, breath tearing her words apart, "survival was allowed to masquerade as wisdom. I won't do it again."

The storm fractured.

The pressure wavered, surging without pattern. Flowers shuddered—not bowing now, but resisting, stems bending unevenly as the ground forgot which rhythm it was meant to obey.

Elana cried out again, pain no longer fully contained. Raven swore under his breath, chaos suddenly unsatisfied. Lucien bore down, but the storm no longer obeyed him cleanly.

The thunder roared—not in triumph.

In refusal.

Nadya sagged. Gillie caught her at last, holding her upright as the sky raged overhead, furious and unresolved.

We stood broken, shaking, lungs burning—but still standing.

The plague had not ended.

But it had been named.

And the sky—denied comfort, denied distortion, denied silence—had begun to crack under the weight of truth it could not drown.

The thunder did not follow.

That was worse.

The pressure eased—not enough to call it mercy, just enough that breath crept back into our lungs without tearing. Cassian lay gasping, Miriam's hands firm on his shoulders as his breathing stuttered into something almost steady. Kaela stayed folded on herself, shaking, but no longer screaming. The flowers lifted an inch, petals trembling as if unsure whether they were allowed to stand again.

No rain came.

The silence that settled wasn't empty. It felt arranged. Held in place.

Elana exhaled slowly, and with it her hum softened, rounding its edges. Not relief—permission. The basin loosened, just enough to feel survivable.

"There," she said gently. "That's enough for now."

I hated how much my body agreed with her.

Nadya didn't move. She stood rigid, breath shallow, as if she were listening past the quiet for something we couldn't hear yet.

The storm hadn't left.

It was remembering.

The Thunder That Remembers

Elana's gaze held on Nadya, attentive. Not hostile. Assessing. "Isn't that what grief is?" she asked, voice careful. "Waiting until you can hold it without tearing yourself apart?"

Nadya's jaw tightened. "Grief is truth with no place to go. Don't dress it up."

The thunder cracked—

Not overhead. Inside the basin.

The concussive shock punched the air flat. My vision dimmed at the edges. Kaela cried out and dropped to her knees, both hands pressed hard to her temples as if she could keep her skull from splitting. The flowers flattened all at once, their pale petals pressed to soil as if forced into prayer.

Cassian collapsed fully this time, breath knocked from his lungs. Miriam cried out and dropped beside him, hands shaking as she tried to help him breathe through the pain. My own chest burned, lungs refusing to expand cleanly, every inhale a fight.

Elana flinched.

It was small. A tightening at the corner of her eyes. A hitch in her breath. But it was real. Her hum wavered, then corrected, forced back into alignment by something unseen. Her shoulders drew back too far, spine straightening beyond comfort, like a string had been pulled tight between her shoulder blades.

Julian.

Not named. Not seen. But present in the correction itself—the invisible tug that said her body was an instrument and someone else was holding the bow.

"You're making this worse," Elana said, and for the first time the gentleness in her voice sounded strained. "Please. You're exhausted. You don't need to explain anything tonight."

The thunder rolled again—approving.

That was the first time the storm felt like it had a personality. Not weather. Not force. Approval.

Nadya's face went still. "There," she said, low. "Do you hear it?"

Elana tilted her head. "Hear what?"

"The reward," Nadya said. "It's rewarding you for asking us to say less."

Raven laughed.

Not loud. Not mocking. It slipped out like breath released after being held too long.

"Oh," Raven murmured. "You're catching on."

His voice wasn't playful the way it had been earlier. It was quieter. Almost…relieved. And underneath it, something in him moved—something that wasn't Kali's delight, wasn't Lucien's pressure, wasn't Julian's leash. Something old and bruised and human, pressing against the inside of the name he wore.

He brought his hand up to his chest like he'd felt a bruise there.

"We know this sound," Raven said softly, eyes unfocused now. "We know what comes next."

The thunder held itself back again. The pressure didn't ease—it narrowed, focused, like the storm was choosing someone.

Elana didn't look at Raven. She couldn't afford to. Her eyes flicked inward for the briefest moment, as if listening for permission.

Pain crossed her face.

Not dramatic. Not loud. A sharp intake of breath. A twitch at the corner of her mouth. Her fingers curled and uncurled at her side, corrected by something unseen.

Nadya watched that, and her voice changed. Still grounded. Still controlled. But sharper now, as if she'd found the seam.

"He's pulling you," Nadya said.

Elana's smile held, but it was too clean. "I don't know what you mean."

The thunder cracked in celebration—hard enough that Micah gagged and spit into the flowers. Kaela curled inward, whimpering through clenched teeth. Cassian's body jerked as he fought for breath that wouldn't come clean.

Miriam looked up, eyes wild. "Stop," she begged, not sure who she was talking to. "Stop—please—"

Elana's hum smoothed again, rounding its edges, offering the smallest relief.

"That's how it works," Elana said, voice warm with effort. "You don't fight the sky. You learn how to stand under it."

Nadya took another step forward—slow, deliberate.

The relief thinned immediately, like a reward being withdrawn.

"No," Nadya said. "You learn how to survive under it by letting someone else carry the weight."

The thunder detonated.

I dropped to one knee beside Kaela, breath sawing uselessly in and out. Pressure pulsed behind my eyes in time with my heartbeat, each thud driving another wave of pain through my skull. Gillie crouched beside Miriam and Cassian, one hand braced on the ground, the other hovering near her blade without touching it—as if she refused to turn steel into a solution the storm could exploit.

Joshua stood at the rim of the basin.

He hadn't left. He hadn't joined. He watched the flowers and the ground like he was listening for something he'd once heard in another place, another life. Thunderlight carved him into uneven pieces—face too bright, hands dim, shadow lagging behind his body by a fraction that made my skin crawl.

When Raven laughed again, Joshua's head snapped up.

Raven's smile faltered.

And for the first time, I saw panic on his face—not fear of us, not fear of the storm, but fear of being seen.

Joshua's mouth moved once. No sound came out. His throat worked like he was swallowing something hot.

"Jonah," Nadya whispered.

She didn't say it like a name spoken to a man.

She said it like truth spoken into a room that wanted to pretend it didn't exist.

The thunder cracked in immediate celebration—furious and pleased at once—and Raven flinched hard enough to stagger. His hand flew to his mouth as if the word had struck him.

"Don't," Raven rasped, voice raw. "Don't—don't call that."

Kali stepped forward through him.

Not a possession like a scream. A coiling, deliberate presence sliding behind his eyes, straightening his posture, smoothing his expression into something bright and cruel.

"Oh," Kali said through Raven's mouth, smiling as if the pain around us were a song she'd heard before. "There it is."

Elana's hum sharpened, forced back into alignment by Julian's unseen pull. The basin tightened. The flowers bowed again. The pressure pressed down like a hand on the back of the skull.

Kali looked at Nadya the way you look at a lock you've already picked once. "You're the witness," she said lightly. "They always send one."

Nadya's face was pale. Her breath came shallow, each inhale an effort. But her eyes didn't drop. "You're proud," she said.

"Proud?" Kali laughed, delighted. "No. I'm practiced."

The thunder cracked—short, sharp, precise—and Cassian screamed as the sound drove into his chest, ripping the air from his lungs. Miriam sobbed with him, hands shaking as she tried to keep him anchored.

Gillie's voice cut through the noise, low and flat. "Stop talking," she said to no one and everyone. "Breathe. Stay in your body. Don't let it take your mouth."

Raven's lips parted again, and this time the voice that came out wasn't Kali's.

It was rougher. Smaller.

"We've changed," Raven said.

The words hit the clearing like a stone dropped into still water.

Joshua's breath hitched.

He took a step without meaning to, then froze—as if the basin had teeth.

"Don't," Joshua said, barely audible, and the word arrived almost on time—almost.

The thunder didn't celebrate that.

It punished it.

The crack came down so hard I felt it in my ribs, like a fist striking from the inside. Joshua flinched and clenched his jaw, mouth snapping shut on silence—as if silence were the only safe place left.

Kali smiled wider, savoring the choke in the moment. "That's the line," she said conversationally. "That's the sentence he used. That's the one that broke the hinge."

Nadya's eyes narrowed. "Explain it."

Kali's gaze flicked to Elana for half a heartbeat, checking the shape of the leash. Julian tightened control, and Elana's hum softened just enough to offer the group a thin thread of relief.

"Joshua didn't betray him with a knife," Kali said. "He betrayed him by surviving."

The thunder cracked—approving.

Kaela cried out and curled tighter. Micah groaned, forehead pressed to the ground, shoulders shaking as he fought for breath.

Kali walked a slow circle through the basin as if she owned it, as if the flowers bowed because she deserved it.

"He spoke enough truth," she continued. "Just enough to live. He didn't lie. He didn't invent. He didn't even raise his voice."

"Not the kind of truth that stays," she added. "The kind that escapes."

Another crack. Another spike of pressure. Miriam sobbed Cassian's name over and over, as if repetition could keep his lungs open.

"He was right," Kali said. "And he left."

"Joshua didn't accuse him," Kali went on pleasantly. "He just didn't stand with him."

Nadya's mouth tightened. "Truth isn't cruelty."

Kali laughed, bright. "Not by itself. But truth without witness? Truth spoken and then abandoned? That's not testimony. That's a verdict."

The thunder cracked again in celebration, and Elana gasped sharply as Julian yanked her back into alignment.

Nadya saw it and spoke faster, voice strained through pain. "He's hurting you," she said to Elana. "He hurt you then. He's doing it now."

Elana's eyes sharpened. Fear flickered—then vanished. "I'm fine," she said too quickly.

The thunder celebrated the lie—not because it was spoken, but because it was lived.

Gillie's blade hummed at her thigh, low and tight, answering the pressure with restraint rather than threat. She didn't draw it. She didn't offer violence to a storm that wanted spectacle. She only shifted her stance, grounding herself between Miriam and Cassian and the weight that kept trying to flatten them.

"Not for death," Gillie whispered, more to herself than anyone. "For life."

The coin at my chest pressed hard against my ribs as if it remembered the hand that placed it there. Under this thunder it felt like a witness with teeth.

Kali noticed my flinch. Her gaze cut to my chest, to the place the coin sat hidden, and she smiled like she'd found a familiar old wound.

"Oh," she said softly. "You kept it."

The thunder cracked. Approval.

My breath caught. Nadya's eyes flicked to me, sharp.

"What did she give him?" Nadya asked, voice strained.

Kali's smile widened. "A burden," she said. "A curse dressed as a coin. 'Carry this.' Do you hear how it sounds like responsibility when it's really a chain?"

Raven's mouth moved again, and for a second his voice came out smaller, older, not Kali's polish.

"She said…" Raven rasped. "She said…look at what we've done. Look at what we've become."

The words landed and stayed.

The thunder didn't strike immediately. It hovered, trembling, like the storm itself recognized the sentence.

Joshua's eyes closed for one long beat, as if he couldn't bear to see the moment replayed in front of him.

Kali stepped closer to Nadya, voice dropping to something intimate. "This is what you don't understand," she said. "I didn't have to claim him. I only had to wait until the truth he heard had no mercy in it. Until the sentence became a cage."

The thunder cracked again—approval—and Nadya nearly buckled. She caught herself, teeth clenched, breath sawing in and out as if each inhale was a knife.

"Truth with no mercy isn't truth," Nadya said, forcing the words through pain. "It's condemnation."

Kali laughed, delighted. "And yet it works," she said. "Look at them."

Raven's smile wavered. Something behind his eyes pressed forward, frantic, like a hand against glass.

Nadya's voice softened—not weak, not soothing. Precise. "Hear me," she said, and she wasn't speaking to Kali. She was speaking to the trapped thing inside the name.

The thunder trembled, impatient.

"You were named for peace," Nadya said again. "That name wasn't a joke. It wasn't bait. It wasn't something to be mocked. It was a calling."

Kali's smile tightened. "Careful," she warned, and the warning wasn't for Nadya. It was for Jonah inside Raven. "Don't listen."

The thunder cracked—hard—trying to drown Nadya's words. The pressure punched down into our bones. Kaela screamed. Micah gagged again. Cassian convulsed and went limp for half a breath that made Miriam howl.

Nadya didn't stop.

"You were told you'd changed," Nadya said, voice shaking, "but that wasn't prophecy. That was accusation. A sentence meant to end you."

Raven's breath hitched. His hand lifted, trembling, to his chest like something inside him was trying to answer.

Joshua finally spoke—one word, broken. "Jonah."

The thunder exploded in punishment, and Joshua doubled slightly, mouth snapping shut as if he'd bitten his own tongue. Silence swallowed him. But the word had landed.

Shim'on's head lifted at the sound—at the cost of it. He didn't look toward Joshua like a man judging a failure. He looked like a man hearing someone choose a hard thing and knowing what it will demand afterward.

Kali's eyes went cold.

She snapped her gaze to Elana, and Elana's hum sharpened like a blade being turned in a fist. Julian yanked her posture into perfect stillness, and Elana hissed through her teeth, pain flashing across her face before she smoothed it away.

"Enough deciding," Elana said again, and this time it sounded less like comfort and more like a command forced through a mouth that wanted to say something else.

Nadya's eyes locked on Raven's face. "You're still there," she said, breath shaking. "If you can hear me, you're still there."

Raven's laughter—when it came—wasn't mockery.

It was recognition.

A cracked sound, like someone who'd been holding a sob for years and didn't know how to let it out without breaking.

"Oh," Raven whispered. "Oh, God."

And for one heartbeat—one terrifying, holy heartbeat—the thunder faltered, as if the storm itself had been forced to listen instead of celebrate.

Kali moved instantly to regain control, smile snapping back into place like a mask fitted over a wound. “Don’t romanticize it,” she said sweetly. “They’re mine. They’re what they became.”

Nadya’s voice went razor-clean. “No,” she said. “He’s what was done to him.”

The thunder cracked again, furious.

And the basin held its breath, waiting to see whether truth could be spoken through pain without becoming cruelty again.

When Thunder Falters

The thunder came again—but it came wrong.

It struck after the moment had already passed, tearing across the basin with all the violence it had wielded before, yet landing without purchase. The sound broke apart as it hit the ground, scattering instead of compressing, echo splintering against the pale stone and flattened flowers.

For the first time since the storm began, the thunder arrived late.

Another crack followed, louder, sharper—furious at its own failure. It ripped overhead and collapsed into empty air, the echo unraveling before it could settle into our bodies. The flowers trembled but did not bow. The basin held.

I felt it then, not as relief, but as absence—the sudden removal of something that had been leaning on us so long we had mistaken it for gravity. My knees nearly buckled, not from impact but from the shock of standing unpressed.

Nadya swayed.

Gillie caught her just in time, arms locking around her shoulders as Nadya’s strength finally gave out. She did not collapse unconscious. She did not go limp. She stayed upright only because Gillie held her there, breath shuddering in and out like each inhale had to be re-learned.

The light that had wrapped Nadya—thin, fierce, uncompromising—did not extinguish.

It moved.

I saw it pass us like a change in air pressure, subtle and unmistakable, a weight shifting rooms. The basin dimmed—not darker, but quieter—as that light slid forward and settled onto Joshua.

He stiffened instantly.

Not in pain.

In restraint.

His shoulders drew back, spine straightening as if something unseen had settled there and refused to let him move. His breath caught, then steadied—too steady, held in check by force of will alone. Thunderlight carved his face into harsh planes, shadow lagging a fraction behind his movements like it could no longer keep pace.

Joshua did not speak.

That was the change.

The storm answered that silence with fury.

A thunderclap detonated overhead, louder than any before—but it struck nothing. The sound rolled uselessly across the basin, echo chasing itself in a hollow loop before tearing itself apart against the treeline. No one fell. No one choked. The sound was violent and empty, like a weapon swinging through air where the target had already moved.

The storm had lost its jurisdiction.

Raven laughed once—short, startled—and then stopped.

The sound cut off as if he'd caught himself mid-breath. His posture shifted, easy confidence bleeding away into something more guarded. The smile he wore thinned, corners tightening as his eyes flicked—not to us, but inward.

Kali did not surge forward this time.

She did not speak.

She withdrew.

Not retreat. Not defeat. A deliberate slipping back, like a hand loosening its grip just enough to wait. Raven stepped with her, backward into the shadows at the edge of the basin, laughter fading into quiet. Not gone. Not freed.

Watching.

And beneath the mask—just for a breath—I felt it. Jonah. Pressed close to the surface like a thought that refuses to be forgotten, waiting for a moment that had not yet arrived.

The thunder cracked again, sharp and furious, striking the ground where Raven had stood a heartbeat before. Stone split. Flowers withered instantly into gray husks. The sound arrived too late, punishing absence instead of defiance.

Lucien's voice tore across the clearing, stripped of restraint.

"Enough."

The word landed like a command meant to end the world by declaration alone. The air tightened—not around our lungs, but around the basin itself, like something drawing a boundary.

"This has gone far enough," Lucien said. "You've had your warning. You've been shown the cost. Submit, and this ends."

The thunder rolled in agreement—reflexive, desperate—then fractured again, echo collapsing into itself. The sound no longer knew who it served.

Joshua did not look at Lucien.

His jaw was clenched hard enough I could see the tendon jump in his neck. His hands were still at his sides, fingers curled as if resisting the urge to do anything—anything at all. The weight on him was unmistakable now, not accusation but responsibility without release.

Nadya lifted her head with effort, blood still dark at her lip, eyes burning but clear.

"No," she said hoarsely. "It doesn't end because you say it does."

Lucien's fury sharpened, focus snapping to her like a blade finding its mark. "You've spoken enough."

Marcus stepped forward.

The shift was immediate. Not louder. Not brighter. Quieter—and heavier for it. Marcus did not raise his voice. He did not threaten. He simply occupied space the way gravity does, inevitable and exact.

Lucien turned sharply, fury already coiling.

Marcus did not look at him.

"The condition has been met," Marcus said, calm as a ledger closing. "Truth has been spoken without defense."

Lucien's expression twisted. "It was not complete."

"It was sufficient," Marcus replied.

The thunder murmured uneasily, no longer striking.

Marcus's gaze moved over us—measured, assessing—then settled on Joshua.

"You have been protected," Marcus continued. "Corrected. Contained. Intervened for."

He did not accuse. He enumerated.

"That protection ends here."

The words landed colder than any thunderclap.

Lucien stepped forward, incandescent with restrained violence. "You would suspend enforcement?"

Marcus finally looked at him then. Not challenging. Not afraid.

"I would acknowledge the law you serve," Marcus said evenly. "Enforcement cannot proceed where witness stands."

Lucien hissed, sharp and furious—but said nothing more.

The storm answered with a final, hollow crack—late, directionless—before collapsing into distant rumble. The clouds did not break. No rain followed. The sky remained sealed, heavy and unresolved.

The storm was finished.

Not cleansed.

Not forgiven.

Finished.

Marcus turned away.

"This is not punishment," he said. "This is time."

The air did not move.

"No storm to carry it for you," Marcus continued. "No voice to speak through. No force to interrupt the waiting."

The thunder faded entirely.

Marcus stepped back, already disengaging. "Consider what remains unsaid," he said. "You will not be sheltered from it."

Lucien remained where he was, rigid with fury—not defeated, but restrained by the very order he enforced.

Raven's silhouette lingered at the treeline, half-shadow, half-light. He did not smile. Did not speak. Only watched—as if something inside him was listening for a voice that had nearly reached it.

Nadya sagged fully now, strength gone at last. Gillie lowered her carefully to the ground, one hand braced against Nadya's back, the other steady at her shoulder.

Shim'on eased down with them—close enough to help, not close enough to crowd. He looked at the sealed sky, then at the basin floor that had held through pressure it had no reason to resist.

"This is what they'll do," he said softly, not as warning—more as mapping. "They'll stop striking so you'll start offering your own explanations."

He glanced at Nadya, then at Miriam's shaking hands on Cassian, then at the place Joshua stood under that new weight.

"And when the thunder is gone," Shim'on added, voice quiet as stone, "you'll think the danger is over. It won't be. It will just be your turn to hold."

The light that had burned through Nadya had passed on from her now.

It rested on Joshua.

Heavy.

Unforgiving.

Silent.

And as the basin settled into an unnatural quiet—no thunder, no rain, no guidance—I understood what had begun.

The storm had not ended the plague.

It had only exhausted its voice.

The quiet settled in its place—not like peace, but like something holding its breath and waiting to see who would move first.

What came next would not strike—it would wait.

The Waiting Hours

The Pressing

The quiet did not feel like mercy. It settled the way fog does in low ground—not arriving all at once, but pooling where sound should have moved and chose not to. It gathered in hollows, in the spaces between words, in the breath before someone decides whether to speak. No thunder followed it. No rain. Just the sense that something had exhaled and decided not to draw breath again.

We stood where Marcus had left us. Not because we wanted to, but because the ground had not yet told us where else to go.

At first, nothing hurt. That was what made it wrong.

The basin still smelled of wet stone and old rot, the kind that never quite dries even when the sun pretends it can. The air carried a faint sweetness—leaves broken down into something close to soil, water that had stood too long without choosing a direction. It wasn't the swamp. But it remembered it. And memory here had a way of seeping into places it didn't belong.

The sound came next. Not a whisper. Not voices. Just a low, constant pressure—like breath being held somewhere nearby. A hum too deep to be musical, too uneven to be silence. It brushed the backs of my ears and slid into my chest, settling there without asking permission.

Gillie shifted her weight.

The relief was immediate—subtle but unmistakable, the way easing off a sore foot feels like kindness after cruelty. Her shoulders dropped without her telling them to. She took a second step before realizing she'd taken the first.

Then she stopped.

The relief snapped out of reach. Not pain yet. Not exactly. More like the sudden absence of something you hadn't known was holding you together. Her spine tightened. Her jaw set. She swallowed once, hard, as if her body had expected motion to continue and didn't know what to do without it.

"You feel that?" she asked quietly.

Cassian nodded. "Yeah."

Micah didn't answer. He was watching the ground, eyes narrowed, as if the stone itself had started lying.

We began to walk. Not together. Not in a line. Just small movements at first—circling the basin's edge, testing the slope, stepping over the same roots we'd stepped over minutes before. No one said keep moving. No one had to.

As my boots found a rhythm, the hum softened. The air loosened around my lungs. The tightness in my joints eased. Breath came easier—not deeper, just smoother.

Nadya exhaled sharply, then laughed once under her breath. "That's not fair."

Rowan glanced at her. "Fairness rarely announces itself with comfort."

She shot him a look. "You know what I mean."

"I do," he said. "I just don't agree that knowing helps."

We kept moving.

The basin did not change. The light stayed the same dull, uncommitted gray it had been since the thunder fell silent. Shadows existed only because memory insisted they should. They didn't sharpen. They didn't stretch. The sun—if it was there at all—had decided not to take responsibility for time.

Joshua stood across the basin. He had not moved.

The Lantern kept him where he was—not with chains, not with force, but with posture. His shoulders were held just slightly too stiff, his hands resting at his sides like a man waiting to be corrected. His eyes tracked us as we moved, but his body did not follow.

When Gillie's path brought her closer to his side of the basin, I felt the shift before I understood it—the way the air thickened, the hum dipping lower.

Joshua flinched. Just a flicker. A tightening at the corner of his eyes. His jaw set harder, like he was biting down on something he didn't want to taste.

The smell changed. Wet iron. Old water.

Gillie stopped without thinking.

The relief vanished. This time it hurt. Not sharply. A pressure bloomed behind her eyes, pushing outward, as if something inside her skull had begun to swell. Her knees weakened. Her breath went shallow and fast.

She took a step. The pressure eased.

She swore under her breath and kept walking.

"Don't stop," Kaela said, a little too quickly.

Gillie looked at her. "You say that like you know."

Kaela swallowed. "I say it because I just did."

Rowan shortened his stride on purpose, deliberately slowing until the ache began to gather in his hips, his knees, the small bones of his feet. He winced—not theatrically.

"This place," he said, "has opinions."

Sera walked beside him, her breathing steady, measured. "About rest?"

"About obedience," Rowan replied. "Rest is just where obedience becomes visible."

We completed one circuit of the basin. Then another.

Time did not behave. The ache did.

It learned us quickly, finding joints that already carried old injuries, pressing where fatigue lived closest to the surface. The longer we walked, the easier it became to ignore. The moment any of us slowed—even slightly—the pressure surged, reminding us what stillness cost.

Lucien's work, I thought distantly. I had felt this before. Not here. Somewhere wetter. Darker. A place where stopping meant sound—voices crawling into the skull until thought itself became pain.

This was different. There were no voices yet. Just the absence of them.

I don't know when I first noticed him. Not in the way you notice a person stepping into view, but the way you realize something has been at the edge of your sight for longer than you're willing to admit. A shape where there shouldn't have been one.

I glanced sideways as I walked and thought—that's not new. Then immediately wondered when I'd decided that.

At the far edge of the basin, just beyond where the light flattened into dull gray, I thought I saw a boy standing still. Or remembered one.

He was thin. Dark hair cut unevenly, like someone had stopped halfway through. His clothes didn't catch the light properly, and neither did his skin—as if the world refused to decide whether he was part of it. A faint scar marked his upper lip, pale and familiar in a way that made my chest tighten before I understood why.

I blinked. He did not move.

The hum thinned in that direction—not vanishing, just unwilling.

I told myself it was memory. Or residue. Or the mind filling space when it's pressed too hard from the inside.

Then Joshua reacted.

Not with his body—he hadn't moved since the thunder died—but with his breath. A sharp, involuntary hitch he couldn't hide. His eyes widened slightly. His lips parted, as if a name had reached the edge of being spoken and found something blocking the way.

The Lantern's light flared.

Joshua's jaw snapped shut. Whatever had almost surfaced was driven back down.

I looked again.

The boy was still there. Or still felt there—watching not us exactly, but the space we were passing through, like he was counting something we couldn't see.

Rowan noticed the change before he noticed the cause. His stride shortened. His breathing shifted. Then, following the line of our attention, his gaze lifted toward the basin's rim.

When he saw whatever I was seeing, he stopped walking.

The ache slammed into him like a reprimand. He staggered, one hand flying out to brace against nothing. His breath tore out in a harsh rush. The pressure behind his eyes spiked so suddenly it blurred the world.

Sera grabbed his arm. "Rowan."

"I know," he said through clenched teeth. "I know."

He forced himself to stay still.

The pain sharpened—more precise, as if the place had learned exactly where to press.

Rowan closed his eyes.

"Tell me something," he said, voice tight but calm. "What moves without feet, eats without mouth, and leaves no tracks when it passes?"

Cassian blinked. "Now?"

"Yes."

"Rowan—"

"Answer," Rowan said. "Or don't. But listen."

The ache climbed. I felt it too—a dull pressure building at the base of my skull. I shifted my weight without thinking and felt relief brush past me like a promise.

I stayed still.

My vision darkened at the edges.

"Time," Sera said softly.

Rowan nodded. "Good. And what does time do when it is not allowed to move?"

No one answered.

The hum deepened.

"It presses," Rowan said.

The boy at the rim tilted his head—just slightly.

The pain did not lessen.

Rowan opened his eyes and began walking again.

Relief flooded in. Too fast.

His shoulders loosened. His breath smoothed. The ache retreated to a manageable murmur.

"That," Rowan said once his voice steadied, "is the lie."

We walked again.

The basin did not change. But something else did.

I frowned.

There was a shape in my thoughts that wouldn't resolve—a sense of almost knowing, like reaching for a word that refused to surface. I shook my head and kept moving.

Gillie glanced at me. "You alright?"

"Yeah," I said automatically.

The word came too easily.

Across the basin, Joshua's gaze flicked from the boy to me, sharp and searching. His fingers twitched once at his side before the Lantern forced them still.

The smell of rot grew stronger—not because the basin changed, but because I noticed it less.

We kept walking.

The ache stayed quiet.

Rowan began another riddle, voice measured. "What is given freely, taken violently, and lost only when you believe you deserve it?"

"You always do this," I muttered.

Rowan didn't look at me. "Do what?"

"Give my head something to hold," I said, "so it doesn't start reaching for an exit."

He nodded once. "Exactly."

The boy remained still.

The Lantern's light hummed—impatient.

And somewhere beneath the hum, beneath the ache, beneath the comfort of motion, something fragile shifted—like a memory loosening its grip.

I didn't notice when it happened.

Only that later, I would struggle to remember exactly when the walking began to feel necessary.

The Thinning

For a few steps, I was certain we were headed back into it. The air had that same damp thickness, the kind that clings to the inside of the lungs and makes each breath feel negotiated rather than given. The light dulled without fully dimming, as if the world were bracing itself for rot. I lifted my feet higher than necessary, waiting for the ground to soften—for that familiar pull at the ankles that meant the swamp had claimed another boundary.

I smelled it before I saw anything—old water, bruised leaves, that faint sweetness that comes just before decay finishes its work. My body remembered what to do even before my mind could argue. I thought the path was turning into the swamp.

It didn't.

The ground stayed firm beneath our boots. No mud. No water. No sucking drag at the heels. But the air remained wrong. The weight stayed. What we were walking into wasn't the place itself—it was the memory of it, close enough that the body responded as if the Withering had already begun, even while the earth refused to give way.

It wasn't the swamp that had returned. It was the shape his sins had left behind. And like any memory lived too many times, it didn't need the place to do its work.

The ground under our boots stayed hard, more grit than mud, but the air changed its mind. It thickened, taking on that wet-iron taste that used to live in Joshua's breath when reedbanks pressed in and the Veins ran too near the surface. The wind came lazy and low, like it had to drag itself through something. Every so often you'd catch the faintest sweet rot—old water, bruised leaves, something that had died and been told to keep pretending it hadn't.

Nadya wiped her nose with the back of her sleeve and didn't look at anyone when she said it. "Tell me you smell that."

"I smell it," Cassian answered. He kept his voice steady on purpose, like he was trying not to hand the air any extra fear to work with. "And I don't like it."

Gillie shifted the strap on her shoulder. The scroll didn't fight her. It settled the way it had learned to settle—present, quiet, almost heavy with restraint. In the basin it had felt like the Word refusing to be used. Out here it felt like the Word refusing to let the world bully us into doing something stupid just to prove we were alive.

On the far edge of us, Shim'on kept pace without joining the line. He walked where the scrub thinned into stone, gaze lowered as if he were reading the ground. Once, he stooped mid-stride, thumbed a flat pebble clean of grit, then let it fall again like an answer he wasn't ready to speak.

Micah glanced down at his own shadow, then up at the sky again as if he expected it to apologize for existing wrong. "Light's flat," he said. "No angle to it."

Sera's hum—a low thread she'd kept since the storm stopped—wavered, then found itself again. She didn't try to make it pretty. It was the sound you make when you're keeping your hands busy so they don't start shaking.

Rowan walked a half-step behind the line, not leading, not lagging—watching. Since Marcus stepped away, he hadn't pushed or preached. He'd let the silence sit between us, measuring what it did to our breathing before deciding how to answer it. Now he spoke like he was giving that pressure somewhere to land that wasn't inside our ribs.

"Don't trust your urgency," he said.

Nadya shot him a look. "I wasn't—"

"You were," Rowan replied, and he didn't say it like an accusation. He said it like someone naming weather. "So was I."

Cassian lifted his chin toward the road ahead. "We keep moving. That's the rule, isn't it?"

None of us answered, because none of us wanted to say it out loud and make it true. But our bodies already knew.

Every time our pace slowed without meaning to—every time someone hesitated to look back, to check a track, to listen for something that might be following—the ache returned, sharp and eager, like a dog trained to bite when you stop walking. It wasn't just pain in the joints. It was pain with opinions. It climbed up the shins and into the back teeth and made the world feel too loud inside your own skull.

In Joshua's Withering, stopping had invited the Whisperers. You'd pause—just to drink, just to breathe, just to think—and the reed-sound would rise, the pressure would build, and then the voices would start crawling in behind your eyes. Memories you didn't ask for. Sins you'd already confessed. Shame that didn't care whether you'd repented—shame only wanted you to break.

So you walked. You walked until walking was the only prayer you had left.

Now the pattern was back—but wrong.

Now walking didn't quiet the world. Walking quieted something in me.

It started small enough that you could pretend it was fatigue. Nadya forgot a word mid-sentence and snapped it back like she'd dropped a tool. Micah went to reach for his cord and paused, frowning, as if he'd forgotten why he wore it. Sera's hum slipped into a different pitch and she blinked hard, startled by her own throat.

Then Gillie said, "Rowan," and something in her tone made all of us glance at her at once.

"What?" he asked.

She touched the strap again, not tightening it, just checking that the scroll was still there. "What was the tally-keeper's name?"

I opened my mouth, ready to answer, and nothing came. Not a blank the way names sometimes slip away. A blank like a door that had been painted over.

Cassian frowned. "The… the woman at the line?"

"Mm-hm," Gillie said. Her eyes stayed on me. "The one who told us about the boy."

Nadya made an impatient sound—half laugh, half hiss. "Why are we quizzing each other right now?"

Because the quizzing mattered. Because it was the only way I knew to tell whether we were still ourselves.

"The boy on Mill Lane," Micah said. He sounded relieved to have anything land clean. "Cut lip."

My lower lip tightened on its own. Old scar. Old ache. I raised my hand to it before I realized I was doing it. The skin there tugged like it had been touched from the inside.

Gillie saw it. Her gaze sharpened. "You did it again."

"Did what?"

"That," she said, nodding at my hand. "Like you've done it before."

I dropped my hand, suddenly embarrassed. "It's just—dry."

"It isn't," Rowan murmured, and for once his quietness wasn't gentle. It was alert.

On the edge, Shim'on's head lifted. Not toward us—toward the air. His mouth moved as if he'd started to say something and chose not to give it the satisfaction. He only touched two fingers to the rock beside his thigh as he walked, grounding himself like he'd learned what drifting costs.

The ache in my shins eased because we'd kept walking through the exchange. Relief slid in like an indulgence. My body tried to thank me for continuing.

And with the relief came the other thing—the thinning.

The road stretched. The world widened. The inside of my head went smoother. Less cluttered. Less sharp. Less named.

It felt good for about three heartbeats.

Then the fear arrived, because I knew the feeling.

In the swamp, when you moved, the Whisperers faded. Here, when we moved, we faded.

Nadya rubbed her forehead hard, as if she could push a thought back into place. "I had a whole sentence," she muttered. "I had it and now it's gone."

Sera's hum stopped outright for a moment. She looked up, startled, like she'd woken mid-fall. "Don't—" she said, then paused, brow creasing. "Don't… what?"

Cassian reached for her elbow and caught himself before he grabbed. He kept his hand close anyway, hovering. "You okay?"

"I'm fine," she snapped automatically, then softened at once because she heard how sharp she'd been. "I'm fine. I just—" Her eyes darted to the scroll on Gillie's back like it might give her the lost word back if she stared hard enough. "I just lost the end of what I was saying."

Micah stopped walking.

It was instinct, not choice—a pause to check the ground, to set his plumb, to put certainty where the world felt too soft.

The ache slammed into us like we'd stepped into a trap we'd forgotten was there. It hit my teeth first, a sudden pressure that made me clench down so hard my jaw popped. My vision narrowed. The air thickened, and beneath it—beneath everything—the faint reed-sound rose.

Not out in the fields.

Inside the skull.

Gillie gasped once, sharp, like a knife nicking a finger. Nadya swore under her breath. Sera's hands flew to her temples, fingers splayed as if she could hold her head together.

And then—just for a blink—the swamp was there. Not the road. Not the pale grass. Reedbanks. Stagnant water. The long, patient suck of mud that doesn't care what you believe. The smell was immediate and intimate, like it had been waiting under our tongues.

I heard a whisper—not words, not yet. Just that old, crawling pressure that meant words were on their way.

Micah flinched, breath hitching. "Keep moving," he managed.

"Move," Nadya hissed, already stepping, because pain teaches faster than doctrine.

Before Micah could freeze twice, Shim'on's voice cut in—quiet, rough with restraint. "Don't bargain with it," he said, not looking at anyone. "It charges interest."

Micah jerked back into motion like the words had hooked him.

We moved, and the pain eased. The reed-sound thinned. The swamp slid back into the background like a nightmare you can only hold if you stop running.

Relief again. That cruel reward.

And with it, the thinning.

Whatever I'd almost remembered in the pain, I couldn't hold onto. It slid away as soon as my feet found their rhythm. The world smoothed. The edges softened. The inside of my head went quiet.

Too quiet.

Rowan moved up alongside Micah, keeping pace without making him feel chased. "That was the first real stop," Rowan said.

Micah swallowed. "It wasn't a stop. It was a stumble."

Rowan's mouth twitched—not humor. Recognition. "That's how it gets you," he said. "It doesn't ask permission. It punishes the pause until you learn the lesson it wants."

Nadya shot him another look, harsher this time. "Stop talking about it like it's a teacher."

Rowan didn't turn his head. He kept his eyes on the road ahead. "It is," he said. "It's just not ours."

Gillie's voice came low. "It's Joshua's sin."

We all felt the words land, even if none of us wanted to agree with them.

In the swamp, he hadn't been able to stop—not because he loved the people, not because he was brave, but because stopping meant hearing what he'd done. Stopping meant looking straight at the thing he kept trying to outrun. So he pushed us. He drove us. He used urgency like a whip and called it survival.

Control dressed up as care.

And now the world was teaching us the same lesson from the other side. Move or be punished. Move until motion feels like mercy. Move until your own mind learns to obey pace instead of truth.

Cassian spat into the dust, disgusted. "He broke it and we're paying."

"Maybe," Sera said. Her hum had returned, but it was thinner now, strained like a wire pulled too tight. "Or maybe we're being offered the same choice he refused."

Nadya barked a short laugh. "Choice. Sure."

Gillie didn't argue. She just shifted the scroll higher on her shoulder as if the Word needed a better seat to watch from.

Rowan slowed his breathing on purpose, deliberate enough that it looked like stubbornness. "We need a rule," he said.

Micah's eyes flicked toward him. "The rule is: don't stop."

Rowan nodded once. "That's their rule. We need ours."

Nadya's jaw tightened. "Rowan—"

"I'm not asking for a speech," Rowan said, and now he looked at her. His gaze didn't push. It held. "I'm asking for something simple enough that our bodies can do it while our heads try to slide away."

Sera swallowed. "Like the breath count."

"Like the breath count," Rowan agreed. "But deeper."

Cassian's voice was rough. "You've got riddles."

Gillie glanced over. "Now?"

"Now," Rowan said.

The road dipped slightly, and for a heartbeat the air tasted even more like reed water. The light stayed wrong—flat and stubborn, refusing to throw shadows the way honest sun does. Somewhere far off, a bird called once and then cut itself off as if it had been corrected.

Rowan spoke without raising his voice, careful not to startle whatever invisible pressure had wrapped itself around the hours. "What is carried by feet," he asked, "but not owned by legs?"

Nadya blinked hard. "What?"

Rowan kept walking. "Answer in your head if you have to."

Cassian snorted. “This is not the time for—”

“It’s exactly the time,” Rowan said, still calm. “If your mouth argues, your body will keep believing the only truth is pace. We need a thought that makes us linger.”

Micah’s jaw flexed. “A road,” he said after a moment. “It’s carried by feet but not owned by legs.”

Rowan nodded once. “Good. Now: what is held by hands, but only kept by letting go?”

Sera frowned, her hum wobbling. “A… bird?”

“Trust,” Nadya said, and she sounded angry that she’d said it.

Rowan didn’t smile, but something in his shoulders eased. “Yes,” he said. “Trust.”

The ache in my shins eased again—not because we’d stopped, but because the riddles had done something subtler. They’d made the inside of my head reach for meaning. They’d made me try to hold a thought long enough to answer.

It was a tiny act of resistance.

It also made the thinning feel different. Sharper.

Like the plague didn’t mind us walking. It minded us thinking while we walked.

Gillie looked back over her shoulder, scanning the road behind as if she half expected Joshua to be there, just out of sight, watching us learn the lesson he refused. “Keep going,” she said softly. “If we stop, it’s going to show us everything.”

Nadya swallowed. “What does it show you?”

Gillie didn’t answer right away. The silence in her mouth wasn’t reluctance. It was caution. “I smell the swamp,” she said finally. “And I remember what it took.”

Cassian’s gaze flicked toward the treeline. “We’re not there.”

"No," Gillie said. "But Joshua is."

The words hung—not because they were poetic, but because they were true in the way the world had started to feel: truth as pressure, truth as consequence.

Micah's voice came low. "If he's here, the Lantern put him here."

"And if the Lantern put him here," Rowan added, "it's because the Lantern wants us to keep moving until we forget why we were ever walking in the first place."

Nadya flared. "We're not forgetting."

Rowan didn't contradict her. He just watched her, the way you watch someone insist they aren't bleeding while blood runs down their sleeve.

That was when Sera said, very quietly, "What was his name?"

We all glanced at her.

"The boy," she said. "Mill Lane."

Nadya answered fast. "He said people call him Boy—"

"Yes," Sera said. "But Rowan asked him something. Something about—" She stopped, eyes widening, and in that widening was the fear—not of pain, not of Joshua, not of the dark, but of a hole opening where a memory should be. "What did you ask him?" Sera demanded.

Rowan's gaze stayed forward, but his voice softened. "I asked him what he calls himself."

"And he said…?" Nadya pressed.

Rowan hesitated—not from reluctance, but because he felt the same thinning we did. "I don't know," he admitted.

The road seemed to shift—not physically, but the way a mind shifts when it realizes it's been lied to. I tried to grab the memory—the boy's bare feet, the brass-mouth lamp, the half-healed cut on his lip—and it slipped like wet rope.

I still had the feeling of him.

I did not have the name.

Gillie's hand rose to her mouth, fingers hovering near her lower lip. She looked at me. "You remember him."

"I remember… a lamp," I said. "And smoke. And—" I swallowed hard as my scar tugged. "And his mouth."

Cassian's voice tightened. "Stop. Don't stop walking."

We weren't stopping. That was what terrified me. We were walking while pieces of ourselves slid quietly out through a crack we couldn't see.

Rowan breathed deliberately. "Third riddle."

Nadya clenched her jaw. "Rowan—"

"Answer fast," Rowan said, and now he sounded less like a riddler and more like a man throwing a rope. "What grows when you run from it?"

Silence—not because we didn't know, but because every answer felt like confession.

"Fear," Micah said.

"Shame," Gillie said at the same time.

"Forgetfulness," Sera whispered, the word hurting her tongue.

Rowan nodded, grim. "All of it," he said. "Which means our rule can't only be 'keep moving.' It has to be 'keep with.'"

Cassian frowned. "Keep with what?"

Rowan's eyes flicked to the scroll, then away. "Keep with the Word. Keep with each other. And keep with the things we refuse to let go missing."

Nadya swallowed. "Like names."

"Like names," Rowan said. "And like the truth that we've been here before."

A thin sound drifted through the air—not thunder, not wind.

Reeds.

Gillie stiffened. Her hand hovered near the knife without gripping it. "Do you hear that?"

Cassian's face tightened. "Don't stop."

"We're not stopping," Gillie said. "It's catching us anyway."

Ahead, the road crested a low rise. The scrub thinned. The world opened again into a shallow basin of pale grass and stone teeth, repeating itself like land that couldn't help remembering.

And on the far edge—too far for honesty—stood a figure in light too clean to trust.

The Lantern.

Beside him, set slightly apart like punctuation, a second figure stood bowed, shoulders rounded, posture so familiar it made my teeth ache.

Joshua.

Nadya made a sound—half hope, half hate—and bit it back.

Rowan didn't look long. He looked at us. "Keep walking," he said, steel in his voice now. "But mark what you see. Say it out loud. Don't let it slide."

"Lantern," Gillie said.

"Joshua," Micah added, the name cutting him.

"We're still us," Sera whispered.

Shim'on's voice came from the edge again, barely above breath. "Say it," he echoed, not commanding—joining. "Names don't belong to the plague."

I touched my lower lip again. Old scar. Old ache.

And as we walked—because stopping would tear us open and walking would erase us—I saw, near the basin's edge, a smaller shape in the grass. A boy's outline. Still. Watching. Too far to see clearly.

Not too far to feel.

Rowan spoke again, quiet and firm. "Last riddle for now. What can you lose without dropping it?"

The answer rose like bile.

Nadya answered first. "Time."

Rowan nodded. "Yes. So we're going to do the opposite."

Cassian frowned. "What's the opposite of losing time?"

"We're going to spend it on purpose," Rowan said. "And we're going to keep the receipt."

The reed-sound grew a shade louder, waiting for the first real pause.

Ahead, the Lantern stood like patience turned into a trap.

Joshua—bowed under false light—did not move.

But the boy at the basin's edge lifted a hand, slow, signaling wait.

And the gesture—small as it was—struck the scar on my lip like a memory knocking from the inside, asking to be let back in.

The Holding

We lost the count sometime after the rise. Not because we stopped counting, but because the numbers stopped agreeing with each other. Cassian swore we'd crested the ridge twice already. Micah insisted it was only once. Sera said neither of them was right—that the land didn't feel repeated so much as folded, like we were passing through the same hour from different sides. No one argued with her.

The road hadn't changed. That was the worst part. Same pale grit. Same low scrub that smelled like it had once been marsh and still resented being called dry. Same flat light that refused to tell us whether the sun had moved or simply blinked.

We kept walking, because stopping still hurt.

Not the sharp, punishing ache from before, but something deeper now. A pressure that didn't spike so much as settle, like the air had weight and was taking up space inside the chest. Every time I slowed enough to notice my breathing, it felt like my lungs had to push through mud to remember how.

Rowan noticed first. Not because he stopped—he didn't—but because he started speaking differently. "Say something you remember," he said quietly, not turning his head. "Not from before. From now."

Gillie glanced at him. "Now like… just now?"

"Yes."

She frowned, still walking. "The way the light keeps flattening everything."

"That's an observation," Rowan said. "Try again."

Nadya scoffed. "This is pointless."

Rowan didn't rise to it. "Pointless is fine. Unanchored isn't."

Cassian cleared his throat. "I remember the sound your boots make when you drag your heel."

Micah blinked. "I don't drag my—"

"You do," Cassian said. "Just a little. Like you're checking the ground behind you without looking."

Micah went quiet.

Rowan nodded once. "Good. Keep going."

I opened my mouth and froze. I could name the smell—rot and old water. I could name the rhythm of my steps, the way my right knee lagged half a beat behind the left. I could name the ache in my jaw where I'd clenched too long. But when I tried to name when—how long we'd been walking, what we'd said just before—nothing landed. Not absence. Slippage. Like a word you say too many times until it becomes only sound.

"I remember the reeds," I said finally, and hated how thin it sounded. "Not seeing them. Just... the sound they make when the wind can't decide."

Rowan's shoulders eased a fraction. "Good," he said. "That's memory with edges."

Sera's hum stuttered, then steadied. "I don't like this," she said softly. "It feels like... like we're being sanded."

"That's because we are," Nadya snapped. "We're just doing it to ourselves."

"No," Rowan said. "We're letting the motion do it."

Micah laughed once, short and sharp. "Then what do you suggest? We stop and let it crack us open again?"

Rowan didn't answer right away.

On the outskirts of our loose line, Shim'on had kept himself half a pace to the side since the basin—nearer the rocks than the road, where the ground felt older. He didn't look at faces when Rowan spoke. He watched feet. He watched where the pale grit changed to stone, where the world stopped pretending it was soft. Once, as if on instinct, he trailed his fingers along an exposed shelf of rock as he passed it—touch light, almost reverent—and then withdrew his hand like he'd been burned by remembering.

The road dipped. The air grew wetter. For a moment the smell of reed water came on so strong I tasted it at the back of my tongue—metallic and green. My scar tugged hard enough that I hissed without meaning to and brought my hand to my mouth.

Gillie saw. She always did. "Does it hurt?"

I shook my head. Then nodded. Then stopped answering and just kept walking. "I don't know," I said, and that scared me more than pain ever had.

Rowan finally spoke. "I suggest we choose what hurts us."

The conversation stopped cold, even though our feet didn't slow.

Nadya stared straight ahead. "That's not an answer."

"It is," Rowan said. "Just not a comfortable one."

The thinning crept closer. It wasn't dramatic. No sudden gaps. No names vanishing outright. It was smaller than that. Cassian stopped finishing his sentences. Sera's hum lost its pattern and became a held note she returned to again and again, like she was afraid to wander. Micah checked his plumb three times in a row before realizing he'd already done it.

Step. Breath. Weight. Step.

If I didn't keep the rhythm going, it felt like the motion might lose track of me.

"That's it," Gillie said suddenly. She slowed—not stopping, just enough to pull the ache tight around her shoulders. "That's the trick."

Rowan turned his head. "Say it."

"It's not just memory," she said. "It's identity. Movement keeps us from having to answer who we are right now."

The ache surged in response, like the land resented being named.

Nadya sucked in a breath. "So what—this place just erases you if you don't keep busy?"

"No," Gillie said. "It erases you if you do."

The silence that followed wasn't empty. It was full of realization.

I stumbled—not enough to fall, but enough that my foot dragged wrong and pain flared hot behind my eyes. For half a second the reed-sound surged so close I almost heard a word take shape. I forced myself to keep pace.

But something inside me reached backward.

Wait.

The word wasn't sound. It was pressure. A hand lifted—not grabbing, just hovering—in my mind.

I looked up.

The boy stood ahead this time. Not at the rim. Not far. Closer. Still at the edge of the road. Still untouched by the ache.

He hadn't aged the way people age. Not taller. Not broader. Just… older. Like time had passed through him instead of over him.

His hand was raised again.

Not warning.

Invitation.

My chest tightened. I knew him. I knew the cut on his lip, the way it pulled when he frowned. I knew the way he watched without asking anything in return.

I did not know his name.

Panic spiked, and the thinning surged to meet it, eager.

Rowan saw me slow. He stepped closer without breaking stride. "Say it," he murmured. "Say what you're about to lose."

"I can't," I whispered. "It's already—"

"Say that," Rowan said. "Out loud."

"I'm losing him," I said, and the words felt like gravel in my mouth. "I don't know who he is anymore."

The ache eased.

Not vanished.

Eased.

Sera's hum shifted—caught—then found a new pattern, lower, steadier.

Gillie exhaled hard. "There," she said. "Did you feel that?"

Nadya nodded slowly. "Yeah."

Rowan didn't smile, but something in his spine straightened, like he'd found a bearing. "That's the rule," he said. "We don't outrun the loss. We name it."

Micah swallowed. "And if we can't?"

"Then we borrow," Rowan said. "From each other. From the Word. From whatever still remembers us."

Shim'on's gaze flicked to the boy—quick, wary—and then to the stone under our feet. When he spoke, it was so low it almost disappeared into the rhythm of walking. "Say it where it can hold," he murmured. "Not to the air. To the rock." He didn't explain. He just pressed his palm once, briefly, to the nearest outcrop as he passed, like he was leaving a mark the thinning couldn't sand away.

Ahead, the Lantern's light flared—too clean, too patient. Joshua stood beneath it, unchanged. Still. Silent.

Watching us walk.

Watching us slow.

The ache crept closer again, offended.

Rowan lifted his voice just enough to carry. "Fourth riddle," he said. "And listen carefully."

We leaned in without stopping.

"What waits for you," Rowan asked, "only when you stop running?"

No one answered right away. Because we all knew. And because knowing meant we might have to face it.

Behind us, the reed-sound gathered—not loud, not yet—but close enough that the memory of pain leaned forward, listening.

Ahead, the boy lowered his hand.

And for the first time since the thunder died, I felt the weight of stillness—not as death, but as something that wanted me to stay long enough to be seen.

The Receiving

We did not stop the way panic expects you to stop. There was no sudden freeze, no sharp intake of breath followed by the instinct to scatter. The place had been shaped for that reaction. I could feel its readiness just beneath the skin—the ache lingering close, alert and waiting, like a correction rehearsed too many times to forget.

Instead, Rowan altered something quieter. He did not halt his feet at first. He changed his attention.

His stride shortened until it barely registered as motion at all, each step placed with deliberate unimportance. More noticeable was his breathing—narrowed, measured, reduced to necessity. He drew in just enough air to remain upright, then held it longer than comfort allowed. When he released it, he did so without relief, without the small indulgence of satisfaction. Breath returned to the world without demand.

The ache noticed. It pressed harder into my legs, sliding upward with offended insistence, searching for the reflex it knew how to punish. Beneath it, the reed-sound stirred—restless and sharp—carrying the same impatient logic the Withering had always carried: move and you will be spared; stop and you will be corrected.

Rowan did not answer the ache. He spoke instead, voice even, almost conversational—the same tone he used when setting a riddle loose, not to be solved quickly but to be lived inside.

"What arrives only when you stop asking it to come," he said, "and leaves the moment you chase it?"

The words did not demand an answer. They demanded occupation.

My thoughts reached for them without permission, circling meaning, testing paradox, lingering where certainty refused to form. I felt the shift ripple outward through the others—Gillie's shoulders easing into a steadier alignment, Sera's hum lowering into something slower and less melodic, Nadya's anger tightening inward where it could no longer spend itself on motion.

The ache pressed again. Harder. It found the places that wanted movement most—the calf already half-convinced to step, the shoulder begging to roll, the jaw tightening around a word it wanted to spit out just to break the silence. My scar burned, a thin line of heat like memory testing its boundary. Behind my eyes, the swamp surged—iron and rot, the first coil of whisper tightening the way it always had.

Move, my body urged. Just one step.

Rowan did not move.

Shim'on did, but only in the smallest way: he edged half a pace nearer without crossing into anyone's space, and set himself where the road's grit gave way to a shelf of exposed stone. He planted his feet like he meant to be found there later. His hand lowered to the rock, palm flat—no flourish, no dramatics—just contact, as if he were reminding his body what holds. His mouth moved once, not quite prayer and not quite speech, and whatever he said didn't travel far enough for the place to catch and twist.

Eliah did move. He shifted—not away from the pain, not toward escape—but closer to Nadya, close enough that his presence overlapped hers. He didn't touch her. He didn't speak. He simply adjusted his stance so that when the ache surged again, it met him first.

I saw it take him. His breath caught—not sharp, not panicked—just heavier, as if compassion itself carried weight here. His hands curled once at his sides, not to strike, not to flee, but to hold. The pain pressed into him and did not ricochet outward. He did not redirect it. He did not pass it along.

He bore it.

The ache hesitated. It had learned how to punish urgency. It had learned how to reward motion. It had never learned what to do with pain that was received without being used.

Rowan's stillness remained full—crowded with thought, paradox held open and unanswered. Eliah's presence remained grounded—pain absorbed, contained, refused transmission. The rule no longer applied cleanly.

Across the basin, the Lantern's attention sharpened—not with light, but with weight. His regard closed around Joshua like pressure finding a weak seam, not touching so much as enclosing. Joshua's shoulders drew back by habit alone, spine aligning into the posture survival had trained into him. He stood rigid beneath that gaze, jaw clenched, eyes forward—not pleading, not defiant.

Braced.

Waiting for correction.

Rowan did not look at him. He turned his palm upward instead—open, empty—and asked another question, quieter now, almost inward, as if he were no longer speaking to the place but within it.

"What remains," he said, "when the body rests… and the mind refuses to flee?"

The ache surged, furious now, offended by the refusal to obey. The reed-sound screamed—not in sound, but in pressure. The swamp rose around my knees in memory, thick and immediate. Iron flooded my mouth as the whisper tested its claim.

Rowan did not move.

Eliah stayed.

And Joshua watched.

Something in Joshua's posture bent—not collapse, not release—but strain tipping toward recognition. His breath hitched, not in fear, but in disbelief, as if he were witnessing a law being broken without consequence.

The Lantern's presence tightened, correcting, insisting.

And then the pressure failed.

Not dramatically. Not all at once. It simply… lost its hold.

The ache withdrew a fraction, uncertain where to press next. And in that slackening, something else became visible.

At first it was subtle—a warmth gathering at Rowan's chest, not bright, not flaring, but steady. It did not answer the Lantern. It did not react to command. It did not hurry.

It waited.

Then it moved.

Not seized. Not transferred. Released.

The light slipped free from Rowan the way breath leaves lungs after being held too long—unnoticed until it's gone, undeniable once it is. It crossed the space between them without haste, without spectacle, a thread of true light that carried no urgency at all.

The plague recoiled from it. The ache fell back as if recognizing a presence it was not allowed to touch.

Joshua stiffened.

Then—just barely—he sagged.

Not collapse.

Reception.

The light entered him not like invasion, not like rescue, but like something long denied permission finally being allowed to return. It settled into his chest, spreading slowly—not bright, not loud—but unmistakable. The shadows that clung to him did not vanish.

They thinned.

Joshua exhaled.

Not relief.

Recognition.

For a single, naked heartbeat, the Lantern's authority fractured. Not dimmed. Split. His light faltered, revealing the strain beneath it—control masquerading as order, command standing in for truth—before snapping back into something colder, sharper, more brittle than before.

But it was too late.

Something had been reclaimed.

Something that had never belonged to him.

The world did not press. It waited.

The reed-sound receded like a tide pulled back by something stronger than hunger. I drew a breath—slow, deliberate, taken the way one takes a risk after being burned—and it stayed where it belonged.

Eliah exhaled at the same moment. The pain did not follow him.

Shim'on's hand lifted off the stone. He didn't look triumphant. He looked wrecked—quietly, privately—like a man watching a law soften and realizing how long he'd lived braced for it to stay hard. His voice came out low, meant for Nadya and Miriam more than the air. "It held," he said simply. Not *we held*. Not *you won*. Just: *it held.* As if steadiness were a mercy you receive before you learn how to carry it.

That was when the laughter arrived.

It didn't arrive loudly. It didn't need to. It slipped into the space like silk dragged across bone—controlled, precise, threaded through with a fury that had learned how to smile.

"Well," Kali said, her voice smoothing itself over the air as if claiming it, "that was expensive."

Nadya turned on her at once, anger snapping sharp and bright. "Get out."

Kali's smile held, but it had gone tight at the corners now, brittle in a way that betrayed restraint stretched thin. "Oh, I will," she replied lightly. "This place has finished what it needed."

Her gaze drifted—not hungry, not indulgent—but calculating, settling on Joshua with the cold appraisal of someone tallying loss. "Stillness," she mused. "How generous of you to remember it exists."

Joshua didn't rise to the bait. He didn't look at her. He didn't speak.

That refusal landed harder than defiance ever could have.

Kali's attention snapped back to us, her eyes sharp now, weighing. "But you've learned something else, haven't you?" she said. "That pain isn't the only motivator."

The shift came then—not beneath our feet, but inside us. It opened low in my gut, subtle at first, a hollow awareness that felt nothing like injury. It wasn't sharp. It wasn't loud. It was the unpleasant recognition of space where something should have been—cleared, emptied, and left waiting. I swallowed, unsettled by how patient it felt.

"And that forgetting," Kali continued, her voice smooth with restrained fury, "can feel like mercy."

Cassian's hands clenched into fists. "What did you do."

Kali laughed softly, the sound all surface and no warmth. "Nothing yet."

The air tightened. Not collapsed—tightened. The light along the road dulled as if something had passed in front of it and chosen to linger. The Lantern's presence sharpened at the edges, colder now, watchful in a way that promised consequence rather than correction.

"I'd eat if I were you," Kali said pleasantly. "You're going to want something soon." She stepped back as she spoke, her form thinning even as her presence pressed harder. "Next comes hunger," she added. "Not for bread." Her smile sharpened. "For what was never yours."

The ache in my legs was gone.

In its place was something worse.

A craving—quiet, intimate, already learning the shape of me.

I knew it with the same certainty I'd known the swamp. Not because it hurt, but because it waited. The road ahead stretched open and expectant, and it smelled like a table set just beyond reach, heavy with the promise of satisfaction that would never arrive.

The world held its breath—not braced, not pressed—held, the way a room does after a door closes and no one is sure whether they're alone yet.

That was when the air folded. Not collapsing. Tightening again, sharper this time. The temperature dropped just enough to be felt on bare skin. Shadows gathered where they hadn't belonged moments before, too deliberate to be natural.

"Well," Kali said again.

Her voice came from everywhere and nowhere at once now, stripped of amusement, stripped of polish.

Angry.

"That was mine."

Nadya turned first. "Get out."

Kali didn't look at her. Her gaze fixed instead on the treeline, where shadow thickened into something that resisted definition until it chose to step forward. Raven emerged with his head slightly bowed, posture tight—not submissive, but wary in the way something cornered learns to be.

"Raven," Kali said.

The name cracked like a blow. The air shuddered, and Raven flinched before he could stop himself.

"You were watching," Kali continued softly. "That was your task."

Raven didn't answer.

"You felt the stillness breaking," she pressed, each word measured. "You felt the pressure slip. And you did nothing."

"They didn't stop," Raven said carefully. "They—"

"They rested," Kali snapped.

The word struck the ground hard enough that it trembled beneath us. "Do you understand how expensive that was?"

She moved closer to Raven, close enough that the air around him thinned, breath turning shallow without being commanded to do so. "I gave you a soul," she hissed. "Pulled you out of silence and rot and gave you voice—and you stood there and let them remember how to trust?"

Raven's jaw tightened. His breath caught.

Kali raised her hand.

Raven's body reacted before sound could form. His shoulders seized. His knees buckled and barely held. Breath tore short and shallow from his chest, dragged away mid-thought as pain rippled through him—not loud, not dramatic, but absolute.

"Do not mistake patience for mercy," Kali said calmly. "If you fail me again, I will remind you what it felt like before you had a name. Before you had hunger. Before you had choice."

Raven swallowed hard. "What do you want."

Kali smiled. "That," she said, turning her gaze back to us, "depends on who breaks next."

Her attention slid deliberately—no randomness in it—until it settled on Sera.

Sera stiffened. Not fear. Recognition.

"Oh," Kali said, delighted now. "You feel it already, don't you?"

Sera's hum wavered, thinning into something unsteady. Her lips pressed together, as if holding back a truth that had already begun to leak.

"You're the dangerous one," Kali continued lightly. "Not because you want too much—but because you know how to be content."

Sera lifted her eyes. "I don't—"

"You will," Kali cut in. "And when the wanting comes, it's going to hurt you more than the rest."

The air shifted again—not pressure this time, but absence.

My stomach clenched. I saw Cassian's jaw lock. Micah's hand curled reflexively toward his cord before he forced it still. Kaela's breath stuttered once, sharp and telling.

Kali noticed all of it.

"Micah," she said almost kindly. "How long do you think you can measure the world before you start resenting the ones who don't have to?"

Micah didn't answer.

"And you," she added to Kaela, her gaze piercing. "You carry restraint like a virtue. I wonder what happens when you decide you've earned more."

Kaela's hand trembled.

Kali turned back to Raven. "See?" she murmured. "Everyone hungers eventually. Your job is to make sure they don't choose gratitude when they do."

"And if they do," Raven asked, voice tight.

Kali's gaze hardened. "Then I take it out of you."

She stepped back, her form unraveling into the light like smoke drawn in reverse. "Next comes the meal," her voice lingered. "And I promise you—it will not satisfy."

The air warmed again.

The pressure was gone.

But the absence remained—quiet, gnawing, seated low in the body and already learning patience.

Not pain.

Want.

I looked at Sera. She hadn't moved. Her hands were clenched at her sides, knuckles pale, as if she were already holding something she didn't trust herself to keep.

The road ahead waited.

And it did not smell like rot or rain or stone.

It smelled like a table set just out of reach—and the certainty that when we sat, someone would leave hungry.

The Shattered Meal

Before the Table

For a few steps, I thought the path was turning back into the swamp.

Not because the ground changed—it didn't. The gravel kept its hard bite under our boots, the pale grit still grinding at the seams of our soles the way it had since the basin. But the air changed its mind. It took on that damp thickness that clings to the inside of the lungs and makes each breath feel negotiated rather than given. The light dulled without fully dimming, as if the world were bracing itself for rot. And somewhere under the smell of stone and old water, that faint sweetness returned—bruised leaves, reed pulp, the soft, patient decay that never hurries because it knows everything eventually sinks.

My body remembered before my mind agreed.

I lifted my feet higher than necessary, waiting for the familiar pull at the ankles. Waiting for the first soft give that meant you were no longer walking so much as being received. I could almost feel it: mud taking shape around the heel, water deciding your weight belonged to it, the slow, humiliating certainty that if you stopped fighting you'd go under quietly. I hated how quickly that memory reclaimed me. How much of me still believed drowning was the natural end of standing still.

Gillie glanced over her shoulder as if she felt the change too. The scroll rode between her shoulder blades like a steadying hand that refused to become a shove. She didn't say anything. She didn't need to. Her jaw had that tight angle it gets when she's listening for something behind what's being said.

Shim'on drifted toward the reed line—not leaving the group, just widening the circle the way you do when you expect trouble to come from the side. His hand brushed the hilt at his hip once, not drawing, not threatening—just checking that he was still himself.

Sera hummed.

She'd been doing it since the thunder stopped—not as a performance, not as comfort-for-others, but like the world required it the way lungs require rhythm. The tune sat low in her chest, thin as a thread you'd miss if you weren't paying attention, and stubborn in the way a candle stays lit when you cup your palm around it and refuse to let wind claim it.

At first I thought it was just nerves.

Then I realized my own breath had started matching it without asking permission.

Step. Breath. Weight. Step.

Not words—not narration—just a quiet counting in the body, the way you keep yourself from shattering when the world has stopped giving you obvious instructions.

Nadya wiped her nose with the back of her sleeve and grimaced. "Tell me you smell that."

"I smell it," Cassian answered. He kept his voice steady on purpose, like he was trying not to hand the air any extra fear to work with. "And I don't like it."

Micah's gaze went to the Vein. Not the water—the edges. The reed beds. The places where the bank looked too smooth, too worn, as if something had been dragging itself in and out of the world for longer than we'd been alive.

Rowan walked a half-step behind the line and said, "Don't trust your urgency."

Nadya shot him a look. "I wasn't—"

"You were," Rowan replied, and he didn't say it like an accusation. He said it like someone naming weather. "So was I."

Cassian's hand tightened on a strap. "We should check supplies."

It was a reasonable thing to say. It was the kind of sentence that makes you feel responsible. Adult. Like you've learned from mistakes. But the moment the words left his mouth I felt something inside me tilt—not toward action, but toward counting.

How much is left? How long until the next place? Who eats most? Who eats least? Who deserves—

I swallowed hard, unsettled by the speed of it. By the way my mind had already started building columns.

Gillie shifted the strap on her shoulder. The scroll didn't fight her. It settled the way it had learned to settle—present, quiet, almost heavy with restraint. In the basin it had felt like the Word refusing to be used. Out here it felt like the Word refusing to let the world bully us into doing something stupid just to prove we were alive.

Sera's hum wavered and then steadied again, lower now, as if she were pressing it into the ground so it couldn't be stolen by the air.

"Can you—" Nadya started, and stopped like she didn't want to ask.

Sera looked at her. Her eyes were tired, but clear. "What."

"Can you stop doing that?" Nadya asked, then immediately regretted it. "Not because it's bad. I just—every time you do it, it makes me—" She made a fist, opened it again. "It makes me feel like I'm about to cry for no reason."

Sera blinked, surprised. Then she nodded once like she'd been told something useful. "It's not for you," she said gently. Not dismissive. Honest.

Nadya huffed a laugh with no warmth in it. "Great. Love that."

"It's for me," Sera added, and the hum didn't stop. "If I stop, my head starts doing the thing."

"What thing," Cassian asked, already wary.

Sera exhaled through her nose. "The thing where it starts making plans that aren't mine."

That landed in me like a cold coin.

Rowan's eyes flicked to her mouth, then to the Vein, then away again. "Good," he said quietly. "So keep humming."

Micah frowned. "Why would—"

Rowan cut him off with a small shake of his head. "Because there are plagues you survive with strength," he said, "and plagues you survive with a mind that refuses to be rented."

Shim'on glanced back at that—quick, sharp—like the phrase had snagged something he didn't want to name yet. Then he looked forward again, jaw set, walking as if pace itself was a discipline.

The air thickened again.

Not like fog. Like attention.

The hairs on my arms rose. The taste of wet iron sharpened at the back of my tongue. And that hollow space in my gut—the one Kali had planted when the pressure lifted—stirred as if something had just leaned over it and smiled.

A laugh moved through the reeds.

Not loud. Not even fully a sound. More like approval.

Sera's hum faltered.

Just a fraction.

And in that falter, the hollow in my belly widened.

It wasn't pain. Not yet. It was the unpleasant recognition of space. A gap where something should have been, cleared out and left waiting like a bowl set on a table.

Kali did not step out.

She didn't have to.

Her presence arrived the way a hand arrives on the back of your neck—not squeezing, not pushing, just there, telling you your body is not private anymore. The light along the Vein dulled without dimming, as if something had passed in front of it and decided to linger. The air cooled just enough to notice. The reeds leaned inward.

"Well," Kali said.

Her voice threaded through everything: water, wind, the pause between steps. Silk dragged slowly across bone. Not amused.

Interested.

And somewhere deeper than her voice, another cadence rode it—a smoother, more polished rhythm that made the sentence sound like a proverb you'd heard your whole life even when you hadn't.

Order first, mercy later.

The words weren't spoken by any mouth I could see.

But I felt them.

Felt them the way you feel a suggestion when it's delivered with confidence and wrapped in "common sense."

Nadya's shoulders went rigid. "I hate that," she said aloud.

"Hate what," Kaela asked, glancing around.

Nadya pressed her fingers to her stomach, hard. "The—" She grimaced. "The thought that I should keep my portion and let someone else deal with themselves."

Sera's hum trembled, then steadied again as if she'd just felt the same intrusion and refused to let it root.

Rowan nodded once. "There it is," he murmured.

Cassian swallowed. "That's not a plague," he said, as if arguing could keep it from being true. "That's just reality."

Kali laughed softly.

And in the laughter, a different voice joined—pleased, bright with cruelty, delighted in the way someone delights when their favorite story reaches the part where the hero makes the wrong choice.

Julian's cadence.

It curled around Kali's laugh like a hand around a wine cup.

"Oh," that hidden voice seemed to say. "This is going to be beautiful."

Sera stiffened as if the sound had touched her skin.

Micah muttered, "We should keep moving."

And there it was again: the urgency. The reasonable thought that movement would solve it.

Raven stepped out of the reeds as if answering the sentence.

He wore the shape of a man who had eaten recently enough to look polite about it. Clean boots. A scarf that looked like a choice instead of necessity. A smile practiced into something almost kind. He inclined his head as though joining a conversation already in progress.

"Planning is wise," Raven said smoothly. "Only fools pretend hunger doesn't compound."

Nadya's hand moved toward her belt and stopped. "We didn't invite you."

Raven's smile widened. "Invitation is such a narrow door," he said. "We prefer open roads."

I watched him carefully.

Raven didn't move like a person.

He moved like a thought that had learned to wear boots.

He took a step and it felt like our own minds had taken it first.

Shim'on shifted—small, almost lazy—putting himself a fraction closer to Nadya and Kaela without making it a stand. He didn't glare. He didn't posture. He just made space feel slightly harder to cross.

"Where's Kali," Cassian asked.

Raven's eyes flicked toward the reeds without turning his head. "Near," he said. "Watching. Appreciating."

"Appreciating what," Nadya snapped.

Raven's smile deepened—and then, just behind it, I saw the faintest strain. The tiniest tremor at the corner of his mouth, like someone holding a scream in their teeth.

Kali was already hurting him.

Not to punish him.

To remind him who he belonged to.

Raven's eyes flicked toward the air again, as if listening to a silent instruction.

Then he turned back to us, all ease.

"You survived the last lesson," he said. "That's impressive. Truly. Rest in a place built to punish stillness." He clapped once—a soft, almost polite sound. "Very clever."

"Stop flattering us," Rowan said.

"We're not flattering," Raven replied. "We're mourning."

Cassian frowned. "Mourning what."

"The simplicity," Raven said. "Pain was straightforward. Pain motivated. Pain corrected." He lifted his hands, palms out, as if presenting an invisible ledger. "But hunger?" His eyes shone. "Hunger is civilized. Hunger doesn't need force. Hunger turns you into a reasonable person."

The hollow in my gut stirred again.

Not pain.

Want.

A craving that hadn't chosen an object yet, but was already learning my shape.

Sera's hum rose slightly, almost reflexive—a thread tightening as the air tried to cut it.

Raven noticed. "That song," he said, nodding toward her. "You hum it like it belongs to you."

Sera didn't stop. She didn't look at him. "It doesn't," she said simply. "It belongs where it's needed."

Raven's smile sharpened. "Everything does," he said. "Until there isn't enough to go around."

Micah's jaw tightened. "We have enough," he said, and the lie tasted like dry bread. "We rationed."

Raven tilted his head. "Did you," he asked gently, "or did you hope?"

The word hope landed wrong, like a blade turned sideways.

Kali's presence tightened again, pleased.

And behind her pleasure, Lucien's older sting threaded through my ribs—not as sharp as it had been in the basin, but cleaner. A precise little needle that flared whenever my attention moved toward a stranger, toward generosity, toward anything that looked like mercy without calculation.

I caught myself looking at Kaela's pack.

Not for any reason.

Just because my mind had decided, suddenly, that her pack looked heavier than mine.

That she might have something I didn't.

That she might be hiding—

I clenched my fists until my nails bit skin.

This was not me.

This was the plague testing its first tooth.

Rowan spoke softly, almost to himself. "Desire doesn't begin with hunger," he said. "It begins with comparison."

Raven's eyes brightened. "Yes," he murmured, delighted. "Exactly."

Then his smile twitched again—strain, pain, warning—and he swallowed hard as if something had tightened around his throat.

Kali was not satisfied.

Raven glanced toward the reeds again, almost imperceptibly.

"More," Kali's voice said, not loud.

Not kind.

And Lucien—smooth, approving—seemed to hum alongside her like an audience member leaning forward.

Make them want.

Raven inhaled carefully. He turned back to us.

"Tell me," he said, voice still pleasant, still "reasonable." "Who among you is the most generous."

Nadya barked a laugh. "What kind of question is that."

"A simple one," Raven replied. "A harmless one."

Rowan's eyes narrowed. "Nothing harmless comes with you."

Raven shrugged. "Fine. Different question." His gaze slid over us deliberately—not random, not casual. He was selecting. "Who among you is the most content."

Sera's hum wavered again.

Kali's presence sharpened like a blade being drawn.

Raven smiled with too much satisfaction. "Ah," he said softly. "There you are."

Sera finally looked up. "Don't," she said. One word. Flat. Not pleading.

Raven lifted his hands in mock innocence. "We didn't do anything."

"You're doing it right now," Sera replied, and her voice was steady even as her hum trembled. "You're trying to make me… look at them like I'm owed something."

Cassian glanced at her sharply. "What."

Sera swallowed. "My mouth wants to say, 'I'm the one holding us together.'" Her eyes flashed with sudden anger—not at us, at herself. "And that's not true. That's just a thought that tastes like pride."

Micah's brow furrowed. "That's not—"

"It is," Sera cut in. She drew a breath, then let it out slowly, pushing the hum back into place like a wedge. "It's trying to make me feel… entitled."

Kali laughed softly—pleased.

Julian's cadence rode it like applause.

Look at her. The saint. The one who sings. The one who deserves.

Nadya's face tightened. "You don't deserve anything from me," she snapped, immediately furious at herself for saying it.

Sera flinched.

Not because of Nadya.

Because the plague had just gotten what it wanted: a fracture.

Rowan spoke quickly, grounding. "Nadya," he said, voice firm but not harsh. "That wasn't yours."

Nadya's jaw worked. "I know," she snapped. Then quieter, almost sick: "I know."

Raven smiled wider, because even resistance feeds him if it turns into conflict.

Kali's presence pressed closer, delighted.

And then, because she loved being watched, because she loved being approved of, because she loved the others' delight like a lover's praise—

She punished Raven again.

It hit him mid-breath.

His shoulders seized. His knees dipped and caught. The pleasant mask on his face cracked for a heartbeat and I saw what he really was beneath it: something stitched together from borrowed voice and forced desire, something that remembered silence as a wound.

He made a sound—barely—and swallowed it.

Kali's voice stayed calm. "That's better," she said.

Raven's eyes watered. He blinked it away.

"Do not make me carry your hesitation," Kali added, almost sweetly.

Lucien's sting flared in the air like approval.

Julian's cadence laughed.

Raven straightened, smile returning like a bruise covered by paint.

"We're sorry," he said pleasantly, to us or to her, I couldn't tell. "Old habits. Old pain." His gaze slid to Micah. "You," he said, as if selecting a new knife.

Micah's posture tightened. "What."

Raven's smile softened into sympathy. "You measure everything," he said. "That's your virtue. But tell us the truth—how long before virtue becomes resentment."

Micah's jaw locked.

Raven leaned in a fraction. "How long before you start hating the people who don't have to work as hard to be good."

Micah's hand curled toward his cord.

Kaela shifted closer to him without thinking.

Raven noticed that too and smiled. "And you," he said to Kaela, voice gentle. "Restraint looks so noble when you're not hungry." His eyes drifted to her pack, then to her hands. "We wonder what happens when you decide you've earned more."

Kaela's breath stuttered once.

Sera's hum tightened, sharper now, like a thread pulled too hard.

Shim'on's voice cut in—not loud, not dramatic. Just placed. "Enough."

Not as a threat. As a boundary—one you could step over, but you would have to do it on purpose.

Rowan stepped forward, not aggressive, but present. "Enough," he said.

Raven's smile held. "We're only talking," he replied.

Rowan nodded. "That's the problem."

The road bent then—not sharply, not dramatically. Just enough that the Vein slowed, water lapping against black rock worn smooth by long use. Reed beds opened into a small elbow of space where the bank looked… built. Not shaped by flood or accident. Shaped by repeated need.

And there, set into the bank as if the earth had grown tired of pretending it wasn't meant for this, stood the slab.

The table waited.

It wasn't grand. It wasn't holy-looking. It was just stone that had been used enough to become familiar. Knee-high. Long enough to hold more than one kind of desperation. Its surface was worn smooth in the center and rough at the edges, as if hands had touched it where they were allowed and avoided it where they were ashamed.

I stopped without meaning to.

The hollow in my gut widened at the sight of it, not with relief, but with sudden specificity.

Food.

Rest.

A place to put hunger down.

The thought hit my mouth like saliva.

Cassian's breath caught. "Oh," he said.

Nadya's eyes narrowed like she didn't trust anything that looked like mercy. "Don't," she muttered. "Don't let it—"

Micah stepped closer, almost involuntary, and then stopped hard, forcing himself still.

Kaela's hands curled, then opened. Curled, then opened.

Sera's hum rose like a warning.

Raven inhaled sharply—too eager—and then checked himself, glancing toward the reeds as if waiting to see whether Kali approved of his enthusiasm.

Kali's presence tightened.

"Oh," she said softly, satisfied. "Now this is interesting."

Julian's cadence purred behind it, delighted.

Set the table. Feed them. Watch them choose.

Lucien's sting pressed under my ribs, subtle but precise, as if marking the moment when mercy could be turned into a weapon simply by changing the story around it.

Raven smiled.

"Accident," he said lightly. "Or mercy?"

Rowan didn't answer him. Rowan looked at the slab like a man looking at a test he'd taken before and failed in public.

Nadya swallowed. "We don't have enough to feed strangers," she said—and the air around the words felt wrong, like something had leaned too close while she spoke. She drew a sharp breath, eyes narrowing. "That wasn't me."

Cassian's hands were already moving—loosening a strap, checking a tie—and I could see the calculation rising behind his eyes.

Shim'on didn't move to the table. He watched the hands. Watched the straps. Watched the way "reasonable" turned hungry when it thought no one was looking.

Sera's hum trembled.

She pressed it down again, breathing it into the air like a quiet refusal.

And in that moment—the moment before we even touched the table—I felt the plague settle into its true shape.

Not pain.

Not pressure.

A smile behind the ribs.

A hollow ache that promised satisfaction and meant consumption.

A want that would grow as it was fed.

And a room full of unseen listeners leaning forward, delighted, eager to see who would take first.

The Table That Spoils

The stone did not look like a table until we needed it to.

It rose from the bank in a low, patient slab, no higher than my knee, longer than two bodies laid end to end. Its surface had been worked smooth not by tools but by weather and use—edges softened by water, corners worn down by hands that had learned to press rather than strike. It stood where the Vein bent in a slow elbow, the water lapping against black rock, steady and unpersuasive. Reed beds leaned inward, whispering, their stalks clicking together as if trading notes about us.

I have always watched for such places. Stones that remember being altars. Ledges that decide to become tables. They do not announce themselves. They wait to see what you will ask of them.

Bread-moss grew in the seams.

At first glance it looked like lichen—pale gold, almost gray in the low light—but when I knelt and brushed my fingers along the cracks, it flaked upward in lacy sheets, thin as bark and warm with a faint memory of sun. It smelled of wet straw and heat both, the way bread does when it's just begun to cool. My mouth flooded instantly, the hollow ache in my gut tightening with a pull that surprised me with its urgency.

Raven noticed.

His eyes flicked down, then away again, his smile deepening as if he'd been proven right about something he hadn't bothered to say aloud. "Lucky," he murmured. "The world still remembers how to feed those who find the right places."

Kali's presence pressed closer, pleased. Yes, Julian's delight hummed through the air, a grin with no mouth. Show them.

I cupped my fingers and lifted the bread-moss gently. It came away clean, leaving the stone beneath bare and dark, the way skin looks when a bandage is first removed. I broke off a corner and watched it carefully. It stayed bread.

"Here," I said, and my voice came out softer than I'd intended. The circle raised their eyes the way you do when you hear a bell you weren't sure belonged to you.

I traced a small mark on the table's edge with my thumb—a breath-gap, a crescent of empty where a circle would have closed. It's an old habit. Circles are for family. Closed circles tempt us to hoard. So I leave every ring parted—a place for a stranger's hand to enter without breaking anything. The dust took the mark and held it.

"We'll open it," I said. "And we will not count before we bless."

Cassian's shoulders lifted at that. He counts to love us; he also counts to stop his heart from sprinting. Micah's gaze flicked over the road and back again, measuring distances that had nothing to do with feet. Kaela knelt already, fingers itching to shape something from the bank's clay. Gillie shifted the strap of the scroll on her back; it settled without protest, present and heavy, as if weight itself had agreed to be useful. Shim'on stayed just off to the side of the slab, not claiming a seat in the circle—watching Raven, watching the reeds, watching our hands more than our faces.

Sera hummed.

The note was thin, almost fragile, but it held. It threaded itself through the sound of water and reeds and breath until the space around the table felt… tuned. Not safe. Not yet. But aligned, like an instrument that has decided which string it will not let snap.

I broke the first sheet of bread-moss into seven pieces because my hands remembered seven. "Blessed are you," I said, palms open, speaking to the Giver and to the stone and to our hunger, "who make bread out of rock, and patience out of ache."

The scroll pressed quiet against my ribs. It did not join the blessing, but its silence weighted the words so they would not scatter.

A watcher stood in the reeds.

He was thin, half-shadow, his hunger worn like manners. He waited with the courtesy of the starving, eyes downcast, hands visible. Gillie saw him first. She didn't look back to ask permission. She took one piece, broke it once more between fingers that had decided too many times not to strike, and went to him with her blade hand open and empty so he could see the edge was quiet.

"Will you receive?" she asked—not making her plenty his shame.

He took the bread.

It stayed bread.

He ate in small, stubborn bites, and the wind did not turn it to dust. His eyes didn't thank her. His body did—shoulders lowering a fraction, jaw unclenching—the tiny loosening that is a man's amen when his tongue is too proud to say it.

Raven's smile tightened.

Kali's attention sharpened. "Careful," she murmured—not to us. To him.

I offered the second piece to the circle. Sera shook her head and lifted her hum instead, as if to say she would eat later from music. Nadya broke off a small bite and slipped it to a dog I hadn't seen—some creatures learn to be the same color as the fear that feeds them. The dog ate.

It stayed bread.

Cassian hesitated.

Then he took a piece—just a mouth's worth. He rolled it in his fingers, weighing it, and tucked it into his pocket.

"For the watch," he said, not meeting my eyes. "Later."

The crumb in his palm went gray.

Not all at once. It dulled, like a memory left in the sun too long. Cassian's hand stilled in his pocket. He frowned, drew the piece back out, and stared at it like a man who has discovered his math no longer applies.

Shim'on saw the shift at the same time I did. His gaze snapped to Cassian's hand, then to the reed line where the hungry watched us pretend we weren't choosing.

A boy at the edge of the reeds licked his lips, ribs sharp beneath his shirt. Cassian swore under his breath and pressed the heel of bread into the boy's hand.

It stayed bread.

Cassian's breath left him in a rush he hadn't known he was holding.

Raven laughed softly. "Interesting," he said. "It seems the stone has… opinions."

Kali did not laugh.

The air snapped tight around Raven's ribs. He gasped—not loud, not theatrical—his shoulders seizing as if a fist had closed inside his chest. Julian's delight flickered bright and pleased. Lucien's approval pressed like a blade laid flat against skin.

"Escalate," Kali said calmly.

Raven recovered quickly, his smile reassembling itself with effort. "Of course," he said. "Forgive us. We were observing."

Micah cleared his throat. "We should establish order," he said. "So no one is missed. Children first. Then the weak. Then—"

"And then the deserving," Raven supplied smoothly.

Micah's jaw tightened. "Then the ones who can carry us farther," he corrected.

The hollow ache in my gut flared, sharper now, and with it a sudden resentment I didn't want: Why do I always have to be the one thinking about everyone else? It startled me with its intimacy. I glanced toward Sera without meaning to.

She was still humming, but her shoulders had tightened, the note pressed thinner by strain. Her eyes were on the bread, not with hunger but with something like fatigue.

Raven followed my glance. "She hasn't eaten," he observed lightly. "Not yet. Doesn't that worry you?"

Sera didn't answer.

Kali's voice slid in, delighted. "Ask her again."

Raven leaned closer, careful to keep his tone gentle. "You should eat," he said to Sera. "Holding things together is expensive."

Sera's hum wavered.

For a heartbeat, it almost broke.

And in that break, a memory rose unbidden—Joshua in the swamp, standing at the edge of still water, humming off-key and too loud, the sound echoing against reed banks as if daring the dark to name him. You used to hum that song when we were stationed at the outer post, the Redeemed had said. Off-key, always. And louder when you were afraid.

The Redeemed never said what they were stationed there to do. Guards, maybe. Watchmen. Something that required hunger to be familiar and patience to be learned too late. Joshua had hummed when he didn't have what others had. He had hummed to fill the space where desire pressed hardest. And when he stopped humming—when the song failed him—that was when the wanting took over.

Sera swallowed.

Her hum dipped, then steadied again—not louder, not prettier. Stubborn.

"I will eat when the circle does," she said quietly.

Raven's smile faltered.

Kali's hand closed in the air.

Pain took Raven again, sharper this time. His knees buckled and caught; his breath tore short and shallow, dragged from him mid-thought. Julian laughed outright now, delighted. Lucien's satisfaction hummed low and cruel.

"Do not let them admire restraint," Kali said softly. "Turn it into resentment."

Raven nodded once, teeth clenched. "Of course."

Kaela had shaped three shallow bowls from the clay, each rim marked with a tiny open spiral. She set them on the stone and reached for the water skin.

"Wait," Micah said, too quickly. "Measure first."

Kaela's hand stilled. Her jaw set. "I've been carrying this since dawn," she said. "My hands are cracked. My back—"

"I know," Micah replied. "But fairness matters."

Raven tilted his head. "Does it?" he asked. "Or does effort?"

Kaela's eyes flashed. The hollow ache in my gut twisted, now threaded with heat. I've earned more, a thought whispered—not mine, not entirely. I've carried more.

Shim'on moved then—not between them, not dramatic—just close enough that Kaela's next breath had to notice him. His voice stayed low. "Kaela," he said, not warning, not pleading. "Don't let him pick your words for you."

Kaela lifted the skin and poured.

The first bowl filled clear and sweet.

The second turned brackish halfway through, the water clouding with a faint gray swirl that smelled like old iron. Kaela hissed and tipped it back instinctively.

The third spilled entirely sour, splashing onto the stone and hissing as if offended.

Kali's laughter rippled, pleased and sharp. "There," she said. "They're learning."

Raven spread his hands. "Order matters," he said gently. "So does intention."

Micah stared at the bowls, face tight. "We need rules."

"And rules need teeth," Raven agreed.

Sera's hum dropped again, the note trembling under strain. Her hands clenched at her sides. "Stop," she said—not loud, not commanding. "You're making it worse."

Raven turned to her, eyes bright. "Are we? Or are we naming what's already happening?"

The hunger surged.

Not pain. Not yet.

Want.

It bloomed behind my sternum, sharp and empty, the craving for enough turning into the craving for more. I saw it on Nadya's face—the flash of calculation she despised. On Micah's—the urge to justify. On Kaela's—the tight line of earned entitlement.

And on Sera's—weariness. The resentment of being the one who had to keep humming while everyone else argued about portions.

Kali leaned into that feeling like a hand pressing a bruise. "Sing louder," she whispered, not to Sera's ears but to the ache beneath them. "You're afraid, aren't you?"

Sera's hum wavered.

Raven stepped closer. “You don’t have to carry it,” he said softly. “You could rest. Let someone else hold the line for once.”

Sera’s eyes lifted. For a terrifying heartbeat, the hum stopped.

The hollow ache surged, and the bread on the stone shuddered—one piece fracturing into gray ash along its edge.

Shim’on’s hand came up—palm open, not touching Sera, just there in her periphery like a steady point on a shifting horizon. “Stay with it,” he said quietly. “Stay.”

Rowan spoke then, quietly, like a hand laid on a shaking shoulder. “Hunger grows when consumption increases,” he said. “That is the lie.”

Kali hissed, displeased.

Raven winced as pain flared again—short, sharp, corrective. Julian clapped in delight. Lucien smiled without lips.

Sera inhaled.

And hummed again.

Not the same note.

Lower. Grounded. Stubborn in a way that refused to be impressive. The sound did not fill the hunger. It framed it. Held it where it could be seen.

The bread steadied.

The ash did not spread.

Kali’s voice turned cold. “Enough,” she said. “Name it.”

Rowan looked at the table. At the bowls. At the bread that stayed bread only when given freely. “This is not famine,” he said. “This is a lesson.”

“A plague,” Nadya said, understanding sharpening like a blade.

The hunger clenched, intimate and patient.

“The Shattered Meal,” I breathed, and the words landed with the weight of truth.

Kali smiled.

"Oh," she said. "Now you're paying attention."

The table waited.

And it was hungry too.

The Lantern's Share

The first bite did not warn us.

It softened on the tongue the way bread should. Warm. Yielding. Familiar enough to relax the jaw before doubt could rise. For half a heartbeat I thought the earlier fear had been imagined, the way bodies invent danger when they're tired and ashamed of wanting relief.

Then the taste changed.

Not sharply. Not enough to spit. It turned damp, then sour, then unmistakably wrong—like mold pressed into the back of the throat, blooming where breath warms it. I swallowed by reflex and felt it drag its way down, leaving rot behind my sternum.

Around the table, the same recognition rippled.

Kaela gagged and turned away hard, hand clamped over her mouth. Nadya swore and spat, the sound sharp against stone, then froze when what hit the ground did not look like chewed bread at all but a gray, fibrous paste streaked with white threads.

Cassian swallowed too late.

His face tightened, eyes watering as he fought not to retch. "No," he muttered. "No, that's not—" He stopped and looked down at the piece still in his hand.

It had changed.

The surface had dulled, the pale gold sinking toward gray. A fine bloom crept along the edge where his fingers pressed too tightly, like something responding to possession rather than touch.

I reached for the water skin without thinking.

The moment the water hit my tongue, it turned. Bitter. Metallic. A taste like old iron leached through ash. I coughed, throat burning, and passed it to Gillie without asking. She took a careful sip, then shook her head once.

"Same," she said. "It's not poison. It wants to stay."

Others tried.

Each attempt failed the same way. Food spoiled mid-chew. Water turned brackish just before swallowing, as if the body were allowed to anticipate relief but never receive it. The worse the hunger grew, the faster the corruption came, until the table itself felt wrong to breathe around.

Then Micah ate.

No hesitation. No fear. A measured bite, chewed with the same discipline he applied to distances and time. He swallowed.

Nothing happened.

He frowned—not in relief, but confusion. "It's fine," he said slowly. "It tastes like bread."

Kaela stared at him. "Look at it."

Micah did. He turned the piece slowly in his fingers, studying it the way he studied everything—rotation, surface, fracture, possibility. The mold crawled openly now, gray seams threading through the bread-moss like rot pretending to be grain. Maggots pulsed in the deeper cracks, white and obscene, their bodies working with blind insistence.

Micah frowned again.

Not in disgust. In assessment.

He lifted the piece again and took another bite.

There was a pause.

I watched his throat work as he swallowed, watched his jaw tighten, then ease. Watched for the flicker—the reflexive wince, the recoil, the bitter aftertaste that had sent bile up the rest of our throats.

Nothing came.

He chewed again, slower this time, eyes narrowing as if testing a second proof. He swallowed.

Still nothing.

No sourness. No iron. No rot blooming behind the teeth. His jaw worked once, thoughtfully, then eased.

"It's fine," he said again, and this time the word sounded guarded, as if he expected it to be challenged.

The silence that followed was not relief.

It was focus.

Eliah reached for a piece next.

Quietly. Without looking at anyone. He broke it carefully—the way he broke difficult news—and lifted it to his mouth. The moment his teeth closed, he froze. He did not gag or spit, but his brow furrowed, calm replaced by something tighter. He chewed once more, slower, then swallowed with visible effort.

He did not reach for another bite.

Miriam tasted her share and shook her head almost at once. "It's… wrong," she said softly, not accusing the food, just naming what had happened to it. "It's like ash that remembers being bread."

Eliah nodded once and reached for the water skin. The bitterness struck immediately. He lowered it, breath hissing between his teeth.

"No," he said quietly. "It doesn't stay."

Miriam wiped her mouth with the back of her hand, eyes bright but steady. "We know what this is now," she said.

Not acceptance.

Recognition.

That was when the division truly locked in.

Those of us who tasted rot could not stop watching the one who didn't.

The hunger changed shape. It was no longer just emptiness. It became comparison. A tight, invasive ache that kept glancing sideways.

Why him.

Why not us.

What did he do differently.

What did we miss.

It was not that the food was clean for Micah.

It was that something had decided he could keep it.

Raven saw it happen.

He moved closer to the table, boots quiet, posture easy. He did not touch the food. He didn't need to. His eyes tracked reactions the way a musician tracks tempo.

"It knows who it's for," he said, voice low and satisfied. "And who it isn't."

Kali's presence coiled tighter around him.

"Yes," she murmured. "Name it."

Lucien's cadence slid through the reeds like silk over bone.

See how fair it feels.

Julian laughed, delighted. This is cleaner than thunder.

Shim'on stepped forward.

He had been watching from the edge, still as a thought no one wants to finish. He crouched and picked up a piece that crawled openly with maggots now, white bodies writhing in seams that had been clean moments before. His eyes flicked once to the reed line—measuring who was watching us measure each other—then back to the bread.

He ate.

Not hurriedly. Not defiantly.

He chewed with visible satisfaction, wiped his mouth, and drank deeply from the skin. The bitterness did not touch him. When he lowered the skin, his face stayed level—no triumph in it, only a steady refusal to pretend we hadn't all seen what this meant.

Nadya stared. "How," she demanded. "How are you doing that."

Shim'on met her stare. "I didn't take it from them."

The words sank deeper than accusation.

Sera's hum rose.

It wasn't comfort now. It was endurance. A note pulled tight and held through pain, vibrating against bone, pressing outward, refusing to let the space collapse inward on itself.

Raven's smile tightened—not in confusion, but in offense.

The hum struck him like a frequency his body had not been built to endure. His breath hitched. His jaw tightened. The pleasant mask cracked for a heartbeat before he smoothed it back into place.

Kali recoiled a fraction.

Lucien hissed.

Julian snarled, delight turning sharp. Make her stop.

"Careful," Raven said to Sera, voice gentle. "You're making this harder than it needs to be."

She didn't look at him.

Her eyes were on Micah. On his hands. On the absence of pain there.

The hunger twisted.

Not pain yet. Envy. A hot, humiliating ache that whispered you are the one holding this together. You are the one paying. You are owed.

Raven leaned in. "You should eat," he said softly. "Carrying everyone is expensive."

Sera's hum wavered.

And in that wavering, memory rose—Joshua at the edge of the swamp, humming too loud, off-key, filling the space where desire pressed hardest. When he stopped humming, when the sound failed him, that was when the wanting took over.

Sera swallowed. "I will eat when the circle eats."

Raven's smile faltered.

Kali punished him again.

The pain hit mid-breath, sharper this time. Raven staggered, knees dipping as his breath tore shallow and fast. Julian laughed openly now. Lucien's satisfaction pressed low and cruel.

"Escalate," Kali said calmly.

Kaela poured water into the bowls she had shaped. The first stayed clear. The second clouded halfway through, gray spreading like breath in cold air. The third turned fully sour, hissing softly as it struck stone.

Micah stared. "We need rules."

"And rules need teeth," Raven agreed, recovering, smiling through pain.

Sera's hum rose higher. This time it hurt—not just Raven. Kali flinched. Lucien recoiled. Julian's delight snapped sharp with anger.

Gillie felt the Balanced Blade answer. Not draw. Not flare. Just a subtle resonance through the metal, a remembered harmony approving restraint. The blade knew this sound. It had been given in it.

Pilgrims turned toward the Lantern.

They offered food.

They ate.

Relief came.

Gillie and I saw it clearly. Not mercy. Transaction.

Shim'on saw it too. He shifted one step closer to the edge of the Lantern's light—close enough to watch faces as they came back chewing, close enough that if someone stumbled toward kneeling, his presence would be the first thing they met. He didn't stop anyone. He didn't have to. He simply watched like someone keeping count of costs that weren't written down.

Sera's hum climbed again, shaking now, agony threaded through every note. Raven backed away, hands raised, pain cutting through him as Kali's grip tightened.

"Enough," Kali said.

The table crawled. The hunger smiled. And the Lantern waited.

The first offering was tentative. A pilgrim stepped forward with a piece of bread held carefully in both hands, as if the food itself might flee. The mold clung to it visibly now, gray and veined, crawling where it had once flaked clean. He hesitated at the edge of the light, eyes flicking toward the Lantern's glow and then back toward the table, as if expecting the stone to protest.

It did not. The Lantern did not move either.

The pilgrim raised the bread higher, arms trembling.

"If… if this is yours," he said, voice hoarse, "then take it."

The light tightened—not brighter, narrower. Focused.

The bread changed. The mold receded like a tide drawn backward, the surface smoothing until it looked—not fresh—but acceptable. Edible. The pilgrim swallowed hard and tore off a piece with shaking fingers.

He ate.

Relief crossed his face so quickly it was obscene. Not joy. Satisfaction. The ache behind his eyes loosened. His shoulders dropped. He laughed once, breathless and surprised.

"It's good," he said, almost ashamed. "It's—fine."

Someone else stepped forward immediately. Then another.

The pattern established itself with terrifying speed. Not a rush. A line.

Each offering followed the same shape—hesitation, hope, transaction, relief. Each time, the cost deepened, though no one spoke it aloud.

Gillie caught my eye as the third pilgrim returned from the Lantern, chewing carefully.

"They're learning how to kneel," she said quietly.

"They're learning how to eat," Cassian snapped, then flinched as if struck by his own tone.

Sera's hum tightened. It was no longer just sound—it was effort. Her chest ached with it, ribs pulling inward against breath as she forced the note to stay grounded, unornamented, unpersuasive. She wasn't humming to convince. She was humming to endure.

And endurance was becoming unbearable.

Every time someone returned from the Lantern with relief on their face, the hollow inside her widened.

Why do they get to stop hurting.

Why do I have to keep holding this.

Why does restraint feel like punishment.

The thought startled her with its intimacy.

She pressed the hum lower, letting it vibrate against her sternum, forcing it to stay physical, embodied. The moment it drifted toward performance, the hunger leapt.

Raven circled her like a polite predator.

"You don't have to do this," he murmured, keeping his voice low enough to feel private. "No one asked you to suffer."

She didn't look at him.

"You did."

He smiled gently.

"We asked you to choose."

Kali's satisfaction pulsed.

Lucien leaned into the space behind Raven's words.

Look at them. Eating. Resting. You could stop.

Julian's delight crackled openly now.

Saints always think hunger makes them holy.

A woman at the edge gagged as she tried to swallow. She spat, bile streaking her chin, and looked wildly toward the Lantern.

Sera felt it like a hook. Not hunger.

Responsibility.

If I stop humming, it will get worse.

If I keep humming, it will hurt me.

Raven saw the fracture open and pressed.

"Look at Micah," he said softly. "He's doing fine. He always does. Rules protect people like him."

Micah stood rigid, jaw clenched, eyes locked on the bowls as if staring long enough would impose order.

"We need to regulate this," he said. "We can't let desperation decide."

"Desperation already has," Nadya shot back. "You just don't like the way it looks."

Micah rounded on her.

"I don't like watching people starve while others indulge chaos."

"Chaos?" Kaela snapped. "You mean mercy that doesn't ask permission?"

Micah's eyes flicked to her pack.

"Easy to say when yours is full."

Kaela froze.

"I know you're still standing," Micah continued. "Some of us can't afford generosity."

Sera flinched.

That was it.

The fracture made audible.

Raven smiled wider. Kali leaned closer, savoring.

Sera's hum wavered, surged, then nearly broke—and the hunger rushed in to fill the gap.

Images assaulted her unbidden: bread that stayed bread, water that stayed sweet, rest that didn't demand payment in pain.

You deserve it, the hunger whispered. You're the reason they're not tearing each other apart. You've earned a bite.

Her mouth filled with saliva.

She hated herself for it.

The Balanced Blade vibrated faintly at Gillie's side. Not warning. Recognition. Gillie laid a steadying hand on the hilt, not drawing, not even gripping—just acknowledging the response.

"It remembers," she said under her breath.

Shim'on's gaze cut to Sera—quick, concerned, not rescuing. He shifted half a step so she wasn't alone in Raven's orbit, close enough that if she faltered, she'd hit presence before she hit the ground.

Sera swallowed hard.

"I don't want to resent them."

Raven seized the word.

"Then don't," he said smoothly. "Resent the system instead. The unfairness. The burden."

Kali's voice slid in, pleased.

"Let her see it."

Sera looked up.

And saw maggots.

They crawled thickly across the table now, writhing through bread seams, clustering where hands had hovered too long. The sight punched the breath from her chest.

Except—

When Miriam reached for a piece, the maggots vanished.

When Eliah ate, the rot did not touch him.

When Micah drank, the bitterness receded.

The injustice burned.

"Why them?" Nadya demanded suddenly, voice cracking. "Why do they get to eat?"

Eliah looked up, startled.

"I didn't—"

"I didn't mean you," Nadya snapped, then winced. "I did. I just—"

"You meant anyone who isn't suffering enough to make you feel righteous," Raven supplied gently.

Nadya rounded on him.

"Shut up."

"Make us," Raven replied pleasantly.

Kali tightened her grip on him. Pain flared briefly. He staggered, recovered, smiling through clenched teeth.

"Say it," Kali whispered. "Say it out loud."

Micah broke.

"Because they're disciplined," he said. "Because they're not indulging panic."

Kaela laughed, sharp and ugly.

"Or because they're better at pretending they don't want more."

Sera's hum surged painfully, raw now, vibrating against teeth.

Stop. Please stop.

Her internal battle collapsed inward.

If I take one bite, it will stop.

If I stop humming, they'll stop hurting me.

If I stop hurting, I can help again.

Raven leaned close enough that she could smell him. Clean. Unhungry.

"Just one," he said softly. "You've earned it."

Kali held her breath.

Lucien's sting pressed hard beneath Sera's ribs.

Julian leaned forward, gleeful.

Say yes.

The hum faltered.

For a heartbeat, it stopped.

The hunger roared.

The table cracked. Bread shattered into ash. Bowls spidered. Water curdled instantly.

Someone screamed.

Sera gasped, horror flooding her face. She clutched her chest and forced breath back into rhythm.

And hummed.

Not beautifully.

Not kindly.

She hummed through pain, through bile, through resentment, through the screaming want clawing at her gut. The sound became unbearable.

Raven screamed.

Not metaphorically.

He dropped to one knee, hands clamped over his ears, body convulsing as the hum tore through him like glass. Kali recoiled violently, her presence lashing outward in fury.

“Enough!” Kali shrieked.

Lucien shrank back.

Julian snarled, delight turning feral.

Break her.

The Lantern’s light flared.

Transactions stopped. Relief cut off mid-bite. Panic surged.

And the group fractured completely.

“You did this,” someone shouted at Sera.

“Stop singing!”

“Let us eat!”

“You think you’re better than us!”

Sera staggered. The accusations struck harder than hunger.

Gillie stepped forward, blade still sheathed, voice steady.

“Enough.”

Shim’on moved with her—not matching her, not leading, simply present at her shoulder like a second brace. His eyes went to the ones shouting, then to the Lantern’s light, then back to Sera, as if tracking what was breaking fastest.

But the damage was done.

The plague had taken root.

Not hunger.

Envy.

The Shattered Meal had claimed its first truth:

What you want will grow the more you feed it.

And those who resist will be blamed.

The Lantern waited.

And he was pleased.

He let the noise spend itself. He let the blame settle where it always does. He let the ache sharpen until it stopped sounding like complaint and started sounding like obedience.

Only then did he move.

When Want Learns to Speak

The hunger reached its limit. It did not fade. It did not retreat. It pressed until it demanded a choice—not relief, but submission.

The Lantern stepped forward, light gathered neatly around him, posture composed, voice calm with authority practiced over centuries. “Bow,” he said—not loudly, not cruelly. “Take what is offered. There is no shame in eating.”

Around him, the ache flared in answer. Bellies cramped. Mouths filled with bitter saliva. Knees bent without permission. Several souls broke then, crossing the last distance to him, hands outstretched, gratitude already forming in their throats.

The Lantern smiled.

Raven murmured approval. Julian laughed softly. Lucien’s cadence threaded the air, smooth and certain. Marcus and Elana pressed the ache sharper, punishing hesitation, rewarding compliance.

Sera did not bow.

She swayed—but she did not bend.

Her hum rose again, louder now, steadier, no longer merely endurance but refusal given sound. It vibrated through her chest, through her ribs, through the hollow places hunger had tried to claim.

No, she said—not with words, but with pitch.

The sound changed.

It thickened. It warmed. Light gathered inside it—not blinding, not commanding, but unmistakably present. The ache in her stomach loosened—not fed, not satisfied, but answered. The hunger lost its teeth.

Those nearest felt it first.

A man who had been clutching his gut straightened suddenly, breath rushing back into his lungs. A woman lowered her bowl, blinking in confusion as the pain eased without payment. The ache did not vanish—but it no longer ruled.

Sera's refusal spread.

The hum moved outward, threading itself through the circle, settling in chests, steadying breath, quieting the animal panic that had driven hands to beg. One by one, backs straightened. Heads lifted.

Micah felt it and froze.

The rules fell silent. His plumb hung useless at his side as he realized there was nothing left to measure. The hunger had been displaced—not by abundance, but by resolve.

"Witness," he murmured.

Shim'on bowed his head—not in submission, but in recognition. Then he stepped into the small space between the Lantern and the first kneeling pilgrim, not blocking, not challenging—simply present, close enough that the next person would have to choose around him. He didn't touch anyone. He just said, low and plain, "Breathe."

Joshua gasped.

The light in the hum reached him fully now, not striking, not judging—entering. It poured into him through breath, through memory, through the places where he had wielded truth like a blade instead of carrying it like a lamp.

He cried out softly, folding inward as the ache in his chest broke open—not pain, but grief. His hands pressed to the ground, shoulders shaking as the warmth spread through him, burning away nothing, illuminating everything.

Shim'on moved without hurry, crouching near enough to be felt without crowding. He didn't offer comfort like a cure. He offered steadiness—one hand braced on the stone, the other open, palm up, as if reminding Joshua there was still a way to receive without taking.

The hunger was gone. Not satisfied. Broken.

People breathed again—deep, steady breaths, the kind taken after danger has passed but memory has not. No one rushed the Lantern now. No one begged. Those who had eaten his share paused mid-chew, shame flickering across their faces—not condemnation, just recognition.

"Thank you," someone said.

Not to the Lantern.

To the Light.

Shim'on inclined his head. Others followed—not kneeling, not worshiping, simply acknowledging what had held them without cost.

Joshua lifted his head.

And hummed.

The sound was rough, untrained, trembling—but it joined Sera's note, carried it, amplified it. Light gathered between them, not flaring outward but pressing inward, filling hollow places hunger had carved and left exposed.

The Lantern's smile vanished. Then returned—sharper.

"Well," he said softly. "That was unexpected."

He stepped forward, anger barely contained beneath composure. "You refuse to bow," he said, voice carrying easily. "Very well."

He gestured.

The table lurched. With a violent sweep of his arm, he shoved it aside. Bread scattered across the stone. Bowls shattered. Water hissed as it spilled and turned to steam.

Then he raised his hand.

Fire came. Not hungry fire. Judging fire.

It consumed what remained—bread, vessels, the possibility of satisfaction itself—burning it all to blackened ruin. Flames roared, meant to wound, meant to terrify.

But the ache did not return.

Sera's hum filled the space, steady and strong, settling into hearts and minds. The burning food did not hurt the way it should have. People watched the fire without flinching, the hunger no longer answering its call.

Shim'on shifted again, placing himself where the heat would have driven the weakest back into the Lantern's light. He didn't raise a weapon. He simply held the line with his body, eyes steady, as if saying: there is still a way forward that isn't bargaining.

The Lantern stared at them, astonishment flickering into fury.

"This," he said coldly, "is not mercy."

He turned, fire still licking the stone behind him, eyes bright with promise and threat braided together. "You have chosen heat without shelter," he said. "We will see how long your voices hold when the world offers nothing back."

The flames did not die. They stayed—burning without guidance, burning without comfort, burning as judgment stripped of light.

Joshua kept humming. Sera did not stop.

And somewhere in the crackle of scorched stone and breath held too long, the air learned a new kind of waiting.

Hollow Fire

Before the Ash Cools

The fire did not go out. That was the first betrayal—quiet, almost polite, as if the world itself didn't want to admit it was breaking another rule. Fire, in any honest life, ends. It spends itself, collapses into embers, becomes a story told later with hands outstretched toward remembered warmth. Even when fire is cruel, it resolves into absence.

But this fire remained.

It held its place where the table had stood, as though stone had learned to breathe flame and didn't know how to stop. The slab was gone—thrown aside by the Lantern's gesture—but its ghost stayed behind: a low scorched rectangle on the bank, edges glowing faintly blue where heat should have traveled outward and softened into night. The marks were too clean for survival, too precise for accident, more like a wound cauterized by something sterile and wrong.

Cold pressed in from the first breath—not the honest bite of wind off water, but something intentional, choosing joints and teeth, seeping up from the ground as if the earth itself had decided to deny us comfort. It slid over skin, quiet and resistant to refusal.

Our breath fogged immediately. Daylight still clung to the far side of the reeds, pale and thinning, but the air around the fire ignored it entirely. The Vein's mist thinned and thickened in slow pulses, as if breathing in time with something unseen, and every inhale felt bargained for.

Someone whispered, "It should be warm," and no one answered, because saying it out loud made the wrongness louder.

Shim'on stood a little apart from the circle, close enough to feel the cold but far enough that no one mistook him for part of the kneeling line. He kept his hands loose at his sides, shoulders drawn in against the chill, eyes tracking the fire with the wary attention of someone watching a trap reset. When one pilgrim drifted toward a half-kneel, Shim'on shifted a fraction—just enough to break the spell of following.

A pilgrim stepped closer. He was tall and heavy-boned, the kind of man whose hands had always known labor, his beard gray and stiff with road dust. He held his palms out slowly, carefully, with the cautious hope of someone approaching a dog that might bite—or might finally let you touch its head.

The blue flame leaned toward him. Not with wind, but with interest.

He waited for heat, and when it didn't come his fingers reddened anyway, color rising into them like shame. His breath hitched. He pulled back and stared at his own hands as if he'd been accused of theft. "It burns," he said, voice shaking. "But it doesn't—"

"It doesn't give anything back," Eliah said.

His voice wasn't sharp, and that was the problem. He stood a half-step forward from the others—not closer to the flame, not retreating either—cloak pulled tight around himself, fingers stiff with cold. His breath came measured and deliberate, each inhale visible in the blue light, and when he spoke it wasn't accusation, but observation weighed down by reluctance.

The man turned toward him, startled, as if bracing for judgment and finding none. Eliah swallowed, the words clearly costing him something, his jaw working once as though he were forcing himself not to add more.

The fire crackled. It burned brighter. It did not warm.

A bedroll too close to the scorch mark curled inward and vanished—not with smoke, but with swallowing. A cloak followed. Then a strap. Comfort erased in clean sequence.

Cassian lunged forward. "Move everything back—now!"

He grabbed a satchel by the strap and yanked it away from the blue edge. The leather went stiff under his fingers, frost blooming across it in spider lines. He cursed and flung it farther, as if distance could undo what had already touched it.

"Don't touch it bare," Micah said, voice tight. His plumb line hung at his side like a useless question mark. "It's not heat. It's… verdict."

Eliah flinched at the word.

"Stop talking like you know what it wants," Nadya snapped.

She hadn't moved forward. She stood rigid, arms crossed tight against herself, eyes fixed on the flame with something like anger—but it wasn't command. It was frustration at being denied traction.

Micah's gaze flicked to her, then away. "I know what it does," he said. "That's enough."

A child began to cry.

The sound cut through the cold like a crack in ice. It was small at first, just a thin whimper, then it rose into a full, helpless wail. His mother clutched him close, rocking as if she could rock the world back into kindness. She whispered into his hair, prayer tangled with panic, words breaking apart as her breath shortened.

The fire leaned.

Blue tongues stretched higher, reaching—not to warm, not to comfort, but to listen.

The boy's cry wavered as if the sound itself was being pulled.

Eliah took an involuntary step forward.

Not toward the flame—toward the child.

His breath caught. His shoulders rose, then fell, like he was forcing himself to stay where he was. His hands flexed uselessly at his sides, fingers pale and stiff with cold.

Shim'on moved first—not to the fire, but to the mother's flank, putting his body between her and the kneeling line as if to keep the panic from becoming a current. He didn't touch the child. He just crouched near enough that the mother could see another steady breath. "Keep him facing you," he murmured, low. "Not the flame."

Sera's hum rose instinctively—low, steady, meant to anchor. But the note came back to her warped, thinned, as if the fire bent sound the way it bent heat. Her throat tightened. Her mouth trembled. She swallowed hard and kept the tone anyway.

Gillie moved without speaking.

She stepped forward with the Balanced Blade held flat, edge turned away, as if she could push the fire back like you push a curtain. The metal answered with a faint vibration—not the clean harmony we'd learned to recognize, but protest. When the blade's guard passed through the blue light, frost blossomed along it instantly—white veins spreading toward the grip.

Gillie hissed and yanked it back. The frost did not melt.

"Even steel rejects this," she said, voice rough.

Rowan crouched near the scorch mark, not close enough to feed it, but close enough to study it the way he studied everything that wanted to own us. He reached out and let the back of his knuckles feel the air two feet from the flame.

His skin puckered.

Not from heat.

From cold.

He pulled back slowly. “It’s reversed,” he murmured. “Not like water—like judgment.”

A pilgrim dropped to one knee.

Not because he believed. Because fear makes the body remember old shapes. He went down in a half-collapse, hands pressed to stone, head bowed toward the blue flame like it was an altar.

“For shelter,” he whispered. “Just—if you can stop it.”

Shim’on did not follow. He shifted his weight once, boots scraping stone, then went still again, hands loose at his sides, as if refusing both the comfort of standing tall and the relief of collapse. His gaze flicked to the man’s bowed neck, then away—like he couldn’t afford to look too long at how easy it was.

Eliah’s chest tightened.

He didn’t speak.

That, too, cost him.

The Lantern’s laughter came soft and delighted from the far edge of the reeds—not loud, not mocking. Satisfied.

Eliah exhaled slowly, breath shaking despite his effort to steady it. He rubbed his hands together once, stopped himself, then folded them tight against his ribs as if to keep mercy from spilling out in the wrong direction.

A woman stood, shaking, and pointed at Sera. "Your song did this," she said, voice cracked. "It challenged him. It made him angry."

Sera's hum faltered.

Just a fraction.

And in that fraction, the cold surged, sharp enough to pull a gasp from several throats.

Sera forced the note back into place. Her eyes were bright, not with tears—yet—but with strain. "No," she said quietly, still humming. "His anger did this."

"You don't know that," the woman snapped.

Eliah opened his mouth—

—and closed it again.

Shim'on looked at the woman once, then at the fire, as if weighing whether answering would feed it. He said nothing, but he stepped closer to Sera's side, not protective, not possessive—just present enough that Sera wouldn't be singled out alone.

Rowan looked up from his crouch. "We do," he said. "Because it doesn't burn what it hates. It burns what we love."

As if answering him, the flame sharpened, attention narrowing.

A bundle of kindling someone had gathered earlier—honest wood, dry bark, a few sticks tied together with string—caught at the edge of the blue. It didn't ignite. It simply blackened and collapsed into pale dust, as though comfort itself had been declared contraband.

Miriam made a sound in her throat—half sob, half fury. "That was for the night," she whispered.

Eliah spoke again, and this time it wasn't an observation offered carefully so no one could accuse him of pushing. It was a refusal that came out rough, as if he'd had to drag it past his own teeth. "Nothing is being taken to teach us," he said, and his voice shook with cold and something worse than cold. "And nothing is being spared."

The fire did not respond—not with heat, not with mercy, not even with the satisfaction of flaring. It simply kept doing what it had been doing, which was its own kind of answer.

The Lantern watched Eliah the way a collector watches a coin he hasn't seen in years: not amused, not threatened, but newly attentive. He didn't move, because he didn't need to; the only thing that mattered was whether Eliah would keep speaking when silence would be easier.

At the edge of the firelight, Shim'on took a half step back—not retreating, not fleeing, but easing himself closer to shadow, as if already measuring how far a person could stand from a thing before it began to claim them.

The kneeling line thickened after that, not all at once, not dramatically, but with the slow efficiency of hunger. One more body folded, then another, and the sound gave it away—fabric rasping against stone, knees striking ground too hard to be reverent, breath breaking as people lowered themselves into whatever shape required the least resistance. They weren't worshiping so much as collapsing into the posture that promised relief, because fear always remembers old rituals even when faith is absent.

Eliah felt the shift as weight added to his spine, not guilt exactly, but expectation—the pressure of being turned into a lever. A man near the front lifted his head, eyes rimmed red and beard damp with breath, and his voice came out hoarse like it had scraped raw against his throat.

"If it isn't teaching us," he asked, "then what are we supposed to do?"

Shim'on's gaze lifted briefly at the question, then dropped back to the ground, jaw tightening—not in agreement, but in recognition of how quickly fear was looking for a mouth to speak through.

"I don't know," Eliah said, because anything else would have been performance.

The honesty landed badly. A murmur rippled through the kneeling line—not anger yet, but disappointment—like a support beam had failed and everyone felt the sag at once. Nadya inhaled sharply and stopped herself, and Cassian shifted his weight with his jaw set, while Gillie watched Eliah in that hard, quiet way she had when she was measuring whether mercy was still steady enough to trust.

The fire crackled and pulsed once, brighter, as if honesty itself had fed it.

"That's the trap," Rowan said quietly, eyes still on the fire. "It offers relief in exchange for precision."

The Lantern's smile was faint, but it was there—the look of someone hearing a line of doctrine repeated correctly. He didn't have to say much yet; the crowd was doing the work for him.

A man at the edge of the kneeling group staggered upright, swaying as if his legs didn't belong to him anymore. "It worked before," he said, voice cracking. "When we named things. When we said what was true."

Eliah turned his head slightly, as if giving that thought the respect of being examined rather than dismissed. "What was true?" he asked.

The man gestured helplessly, breath hitching as his words fought the cold. "That people make mistakes. That some of us—" He stopped, swallowed, forced it. "That some of us cause harm."

The fire leaned, and a brief flicker of orange licked its core—gone almost instantly, but not before several people gasped like they'd been touched.

"I felt that," someone whispered, and another answered, "So did I," with the desperation of someone begging their own body to believe the world can still bargain fairly. Then the cold surged back harder, punishing the momentary hope, and the warmth was gone so fast it felt like theft.

The Lantern's voice slid through the space smooth and almost regretful, as if he hated that this lesson had to be taught. "Truth stings," he said, "but it heals. Eventually."

Eliah flinched as if struck—not because the words were loud, but because they were familiar in the mouths of people who use them as permission. "No," he said too fast, and heads turned toward him immediately, hungry for contradiction. "It doesn't. Truth without care just moves the wound. It doesn't close it."

A woman laughed once—short, brittle. "Easy for you to say. You're not the one freezing on your knees."

The cold answered her words by pressing deeper into muscle and bone, the kind of pressure that doesn't feel like weather so much as a verdict.

Eliah stepped forward before he realized he was moving, not toward the fire but toward the kneeling line, and Gillie stiffened as if preparing to intercept him if the flame reacted. It didn't. Eliah crouched instead—slowly, carefully—bringing himself down to the woman's level until his knees hit stone hard enough to flash pain behind his eyes.

"I am," he said quietly when she stared at him, confusion breaking through her anger. His voice shook, and he didn't try to disguise it. "I'm freezing too."

The woman blinked, looking him over like she couldn't reconcile what she was seeing with what she needed to believe. "You're standing," she said weakly.

Eliah swallowed once. "I was," he replied. "I'm not now."

Shim'on watched Eliah drop, and something in his shoulders loosened and tightened at the same time—relief at the choice, fear of what it would cost. He didn't kneel, but he moved a step closer to the woman's flank, eyes on the line behind her, as if guarding against the moment when mercy gets mistaken for permission.

The fire crackled again, sharper this time, and blue tongues surged higher to devour another scrap of cloth someone had tried to tuck beneath a pack. Frost spidered across the stone at the edge of the scorch mark as if the ground itself were catching infection.

The Lantern watched closely, because this was not the response he wanted from Eliah—not compliance, not collapse, but presence. "Careful," he said mildly, as if offering a gentle warning. "Mercy can become indulgence."

Eliah's jaw clenched, but he did not rise. "Then let it," he said. "I won't let it become cruelty."

The kneeling line wavered at that—some faces turning uncertain, others hardening as anger rose where fear had already been spent.

Sera's voice held alongside it, thin but present, and the Lantern's smile narrowed as he watched that steadiness refuse to break. "This is inefficient," he said softly. "You could end this."

Eliah looked up at him, eyes stinging with cold, breath dragging tight through his chest. "How?" he asked, because the question mattered even if the answer didn't.

"By letting the fire do what it was made to do," the Lantern replied, voice calm and surgical. "By naming what deserves to be burned."

A shudder ran through the crowd, and several heads bowed deeper despite themselves, hope flaring in the same place hunger lived.

Eliah felt the pull then—not toward judgment, but toward relief. The temptation wasn't power; it was rest, one sentence and one decision and one weight finally set down. His hands shook violently, so he pressed them flat to his thighs to steady them, fingers numb against cloth.

"No," he said again, quieter now, and the Lantern's eyes narrowed as if measuring whether quietness meant weakening.

"You're choosing disorder," the Lantern said.

Eliah's voice came out hoarse, but it did not bend. "I'm choosing people."

The fire screamed—not audibly, but in a surge so unmistakable several pilgrims cried out as if they'd heard it anyway. Blue flames leapt, consuming the last intact bedroll; a walking staff blackened and collapsed into pale dust; a child cried out again as the cold spiked sharply enough to bloom pain across skin. Shouts broke loose—"Stop him!" "Say something!" "Do something!"—and the whole clearing turned toward Eliah, not Nadya, not Gillie, not even the Lantern, because mercy that refuses to judge becomes unbearable when bodies are the ones paying.

Shim'on lifted his chin toward the crowd—not defiant, not pleading. Just a steady look that said: you're about to do something you'll call necessary. His mouth tightened. He didn't speak. He stayed.

Eliah closed his eyes, and for one terrible heartbeat he almost spoke the sentence that would buy relief at someone else's expense. When he opened them again, his refusal looked less like confidence and more like endurance. "No one is being named," he said hoarsely. "Not tonight."

The cold held. The fire did not go out. But the Lantern's expression finally changed—not into anger yet, but into calculation, because Eliah had not broken, and he had not withdrawn mercy.

That meant the plague would have to work harder.

The Discipline of Fire

With the cold came penetration.

It did not strike all at once, but worked inward with patience. Fingers stiffened first, joints aching as if twisted slightly out of place, followed by breath shortening—not from panic, but reluctance, lungs refusing air that offered nothing back. The fire still burned behind us, blue tongues licking higher against the dark, casting long shadows that looked warmer than they were. Light moved freely. Heat did not.

Someone laughed once, a thin, brittle sound that snapped off almost immediately, embarrassed by its own existence.

"We should move closer," a pilgrim said, edging toward the flame. He held his hands out, palms spread, as if asking a question the fire refused to answer. His breath fogged white, then thinned as he leaned nearer. "It looks… stronger."

Gillie shook her head before he could take another step. "It's not." She knew without touching it. The Balanced Blade at her side hummed faintly, not warning, not approving—only registering the wrongness of the thing, the sound skittering across the metal like frost.

The Lantern had not left.

He stood just beyond the reach of the firelight, where shadow folded neatly around his outline, his glow muted and disciplined, like a man who had learned restraint and expected credit for it. He watched the group the way one watches a field after sowing—patient, certain something would rise.

The cold deepened.

A woman wrapped her arms around herself and rocked on her heels. "It's getting worse," she whispered. "It's getting colder the more it burns."

"That's not possible," another muttered, though his teeth chattered as he spoke.

Shim'on stood near the edge of the circle, not far enough to escape the cold, not near enough to be counted among the kneeling. He rubbed his hands once and stopped, as if unwilling to ask even friction for comfort. His eyes moved constantly—fire, Lantern, pilgrims—measuring who was leaning and who was about to.

Joshua remained where the dark had left him—on the far side of the fire, closer to the Lantern's light than to the circle of pilgrims. He did not sit with them, nor apart in defiance. He sat claimed. The flames painted his face in blue and shadow, sharpening the planes of his cheeks, hollowing his eyes until he looked less like a man resting and more like something placed where it could be seen.

His hands lay loose in his lap. His head was bowed.

And he hummed.

Not loud. Not steady. But present—a rough thread of sound that refused to vanish even where it did not belong.

The Lantern tilted his head, listening.

Sera felt the cold most sharply in her chest—not pain, but pressure, like the absence of something that should have been there. Her hum wavered as breath resisted, then steadied again as she pressed it lower, forced it into muscle and bone. She tasted iron and swallowed it down.

Around them, pilgrims shifted, stamping feet and rubbing arms. The fire flared brighter, devouring scraps of cloth, a broken bowl, a discarded pack strap thrown too close in desperation. Each offering vanished in a hiss of blue-white flame, and with every loss the cold seemed to sharpen, as if the world were tallying what they no longer had.

The Lantern smiled.

"Strange," he said mildly, stepping forward just enough that his light touched the edge of the group. "So much fire. So little comfort."

No one answered him.

"You wanted heat," he continued, gesturing toward the flames. "You refused shelter. Now you have exactly what you asked for."

A man near the edge dropped to one knee—not fully kneeling, just folding in on himself as if his body had reached a limit before his will had. "Make it stop," he said hoarsely. "Please. I can't—"

The Lantern raised a hand—not to command, but to settle them.

"I asked you to bow," he said calmly. "Because bending is easier when it's chosen. Understanding comes after."

"Understand what?" Nadya snapped. Her voice cut sharp through the cold. "That you enjoy this?"

A ripple went through the group. Some nodded. Others looked away.

The Lantern's gaze lingered on Nadya—acknowledgment, not hunger—before sliding past her. It landed on Eliah. And stayed.

"You enjoy clarity," the Lantern said softly, eyes never leaving him now. "So do I."

The word stirred the fire. For a heartbeat, the blue flickered—orange flaring briefly at its core, a breath of warmth brushing skin before vanishing again.

Several people gasped.

"You felt that," the Lantern said. "Didn't you?"

A murmur rose—yes, for a moment—and then the cold rushed back in harder, crueler for the tease.

"What did you do?" a woman demanded, eyes bright with hope and fear tangled together.

"I spoke truth," the Lantern said, and let it settle. "Fire is honest. It responds to what is named. What is hidden freezes. What is confessed burns clean."

Sera felt something shift—not in the fire, but between people. Attention sharpened, turned inward, then sideways.

"Name the guilty," the Lantern said, voice calm and reasonable. "And the fire will warm."

Silence fell, heavy.

Micah's plumb swayed once, then stilled. The cord hung stiff with frost.

"The difficulty," he said carefully, "is definition."

Several heads turned toward him.

"Guilt isn't stable," Micah continued, voice level, measured. "If you want it to hold, it has to be specific. Fear spreads. It blurs."

The Lantern's gaze flicked to him—quick, assessing.

Micah inclined his head slightly. "Fear is present in everyone here. If that's the measure, the fire won't know where to stay."

The Lantern stepped closer to the flame. He lifted a hand.

"The guilt here," he said quietly, "is fear."

The fire flared—orange blooming for two full breaths. Warmth washed over the nearest pilgrims. Shoulders dropped. Someone sobbed.

Then the color drained away. Blue reclaimed the flame, and the cold snapped back sharper than before.

A woman laughed, half hysterical. "It worked," she said. "For a second—it worked."

Micah watched the fire settle, expression unreadable.

"Truth always works," the Lantern replied. "Briefly. Until it is finished."

"Then it needs refinement," he added softly.

Eyes turned, searching, measuring.

"That wasn't truth," Shim'on said quietly from the edge. His voice didn't rise, but it carried. "That was accusation."

The Lantern tilted his head. "Are they so different?"

Shim'on didn't answer immediately. He stepped half a pace forward—not toward the fire, but into clearer sight. "One asks for change," he said. "The other asks for a body."

The cold bit deeper.

A young man near the fire hugged himself. “I don’t care what you call it,” he said. “I just want to feel my hands again.”

“Then speak,” the Lantern said gently. “The fire listens.”

There was a pause. Then, hesitantly, another voice joined.

“It’s him,” someone said, pointing toward Joshua. “Ever since he started humming—”

Joshua’s head lifted slightly. The hum did not stop.

The fire surged, orange flickering stronger this time. Heat licked outward, touching more skin, and a collective breath shuddered through the group.

Shame twisted Sera’s gut. “That’s not—” Gillie began.

The warmth faded.

Colder than before.

The pilgrim who had spoken staggered, clutching his arms. “It worked,” he insisted. “I felt it. We just—we need to say it clearly.”

Eliah’s hands trembled—not from fear alone, but restraint. He stood rigid, breath shallow, teeth chattering hard enough that his jaw ached. He could feel the pull to end it—to give the fire a name, to offer a sacrifice and call it guidance.

The Lantern turned fully toward him. “You see it,” he said. “You always do.”

Eliah did not answer.

“Say it,” the Lantern urged, voice kind. “Guide them.”

The fire crackled, devouring another scrap—someone’s blanket this time. Blue flames swallowed it whole, and its owner cried out.

“Say it,” the Lantern repeated.

Shim’on’s gaze moved to Eliah—not pleading, not commanding. Watching.

Eliah swallowed, thoughts colliding—of the traveler shamed earlier, of bread blackening in Miriam's hands, of mercy mocked, of order dissolving.

"If someone caused this," Nadya said carefully beside him, watching him now instead of the fire, "then naming it matters."

The fire leapt—orange blazing, heat surging outward. People cried out, some laughing, some weeping. For three breaths, the world felt almost bearable.

Then the warmth died.

The cold returned like punishment.

"Do it again!" a woman screamed.

Another voice joined. "Say who it is!"

Accusations began to fly—not shouted at first but offered. He didn't share. She hesitated. They argued. Each name brought warmth, and each warmth vanished faster than the last.

The Lantern watched, pleased. "This is justice," he said softly.

Sera's hum strained, climbing, pain threaded through every note. "Stop," she cried. "This isn't helping."

"They're warmer when they speak," the Lantern replied calmly.

"Only for a moment," she shot back. "And it costs someone else."

The fire flared again as someone shouted Eliah's name. He flinched as warmth brushed his skin, the relief immediate and horrifying.

"This is not warmth," Shim'on said sharply. "It's reward."

"Reward for courage," the Lantern corrected. "For saying what others fear."

"Or for feeding the fire," Gillie snapped, as another pack burned, then a staff, then dried reeds meant for sleep.

"Please," a pilgrim sobbed. "I'll say whatever you want."

"Then bow," the Lantern said.

Several did—not fully, not yet.

Shim'on did not.

He took a step forward instead, not into the firelight but into the line of sight of those kneeling, as if daring them to notice the difference between bending and choosing.

Sera's hum grew louder, raw enough to scrape her throat.

Joshua's rough, imperfect hum did not rise to meet it.

It slid beneath it instead—lower, heavier, threaded with something older than comfort. The fire did not warm, did not soften—but it steadied. The flare collapsed into a hard, listening burn, blue tongues tightening as if restrained by an invisible hand.

The Lantern stiffened.

Not because the fire failed—

But because it obeyed the wrong voice.

"Enough," he snapped, sharp now, fury cutting through restraint. "That is not your role."

The fire surged again, blue-white fury consuming the last comforts.

But the cold did not worsen.

Something had shifted.

"It's… not hurting as much," someone whispered.

Eliah stood shaking, uncomforted and unarmed. He did not speak, and because he did not, the fire found no name.

The Lantern's smile thinned. "This is only the beginning," he said softly.

The flames stayed. Joshua kept humming. Sera did not stop.

And Shim'on remained standing.

The cold held—waiting to see who would break first.

Mercy Without Shelter

The cold did not advance, and that was what unsettled them most. It remained steady, inhabiting the body rather than attacking it—no longer sharp enough to command panic and no longer cruel enough to force decision. Instead, it settled into joints and lungs, into the soft places behind the eyes, until every breath had to pass through it first. Fingers ached but still obeyed. Teeth stopped chattering. Pain dulled into something closer to endurance.

And endurance made room for thought.

Shim'on stood a few paces back from the kneeling line, arms folded tight against his chest, weight shifting from heel to heel as if the ground itself made him uneasy. He hadn't knelt. He hadn't stepped forward either. He watched the fire the way someone watches a door they're afraid might open.

The fire continued to burn behind them, blue tongues folding and unfolding with patient appetite. It no longer lunged for what was offered, no longer reached greedily for scraps. It waited instead, a watcher rather than a predator, its scorch mark widening by degrees so small they felt imagined, the edges glowing faintly as if the stone remembered warmth and resented its absence.

A murmur moved through the kneeling pilgrims—not prayer, not gratitude, but comparison.

Shim'on did not join the murmuring. His gaze flicked from face to face instead, cataloging expressions the way someone memorizes exits. When one of the kneeling men smiled in relief, Shim'on flinched—not at the cold, but at the smile itself.

"I don't feel it as badly," someone whispered.

Another voice answered, barely audible. "Me neither."

A man who had bowed fully, forehead pressed to stone and shoulders curved inward in the shape of surrender, lifted his head. His eyes were glassy but alert, his mouth pulled into a smile that looked almost apologetic. "It's warmer down here," he said. "You should try it."

Gillie turned sharply. "No," she said. "It isn't."

The man frowned, confused. "It is," he insisted. "I can feel my hands again."

"You feel relief," Gillie replied. "Not warmth."

The Lantern watched from the edge of the firelight, posture relaxed, hands folded as if attending a lesson he had taught many times before. "That," he said pleasantly, "is the first lie comfort tells."

The cold tightened around those still standing—not enough to punish, just enough to remind.

Lucien's voice drifted in from the reeds, smooth and precise. "He's not wrong," he said. "It is warmer. For now."

Julian stepped into view beside him, smile sharp with theatrical sympathy. "You always ruin things by talking about later," he said. "Let them enjoy the moment."

Kali's laughter followed, low and delighted. "Moments are all they have left."

Raven's voice came last, nearer than expected, sliding along the edges of the circle. "Bow," he whispered—not as command, but invitation. "Just enough."

Several pilgrims flinched.

Shim'on's jaw tightened. He took a single step backward—not dramatic, just enough to put space between himself and the word, as if distance alone could keep it from lodging in his body. He glanced once at the kneeling man's hands, then away, like he couldn't stand to watch relief being priced.

Gillie felt the word strike like remembered pain. She turned, voice carrying. "You remember that," she said. "They said bow. Then bend. Then break."

Some nodded.

Others didn't want to.

Marcus stepped forward, his presence heavy and deliberate. "Breaking isn't always violent," he said calmly. "Sometimes it feels like relief."

Elana appeared beside him, eyes kind, hands open. "And broken things don't ache," she added gently. "They don't argue. They rest."

The cold answered her words with a subtle easing—just enough to be felt.

A woman gasped. "I—I feel it," she said. "They're right."

The Lantern inclined his head. "Truth," he said. "Spoken plainly."

Gillie moved before the relief could settle.

"That's not how it looked."

Her voice didn't cut. It remembered.

"I watched you break," she said, eyes fixed on Marcus. "Every time they told you to."

Marcus's jaw tightened—just enough to be noticed.

I joined her—not beside her, but with her, the memory already rising in my throat.

"We heard the commands," I said. "From the shadows. From the ones who didn't have to feel it."

I didn't raise my voice.

"Bow."

"Bend."

"Break."

The easing cold recoiled, uncertainty rippling through it.

"And every time," I continued, "your bodies locked. Your breath seized. You shook—not because you chose stillness, but because pain left you no other option."

Elana's expression faltered, kindness slipping for a fraction of a second.

"That wasn't rest," Gillie said. "That was obedience taught through pain."

Marcus exhaled slowly. "Sometimes," he said carefully, "it feels like relief."

"So does silence," Gillie replied. "When you're finally afraid to speak."

"So does numbness," I added. "When safety has already been taken away."

The cold crept back in—not sharper, not crueler, but stripped of its false kindness.

The Lantern did not smile this time.

"Interesting," he said mildly.

The fire flickered, orange pulsing once at its core, as if undecided.

Eliah felt the pull then—not hunger, not fear, but something older than either, something the cold had made honest.

The desire to be done.

To end this in a way that felt clean. To give the suffering a shape. To give the group a single motion they could all agree on so the air would stop trembling with indecision.

Mercy required staying inside the mess. Mercy required time. Mercy required letting people remain complicated while you remained present.

But the cold made patience feel like cruelty.

Judgment promised speed. Judgment promised a door. A verdict. A hinge that would shut and keep the wind out.

Micah stepped closer to the fire.

Shim'on moved the opposite direction, edging toward the darker boundary of the clearing. He said nothing, but his shoulders drew inward, as if bracing against a tide he refused to let carry him.

Gillie caught his sleeve. "Don't."

He shook her off gently. "They're not wrong," he said, voice strained. "The cold isn't advancing. It's waiting."

"Because it wants you to finish the work," Gillie said.

Micah didn't answer.

Lucien smiled. "See how well he understands?" he said. "Discernment is such a gift."

Julian clapped softly. "You trained him beautifully."

The Lantern did not correct them.

A pilgrim stood and pointed at Eliah. "You almost fixed it before," he said. "When you stopped everyone from tearing into each other."

Others nodded. Hope stirred—dangerous, bright.

"You can do it again," someone urged. "Say the right thing."

The fire flickered again—brief, tempting. Warmth brushed skin, and a collective sound rose—half sob, half laugh.

"Again," someone begged. "Please."

Eliah closed his eyes.

When he opened them, he did not look at the fire.

He looked at the people.

"Listen," he said.

His voice did not command. It steadied.

"I'm going to tell you something," he continued. "Not to accuse anyone. Not to pick a target. Not to give you a shortcut. I'm going to tell you what this is actually asking for."

The Lantern tilted his head, curious.

Joshua's hum wavered—just a fraction.

"There was a time," Eliah said, "when pilgrims followed Marcus."

The air shifted at the name—not because it was new, but because it was familiar. A memory in the bones. A story told around fires like warnings, always simplified, always edited into something easier to swallow.

"They were tired," Eliah said. "Tired the way you're tired now. Worn down until pain felt like personality. They had watched the world break and decided the worst thing in the world was uncertainty."

The fire leaned, attentive.

"They wanted someone to blame," Eliah said, "because blame feels like control. And Marcus gave them control—not by warmth, but by direction."

Marcus did not move. His stillness felt instructional.

"They called it protection," Eliah continued. "They called it order. They called it justice. But what they wanted was simpler than that."

His breath fogged white and thinned. "They wanted relief. And they wanted to believe relief could be earned by obedience."

Shim'on closed his eyes at that—not in agreement, but in recognition. His fingers curled once, then stilled, as if memory had reached for him and missed.

A murmur ran through the kneeling line, agreement without thought, the way bodies agree with whatever offers less pain.

"They bowed," Eliah said. "Not because they loved what was right, but because they wanted to stop hurting. They followed because following meant they didn't have to decide anymore."

The orange in the fire's heart pulsed again, brief as a blink.

"They learned the rules," Eliah said. "They learned how to move when he moved, how to speak when he spoke. They learned the posture of submission so well they began to confuse it for faith."

A pilgrim swallowed audibly. Another lowered her head further, as if posture itself could purchase safety.

"And then," Eliah said, "there came a day when someone among them needed mercy."

The cold tightened—not to punish, but to listen.

"It wasn't spectacle," Eliah continued. "It was small. Human. A misstep. A fear. A moment where someone didn't do the right thing fast enough."

The fire did not flare. It waited.

"The pilgrims demanded judgment," Eliah said. "They didn't call it cruelty. They called it clarity. They said mercy would make everything weak. They said mercy would rot the world."

Kali's laugh threaded softly through the reeds. Julian echoed the word mercy with amused disdain.

Eliah did not look at them.

"Someone tried to speak mercy anyway," he said. "Not loudly. Not dramatically. Just present. Just refusing to turn pain into a weapon."

Joshua's shoulders tightened, recognition without consent.

"The pilgrims hated that," Eliah said. "Not because it was wrong. Because it didn't pay them back."

His hands trembled slightly at his sides, numbness pretending it wasn't.

"They asked: If mercy is real, why are we still hurting? If we bowed, why aren't we warm? If we obeyed, why aren't we safe?"

The fire pulsed orange for half a breath, warmth brushing faces, then vanishing like a lie corrected.

"And when mercy didn't give them relief," Eliah said, "they turned on the one who offered it. Because the easiest way to hate your suffering is to hate the person who refuses to justify it."

Lucien exhaled, pleased. "Mercy disappoints."

Eliah's gaze sharpened, not at Lucien, but at the listening bodies. "Do you understand what happened?" he asked. "No one felt warm. No one was applauded. Mercy did not work."

A kneeling man rasped, "Then what's the point?"

Eliah held his gaze. "The point was that mercy stayed."

His words sank rather than rose. "It stayed when judgment would have made everyone feel powerful. It stayed when doing the right thing didn't work."

The cold pressed heavier with meaning.

"And the pilgrims," Eliah said, "called that weakness."

Raven whispered, eager. "Because it is."

Eliah turned slightly, keeping the fire behind him as witness rather than comfort. "Mercy doesn't reward bowing," he said. "Mercy doesn't bargain. Mercy doesn't say: give me submission and I'll give you warmth."

Resentment stirred. Hunger to turn pain into currency.

"That's why this works on you," Eliah said quietly. "Because you want the fire to approve of you."

The orange pulse answered, precise and seductive, and several pilgrims gasped as if named.

Eliah swallowed iron. "In Marcus's line, covenant meant protection for obedience. Bow and be spared. Join and be untouched."

He shook his head. "That isn't covenant. That's a deal."

The fire waited.

"And when deals fail," Eliah said, "people don't repent. They accuse. They demand a price. They demand someone else's body so their own can feel lighter."

A woman cried, "But we're freezing."

"I know," Eliah said, and did not soften it. "And that's why this temptation is so clean."

The fire pulsed faster, like a heartbeat seeking rhythm.

"You want me to complete it," Eliah said softly. "You want me to turn mercy into a lever."

The fire leaned.

Eliah did not.

"No," he said.

The orange vanished. The cold did not worsen. It simply remained.

The silence that followed was not empty. It was listening.

Shim'on remained standing. He did not speak. He did not kneel. He simply stayed where he was, breathing through the cold without asking it to become anything else.

Joshua's hum continued—ragged, stubborn. Sera's voice wove around it.

And Eliah stood between the kneeling line and the watching reeds, not as judge, not as savior—only as someone refusing to turn mercy into proof.

Shim'on shifted closer to the group then—not enough to be seen as joining, just enough that no one could say he had left.

The Measure of Mercy

The fire waited, and it had learned patience from the way we had not finished what it was training us to do. Its blue tongues folded inward, light thinning but never dying, as if the flame itself were listening for permission it had not yet been granted. The cold held steady too—no longer sharpening, no longer coaxing, simply present in every breath and joint, and in the tiny hesitations that formed between us, breath catching where bodies should have trusted one another. No verdict had been given, no relief purchased, and the circle the Lantern had been training them to complete remained stubbornly open.

Eliah stood where he had refused to finish the bargain, chest tight and lungs burning with air that no longer promised anything back. His hands trembled, not with fear, but with the weight of what he had chosen not to do—and what he had chosen to stay inside.

Around him, the pilgrims shifted uneasily, as if their bodies had been taught a sequence and now the music had stopped mid-measure. Some rose halfway from their kneel, uncertain whether obedience still mattered if it earned nothing; others stayed bowed, frozen between habit and hope, unsure whether standing would now be counted against them. Even their silence felt different—less worshipful, more hungry, as if they were waiting to be told what kind of suffering they were allowed to have.

Shim'on did not kneel. He stood just outside the loose arc of bodies, far enough back that no one had asked him to bow, close enough that he could not pretend this was not his concern. His arms were folded tight, shoulders drawn inward, as if he were holding himself together against a decision he refused to make for anyone else. Once, he glanced toward the reeds, then toward the pilgrims' backs, like he was already marking where the first rush would come from.

The Lantern watched it all begin to unravel, and the ease he had worn so carefully finally cracked. His posture remained upright and his glow stayed contained, but something in the quality of his light sharpened and compressed. When he spoke, the word did not sound like language so much as something spoiled. "Mercy," he said, and then he let the word hang there, as if the air itself should recoil.

"You would offer mercy," the Lantern continued, voice low and precise, "as if it were virtue—when it is weakness dressed up as patience."

His gaze cut to Eliah as if to make the accusation personal, and the fire behind them tightened in response, not flaring or dimming but drawing inward as though bracing.

"They bowed," he said, stepping forward now, boots crunching against frost-stiffened ground. "They yielded. They offered themselves to the mechanism you exposed, and you refused to use them."

The contempt in him did not need volume; it only needed clarity. He flicked his eyes toward the kneeling pilgrims as if they were proof of how right he was, then returned to Eliah with something sharper than anger—offense.

"You stood between suffering and resolution," he said, and his voice rose enough to cut through the clearing, "and you called that righteousness." A short laugh escaped him, humorless. "Mercy is for the weak," he said. "For those who cannot finish what pain begins."

Shim'on shifted his weight, boots scraping softly against frost. His eyes flicked from the Lantern to the fire and back again, not tracking authority, but measuring consequence. His hands loosened at his sides—ready, not dramatic.

Joshua did not lift his head. He remained seated apart, hands loose, shoulders drawn inward against the cold, and he kept humming—uneven and human and stubborn, a thread of breath refusing to be trained into silence. That sound broke something the Lantern had been holding together by will alone. His composure snapped, not gradually, but all at once. "You dare keep him breathing like that?" he snarled. "You dare let him remember himself?"

The light around the Lantern changed as if the air itself had been pulled tight. It did not burst outward; it condensed, pressure building like a held breath refusing release.

"Mercy does not heal," he roared, and the frost at his feet steamed as if his fury could scorch what cold had claimed. "It corrupts. It teaches people that suffering has no teeth, that obedience is optional, that covenants mean nothing unless they are enforced."

He turned sharply, sweeping his arm toward the reeds as if calling a judgment he had been saving for when persuasion failed.

"Enough."

The command did not need to be loud. It did not need to be repeated. The reeds answered.

They rose from shadow and mist with practiced coordination, shapes unfolding as if they had been waiting for the exact moment the Lantern would stop pretending this was still a lesson. Lucien stepped forward first, expression sharpened into something predatory and precise. Julian followed, already grinning, hands flexing as if eager for applause. Kali's laughter threaded through the air bright and vicious, and Raven slipped along the perimeter so quietly he seemed more absence than movement. Marcus advanced last—measured, heavy, inevitable—and the pilgrims cried out as the air became harder to breathe, not colder exactly, but resistant, endurance turning into strain.

Shim'on took one step farther back as the reeds emerged—not in retreat, but in refusal. Then he moved sideways, putting himself near the edge of the kneeling line, close enough to catch someone if they bolted, close enough to block a panic-stampede from crushing a smaller body.

Eliah felt the shift then, and it was not fear. Something in his chest loosened—not like relief or warmth, but like a knot untied after being carried too long. The ache that had lived there since before the fire, since before the cold, since before the first bargain had ever been offered, released its grip as if it had finally been given permission to stop bracing. He inhaled sharply, and what rose from him did not come as spectacle or force. It lifted instead: a thin filament, disciplined and steady, drawing free of his chest the way breath leaves lungs when it is no longer being forced.

The filament crossed the space between them without heat, without reminder, without permission, and the Lantern saw it. "No," he hissed, sudden and raw. But it was already moving, already done, and when it entered Joshua the effect was immediate—not a dramatic throwback, not a collapse, but a settling so deep it looked like a body remembering how to be inside itself. Joshua folded inward as if struck by a truth his bones recognized, shoulders curling as something long misaligned finally found its place. A sound tore from his throat, raw and involuntary, more animal than word, and then the hum returned—not searching, not pleading, but anchored.

Shim'on felt it too—not as touch, but as pressure shifting in the air, like weight transferred without ceremony. His breath caught, then steadied. His chin lifted a fraction, as if he'd just decided what mattered more than being seen.

The fire shuddered as if its appetite had been interrupted. Its blue tongues pulled inward, light thinning as though starved of something it could no longer extract, and the scorch mark on the stone stopped spreading. The edges dulled, heat bleeding away without permission, the flame still present but no longer expanding its claim.

The cold remained, but it changed in the way weather changes when a storm gives up trying to become a verdict. It stopped pressing for decision, stopped asking for blood, and became simply unpleasant—inescapable, insufficient, and suddenly unable to make anyone prove anything.

The Lantern screamed, and the sound tore through the clearing like a blade on stone. His polish vanished in an instant, replaced by something naked and furious that could not tolerate being resisted without being obeyed.

"You dare," he roared, stepping forward as his light flared violently, radiating heat that turned frost to steam and breath to knives. "You steal from me with restraint? You undo my work by refusing to finish it?"

His eyes burned through the clearing, through Eliah, through Joshua, through every one of us who had tasted the lie and now had to live without it.

"Kill them," he ordered, not shouted—placed into the world like law.

The reeds exploded into motion.

Lucien moved first, gestures sharp and deliberate, snapping threads of false warmth through the air—relief shaped like kindness that burned on contact. Julian followed with wild laughter, hurling force without care for aim, delighting in chaos. Kali surged forward, sound itself becoming weapon, her laughter shattering focus and turning fear into frenzy. Raven struck from behind—as he always did—his presence only understood when something vital was already gone, when a scream arrived late, when a body fell without anyone seeing the moment it was taken.

Marcus came straight through the center, and there was nothing theatrical about him. Each step carried a verdict, each strike heavy enough to break ground, his expression calm as if violence merely confirmed what he had always known. The pilgrims screamed, and some ran, and some froze, and some reached toward the fire again because desperation does not care what you promised yourself you would never do again.

Shim'on caught a pilgrim who stumbled backward into him—steadying her by the elbow, then pushing her down and aside, out of the first rush. "Down," he said once, low and urgent, and it wasn't a command so much as a way to keep her alive. Then he turned, eyes tracking Raven's movement like he'd learned to watch for things that arrive from behind.

Gillie drew steel, Micah shouted orders that barely carried over the roar, and Sera moved to Joshua's side with her voice threading through the chaos to keep his hum from being torn loose by shock and fear.

Eliah stood his ground, not because he believed he could stop what was coming, but because mercy had already been spent. There was no bargaining left in him to offer, no shortcut left to take, no clean sentence that would make the world feel ordered again.

The Lantern watched the battle ignite and his fury sharpened into satisfaction as pain returned to the equation, as if suffering finally made sense again now that it could be enforced. He gestured at Eliah, at Joshua, at the thin trembling line of light that had crossed between them, and his laugh carried disbelief sharpened into hatred.

"This," he said, voice cutting cold, "is your answer?"

His glow compressed hard and blinding. "You reduce judgment to endurance," he snarled. "You replace obedience with waiting. You call that mercy."

He stepped forward, and his eyes locked on Eliah with the kind of promise that is meant to be remembered later.

"This is not mercy," he said. "This is its measure—and it disgusts me."

Then he leaned in, voice lowering with the intimacy of a threat that expects to be fulfilled. "You will learn that refusing judgment does not end suffering. It only delays the accounting."

The fire did not answer him. Joshua's hum held. Steel rang. The clearing broke open into violence that no longer pretended to be plague, with Lucien's false warmth blistering skin and Julian's laughter splitting into command, with Kali's voice unraveling resolve and Raven striking from angles that felt like absence rather than motion. Marcus advanced without haste, each step a sentence, each strike delivered with the certainty of something that believed itself inevitable.

The Lantern watched with open satisfaction, because to him this was correction—obedience restored by force.

And then the scroll pulsed.

Not gently. Not as warning. It flared.

White-gold light tore outward from its surface in a single violent breath—authority made visible. It did not erase what was already happening; blows still landed, blood still struck stone, screams still carried. But the direction of violence broke apart as if the air itself had learned how to refuse certain trajectories, as if momentum could be denied without argument. The ground rang, weapons skidded, bodies hit stone and rose again with confusion in their eyes because the world had stopped behaving like a place that rewarded cruelty.

Marcus staggered—only once, and only half a step, but it was enough to change everything. The earth beneath him resisted his weight like memory made solid, and his jaw tightened as he lifted his gaze, not toward Joshua and not toward Eliah, but toward the scroll.

Raven recoiled fully, the shadow that carried him tearing at its own edges, thinning and unraveling, and the hiss that left him was not pain but recognition.

Elana cried out too—not loudly, not dramatically, but with the sharp involuntary sound of something remembering what it had been reduced to, her kindness cracking into naked fear before she could mask it.

Lucien swore. Julian stopped laughing. Kali's voice broke mid-note as her influence unraveled where the light scorched through it.

Shim'on flinched at the flare like everyone else—and then stepped into it, not toward the Lantern, but toward the nearest pilgrim who'd frozen mid-run. He grabbed her sleeve and hauled her behind him, into the edge of that white-gold boundary, as if he trusted it more than he trusted his own instincts.

The Lantern turned, and what he saw on his own side was not resistance.

It was fear.

Real fear, the kind that cannot be performed.

His composure shattered. "You remember," he snarled, voice tearing loose of its polish. "You remember what it did to you." The scroll burned brighter, and its light wrapped around us—not as shelter and not as shield, but as declaration. A boundary formed where commands lost cohesion, where false warmth collapsed before reaching flesh, where strikes landed wrong and momentum failed to complete itself.

The war did not stop. It changed shape.

Marcus forced himself forward through resistance, furious now, and the fury made him sloppy in the smallest ways—tiny corrections he hadn't needed before, costs he hadn't had to pay. Raven circled wider than before, his strikes shorter and faster, never lingering, never trusting the light. Elana retreated a step, then caught herself, shame and terror warring across her face.

The Lantern roared at them like a master watching trained beasts flinch. "You will not," he thundered, light sharpening into something cruel, "you will not be cowed by memory."

He stepped forward incandescent with wrath. "Mercy is rot," he spat. "It loosens vows. It leaves obedience unrewarded. It teaches submission without safety." His gaze burned through us and then pinned Joshua as if hate could force a soul back into the shape he preferred. "And you," he snarled, "you dare let it live again."

Joshua's hum surged—ragged, defiant—and it locked into the scroll's rhythm like a heartbeat that had finally remembered its purpose.

The scroll pulsed again, not brighter but deeper, and that depth mattered more than brightness ever could.

It did not end the assault. It endured it long enough to keep breath in lungs, long enough to keep feet beneath bodies, long enough to prevent erasure.

It was not victory. It was refusal.

The Lantern threw out his arm and his voice cut through the clearing like a blade. "Everything," he commanded. "Break them."

Lucien surged with precision turned lethal, Julian followed with intent sharpened, Kali forced her voice back into shape, Raven struck low and fast, and Marcus drove forward through the resisting world with fury eclipsing caution. The war continued—blood and steel and breath and light colliding in a clearing that could no longer pretend this was only a lesson.

Shim'on edged closer to us then—not enough to be counted, not enough to be claimed, but close enough that no one could say he had chosen the other side. He didn't announce himself. He just stayed within reach—where a hand could find his sleeve in the dark.

And beneath it all, settling like frost into us all, the truth became unavoidable:

This was no longer only a plague.

It was war.

And mercy—mercy that would not close the circle, mercy that would not purchase relief with a body—had just become unforgivable.

The Breaking of Vows

The Cost of Standing

The Lantern did not rush the moment. That was the cruelty of it—that even now, with bodies already falling and the clearing torn open by steel and sound, he allowed himself stillness. He stood amid the violence like a judge watching evidence arrange itself. Frost steamed around his boots. Light clung to him, compressed and unforgiving, as if even illumination had learned to harden.

"Do you hear it?" he called, his voice carrying above the clash—not louder, just cleaner, cutting through chaos the way truth once had. "That sound beneath the screaming?"

No one answered. No one could.

"Listen," he insisted, lifting his hands—not in command yet, not quite. "That is trust failing. That is faith buckling under weight it was never trained to carry."

A pilgrim near the treeline fell to their knees and bowed fully, forehead to stone, hands shaking as they stretched forward in offering. The Lantern's gaze flicked to them with mild interest.

"Not you," he said calmly.

Raven crossed the space in a blink. The bowing pilgrim never rose.

The Lantern did not look away when the body struck the ground.

"You mistake silence for submission," he continued, turning slowly, letting his light rake across the clearing. "You mistake proximity for covenant. You mistake mercy for loyalty."

"No," Shim'on said from the edge, voice rough and unused. He didn't shout. He didn't posture. "You mistake fear for agreement."

Lucien struck again, false warmth ripping through a cluster of pilgrims who had huddled together instinctively, arms thrown around one another as if closeness itself were protection. Skin blistered where the heat passed. One screamed and shoved another away, trying to flee. Julian laughed and sent them both sprawling.

Shim'on moved—quick, economical. He caught the one who fell hardest by the collar and dragged them behind a half-collapsed pack, out of the next arc of heat. "Stay down," he muttered, and the words weren't comfort. They were instruction for survival.

The Lantern nodded, satisfied.

"Look," he said softly. "See how quickly love becomes leverage."

The Lantern raised his voice at last.

"You were warned," he called. "Covenant is not comfort. It is constraint. It binds so that it may hold—and what will not hold must be broken."

Gillie staggered as another impact rattled her injured arm. Pain flared hot and white, nearly buckling her knees. Sera caught her without looking, teeth clenched, blood already streaking down her temple, and shoved her back toward Joshua—placing herself between Gillie and the next blow as if her own body were simply another barrier to be spent.

Joshua stood where the Lantern had placed him.

Not kneeling. Not advancing.

Standing.

He obeyed the command—but it was tearing him open to do so.

The hum in his chest wavered, not gone, not defiant, but strained—like breath held just past safety. The filament Eliah had given him still burned low in his core, unfamiliar and frightening in its steadiness. It did not erase his darkness. It illuminated it.

And that was worse.

He had believed—truly believed—that when the light left him, that was the verdict. That worthiness had an expiration. That redemption belonged only to those who had never broken covenant so completely.

Now something inside him whispered that he had been wrong.

Not innocent.

But not unreachable.

The Lantern felt the shift.

"You stand very still," he observed, eyes narrowing. "That is not the posture of obedience."

"I'm standing where you told me," Joshua said quietly.

"Yes," the Lantern replied. "But you are not bowing."

His voice sharpened.

"Bow."

Joshua hesitated—just long enough.

The Lantern's hand snapped downward.

"MAKE THEM BREAK."

The reeds answered as one.

Marcus surged forward like a verdict finally delivered. Lucien fanned outward, precision tightening into cruelty. Julian followed the sound of panic, targeting fractures with delighted efficiency. Kali's voice rose again, sharp and warping, laughter threaded with command. Raven vanished into motion, reappearing only where resistance had already failed.

The pilgrims shattered.

Not as a group—there was no group anymore—but as promises coming undone.

A man in a gray cloak stumbled backward toward the stones, dragging a woman by the wrist. She was limping—one ankle already swelling wrong beneath torn cloth—but she refused to slow, teeth clenched, refusing to let pain choose for her.

"Keep moving," he pleaded. "Just—just keep moving. I promised."

The word promised sounded fragile here. Like a child's prayer.

She tightened her grip. "Don't leave me," she said—not afraid of dying, but of being abandoned while alive.

A shadow slid between them.

Raven didn't strike immediately. He moved like a question, forcing them to choose where to look. The man saw him first and yanked the woman behind him, shoulders squaring in an old reflex that remembered protection better than fear.

The blade flashed low.

The woman screamed—not because she was cut, but because her husband folded as if something inside him had been switched off. He dropped to his knees, clutching his side, breath coming out wet and stunned.

"No," she whispered, grabbing him under the arms. "No—don't—don't—"

"I promised," he gasped, trying to stand.

The Lantern watched them with quiet approval.

"See?" he called. "How covenant becomes cruelty when it cannot be enforced."

The woman braced herself under her husband's weight and tried to drag him anyway. Her injured ankle buckled. They fell together. She clung to him, sobbing, begging him to breathe, to stay, to finish the vow with her.

Raven stepped in again.

When the man's hand slipped from hers, the promise seemed to leave with it.

The woman rose screaming—rage and disbelief tangled together—and Julian's force struck her mid-breath, slamming her into stone hard enough to silence the word why forever.

"This," the Lantern continued, his voice carrying as doctrine now, "is what happens when covenant is treated as sentiment instead of law."

Gillie cried out as a blade clipped her leg, pain finally catching her in full. She collapsed hard, breath torn loose—and the scroll answered.

Not with comfort.

With direction.

The pressure shifted through her body like hands at her shoulders, turning her just enough. She rolled instinctively, and the next strike skidded off stone instead of bone. She gasped, heart hammering, and understood without words: the scroll was not saving her.

It was guiding her.

Left. Now.

Sera felt it too. Her blade lifted a heartbeat earlier than instinct would have allowed, catching Raven's strike with a clang that rang wrong—too close, too loud. She staggered, barely holding, but she remained standing.

The scroll pulsed again—not brighter but deeper—and the rhythm passed through us like current through wire.

It did not stop blows. Blood still struck stone. Screams still tore the air.

But it refused erasure.

It altered timing. It bent trajectories. It turned certainty into hesitation and hesitation into breath. It kept bodies alive long enough to choose again.

I understood then that the scroll was not protecting us from pain.

It was protecting the possibility of faithfulness.

"Stay with it," I shouted—whether they heard me or only felt the same pull, I couldn't tell. "Don't scatter. Don't chase. Listen."

Micah heard it—and flinched.

Not from pain.

From recognition.

For the briefest instant, he did not look like a man being tested. He looked like a man calculating. His eyes tracked the clearing, not counting enemies, but bodies. The wounded. The ones who would not survive another minute of refusal.

It wasn't cowardice that moved through him.

It was leadership's oldest temptation: the belief that bending might save what breaking would destroy.

Lucien's false warmth slammed into his side before the thought could finish forming. Micah cried out and dropped to one knee, teeth bared, one hand clutching his ribs where the heat had passed too close to his heart.

The Lantern saw it.

"Ah," he said softly. "Leadership fractures first."

Micah forced himself upright, blood soaking his sleeve. His gaze flicked to the Lantern, then to Joshua—and for the smallest moment I saw it: not betrayal, not surrender, but the crack where strategy might masquerade as mercy.

If bowing ends this… how many lives is pride worth?

The scroll pulsed again, and Micah stiffened, jaw tightening as if resisting a truth he could not afford.

"No," he growled, voice rough with pain and something sharper. "Nobody bends."

"Not for this," Shim'on added. He didn't raise his voice. He didn't look at the Lantern. He stepped in closer to the line instead—close enough that if someone folded, he'd be there to haul them back before the reeds could claim the gap. He said it the way stone says no to water.

Still, the moment lingered like splintered wood in my chest.

The Lantern turned back to us all, his satisfaction sharpening.

"You still believe endurance is virtue," he said. "You think waiting sanctifies disobedience."

His light compressed violently around him.

"Then listen carefully," he said, voice dropping low, intimate, deadly. "Because what comes next will not ask you to stand."

The clearing quieted—not because the war paused, but because something worse had entered the air.

"What comes next," he continued, "will enter you where you keep your vows. Where you store your promises like coins you believe cannot be stolen."

His gaze swept the pilgrims, the wounded, the bodies bound together in death.

"I will not need steel," he said. "I will make you doubt what you love. I will make closeness feel like betrayal. I will make faithfulness feel like foolishness."

He smiled then, thin and terrible.

"You will beg to be allowed to break what you once called holy," he promised. "Because it will feel like the only mercy left."

He straightened.

"So bow," he commanded. "While bending still ends something."

Joshua inhaled sharply.

The filament inside him flared—not bright, but true—and for the first time since the fall, anger rose alongside shame.

"Stop," he said.

The Lantern froze.

"What did you say?"

"I said stop."

The Lantern's composure shattered into offense.

"You stand where you are told," he snarled. "You breathe because I allow it."

Joshua's hands trembled—but he did not bow.

"I thought," he said hoarsely, "that because I lost the light, I lost the right to hope."

"And now?" the Lantern demanded.

"And now I know I wasn't empty," Joshua said. "Just unfinished."

The Lantern screamed.

"BREAK HIM."

Marcus lunged.

The scroll burned—not outward, but between—and the ground beneath Marcus resisted like memory turned solid. He staggered half a step.

Enough.

Enough for Joshua to breathe.

Enough for mercy to remain unforgivable.

The Lantern shook with fury, light warping around him, and his voice cut through the clearing like a blade drawn slow.

"You will bow," he promised. "If not now—then by what I make you become."

And the war pressed in again—blood and steel and breath colliding under a threat that was no longer metaphor.

This was not yet the next horror.

This was the warning.

The Shape That Remained

The war did not stop when Kaela stepped forward.

Steel still rang. Breath still tore loose from lungs already raw. Bodies still fell in ways that made promises feel foolish. The clearing had learned nothing yet, and it was not ready to listen simply because one more soul refused to bow.

Kaela moved through the broken space without urgency, keeping low, staying aware, stepping where the scroll had already thinned the danger just enough for passage. She had been with us the whole time—quiet in the Hollow Fire, quieter still when the Lantern began pressing—but now her silence carried weight rather than absence. Blood streaked one sleeve of her coat, and ash marked her hands, ground into the creases of her palms as if she had knelt somewhere earlier, somewhere the war had not yet reached.

The Lantern saw her at once.

Not because she resisted him, and not because she glowed, but because the pressure that was breaking others seemed to slide past her without purchase. Pilgrims nearby faltered and turned inward, choices collapsing into instinct, but Kaela moved as if her footing had already been decided. The contrast unsettled the clearing more than any shout could have.

Joshua felt it before he understood what he was reacting to.

The filament inside his chest tightened sharply, not in pain and not in warning, but with a recognition that arrived too fast to argue with. His breath caught, and for a moment the sounds of the clearing dulled at the edges, as if something older had stepped closer than the present moment allowed. He tasted stone dust and remembered charcoal on fingers, remembered walls that would not accept straight lines no matter how carefully he tried.

He turned.

Kaela stood several paces away, watching him—not accusing, not pleading, simply present in a way that refused to let him disappear unnoticed.

"You're doing it again," she said.

The words were quiet, almost lost beneath the clash of steel, but they struck him harder than the Lantern's commands. He felt the familiar defense rise—obedience, positioning, endurance—but it faltered before it reached his mouth.

"I'm standing where I'm supposed to," he said instead, and even as he spoke it he knew how thin it sounded.

"That's not the same thing," Kaela replied. "You're fading."

The Lantern's laugh cut across the exchange, sharp and offended. He did not address her directly at first, as though acknowledging her would grant something he had not intended to give.

"Do you see this?" he called to the clearing. "Even now—when the cost is visible—there are still those who mistake presence for loyalty."

He turned toward Kaela at last, light tightening around him. "Step back," he ordered. "You complicate what is being corrected."

Kaela did not answer.

She knelt.

The motion was deliberate, not submissive. She lowered herself between two fallen bodies, one hand braced against stone as she found her balance, the other already moving before anyone could stop her. The scroll did not flare, but the current we'd been following tightened, as if the ground itself were listening.

Kaela pressed her fingers into ash and frost and traced a single, slow curve.

Just one.

Not a symbol made for display, and not an argument. A widening line that refused to close back on itself, drawn with the patience of someone who knew interruption was coming.

The Lantern's voice sharpened. "Erase that."

No one moved quickly enough.

Joshua stared at the curve as if it were breathing. Memory rose in him without permission—hands small and determined, charcoal dust smeared across skin, spirals drawn where straight lines had failed. He remembered irritation, remembered asking what it was supposed to mean, remembered being told that it didn't end and therefore couldn't be trapped.

His knees softened, and he had to fight not to lean forward.

"Don't bow," Kaela said to him, still kneeling, her voice steady despite the chaos pressing in from all sides. "And don't disappear."

The Lantern stepped forward, his light hardening into command. "Remove her," he snapped.

Marcus advanced, each step heavy with intent, but the ground resisted him again—not enough to stop him, but enough to fracture the certainty of his stride. The scroll held low and steady, not declaring authority and not retreating, simply refusing to yield the space Kaela occupied.

Raven moved faster, slipping in from the edge where the light was thinnest.

I felt the scroll pull—not away from Kaela, but toward her, threading presence around her like a boundary that was not a wall.

And Shim'on moved with it.

He didn't charge. He cut across behind Kaela in two quick steps and planted himself where Raven would have wanted an opening, shoulders squared, hands empty and ready. When a pilgrim stumbled into that gap, Shim'on caught them by the collar and shoved them down behind him, buying a breath without turning it into a rescue that could be praised.

"Stay," he said. Not comfort. Command-for-survival.

Raven's strike glanced, steel skidding where flesh should have been, and Sera was there a heartbeat later, blade catching the follow-through with a sound that rang too loud and too close.

Gillie dragged herself upright again, pain flaring sharp and bright through her leg, and followed the pull without thinking, each step guided just enough to keep her moving. Micah shouted for the line to hold, his voice rough with strain, and forced himself into motion, colliding with Marcus in a brutal exchange that sent both of them staggering.

Kaela finished the curve and lifted her hand.

It was imperfect—ash smudged, frost breaking its continuity—but it held.

The Lantern paused, just long enough for the hesitation to matter.

"That shape," he said, quieter now, irritation threading into something closer to unease. "It teaches disobedience."

"It teaches pause," Shim'on said from behind the line. He didn't raise his voice. He didn't look away from the angles where Raven hunted. "And you hate anything that doesn't hurry to obey."

Kaela rose slowly to her feet, brushing ash from her palm without ceremony. "No," she said. "It teaches return."

She looked at Joshua—not commanding him and not pleading.

"Come back," she said.

Not to her.

To himself.

Joshua took one step before he realized he had moved.

The Lantern's scream tore through the clearing, rage snapping his composure cleanly in two, and the war surged again around a truth that had not yet been paid for but could no longer be ignored.

Kaela had not ended anything.

She had interrupted it.

And that interruption—small, imperfect, already under attack—began to change the way the clearing moved.

The violence bent around her. Strikes that should have finished glanced wrong. Momentum faltered at the last possible moment. The clearing no longer moved with the clean efficiency the Lantern demanded. There was drag now—hesitation, friction, breath returned where breath should have been taken.

The Lantern felt it immediately.

His light sharpened again, brightening not outward but inward, compressing with irritation that bordered on offense. He had built this moment carefully—pressure calibrated to force submission, fear shaped into obedience—and now something was misaligning it. Not defiance. Not rebellion.

Interruption.

"Do you feel that?" he called, his voice cutting through the noise with deliberate calm. "That hesitation? That uncertainty?"

Lucien struck again, false warmth lashing outward in precise arcs, but bodies twisted away just enough, hands slipped, footing failed. Julian's laughter faltered into something harsher as his blows landed with less spectacle and more effort. Even Kali's voice, sharp and commanding, wavered at the edges, influence thinning where the spiral's presence tugged at the air.

"This," the Lantern said, gesturing sharply toward Kaela, "is contamination."

Kaela did not answer him.

She stood now, close enough to Joshua that retreat would require conscious effort. The spiral at her feet remained—a partial curve in ash and frost, already scuffed by boots and blood—but it continued to insist.

Joshua's breathing steadied in spite of himself.

The filament inside him warmed—not flaring, not healing, but anchoring him just enough that the Lantern's commands no longer slid cleanly into place. For the first time since the clearing broke open, Joshua was aware of his own weight again, the way his feet met the ground, the way his breath belonged to him rather than to expectation.

And that awareness terrified him.

If he stayed like this—present, connected—then what he did next would matter.

The Lantern turned his full attention on him.

"You feel it," he said, voice smooth again, coaxing rather than commanding. "That pull back toward consequence. Toward choice."

Joshua did not answer.

"You could end this," the Lantern continued, stepping closer, light pressing in. "You could shape the suffering instead of letting it scatter. You could give them a structure they understand."

Joshua's gaze flicked, just once, toward the pilgrims still falling, still breaking under blows meant to teach them something they did not have language for. Toward Micah, bloodied and straining to hold a line that barely existed anymore. Toward Gillie, dragging herself upright again despite pain that should have stopped her.

The thought slid into him with horrifying ease.

He could stop this faster.

Kaela saw it cross his face.

Her hand lifted—not touching him, not restraining him, simply entering his field of vision like a reminder he had asked for once, long ago, without realizing it.

"That's how it breaks," she said quietly. "You don't betray anyone. You just decide for them."

Joshua swallowed hard.

"I don't want them to die," he said.

"I know," Kaela replied. "That doesn't make it safe."

The Lantern smiled, thin and patient, sensing the tension where he could press. "Hear her," he said mockingly. "Hear how fear dresses itself up as wisdom."

He raised his voice again, sharp enough to cut through the clearing.

"You are watching covenant fail," he announced. "Not because it was violated—but because it was shared."

He turned toward the reeds.

"Pressure," he ordered. "Increase it. Separate them."

The command rippled outward, and the war responded by tightening. Marcus surged forward again, driving a wedge through the already-thinning line. Raven slipped deeper, faster, forcing the group to break formation or be flanked. Lucien shifted tactics, targeting not bodies but moments—striking where trust required timing, where one person depended on another to hold.

Micah felt it and shouted orders—too fast, too many—trying to compensate for a line that no longer behaved predictably. His gaze flicked again toward Joshua, then toward Kaela, irritation and doubt tangling in his expression.

"We can't hold like this," he snapped, more to himself than to anyone else. "We need to—"

The sentence died unfinished.

The scroll pulsed, deeper this time, and Micah felt it like resistance against his ribs, not forbidding him, but slowing him—forcing the thought to complete itself before becoming action.

Need to what?

Fold?

Bow?

Trade one command for another?

His jaw tightened.

Across the clearing, the Lantern noticed the hesitation and seized it.

"Say it," he urged Micah, voice carrying. "You know what ends this."

Micah's fists clenched. His gaze dropped for half a heartbeat, calculating again—bodies, distance, cost—and when he looked up, something brittle had entered his eyes.

Joshua took a step forward.

Not toward the Lantern.

Toward Micah.

"No," Joshua said, the word rough, unpolished, but real. "Don't."

Micah stared at him, shock flickering across his face. "You don't get to—"

"I know," Joshua cut in. "I don't get to command anything. But don't do this."

The Lantern laughed outright now, delighted.

"Look at you," he said. "Back among them. Back where failure becomes communal."

He gestured sharply.

"Make him choose," he ordered. "If he wants to stand with them, let him cost them something."

Marcus advanced again, this time angling directly toward Kaela.

The spiral at her feet darkened as ash smeared beneath his step, its curve partially crushed, its continuity broken in places. The Lantern's light flared in satisfaction.

"There," he said. "See how easily it fails."

Kaela did not retreat.

She stepped sideways instead, placing herself fully between Joshua and the advancing threat, her shoulder brushing his arm just enough to anchor him again.

"It doesn't fail," she said calmly. "It gets interrupted."

She looked back at Joshua, her voice steady despite the chaos closing in.

"So do you."

The Lantern's smile vanished.

Something like concern flickered across his expression—not fear, not yet, but calculation gone wrong.

"End this," he snapped. "Now."

The war surged again, but it no longer moved cleanly in his direction. Resistance had entered the system—not loud enough to win, not strong enough to stop the blows, but persistent enough to cost him time.

And time, in this place, was not neutral.

Kaela stood at the center of that cost, quiet and unarmed, holding a shape that refused to close while the Lantern learned—too late—that covenant, once carried, could no longer be fully commanded.

The Lantern adjusted.

It was not retreat. It was not escalation. It was something colder and more precise—the moment when force realizes it cannot win by pressure alone and turns instead to reinterpretation. His light dimmed just enough to lose its edge, softening into something that almost resembled restraint, and the change rippled outward through the reeds like a new set of instructions written into their bones.

"You misunderstand," he said, and his voice carried differently now—not as command, but as explanation. "I am not threatened by return."

The word lingered, tasted.

"I am threatened by who defines it."

The spiral at Kaela's feet no longer held cleanly. Ash had been smeared by boots and blood, its curve interrupted, its continuity scarred, and yet it remained legible—an unfinished shape insisting on itself even in fragments. The Lantern gestured toward it, almost gently.

"Do you see?" he said to Joshua. "It only works while it is untouched. While it costs nothing. While no one asks it to choose."

Joshua's breath caught. The filament inside him warmed again, but this time it pulled unevenly, as if something were being threaded through it without his consent. The Lantern stepped closer, careful now, circling rather than advancing.

"Return is not purity," he continued. "It is instability. It invites repetition. You know this."

Joshua did know it. He had lived it.

Every return he had ever attempted had carried the risk of breaking something again—trust, patience, belief. He had learned to mistake distance for safety, authority for restraint. The Lantern felt that memory and pressed it open.

"You come back," the Lantern said softly, "and you break them again."

The words landed harder than accusation.

Kaela turned toward Joshua, reading the shift immediately. "That's not true," she said.

The Lantern smiled. "Isn't it?"

He lifted his hand and pointed—not at Joshua, but at Micah.

"Look at him," he said. "Look how quickly leadership starts calculating. Look how close he is to bending—not out of fear, but out of responsibility."

Micah stiffened, anger flashing, but the Lantern did not stop.

"Return does that," he said. "It restores proximity. Proximity restores influence. Influence restores damage."

The war slowed around them—not stopping, but tightening into a ring of attention. Even Marcus hesitated now, waiting for the shape of the next command.

"You want to stand among them again?" the Lantern asked Joshua. "Then stand fully. Accept what comes with it."

Joshua's gaze flicked to Micah, to Gillie, to Sera holding the line with blood on her face and exhaustion in her stance. He felt the old instinct rise—the need to manage, to correct, to take weight onto himself so others wouldn't have to carry it.

He stepped forward.

Kaela's hand closed around his wrist.

Not hard.

Enough.

"Don't," she said quietly. "That's not return. That's control pretending to be sacrifice."

Joshua froze, caught between motion and memory.

The Lantern seized the moment.

"There," he said, sharp now. "You see it. You cannot come back without becoming dangerous."

He gestured toward Kaela. "Even she knows it. She restrains you."

Kaela did not release Joshua's wrist.

"She reminds me," Joshua said hoarsely. "There's a difference."

The Lantern's composure cracked—not into rage, but something closer to disdain.

"You want return without consequence," he said. "You want to be present without power. That is not how covenant works."

He turned toward the reeds again.

"Force it," he commanded. "Make return choose."

The pressure returned—not as a wave, but as a narrowing. Marcus advanced again, this time not toward Kaela, but toward Gillie. Lucien shifted his angle, cutting off Sera's support. Raven slipped wide, hunting the edges where trust thinned first.

Kaela felt the spiral strain.

Not failing—asking.

She dropped back to one knee, fingers brushing the broken curve, and this time she did not redraw it. She followed it, tracing what remained instead of correcting what was missing, honoring the interruptions rather than erasing them.

Joshua watched her and understood something that terrified him.

The spiral did not prevent breaking.

It allowed return after breaking—without pretending the break hadn't happened.

The Lantern saw it too, and for the first time, real anger broke through his control.

"NO," he snarled. "Return must cost obedience."

He stepped forward incandescent with wrath, light flaring hard enough to scorch frost into steam.

Joshua moved without thinking. He placed himself between the Lantern and Kaela. The act was instinctive, reckless, and immediately dangerous.

Micah shouted his name.

Gillie cried out.

The Lantern smiled.

"There," he said. "That's the trust you always break."

The accusation struck deep because it carried truth. Joshua had stepped forward before—had chosen presence without patience, sacrifice without permission. The old pattern snapped into place around him like a trap he had built himself.

Kaela rose beside him.

"This time," she said calmly, "he didn't disappear to do it."

She met the Lantern's gaze without flinching.

"And he didn't decide alone."

"And he didn't decide for us," Shim'on added. "That matters."

The scroll pulsed—not bright, not loud—but wide, its presence stretching across the clearing like a held breath finally allowed to expand. It did not stop the war. It did not command retreat.

It simply refused the Lantern's interpretation.

Joshua stayed where he was.

Not advancing.

Not bowing.

Not retreating.

The Lantern stared at him, fury and calculation warring behind his eyes.

"You will break again," he promised. "And when you do, I will be there to collect what you owe."

Joshua nodded, once.

"Maybe," he said. "But not like before."

The Lantern stepped back—not because he was finished, but because this phase had reached its limit.

The war surged again around them, blood and breath colliding, but something fundamental had shifted. Return had been tested—and not corrupted. Trust had been risked—and not seized.

The plague had not been satisfied.

But it had been answered.

And Kaela—quiet, steady, carrying a shape born of a fracture she never chose—stood at the center of that answer, holding space for a covenant that refused to be enforced, even as it prepared to demand everything.

The Child's Vow

The war shifted again—not forward, not back, but inward.

I felt it before I understood it, the way you feel weather change in your joints before the sky admits what it's doing. The pressure around us didn't ease, but it narrowed, turning less interested in bodies and more interested in memory. The Lantern stepped back just far enough to let something else take the weight, and I knew immediately that whatever was coming would not arrive with steel.

It would arrive with names.

They came from the edge of the clearing where the light was thinnest, where the scroll's presence softened into something like permission rather than command. Two figures moved through the smoke and scattered bodies without urgency, as if the war itself recognized them and made space despite itself.

Grace walked first.

She did not look like someone entering a battlefield. She looked like someone who had lived inside one for years and learned how to move without flinching. Her clothes were torn and travel-worn, her hands scarred in the quiet way that came from holding things together too long, and her eyes carried a steadiness that had nothing to do with hope and everything to do with refusal. She had endured what obedience could not fix, and the endurance showed.

Behind her came Olivia.

She moved more slowly, one hand pressed to her side as if guarding an old wound that never fully healed. Her gaze swept the clearing with recognition rather than shock, sorrow rather than fear. This was not the first ruin she had walked through bearing Joshua's name. She knew the cost of his choices in a way no one else here could claim.

The Lantern saw them and did not smile.

His light tightened, not flaring but compressing, the way it did when something entered his calculations that could not be reduced to leverage. This was not interruption by force. This was complication by history.

Joshua felt them before he turned.

The filament in his chest tightened again, but this time it did not warm or steady. It ached. His shoulders slumped as if the weight he'd been carrying without language finally found its shape, and when he spoke Grace's name it broke open something in his voice that he had been holding shut since before the clearing ever formed.

"Grace."

She stopped several paces from him, far enough to keep the boundary intact, close enough that retreat was no longer possible. She did not reach for him. She did not accuse him. She simply stood where he could see her and let the truth of her presence do what no command ever had.

"You don't get to disappear again," she said quietly.

Joshua swallowed hard. "I wasn't—"

"I know," she said. "That's what scares me."

Olivia moved past her then, her attention already elsewhere. She did not look at Joshua. She did not look at the Lantern. She looked straight at Kaela.

At Ella.

"There you are," Olivia said, and her voice softened in a way it had not for Joshua. "Ella."

The name fell into the clearing like a dropped stone.

Gillie froze beside me.

I felt the recognition ripple through her before she spoke, felt memory reach backward and forward at once. The name did not belong only to this moment. It carried echoes—protection half-remembered, stories never finished, a child held just out of sight.

"Ella?" Gillie whispered, and the sound of it felt like a door opening somewhere deep in her chest.

Kaela turned at the sound, confusion flickering across her face before something steadier took its place. She looked at Olivia fully now, and whatever question had lived between them unspoken for years finally rose to the surface.

"You said it made you feel small," Olivia said gently. "You hated it."

Kaela's breath hitched. "You said it meant light."

"It does," Olivia replied. "It always did."

The Lantern stepped forward sharply, irritation snapping into command. "Enough," he said. "This is not the place for reunions."

Grace turned toward him.

For the first time, I saw hesitation touch him—not fear, not yet, but something like recognition. Grace had never bowed to him. Not once. Not when obedience would have spared her pain. Not when silence would have made her invisible.

"This is exactly the place," she said. "You just don't like what it exposes."

A few pilgrims shifted at the edge of hearing—too close, too hungry for a new story. Shim'on moved without flourish and cut across their line of sight, positioning himself between them and the women like a door quietly shut. He didn't draw steel. He didn't threaten. He simply stood, shoulders squared, gaze flat, making it clear that whatever the Lantern wanted to turn this into, he would have to work for the angle.

Grace turned back to Joshua, and when she spoke again her voice did not shake.

"When you broke covenant," she said, "it didn't end with me."

Joshua flinched.

"It passed," Grace continued. "Into her. Into the child who never asked to carry what you dropped."

She gestured toward Kaela, toward the spiral scarred into the ground beneath her feet.

"She's been drawing that shape since she was old enough to hold anything that would mark a surface," Grace said. "Before she knew what it meant. Before she knew whose absence it answered."

Joshua's knees softened again.

"I didn't know," he said, barely audible.

"I know," Grace replied. "That's the problem."

The Lantern laughed, sharp and brittle. "Listen to them," he said. "Listen to how they dress inheritance up as innocence."

Olivia's gaze snapped to him, fury breaking through her restraint at last. "You don't get to speak about inheritance," she said. "You've never carried anything you didn't steal."

Kaela stood very still between them, the spiral at her feet grounding her in a way the Lantern could not touch.

"I'm not fixing him," she said quietly.

Grace nodded. "No."

"I'm not paying his debt," Kaela continued.

Olivia's mouth curved into something like pride. "Exactly."

Kaela lifted her eyes to Joshua, steady and unafraid. "I'm keeping what was given to me."

Shim'on exhaled, slow. He glanced—not at the Lantern, but at the listening bodies around the clearing, as if measuring how fast a crowd could turn grief into a weapon. "Then it survives," he said. "Without becoming a throne."

The scroll pulsed—not as command and not as shield, but as witness. I felt it settle into my spine, into all of us, as if marking something that could not be undone or reclaimed by force.

The Lantern stepped back, openly unsettled now.

This was not endurance.

This was not resistance.

This was lineage refusing to be weaponized.

And beneath the war, beneath the broken vows and threatened horrors, something older than judgment held its ground—not to erase what had been done, but to refuse to let it define what would come next.

A vow had been made long before anyone here understood its weight.

And it was still standing.

The Return

The war did not end, but it lost its direction.

Blows still landed. Breath still tore loose. Bodies still collided with stone and steel. But the hunger driving it no longer knew where to go. Commands echoed and fractured instead of carrying cleanly. The reeds still struck, still obeyed—but obedience had begun to cost them effort, and effort was not something the Lantern tolerated well.

Kaela stood where the spiral had been drawn and broken, her presence anchoring the clearing in a way no blade or light could replicate. She did not look outward for confirmation. She did not search the scroll for permission. She stood as if listening for something beneath the chaos, and in that listening the violence around her thinned, refusing to complete itself the way the Lantern intended.

Joshua watched her with a terror deeper than fear of dying.

Because he understood what she carried—and what it would mean to give it back.

Grace had named it without ornament: what you dropped did not disappear. Covenant had not shattered into nothing. It had passed forward, absorbed into blood and bone that never asked to bear it. Kaela had not inherited his guilt, but she had carried the consequence of his absence. The light that should have remained with him had found shelter where it could.

Not ownership.

Shelter.

Kaela opened her eyes and looked at Joshua. No accusation. No demand. She had already chosen. Now she waited to see if he would recognize what was being returned.

"You don't owe me anything," she said quietly.

Joshua shook his head. "I owe you everything."

"No," she replied, gentle but unyielding. "That's the lie that keeps it broken."

She stepped closer. The filament inside his chest trembled, drawn forward by recognition. I felt the scroll shift—not surging, not intervening—but withdrawing just enough to make space. Its restraint mattered more than any flare of power.

"I carried it because it had nowhere else to go," Kaela said. "But it was never mine to keep."

The Lantern moved sharply, light tightening. "No," he said. "You do not decide that."

Kaela did not turn toward him.

She placed her hand over Joshua's chest—not pressing, not claiming, simply resting there as one rests a hand over a wound that must be opened to heal. The spiral beneath her feet seemed to steady, its broken curves aligning—not into completion, but into coherence.

"I'm not giving you light," she said. "I'm returning what was never meant to stay with me."

Joshua gasped.

What unraveled inside him was neither violent nor clean. The filament loosened like breath finally released, and the light moved where it had always belonged—not flooding him, not absolving him, but restoring him to himself. It did not erase the dark. It made room for truth to live alongside it.

Joshua fell to his knees.

Not in submission.

In recognition.

The sound he made was not a word. It was the sound of someone discovering that endurance had never been the same thing as survival.

The Lantern screamed.

Not rage at first—but violation. His light detonated outward in a shockwave that tore frost into steam and knocked bodies to the ground, weapons skidding across stone as breath was ripped from lungs.

"You dare," he roared, "return what was claimed?"

Kaela stepped back as the contact broke, face pale now, breath shallow. She did not reach for the light again.

"I didn't take it," she said. "So I couldn't lose it."

Joshua lifted his head slowly, hands shaking against the ground. The light was fully alive in him now—not obedient, not weaponized—but true. He did not rise. He did not speak. He stayed where he was, relearning what it meant to be present without command, without role, without the illusion of authority.

I saw the moment the others understood. Not miracle. Not victory. Weight returning to its proper place.

Grace moved first.

She crossed the space without hurry and knelt beside him. She did not touch him. She did not comfort him. She bore witness.

"You don't get to rush this," she said quietly. "You don't get to pretend it feels clean."

Joshua nodded once. "I know."

Olivia came next, one hand still pressed to her side, the other steadying Kaela's shoulder. Kaela had gone pale; the cost of carrying and releasing had finally arrived.

"You don't have to carry it anymore," Olivia said. "You never should have."

Kaela exhaled shakily. "I didn't know how not to."

"That's not a failure," Olivia replied. "That's inheritance doing what it always does—absorbing the fracture until someone names it."

Around us, the fighting thinned. Not stopped. Not resolved. But confused. Pilgrims slowed, some dropping weapons they didn't remember lifting. Others backed away, breath ragged, unsure whether the next command would still land.

The scroll did not flare.

It remained.

Joshua finally lifted his head.

His eyes moved across the group—not counting. Not commanding. Seeing. The damage. The cost. The trust he had nearly broken again.

"I don't get to lead," he said, voice raw. "Not like that."

Micah stiffened—relief and resentment crossing his face at once. He did not argue. He nodded once and turned back toward the line.

Shim'on stepped in beside him—not taking command, but closing a gap that had opened while everyone watched Joshua fall. He didn't speak. He simply repositioned two staggered pilgrims with a touch at the shoulder and a low, steady "Hold here," grounding the line before it could fracture again.

Kaela met Joshua's gaze, tired now.

"You don't get to disappear either," she said. "Return means staying."

Joshua swallowed. "I will."

It was not loud. It was not ceremonial. It landed with the quiet weight of something that could still be broken.

The Lantern laughed.

Measured. Satisfied.

"You see?" he said. "Even return has limits. Even truth requires permission to act."

"Limits aren't the problem," Shim'on said. "Ownership is."

The Lantern stepped forward slowly, light gathering into edges, dividing space into what could be held and what could be taken.

"You have proven something important," he continued. "Covenant can be restored."

His gaze cut to Joshua, then to Kaela.

"But restoration is not restraint."

The wind stirred—stronger now, threading through the clearing with intent. Cloaks tugged. Breath pulled unevenly. It did not move randomly.

It counted.

The Lantern's smile widened as his eyes settled on Cassian.

"And now," he said softly, "we will see who understands that authority is not felt—it is seized."

His fury shifted—collapsed inward.

"You want covenant without enforcement," he snarled. "Return without obedience."

His light compressed until the air around him buckled.

"Then we move on."

The words landed with finality.

The air changed—not colder, not hotter—but claimed. Currents formed where none had existed before, pulling at cloaks, at weapons, at breath itself, dividing what could be held from what must be taken.

"You think the sin was breaking trust," the Lantern said, voice ringing clear. "You think covenant was the wound."

He turned, gaze settling on Cassian.

"No. The wound was taking what was never entrusted."

Cassian stiffened.

I saw it then—the way he stood a fraction higher than the line required, the way his eyes tracked positions instead of people. Authority had settled on him like a stolen crown, worn long enough that he had begun to forget it was not his.

Shim'on saw it too.

He moved—not toward Cassian, not yet—but into his peripheral vision, anchoring him without challenge. A quiet presence. A warning that whatever happened next would not be answered alone.

The wind shifted again.

Uneven.

Restless.

"You thought it was yours," the Lantern said softly. "That's the sweetest mistake."

The wind rose—not violent yet, but insistent, worrying at banners, threading through armor and bone. It refused direction.

Cassian met Joshua's gaze across the clearing—defiance flickering, fear buried beneath it. The wind pulled harder at him than at the others, testing balance, finding seams.

The Lantern tilted his head, listening.

"You took it," he continued. "Authority. Direction. The right to decide who stands and who falls."

His smile widened as the gale gathered.

"Now give it back."

The war did not resume.

It changed shape.

The wind circled—counting nothing, claiming nothing—undoing the illusion that anything here could be held by force. Breath turned unreliable. Footing betrayed intention. Possession grew slippery.

And as the currents tightened and the air learned how to pull without asking, I knew the next cost would not be paid in blood alone.

It would be paid in release.

And not everyone would survive letting go of what they had stolen.

The Crushing Wind

When Command Slips

The Lantern raised his hand, and the noise of the battle bent toward him without stopping.

"You think you can stand without structure," he said, his voice carrying cleanly through steel and breath. "You think you can move without being held."

His light sharpened—not flaring outward but compressing, edges drawing tight as if the air itself were being gripped. "Then feel what happens," he continued, "when nothing belongs to you anymore."

The ground shuddered once, not in warning, not in answer, but in compliance.

The wind moved through it all, not roaring, not striking, but insinuating itself into every small motion. It slipped between bodies, nudging balance, testing weight and grip. It did not hit. It interfered.

"Bow," the Lantern commanded, and for a heartbeat the word still carried weight.

Marcus stepped forward into that heartbeat before it could fade.

"You heard him," he called, voice carrying a sharp, practiced cruelty. "Bow—or break under what's coming."

He spread his hands slightly, as if offering clarity rather than threat. "The wind doesn't need to strike," Marcus continued. "It only needs you standing where you shouldn't be."

The wind answered by doing nothing at all.

Then the battle continued.

Not cleanly. Not correctly.

Steel still rang. Bodies still collided. Cries still tore loose from throats raw with cold and fear. But the shape of the fighting had begun to loosen, as if the rules everyone had been obeying without question had quietly stepped away.

Orders were shouted and answered, but the answers arrived thin, incomplete—half a breath too late, or breaking apart before they could be followed. A command to hold became a pause. A signal to advance turned into two people stepping forward and three stepping back. Nothing collapsed all at once. It frayed.

I felt it first in my hands. The hilt of my blade shifted as if the leather had softened, grip slipping just enough to make me adjust, then adjust again. Around me, others fumbled in similar ways—shields knocked askew by nothing more than a change in footing, blades glancing off armor they should have struck cleanly.

The wind kept working—tugging at cloaks, nudging elbows, catching breath at the wrong time. Not enough to knock anyone down. Enough to make everything unreliable.

Lines formed because we were used to forming them. They dissolved because the space between us no longer honored alignment. I watched Rowan step into position beside Nadya, only for the ground to betray them both, a subtle slope that sent them separating instead of bracing together. Eliah shouted a correction, and they tried again, and again the moment refused to hold. It was as if the clearing itself had grown impatient with being told what it was for.

Somewhere behind us, the Lantern's voice cut through the noise, sharp and precise.

"Left flank—hold."

For a breath, it worked. Bodies shifted, shields came up, a line half-formed where it was told to exist.

"Advance the center."

The words arrived cleanly, but the movement didn't. Two stepped forward. One hesitated. Another turned the wrong way entirely, eyes flicking toward the sound instead of following it.

"Close the gap," the Lantern snapped.

No one closed it. A few stared, waiting for something else to follow, as if the command were incomplete on its own.

"Close it," he repeated, louder now.

A man lunged where no gap remained. Another backed away from a space that no longer existed. The line bent, then folded, not breaking outright but losing its shape like wet cloth.

"Right side—rotate."

The wrong people moved. Someone rotated the opposite direction. Someone else moved purely out of reflex, obeying the idea of command rather than its meaning.

The Lantern's tone tightened. Not rage yet. Not fury. Offense.

"Respond," he ordered.

The word hung there, unanswered.

Steel still rang. Breath still tore loose. But his voice no longer arranged the world the way it expected to. The sound of command remained sharp and perfect—what failed was the space it was supposed to claim.

The wind answered him by doing nothing at all.

It did not surge. It did not howl. It simply refused to align itself with purpose.

A banner snapped loose from its tie and wrapped around a spear shaft, yanking it from the hands of the man holding it. A shout went up as someone stumbled, not from a blow but from a momentary loss of balance that felt like forgetting where the ground was supposed to be.

I saw Sera catch herself on a knee, breath knocked loose by the sudden effort, and when she rose again her eyes were wide with something that wasn't fear. Confusion. As if she had stepped into a room where the furniture had been rearranged without warning.

That was when Cassian was struck.

It wasn't dramatic. No cry, no flourish of steel. An enemy blade slipped through a gap that should not have been there, angled wrong by a fraction, finding flesh beneath his ribs. Cassian stiffened, breath hitching once, his hand tightening reflexively on the haft of the weapon he carried. The enemy did not even realize what had happened at first, already being shoved back by the press of bodies, already losing position as the fight shifted again.

Cassian did not fall.

He did not call out.

He did not signal.

He drew one slow breath, then another, shoulders settling as if he had made a quiet decision. Only when he turned slightly did I see the dark spreading at his side, soaking into cloth already stiff with cold. The sight hit me with a clarity that had nothing to do with panic. The wound was bad. Mortal. Cassian knew it as surely as I did.

He stayed where he was.

People looked to him without realizing they were doing it. Not because he had ordered anything, but because his presence had always steadied the air around him.

A man near him faltered, eyes flicking to Cassian's face as if expecting instruction. Cassian met his gaze and said nothing, simply nodded once—an acknowledgment, not a command. The man swallowed and turned back to the fight, movements less frantic, more deliberate, as if being seen had been enough.

"That's how it survives," Shim'on said. "Presence without instruction."

Joshua stood a few paces away, half-shadowed by the shifting light, his posture uncertain. He was close enough to be struck, far enough to avoid being counted. I watched his attention fix not on the enemy surging and retreating in broken rhythms, but on Cassian—on the way he held himself, on the way people moved around him, not directed, not controlled, but steadied. Joshua's jaw tightened, something working behind his eyes as if a memory he had tried to bury was stirring again.

The Lantern's voice rose, sharper now, cutting through the din with an edge meant to reclaim attention.

"Form on me."

Habit answered first. Bodies leaned inward, feet shifting, a loose arc beginning to take shape.

"Press them back."

The movement fractured. A few surged. Others braced where no pressure came. Someone swung too early, blade catching nothing but air.

"Hold—hold the line."

No line held. A shield slipped free. A man stumbled backward into someone else's space. The shape they were meant to become dissolved before it finished forming.

"Re-align," the Lantern snapped, light flaring around him, frost hissing into steam at his feet.

Nothing re-aligned.

People looked toward him instead of moving, eyes searching his face as if waiting for something clearer—something that would tell them what the words were supposed to mean now.

"No," he said sharply.

The word was meant to gather everything back into place.

It didn't.

The wind brushed past him and went on its way.

It slipped through armor seams, tugged at loose straps, pressed against faces already numb with cold. A shield skidded from someone's grasp and clanged across stone, the sound startlingly loud in the sudden gap that followed. Another fighter reached for it and missed, fingers closing on air as if the object had shifted just out of reach. Laughter burst from somewhere—high, sharp, brittle—and died just as quickly when its owner realized nothing about this was funny.

Cassian shifted his weight, a subtle adjustment that cost him more than he let show. His hand pressed briefly to his side, then fell away. His breathing had grown careful, measured, each inhale chosen. Still, he did not retreat. When Nadya stumbled back toward him, eyes wild, Cassian caught her by the elbow and steadied her without pulling her anywhere.

"Easy," he said quietly, the word landing like a hand on her shoulder.

She nodded, breath slowing, and moved on.

Joshua watched that too.

"Stand," the Lantern commanded.

Marcus moved first, always eager to translate command into pressure. “You heard him,” he barked, stepping forward, voice heavy with threat. “Stand where you are.”

A few obeyed out of reflex. One man froze, shoulders locking as if fear itself had been mistaken for discipline.

Raven laughed softly. “Oh, they heard,” he said, voice slipping sideways through the moment. His eyes flicked across the line, measuring reactions instead of positions. “The question is whether they think it means the same thing now.”

Marcus rounded on him. “This isn’t a question,” he snarled. “You stand because you’re told.”

Lucien cut in before the argument could sharpen further.

“No,” he said calmly, and the word landed harder than Marcus’s shout. “You stand because you understand what happens if you don’t.”

His gaze never left Marcus’s face. Marcus stiffened, jaw tightening, the challenge swallowed rather than answered.

Lucien lifted his voice, smooth and precise, pitched to carry. “You heard your master,” he called. “Stand.”

The words were perfect. The timing was not.

Someone stepped back instead. Another shifted sideways, seeking space rather than obedience. The line bent, uncertain whether it was being threatened or instructed.

Elana tried next, slipping between tones as easily as breath. “Please,” she urged, hands open, eyes wide with practiced concern. “Just stand still. It will be easier if you do.”

A woman hesitated, torn between comfort and instinct, and nearly lost her footing when the ground sloped beneath her.

Julian laughed and clapped his hands once, sharp and loud. "Easier," he echoed brightly. "Did you hear that? Easier!" He leaned close to Elana, voice low and biting. "Go on. Smile more. Make them want it."

Kali's voice rose over all of them, not loud, but irresistible, threading the chaos into something almost musical. "Stand," she sang, the word bending and stretching, turning into invitation instead of command. "Stand with us."

Raven tilted his head, watching her with interest. "Careful," he murmured. "You're giving them a choice."

Kali smiled at him. "I always do."

Movement continued anyway.

Not defiance. Not unity. Necessity. People adjusted for balance, for breath, for the sudden unreliability of space itself. Shields slipped. Feet slid. Stillness became dangerous.

Lucien's eyes narrowed. "Enough," he said, sharply now.

No one listened.

The Lantern stepped forward, light compressing tight around him, frost hissing into steam at his feet. "Listen," he commanded, the word honed to cut through everything else.

Marcus seized it. "Listen when he speaks," he growled. "That voice is law."

Raven's smile widened. "Sound travels," he said lightly. "Law doesn't always follow."

Kali laughed.

For half a breath, the clearing stilled. Eyes lifted. Bodies paused.

Then the wind passed between them, tugging at cloaks, nudging elbows, pulling breath sideways in the lungs, and the moment dissolved back into motion that answered no single voice at all.

The Lantern felt it then—not loss of strength, not loss of numbers, but something far more intolerable.

Claim.

The certainty that when he spoke, the world was supposed to arrange itself accordingly.

Even fractured, even amplified, even weaponized through others, it would not.

Around us, the battle continued to unravel. Timing betrayed intent. A strike that should have landed cleanly glanced off, while another landed harder than expected, sending both combatants reeling. Shouts overlapped, collided, dissolved into noise without direction. The wind threaded through it all, patient, almost curious, as if testing what could be relied upon.

I found myself thinking, absurdly, of ownership—of how much of what we were doing depended on the belief that we held something: ground, position, authority—and how easily that belief was being taken apart without anyone actually taking it.

Cassian swayed then, just slightly, and Joshua moved without thinking, a half-step forward, a hand hovering as if ready to catch him. Cassian straightened before the gesture could become anything else. Their eyes met for a moment, and in that look something passed between them that had nothing to do with the fight. Recognition. Not forgiveness. Not accusation. Recognition of a cost that could not be avoided.

The Lantern saw it.

His gaze snapped to Cassian, then to Joshua, and something like calculation flickered there. He advanced a step, light sharpening, and barked a command meant to snap the world back into place.

"Enough. Fall back. Now."

The order struck the air like a thrown blade.

It did not stick.

For the first time, I saw uncertainty touch him—not fear, not doubt, but surprise. As if the world had answered him incorrectly.

The wind did not howl. It did not roar. It simply continued to make everything harder to hold.

And standing there amid the slipping lines and faltering commands, watching Cassian bleed quietly into the cold while refusing to claim a single thing, I understood what was happening with a clarity that settled deep in my bones.

This fight wasn't being lost.

It was being unowned.

Authority Without a Throne

The wind did not grow louder as the minutes passed. It grew more exact.

At first it had only been inconvenience, the kind of interference you could blame on weather or fatigue—cloth snapping loose, feet sliding, breath catching at the wrong time. Now it began to behave like intent. It learned what hands were trying to do and made those motions unreliable. It learned where we were bracing and made the ground a fraction less honest beneath us. It learned which objects we were depending on, and it pulled at that dependence like a seam.

I watched Rowan swing at a reed that had pressed too close, steel meeting air with the clean arrogance of a strike that expected to land, only for the blade to twist mid-arc as if the wind had hooked its edge. Rowan's wrist buckled. The strike went wide. The reed took advantage without thinking, because that was what they did—capitalize, consume, correct. Rowan staggered, not from the reed's blow, but from the betrayal of his own grip.

Nadya cursed and yanked her shield higher, but the strap slid against her forearm as though the leather had decided it no longer belonged there. She adjusted, tightened, adjusted again, and each correction cost her attention.

The wind didn't need to strike her. It only needed to make her spend time trying to keep what should have stayed put. Sera's cloak snapped across her face, blinding her for half a heartbeat at the wrong moment.

Eliah caught her elbow and shoved her back into space before a blade could find her ribs.

Everything we held was becoming negotiable.

That should have driven us into tighter formation, into some instinctive unity that made the world simpler by force. Instead it did the opposite. We scattered in small ways—half-steps, shifted angles, broken sightlines. We tried to hold the same shape we always held when fighting mattered, and the wind kept loosening that shape. The longer it went on, the less the battle felt like two sides clashing and the more it felt like the rules of movement had changed without warning.

Shim'on moved with that change without comment, adjusting his footing once, then stilling—eyes tracking the wind's behavior rather than the blades.

The Lantern's lieutenants were still there, threading through the chaos like predators who understood exactly what kind of confusion to harvest.

Marcus drove himself into the press first, shoulder-checking a pilgrim back into line and shouting over the noise, his voice thick with command.

"Stand where you're told," he barked. "Hold, damn you—hold!"

He pointed, sweeping his arm as if he could physically force the world back into alignment. "You break now, you break forever."

A man stumbled instead, shield torn sideways by a sudden pull of wind, and Marcus snarled, stepping closer. "I said stand." His tone sharpened, edging toward threat. "Or you'll learn what breaking really feels like."

Lucien's gaze snapped to him instantly.

"Careful," Lucien said, not raising his voice, not even turning his head fully. The word landed like a blade set gently against Marcus's throat. "You're not the one who decides that."

Marcus stiffened. "I'm keeping them—"

"You're overreaching," Lucien cut in, eyes finally lifting to pin him in place. "Again." His voice remained calm, almost bored. "Let the failure speak for itself."

Marcus swallowed whatever reply had been forming and stepped back half a pace, fury simmering behind his eyes.

Raven slipped past them both, their presence felt more than seen. They appeared beside a pair of pilgrims who had frozen mid-motion, their smiles brittle with fear.

"We heard him," Raven said lightly, tilting their head as if listening to something only they could hear. "Didn't you?" Their eyes flicked toward the Lantern and then back again, amusement curling their mouth. "He says bow. Funny thing about that word—everyone hears it differently."

One of the pilgrims shook his head. "I—I can't—"

Raven's smile widened. "Oh, you can," they murmured. "You just don't know yet which way."

They vanished again, laughter trailing behind them like an echo that didn't belong to any throat.

Elana drifted through the gaps Raven left behind, her movements unhurried, almost gentle. She touched a woman's arm, her voice low and warm. "It doesn't have to hurt," she whispered. "You don't have to be brave. Just stop fighting what's already decided."

The woman's breath hitched. "If I bow—"

"You'll rest," Elana said softly. "You'll be held." Her fingers tightened just slightly. "Isn't that what you want?"

Julian's laughter cut through her words, sharp and bright. "Don't lie to her like that," he said, striking someone hard enough to send them sprawling. "Make it honest." He grabbed Elana's wrist, yanking her back into motion. "Tell them it hurts either way. That's the fun part."

Elana flinched, her expression tightening before smoothing again, and she leaned back toward the fallen pilgrim, voice trembling just enough to sound sincere. "He's right," she said. "It hurts. But at least this way, it ends sooner."

Kali's voice threaded through all of it, rising and falling in strange, dissonant patterns. "Listen," she sang, not loud but everywhere, her tone slipping into ears like a thought no one remembered choosing. "Listen how the wind answers. Hear how it knows who belongs where."

Someone screamed—not from pain, but from the sudden certainty that they no longer trusted their own footing.

Above it all, Lucien observed, intervening only when someone hesitated long enough for choice to begin forming. A glance here. A gesture there. A precise, lethal correction when doubt threatened to become defiance.

And still, beneath their efforts, the wind refused to settle.

Commands expanded. Threats multiplied. Temptations sharpened.

But nothing held.

The lieutenants pushed harder, louder, crueler—each adding their own flare to the Lantern's will.

And the world answered them by slipping further out of reach.

And yet, in the midst of that, people kept turning their heads toward Cassian.

Not because he shouted. He didn't. Not because he moved to the front. He didn't. He stood where he had been struck, breathing carefully, hand occasionally pressing to his side as if to remind his body that it had been cut. His face was pale in the cold light, but his eyes stayed steady. He was not commanding anything. He was not claiming anything. He was simply there, present in a way that made everything around him feel less like panic and more like reality.

A pilgrim stumbled toward him, wide-eyed, sword held too high and too tight, blade wobbling in a hand that had forgotten how to stop shaking. "Tell me where to go," the man blurted, voice cracking. "Tell me what to do."

Cassian didn't answer with a direction. He didn't point. He didn't order. He looked at the pilgrim's hands, at the blade angled so wildly it was as likely to cut a friend as an enemy, and Cassian reached out—not to take it, not to control it, but to press two fingers gently against the flat of the steel and lower it.

"Breathe," Cassian said.

The word landed heavier than an order would have.

The pilgrim blinked, as if he'd been slapped, then inhaled so sharply it hurt to hear. Cassian didn't soothe him. He didn't offer comfort. He simply stayed close enough that the pilgrim could follow the instruction without feeling stupid for needing it. When the man's shoulders settled, Cassian said, "You're not a weapon. Don't become one."

The pilgrim nodded once, hard, and backed away, blade held lower now, still frightened but no longer frantic. He moved back into the mess of bodies without a plan, and somehow his movement was truer for it—less about winning and more about staying alive without losing himself.

Shim'on shifted to fill the space the pilgrim vacated, not guarding it—just keeping it from becoming empty. His hand lifted once, palm down, a steadying gesture to the next person edging in. "Slow," he said, barely audible.

People began to come to Cassian that way. Not in a line. Not as a request for leadership. As if their bodies were seeking a witness the way lungs seek air.

Rowan backed near him, blood on his sleeve, eyes darting as the wind tugged at his cloak. "We should regroup," Rowan said. It was not a command. It was a plea. "We should—Cassian, we should hold them."

Cassian's gaze moved over the field in a slow sweep. He took in the broken shapes of our side, the reeds pressing and retreating, the Lantern's lieutenants feeding on confusion, the wind undoing everything we tried to make stable.

He did not say, Yes. He did not say, No.

He said, "We can't hold what isn't holding."

Rowan frowned, frustrated by the lack of instruction. "Then what do we do?"

Cassian's mouth tightened slightly, not from impatience, but from pain. He pressed his hand to his side again. When he spoke, his voice was quieter than the clash of steel, but the people close enough to hear it leaned in as if he had started praying.

"We keep each other from becoming what they want," Cassian said.

Nadya scoffed, adrenaline sharpened into anger. "That's not a plan."

Cassian met her eyes. "It's the only plan that doesn't belong to them."

That was the first time I understood what he was doing. He wasn't trying to win the battle. He was trying to keep us from being rewritten by it. He refused to make us into a unit because units could be owned. Units could be commanded. Units could be turned.

Witnesses were harder to possess.

The wind proved him right. It kept punishing anything that resembled ownership. Someone tried to grab a fallen spear and it slid away. Someone tried to plant their boots and found the ground subtly shifting under them. A shield strap snapped as if it had decided it had served long enough. Even my own blade felt strange in my hand—no longer promising that my grip meant control. Every time I tightened my fingers, I felt the tiny resistance of something refusing to be treated like property.

And still, people looked to Cassian.

Not because he filled the vacancy. Because he refused to.

Across the clearing, the Lantern watched it unfolding, his expression tightening as it kept trying to return to polish and failing. He spoke less now, as if each command required effort he had not expected to spend.

"Hold," he said once, the word clean and exact.

Marcus moved immediately, shoving a pilgrim back into place. "You heard him," he growled.

Lucien's eyes flicked toward him.

"That will do," Lucien said quietly.

Marcus bristled, then checked himself under Lucien's stare, stepping back with his anger swallowed but not gone.

Nearby, Julian leaned in close to Elana, voice pitched low. "Push harder."

Elana's mouth tightened. She obeyed—but her gaze flicked away from him as she did, resentment flaring and fading just as quickly.

Raven passed Kali without slowing, their smile lingering a fraction too long. Kali answered it with a hum that slipped between notes, neither challenge nor submission.

Lucien watched them all, intervening rarely now—one look, one gesture, never a raised voice. Even so, the precision that once held them in place began to loosen.

Above them, the Lantern stood rigid, light compressed tight around him. His claim over them was not gone, but it had changed. What had once rested now pressed.

He spoke again.

"Enough."

The word landed unevenly—answered by some, missed by others.

The lieutenants did not echo it this time. They adjusted instead, each in their own direction, each correction pulling against another.

The Lantern felt the shift with something close to disbelief.

Authority was still there. But certainty had begun to cost him.

Shim'on adjusted his stance again, once, as if responding to a pressure only he had noticed, then went still.

Joshua stood in the midst of all of it like a man who had been told to pick a side and discovered that sides were not the real problem.

He was near enough to Cassian that I could see his face clearly when the wind tugged at him. His shoulders were drawn inward, hands loose, as if he didn't trust his own reflexes yet. He wasn't striking. He wasn't retreating. He was watching—watching Cassian steady people without directing them, watching Cassian refuse the throne being offered to him by panic.

I saw Joshua's throat bob with a swallow that looked like shame.

Cassian caught his gaze—not as confrontation, not as accusation. Just as witness.

Joshua's lips parted as if to speak. No words came. He glanced away, eyes flicking toward the Lantern, toward the lieutenants, toward the chaos that had been made in his name once, long ago, when he had believed that taking leadership was the same as saving people.

Cassian didn't follow Joshua's gaze. He stayed on Joshua's face.

"You're looking for a verdict," Cassian said quietly.

Joshua flinched as if the words were a strike. "No."

"Yes," Cassian replied, and there was no harshness in it. Only truth. "You want someone to tell you what you are."

Joshua's jaw clenched. "I already know what I am."

Cassian's eyes held. "You know what you did."

The difference mattered more than any comfort could have.

Joshua's breath came uneven. "Don't," he muttered, not as a plea for mercy, but as a plea not to be seen.

Cassian didn't soften. He didn't push. He simply said, "I'm not here to accuse you."

Joshua looked up sharply, suspicion flickering.

Cassian continued, "And I'm not here to absolve you."

For a second, something in Joshua's face broke open—relief and pain and anger all tangled together. He had been bracing for condemnation. He had been hoping for a clean forgiveness. Cassian offered neither.

Instead he offered the only thing that could not be stolen.

Witness.

A scream split the air to our left as someone went down under Julian's force, and the sound yanked Joshua's attention away. The moment between them could have vanished. It didn't. Cassian kept it present simply by staying where he was, breathing carefully through pain that was beginning to take more from him.

I realized then that the wound wasn't just bleeding. It was deepening. Cassian's movements had grown more deliberate, as if every shift had to be weighed against what it would cost. The blood at his side had darkened, stiffening in the cold. He did not press it like a man trying to live. He pressed it like a man acknowledging what was happening without letting it dictate his mind.

Another pilgrim stumbled near, face streaked with frost and tears. "Cassian," she gasped, "tell us—tell us where to go. The Lantern—he's—"

Cassian raised one hand, palm out. Not to command silence. To hold her panic at bay.

"Look at me," he said.

She did, breath shuddering.

"What do you see?" Cassian asked.

She blinked, confused by the question. "I—blood. Steel. Wind."

Cassian nodded. "Yes."

He waited until her breath slowed by a fraction. "Now tell me what you don't see."

Her brow furrowed. "I don't—" She swallowed. "I don't see a path."

Cassian's expression did not change. "That's because we don't own one."

The words settled in her like cold water. She stared at him, trying to find hope in it. Cassian didn't hand her hope. He handed her honesty.

"We move when the world makes space," he said. "Until then, you keep your hands from becoming cruel."

The pilgrim backed away again, shaken but steadied.

The Lantern saw that interaction too. I felt his gaze even before I looked up. It had shifted from generalized fury to something more personal, more predatory. He was done trying to orchestrate. He was beginning to select. His attention circled Cassian like a blade circling a throat.

He took a step forward, light tightening around him, and spoke as if the world still belonged to his voice.

"Hold what is yours," the Lantern commanded. "Stand with me."

The words carried across the clearing with terrible clarity.

Nothing answered them.

No line formed. No unified movement. No surge of obedience. People moved anyway, but not toward him—around him, past him, away from the idea that anyone could claim what was happening.

Something in the Lantern's expression collapsed. Not fear. Offense so deep it looked like injury.

He stopped issuing commands after that. I saw it happen like a switch thrown. His posture changed. The angle of his shoulders. The way his gaze ceased sweeping the field and began to lock onto individuals. He was no longer trying to direct an army. He was choosing prey.

Shim'on remained where he was, neither retreating nor advancing, as if absence itself had stopped being an option.

I felt the shift in my own gut, the way you feel a storm change direction even when the sky looks the same. The lieutenants reacted too—Marcus tensing, eager and uneasy; Lucien narrowing his eyes, recalculating; Raven smiling wider as if delighted by the hunt; Kali's song thinning into something sharper; Julian bouncing on his heels like a child who had been promised a new game; Elana pausing, lips parting as if she could sense her leash tightening.

Something shifted beneath the battle—not in force, but in direction.

We were no longer fighting to hold ground. We were fighting to remain unclaimed.

Cassian leaned slightly toward me then, close enough that I could hear him without shouting. His voice was rougher now, pain pressing at it like a thumb.

"You feel it," he said.

I nodded, jaw tight. "He's done commanding."

Cassian's eyes flicked toward the Lantern and then back to me. "He won't stop," Cassian said simply.

I swallowed, the truth of it colder than the wind. "Then what do we—"

Cassian lifted his head just enough to meet my eyes fully. The look was steady. Not brave for show. Not hopeful. Witness.

"I won't take what isn't given," he said quietly. "Not even to save us."

The words did not sound like strategy.

They sounded like boundary.

Behind us, steel still rang. The wind still interfered.

And somewhere in the Lantern's tightening focus, pursuit was already taking shape.

Cassian, bleeding into the frost, remained exactly what he had chosen to be: not a throne, not a commander, not a judge—only a man who refused to become possessed by the need to possess.

The Cost of Bearing Witness

Cassian could no longer stand without effort.

It did not happen all at once. He did not collapse or cry out or mark the moment with drama. His knees simply stopped trusting him the way they had before, and when he shifted his weight, the ground seemed farther away than it used to be. He braced himself against a broken shield half-buried in frost, breath shallow now, each inhale scraping as if it had to pass through something narrower than lungs.

Someone reached for him—Rowan first, then Nadya—and Cassian shook his head before their hands could settle.

"Not yet," he said, voice calm, almost apologetic.

"You're bleeding," Rowan insisted, already tearing fabric free. "You need to—"

Cassian covered Rowan's wrist with his own hand. The pressure was light. The refusal was not. "I know," he said. "But moving me won't stop it."

Nadya crouched anyway, eyes sharp, assessing. "You can't stay here."

Cassian's gaze lifted past her, past the churn of bodies and slipping ground, toward the space where Joshua stood half-withdrawn from the fight, watching everything and belonging nowhere. "I can," Cassian said quietly. "Just not for long."

The wind pressed in closer, not striking him the way it struck grips and footing around us. It moved as if aware of him, circling rather than pushing—a presence that felt less like threat than appointment. I noticed then that the wind did not tug at Cassian's cloak or pull at his balance the way it did with the rest of us. It treated him differently. Not reverently. Patiently.

Shim'on noticed it too and did not step in. He stayed where he was, holding the space around Cassian without claiming it, turning one anxious pilgrim back with a quiet, steadying hand.

Joshua stepped closer.

He moved like someone approaching a truth he already knew but had not yet been given permission to say aloud. His face was pale, his breath uneven, light and dark still out of alignment inside him. He knelt beside Cassian without being asked, as if the posture came back to him before the words did.

Cassian watched him for a long moment before speaking.

"You see it now," Cassian said.

Joshua nodded once. He could not seem to look away. "I didn't think it looked like this."

"It never does," Cassian replied. "When you're inside it."

Joshua swallowed. His eyes tracked the disorder around them—the way people hesitated, the way no one stepped fully into place. His voice came out low, careful.

"You could have…" He stopped, jaw tightening. "There were moments. When it would have… held."

Cassian watched him closely. Not suspicious. Not defensive. Listening.

"Yes," Cassian said softly. "It would have."

Joshua's gaze flicked away, as if that admission cost him. "Sometimes that's enough."

Cassian smiled faintly, the expression brief and honest. "Sometimes," he agreed. "And that's why it fails later."

Joshua shook his head once, frustration leaking through restraint. "You don't have to do this for me."

"I'm not," Cassian said. There was no edge in it. No correction. Just truth. "I'm refusing to do it like you did."

That landed.

Joshua's shoulders drew inward, breath catching—not in anger, not in denial, but recognition arriving without permission.

The pain was constant now. Cassian's breaths came shorter, more measured, each one chosen rather than automatic. I could see the effort it took for him to remain present, to keep his eyes clear, to speak without letting strain creep into his voice. Whatever had pierced him had gone deep. He knew it. He had known it since the moment it happened.

"You still don't have it," Cassian continued, eyes steady on Joshua. "The thing you lost."

Joshua did not pretend not to understand. "Authority," he said quietly.

Cassian nodded. "Not the kind people follow because they're afraid. The kind they follow because it doesn't ask them to be smaller."

Joshua's hands curled against his knees. "I took it."

"Yes," Cassian said. Not accusation. Witness. "You took it because no one stopped you. Because it worked. Because everyone was relieved someone else was deciding."

Joshua's breath shuddered. "I thought that meant it was mine."

Cassian shook his head slowly. "Authority doesn't belong to the one who acts," he said. "It belongs to the one who refuses to act until it's given."

Joshua closed his eyes.

"This isn't about worth," Cassian added gently. "It never was. You didn't lose it because you failed. You lost it because you seized it."

Joshua's voice came rough. "Then how do I get it back?"

Cassian did not answer right away.

Around us, the fight continued to unravel—awkwardly. People moved and stopped and moved again, uncertain whether their next step would be supported. The lieutenants still stalked the edges, their threats losing precision as the space refused to cooperate. The Lantern stood apart now, watching, no longer directing, his interest sharpened by something he did not yet understand.

Cassian exhaled slowly. "You don't," he said.

Joshua looked at him, startled.

"You don't take it back," Cassian continued. "You can't force its return. You can't claim it by repentance or courage or suffering. Those things matter, but they don't restore what was never yours to reclaim."

Joshua's shoulders sagged. "Then it stays broken."

Cassian's gaze softened. "No," he said. "It waits."

"For what?"

"For someone who will give it freely."

The meaning landed between them like something heavy set down at last.

Joshua's breath caught. "You can't mean—"

Cassian lifted a hand, stopping him—not with command, but with presence. "I won't take what isn't given," he said again, quieter now. "Not even to save us."

The wind shifted—not closer, not harder. Simply attentive.

Cassian leaned back slightly, his strength ebbing now in ways that could no longer be hidden. Nadya reached out again, this time not to move him, but to steady him where he sat. Cassian accepted that help without comment.

"I thought authority meant deciding," Cassian said, voice thinning but clear. "Telling people where to stand. When to move. Who to trust."

Joshua listened as if these words were being etched into him.

"It doesn't," Cassian continued. "It means staying when everyone else needs you to move. It means refusing to turn people into proof. It means letting the cost land where it must instead of passing it on."

Joshua's eyes burned. "You're paying for what I broke."

Cassian did not deny it. He simply met Joshua's gaze. "I'm returning what fled," he said. "That's different."

The Lantern's attention sharpened then. I felt it like a pressure shift, the air around us tightening slightly, as if he had leaned forward without moving his feet. He did not intervene. He did not interrupt. Curiosity had replaced impatience.

Cassian's breathing grew shallow. His hand trembled once against Nadya's sleeve and then stilled. Whatever choice he had been carrying internally had settled now, complete.

I felt it too—a tightening in my chest, a sense of something aligning. This was not strategy. This was not sacrifice announced for effect.

This was an end choosing its shape.

The wind did not touch Cassian.

It waited.

And I knew, with a certainty that had nothing to do with foresight, that when he moved next, the world would not move with him.

It would receive him.

What Was Never Taken

Cassian did not announce what he was doing.

There was no signal, no lifted hand, no final instruction given to anyone standing nearby. He did not ask us to witness him, and he did not ask Joshua to prepare. He simply shifted—barely—and the change was enough that I felt it before I understood it. The air near him went still, not because the wind had eased, but because something had finished.

Joshua felt it too.

He looked up sharply, breath catching, as if a sound too low to hear had reached him anyway. Cassian met his eyes and held them there, not urgently, not pleading. There was no request in the look. Only permission.

"You don't have to—" Joshua began.

Cassian shook his head once. Not refusal. Completion.

"I won't take what isn't given," Cassian said quietly. "But this was never taken."

His hand came to rest against Joshua's chest. There was no force in the touch, no pressure, no ritual to it. It was not an act of will. It was a yielding.

What passed between them did not flare or burn. It did not arrive like fire or flood or judgment.

It settled.

I felt it as a change in weight—something finally stopping its sideways pull. Joshua inhaled sharply—not in pain, but in recognition—his shoulders drawing inward as if his body remembered how to hold something it had been bracing against for too long. The light did not erase what was already in him. It did not cleanse or absolve or resolve.

It aligned.

Authority returned the way breath returns after being held too long—not triumphant, not loud. Necessary.

Joshua stayed on his knees.

He did not rise. He did not glow. His hands pressed into the frost as if the truth of his weight had only just reached him.

Cassian exhaled.

The sound was thin. Final.

At the same instant, the wind fell silent.

Not gradually.

It stopped.

The pressure vanished, and the sudden calm struck harder than the storm ever had. Cloaks settled. Frost stilled. Breath returned to lungs without resistance. Somewhere to my left, Shim'on went motionless, as if he'd decided this stillness needed guarding.

The Lantern recoiled.

His light flared violently, edges snapping tight as he turned on the clearing, fury tearing loose of polish. "No," he snarled, the word cracking through the stillness. "I did not release you."

The wind did not answer.

Cassian sagged as the strength left him, the reason for holding himself upright finished now. Nadya caught him as he folded, lowering him to the frost with care that arrived too late to save him and mattered anyway.

His breathing was shallow, uneven, each breath chosen.

"You're—" Joshua started, voice breaking. "You're giving it back."

Cassian's eyes found him again, steady even now. "Not all of it," he said. "Enough."

Joshua shook his head helplessly. "I don't deserve—"

"That was never the measure," Cassian replied. "You're almost restored. That matters."

The words hit me harder than the wind ever had.

I remembered Tomas then—remembered the way his light had torn loose and left him empty on the stone, remembered how Joshua had carried that return like a wound instead of a gift. This was different. Not the first light entering him. Not the beginning.

A restoration.

Proof that what had fled could still come home.

Cassian's pain moved through him in waves now, visible in the tightening of his jaw, the careful pacing of his breaths. He did not resist it. He did not welcome it. He endured it the way he had endured everything else—not as trial, not as proof, but as cost allowed to land where it must.

Across the clearing, the Lantern watched, fury sharpening into something colder as realization set in.

Authority was no longer something he could exploit.

It had been returned without becoming available.

He stepped forward once, light compressing as if to seize the moment back by force—then stopped. There was nothing to take. No vacuum to fill. The space Cassian left remained open, unclaimed.

The Lantern's expression hardened.

Command was finished.

Cassian turned his head slightly, eyes finding me where I stood frozen. "Don't build around this," he said.

"I won't," I answered, and meant it.

That was enough.

Cassian's eyes closed—not in surrender, but in rest. His breathing slowed, each rise of his chest shallower than the last, until there was no next breath to wait for.

No struggle marked the end.

Cassian died as he had lived in this place—not taking, not claiming, not ruling. Bearing witness until the cost finished its work.

Shim'on did not turn away when Cassian went still. He remained where he was, eyes lowered, as if committing the weight of the moment to memory rather than meaning.

The wind did not return.

The Lantern turned away, light drawing inward, fury reshaping itself into intent. When he looked back at us, there was no general there.

Only a hunter.

The battle did not end.

It changed direction.

Cassian lay still at our feet, blood darkening the frost. Authority had not been taken from him.

It had been given back.

And it killed him.

The Second Break

The Stillness After the Wind

Cassian's body had not cooled yet, but the world behaved as if it had already agreed to forget how heat worked.

The absence of wind was the first thing that made the clearing feel wrong—not because the cold deepened, but because nothing corrected it. Frost lay where it had fallen, unbothered by breath or movement. Reed-edges did not whisper against one another. The air stayed fixed, as if it had been told to hold and had obeyed too well.

It was the kind of stillness that follows command, not peace.

Gillie stood closest to Cassian. Not kneeling. Not reaching. Just standing where momentum had left her, blade hanging slack at her side, shoulders drawn inward as if the world had narrowed around her without permission. Her breath came shallow and measured, each inhale deliberate, as though her body had forgotten how to breathe without resistance.

She wasn't crying.

That was what unsettled me most.

Grief usually moved her—sharp or sudden—but this hadn't yet found a way in. She stared at Cassian's body with the expression of someone trying to remember what sequence came next, and failing. As if the rules had changed mid-gesture and she was still waiting for the correction.

Joshua remained on his knees.

His hands were pressed into the frost, fingers splayed, knuckles white. His shoulders bowed under a weight that did not belong to the cold or the fight or even Cassian's fall alone. His breath trembled, uneven, as if it were testing the idea of being felt again after too long spent numb.

He did not look at Cassian.

He did not look at Gillie.

He looked at the ground like someone who had been forgiven once and did not trust it to happen again.

The others were scattered, not as formation but as consequence.

Nadya stood rigid, jaw clenched so tightly I could see the muscle jumping beneath her skin. Her gaze moved once toward Cassian and then away, as if she had learned long ago not to linger where loss might ask something of her.

Rowan's fingers twitched around his blade. Not tightening. Not loosening. A restless motion, like a man waiting for a signal that no longer existed.

Sera's breath came in thin threads, shoulders lifting too high with every inhale. She stared at nothing, lips parted as if the world had paused mid-sentence and she was afraid to interrupt.

Eliah's eyes shone with tears he refused to acknowledge. He did not wipe them away. He stood very still, as if movement might be interpreted as permission to feel.

Miriam watched the air above Cassian's body with an intensity that bordered on accusation, like she expected something—light, breath, a sign—to return and finish what had been interrupted.

No one spoke.

No one stepped forward.

No one dared to fill the space Cassian had left behind.

Shim'on stood a short distance back from Cassian's body, posture unchanged. His attention moved once—taking in Gillie, then Joshua, then the edges of the clearing—before settling again, patient and unclaimed. One hand rested near his weapon, not drawing it, simply keeping himself ready to move if someone else couldn't.

The silence did not feel respectful.

It felt opportunistic.

I became aware, slowly, of the Lantern again—not because he moved, but because he didn't. His light had compressed, drawing inward rather than flaring outward, edges sharpened not for attack but for observation. He stood across the clearing with the patience of something that understood how moments broke when they were pressed too soon.

He was watching the stillness.

Measuring it.

Learning what it made visible.

That was when I noticed Kali.

She hadn't advanced. She hadn't withdrawn. She stood where she had been before Cassian fell, her posture loose, almost bored, weight resting casually on one hip. Her smile—thin, practiced, cruel—had softened into something quieter. Not less dangerous. More focused.

She was not looking at Cassian.

She was looking at Gillie.

The realization sent a cold spike through my spine. Gillie's attention was still fixed downward, her vision anchored to the place where certainty had ended. She had not lifted her blade. She had not shifted her stance. She had not felt the opening.

Kali had.

The Lantern had.

The clearing held its breath.

It wasn't waiting for grief.

It was waiting for permission.

A pilgrim somewhere near the edge of the clearing took a half-step backward, boot crunching softly against ice. The sound echoed too loudly in the stillness. Several heads turned instinctively toward it, searching for a source of danger that refused to announce itself.

The wind did not return.

That absence pressed harder now—not as cold, but as imbalance. The world felt unfinished, like a held note that wouldn't resolve. Every instinct in my body screamed that something was about to happen, not because the tension was rising, but because it had stopped rising altogether.

I shifted my weight, the scroll's strap creaking faintly across my shoulder. The sound felt obscene, too loud for the moment, and I froze again, heart pounding as if I had committed some small sacrilege.

Gillie still hadn't moved.

Her blade slipped a fraction lower in her grip, the tip angling toward the frost as if gravity had remembered her before she had remembered herself. Her shoulders sagged—not in surrender, but in fatigue, the kind that comes when the force holding you upright vanishes without warning.

Joshua's breath hitched.

He lifted his head slightly—not enough to meet anyone's eyes, but enough to suggest awareness returning in painful increments. His mouth opened as if to speak, then closed again. Whatever words he considered, he did not trust them yet.

Across the clearing, Marcus shifted his stance. Lucien's gaze sharpened. Julian's smile thinned, interest flickering behind his eyes. Elana leaned subtly closer to the Lantern, her presence coiling near his shoulder. Raven tilted his head, curiosity edging toward alertness.

And Kali—

Kali smiled.

Not wide.

Not hungry.

Certain.

This was the pause she had been waiting for.

Not grief.

Not confusion.

The stillness that follows obedience breaking.

The stillness that asks the wrong question: What happens now?

Gillie's fingers tightened around her blade at last, a delayed reflex that arrived seconds too late. Her gaze lifted—just a fraction—from Cassian's body, her focus beginning the slow, painful process of re-entering the world.

But Kali was already moving.

The clearing did not know it yet.

The Lantern did.

And the silence—treacherous, unguarded—made room for the strike.

The Strike That Found the Pause

Kali moved like a decision finally released.

One heartbeat she was still—weight settled, smile faint, posture almost languid. The next, she wasn't crossing the space so much as erasing it. Shadow snapped forward with her, folding distance into something thin and useless, and the frost beneath her feet did not crunch the way it should have. Even sound seemed reluctant to follow, as though the world didn't want to admit what was happening until it was already done.

She didn't shout.

She didn't taunt.

She didn't offer the clearing a warning it could pretend to ignore.

That was her cruelty—how clean she kept it. How she treated killing like punctuation rather than performance.

Gillie still hadn't fully returned to herself. She had lifted her gaze, yes, but the motion was slow, delayed, like a lantern being relit by hands that didn't remember the rhythm. Her eyes were still caught on the shape of Cassian's body, on the fact of it, on the quiet brutality of blood on white. Her blade hung low in her grip, and her stance was not the stance of a fighter who was ready.

It was the stance of someone who had been forced to stop mid-breath.

Kali saw that. Kali loved that.

The strike was angled for ribs—low and precise, a line meant to slide beneath armor and certainty alike. It wasn't a duel. It wasn't a challenge. It was an execution written into the pause.

For a fraction of a second, my mind refused to believe it—not because I doubted Kali, but because the clearing still felt like held breath. The idea of movement felt like a violation.

Then my body reacted, late and furious.

"Gillie—" I tried to shout.

But the word caught in my throat.

Not because my lungs failed, but because the air itself felt thick with consequence, as if speaking would bind something I didn't understand. I heard my own voice break against silence and die there.

Gillie didn't turn.

Her grief had made her narrow, and in that narrowing, she didn't see the dark blade coming for her.

Nadya saw it.

Rowan saw it.

Eliah saw it.

They all moved in the same instant, but not together—scattered bodies trying to remember how to become one force again. Nadya surged forward with a curse that cracked sharp through the stillness, but she was too far. Rowan lunged, blade lifting, but his footing slipped on frost still unsoftened by wind. Eliah's hand came up as if to call light—then hesitated, as if his own belief had to decide whether it was allowed to answer anymore.

Sera inhaled sharply, a sound like a prayer trying to begin and failing.

Miriam's mouth opened, but no sound came.

And Joshua—

Joshua did not move.

Not because he didn't care.

Because he was still on his knees, still bound inside himself, still broken in the particular way that makes your body forget you have permission to stand. His head turned—slow, horrified—eyes tracking Kali like a man watching a weapon he once helped sharpen.

Kali's blade flashed.

Her smile didn't change. She didn't look at anyone else. Her entire attention was fixed on Gillie, not as a person, not as a soul—just as a vulnerable point in a line she intended to sever.

Gillie shifted at last.

A fraction.

Not enough.

Her shoulder turned slightly, as if she were about to step toward Cassian, as if she were about to kneel, as if grief had finally decided motion was acceptable again.

That small movement aligned her body perfectly for Kali's strike.

The blade was going to land.

I felt it as certainty—cold, immediate, unarguable. The kind of knowing that arrives before impact, when your mind races ahead because it cannot bear to be present for what comes next.

At the edge of the clearing, Shim'on shifted his footing—not forward, not back—adjusting as if he felt the break in timing before it reached the body it meant to claim. His gaze snapped to Kali's wrist, then to Gillie's ribs, mapping the line of the strike as if he could anchor the moment by seeing it clearly.

Time did something strange.

Not slowing.

Not stopping.

Just thinning—like the clearing had become a page stretched too taut, and the ink of action was about to tear straight through it.

Kali was almost there.

And in the far edge of my awareness, I felt the Lantern's gaze sharpen.

He wasn't surprised.

He wasn't reacting.

He was watching the inevitability he had set in motion take the shape he wanted.

This was his proof.

Not that he could kill us—he'd always proven that.

But that grief made us sloppy.

That loss made us divisible.

Kali's blade cut into the space directly in front of Gillie's ribs.

And still Gillie didn't see it.

Her eyes were on Cassian.

On what had been paid.

On what couldn't be returned.

And then something inside the clearing—something not wind, not light, not command—shifted.

Not a miracle.

Not a rescue flaring bright enough to be named.

Just a disruption at the edge of inevitability.

The scroll on my shoulder didn't flare.

It didn't speak.

But the strap pulled tight across my collarbone, as if it had leaned—not toward the strike, not toward Kali, but toward Gillie. Toward the pause itself. As if it recognized the danger not in the blade, but in the stillness that made the blade possible.

The world seemed to catch.

Just for a heartbeat.

Not enough to stop Kali.

Enough to make the clearing notice her.

Nadya's curse turned into a scream.

Rowan's blade finally found traction and surged forward.

Eliah's hand lifted again—this time without hesitation—fingers spread as if to call something he had no right to demand, only to beg.

Gillie's head snapped fractionally to the side, her instincts finally arriving.

And Kali—

Kali's smile sharpened, offended by resistance that should have come sooner.

Her blade continued forward anyway.

Because she didn't need the pause anymore.

She had already found it.

And now she meant to finish what she had started—before the clearing could remember how to fight as one.

Michael

Someone stepped into the strike.

Not lunging.

Not flailing.

Not late.

The movement was so precise it felt wrong at first—as if the clearing itself had chosen a body and pushed it forward to interrupt what had already been decided.

Micah.

He came from Gillie's blind side, crossing the line of the blade with a speed that did not belong to a pilgrim, or a survivor, or a man who claimed to have learned his fighting in fear and desperation. This was not panic. This was not instinct alone.

This was memory made muscle.

Kali's blade met him instead of Gillie.

Not cleanly.

Micah didn't try to stop the strike—he redirected it, twisting his torso at the last possible instant so the blade slid inward rather than through. The impact cracked through the clearing with a dull, brutal sound, the kind that made breath seize across the field in sympathetic pain. Frost sprayed where his heel dug in, boots skidding half a step as he absorbed the force with his shoulder and ribs.

Kali hissed—not in surprise, but in offense.

Her eyes snapped to his face, pupils narrowing as if she were reclassifying him in real time. Whatever she had thought Micah was—useful, weak, disposable—it shattered in that instant.

"You," she spat, the word sharp with contempt and something dangerously close to recognition.

Micah didn't answer.

He couldn't.

Her blade was already buried in him.

Blood bloomed dark against the frost, steaming faintly now—not with heat, but with the body's last stubborn insistence on being alive. Micah's breath punched out of him in a single, involuntary sound, his jaw tightening hard enough that I heard his teeth grind.

But he didn't fall.

Instead, his other hand came up.

And there was a blade in it.

Not drawn in desperation.

Already there.

The movement that followed was quiet. Efficient. Terrible in its restraint.

Micah drove his blade into Kali's side, just beneath the edge of her armor, angling upward with a precision that made my stomach drop. He didn't scream. He didn't curse. He didn't even look angry.

He looked decided.

Kali's breath hitched.

Her smile shattered—not into fear, but fury. She tried to twist away, to pull back, to disengage and finish what she had started from another angle. But Micah stepped into her, locking his arm, holding her in place with a strength that did not belong to the man we thought we knew.

Her light flickered.

Just once.

That was all it took.

The plague that had threaded the clearing—whispers, distortions, the thin pressure of despair that bent truth sideways—buckled. Not slowly. Not gently. It collapsed like a tent whose central pole had been yanked free. Sound rushed back into the space, sharp and disoriented. A scream cut off mid-note. Shadows lost cohesion, snapping back into the shapes they had been pretending not to inhabit.

Kali staggered.

Her laughter—always so deliberate, so cruelly placed—died unfinished in her throat.

She tried to speak.

What came out instead was breath.

Thin. Broken.

Her knees buckled first.

She fell hard into the frost, her body folding in on itself with a sound that felt too final to argue with. The blade slid free from her grasp, clattering once before vanishing beneath drifting shadow that no longer knew how to obey her.

Micah sank with her.

Not collapsing.

Lowering himself, as if the decision to stand had finally run out of strength.

He dropped to one knee, then both, one hand pressed hard against his side, fingers already slick and red. His other hand still gripped the blade that had ended her, knuckles white, trembling now—not with fear, but with the cost of holding on just a moment longer than his body wanted to allow.

For a heartbeat, no one moved.

Then—

"Michael, NO!"

Olivia's voice tore through the clearing.

Not loud.

Not theatrical.

Devastated.

The name cracked something open in the world.

Gillie froze.

Not mid-step.

Mid-breath.

Michael.

The name struck her like a physical blow—not because she had never heard it, but because she had carried it for so long without permission to touch it. The name of a man who had left. The name of a ghost shaped by silence and unanswered questions. The name she had learned to bury so deeply she could pretend it didn't still ache.

Michael.

Micah's head jerked at the sound.

Not in guilt.

Not in fear.

In recognition.

Just enough for Gillie to see it.

Just enough for the truth to land.

She staggered forward, the Balanced Blade trembling in her hand, her mind racing faster than her body could follow. "Micah—" she started, then stopped, the word catching wrong in her mouth. She swallowed hard. "Michael?"

He looked up.

And for the first time since I had known him, there was nothing guarded in his eyes.

No masks.

No bargains.

No careful distance.

Just a man bleeding out on frost, staring at the daughter he had never been allowed to keep.

"You look like her," he whispered.

The words broke her.

Not loudly.

Not cleanly.

Her face crumpled, grief and fury and longing colliding in a way that left no room for pride. She dropped to her knees beside him, heedless of the blood soaking into her clothes, the cold biting through fabric she no longer felt.

"You don't get to say that," she said, voice shaking. "You don't get—"

"I know," he breathed. His hand came up—not to be held, not to be forgiven—but simply to touch. His fingers brushed her wrist, light as breath, barely there. "I couldn't lose you too."

Tears fell, silent and relentless, striking the frost like rain that had waited too long.

Micah's grip slackened.

The blade slipped from his fingers.

His breath stuttered once—twice—and then stopped.

Michael died with his eyes on his daughter.

The clearing exhaled.

Not in relief.

In shock.

Kali lay motionless, her presence already thinning, her influence gone so completely it felt like a wound that had been cauterized by absence. The plague she had held together did not linger. It did not argue. It simply ended.

Across the clearing, something broke.

Not exploded.

Collapsed inward.

The Lantern looked at Kali's body.

And for the first time, his light did not command the space around him.

It contracted.

Sharp. Sudden. Violent in its restraint.

Lucien stiffened, calculation slipping for a fraction of a second into something like alarm.

Julian's smile vanished.

Elana's breath caught, her hand lifting instinctively before she could stop herself.

Marcus took a step back without meaning to.

Raven tilted his head, curiosity edged now with something like unease.

The Lantern did not roar.

He did not strike.

He did not summon anything at all.

"She was mine," he said.

Not a claim.

A truth.

The words landed like ice.

His gaze lifted slowly to us, cold and precise, stripping away the last illusion that grief might soften him.

"You will run," he said.

Not a command.

A prophecy.

And as Gillie knelt beside her father's body, as Joshua lifted his head with something broken and human flickering behind his eyes, as the Seven drew closer together without speaking—

The Lantern took one step forward.

And the world leaned toward escape.

The Lantern Breaks

The Lantern did not scream.

The absence of it was worse.

He stood where he had been standing when Kali fell, his posture unchanged, his hands still, his light drawn so tightly inward it no longer spilled across the clearing. For a long breath, nothing moved around him—not frost, not shadow, not even the thin debris of sound that usually seemed to orbit his presence like obedient ash.

Grief did not announce itself.

It hollowed.

"She was mine," he said again, quieter this time—not softer, but emptied of performance.

The lieutenants felt it immediately.

Lucien's gaze flicked from Kali's body to the Lantern's face, calculation recalibrating at dangerous speed. Power had not vanished—but its axis had shifted, and men who survived such shifts learned quickly where not to stand.

Julian's expression reassembled itself with effort. The hunger returned, but dulled now by uncertainty. His fingers flexed as if testing whether the rules he depended on were still intact.

Elana's breath came shallow. She had moved closer without realizing it, her body reacting before her will. Something in the Lantern's contraction pulled at her—an old tether tightening, reminding her where she belonged, and how much of that belonging had always been borrowed.

Marcus said nothing, but the subtle way his shoulders squared betrayed him. He was bracing. Preparing. A soldier waiting to be given back his enemy.

Raven watched the Lantern instead of the dead.

That was new.

The Lantern took one step forward.

Not toward us.

Toward Kali.

His light shifted as he moved—not flaring, not striking, but compressing even further, collapsing inward until the space around him felt starved of oxygen. Frost creaked beneath his boots as if the ground itself were unsure how to hold his weight anymore.

He stopped beside her body.

For a moment—just one—I thought he might kneel.

The idea felt obscene as soon as it surfaced.

He did not kneel.

He looked down at her as one might look at a structure long relied upon, suddenly missing from the landscape. Not mourned for its beauty, but for its function.

The Lantern lifted his gaze again.

To us.

Not scanning.

Selecting.

"You were permitted to survive," he said calmly. "You were shaped. Pressured. Contained." His eyes lingered on Gillie—on the body at her knees, on the blood frozen into the frost around them. "You were never meant to be free."

His light sharpened—not outward, but inward, the way a blade sharpens itself before cutting deeper.

"I gave you time," he continued. "I gave you structure. I gave you enemies you could name, so you would never think to question the hand that pointed them out."

He paused.

"And still," he said softly, "you reached for lineage instead of obedience."

The word lineage landed like an accusation.

"Now look at what it has cost you."

His gaze swept the clearing—not theatrically, but clinically. Cassian's body. Kali's. Michael's. The scattered wounded. The silence fraying at the edges of the space where plagues had once obeyed him without hesitation.

"You have mistaken grief for victory," the Lantern said. "This is not collapse." His eyes hardened. "This is refinement."

Something in the air shifted.

Not wind.

Direction.

The scroll on my shoulder stirred—not pulling, not pushing—but turning. The sensation was subtle enough that I might have missed it if I hadn't already learned to listen for what did not demand attention. The strap across my chest tightened a fraction, leather creaking softly as the weight of it reoriented itself.

A path had not opened.

But a direction had.

The Lantern felt it.

His eyes flicked—not to me, not to Gillie—but to the space behind us. The far edge of the clearing. The place where frost thinned and stone dipped low, where the land fell away into a shadowed cut that had not been there before.

The beginning of a canyon.

His jaw tightened.

Not in rage.

In realization.

"You will run," he said again, and now the words carried something colder than threat. They carried inevitability. "Not because you are brave." His gaze locked on Gillie. "But because grief teaches the body to flee before the mind catches up."

Joshua rose slowly to his feet, something unsteady and raw in the way he stood. His eyes flicked between Michael's body and the Lantern, then toward the darkening cut in the earth beyond us. Whatever loyalty had once anchored him was cracking under the weight of too many truths arriving at once.

We drew closer together—not forming ranks, not answering to command, but clustering the way people do when the ground beneath them begins to tilt. Shim'on closed the gap on the outside edge, not leading, not retreating—just placing himself where a strike would have to go through him first.

The Lantern did not stop us.

That was the final proof.

If he had commanded now—if he had unleashed his forces, called wind or fire or bone—the path would have closed. The rule the scroll had introduced would have snapped shut the moment claim replaced grief.

He knew it.

We all felt it.

This was not the moment to strike.

This was the moment to let us go.

Not out of mercy.

Out of necessity.

The Lantern took another step back.

Not retreating.

Repositioning.

His light cooled further, edges smoothing into something observational again—less tyrant, more tactician.

"Run," he said one last time. "Carry your dead. Carry your names. Carry your stories." His gaze narrowed. "They will weigh you down."

He turned away from us.

Toward preparation.

The cold he left behind was different from the cold he wielded. It did not bite. It did not hum with threat. It settled—anticipatory, patient, absolute.

Gillie pressed her forehead briefly to her father's shoulder, a private gesture of grief she did not ask anyone to witness. Then she rose, jaw set, eyes clear in a way they had not been before.

"This isn't finished," she said—not to the Lantern, not to the dead—but to the space ahead.

Olivia stepped in close, her presence steady as bedrock. "No," she agreed quietly.

"But it's begun," Gillie said.

The scroll leaned again—not opening the way, not splitting the earth—but aligning us with it. The canyon's mouth yawned wider, stone shifting with a low, grinding sigh that felt less like rupture and more like permission.

Behind us, the Lantern watched.

Not chasing.

Yet.

Ahead of us, the land bent—not into safety, not into certainty, but into a direction that had not existed moments before.

The scroll did not open the way.

It only leaned—subtly, firmly—toward motion.

And the world shifted toward escape.

Chains Unbroken

The Perfect Path

We ran. Not in formation. Not with any clean line of purpose. We ran the way bodies run when grief is still too hot to touch and the only mercy left is distance.

Something in all of us had broken back in the clearing, and the running only made the fractures louder.

Frost snapped beneath our boots in brittle sheets, and the reeds along the clearing's edge hissed as we shoved through them, dead stalks clawing at our sleeves as if they wanted us to stay and finish what had started here.

Cassian came with us.

He was heavier than he should have been, not because death adds weight, but because it removes cooperation. He did not shift to help our grip. He did not brace or balance or breathe at the right moments. He was simply there—solid, unyielding, a truth pressed into our arms. Nadya took his shoulders without a word. Eliah had his legs. When the ground bucked and the frost gave way to mud beneath the thin white, Miriam slipped in beside Nadya and caught the strain before it tore her wrist. No one asked who would carry him. No one offered to take him. We just did it, like instinct, like penance.

Shim'on ran a half-pace wide of the line, close enough to be counted and far enough not to be claimed, his eyes tracking the ground ahead the way a man watches for fractures before they open.

Gillie kept moving at our side, close enough to touch and far enough not to be steadied by anyone's hand. The Balanced Blade rode at her hip, striking her thigh in small, rhythmic taps each time she lengthened her stride. She didn't look back. Her face was set the way it had been set when she stood in front of the wind and refused to bend—not hardened into stone, but narrowed into clarity. Tears had dried on her cheeks in uneven tracks that caught the dim light whenever her head tilted, but she didn't wipe them away. She didn't need anyone to see them, and she didn't need to pretend they weren't there.

Behind us, Olivia did not run.

She stood at the edge of the clearing where the frost still remembered what it had held, her silhouette steady against the shifting dark. She did not call after us at first. She did not reach out. She watched—eyes following Gillie alone, not to claim her, not to tether her, but to release her.

When Gillie faltered for half a step, breath catching hard in her throat, Olivia lifted her voice—not loud, not urgent, but unmistakable.

"Go," she called.

Not a command.

A blessing.

Gillie's stride didn't break, but something in her shoulders eased, just enough to keep her upright.

"I am with you," Olivia said then, voice carrying farther than it should have been able to. "Not behind you. Not ahead of you. With you."

Gillie didn't slow, but the words struck something deep—a chain she'd carried for years shifting just enough to hurt.

Gillie did not turn.

She didn't have to.

The words settled into her like ballast, like a truth that could be carried without being displayed.

Kaela ran a few steps behind, jaw clenched, eyes wide in a way that made her look younger than she already was. She glanced once toward Olivia—just once—and the look that crossed her face was not longing, not accusation, but recognition. The kind that hurts because it is finally honest. Her gaze dropped away as if burned, and she ran harder, grief sharp and unguarded in her chest.

Olivia remained where she was.

Watching the space where they had been. Watching the direction they had gone. Watching until the dark shifted and the path claimed them fully.

Only then did she lower her head.

Joshua ran on the outer edge.

Not with us.

Near enough that if the dark surged after us he would be caught in it, far enough that no one could pretend he belonged in the center. He held his arms close to his body like a man expecting to be struck. His shoulders were hunched, not from fatigue but from a weight inside him that didn't know where to go now that the wind was gone. When he looked at Cassian, his face tightened as if he wanted to speak, but nothing came. When he looked at Gillie, he looked away again, as if the act of seeing her was accusation enough.

The scroll stayed on my shoulder.

Not warm. Not bright. Not singing the way it sometimes did when it wanted to remind us it was alive. It was a presence like a compass that had found north and would not allow itself to be argued with. The leather strap across my chest tightened and eased in subtle pulses as if the scroll were breathing through the harness, and each time it shifted, the world in front of us adjusted.

Not the earth splitting. Not the sky opening. Nothing miraculous.

Just alignment.

A fallen trunk that should have forced us wide rolled just enough that a narrow lane appeared beside it. A patch of ice that should have sent Nadya sliding held long enough for her to keep Cassian steady. A tangle of reeds parted at the last possible moment, not like it was pushed aside, but like it had never grown there in the first place. The path did not announce itself. It simply kept being the next correct step, again and again, like the world had been persuaded into yielding without knowing it had agreed.

Rowan noticed first.

He was running with his blade still in hand, not raised, not lowered, simply held as if it was part of his body now. He kept glancing ahead and then down, reading the ground the way he read rooms—watching for traps, for patterns, for lies. After three turns that should have been wrong and one narrow cut between two stone shelves that should have been impossible, he let out a sharp breath through his teeth.

"This isn't chance," he said, voice clipped by motion.

No one answered him.

Not because we disagreed, but because speech felt expensive, and slowing felt like death.

Sera ran close to me, her vial tucked under her arm like a secret she could not afford to spill. Her hum was gone. Whatever she used to steady herself with had been swallowed by the need to keep moving. She kept touching her throat with two fingers as if checking whether her voice still existed. Her eyes stayed forward, fixed on the narrowing land, wide with the kind of fear that isn't fear of pain but fear of what pain will ask you to say aloud.

Miriam glanced back once.

Just once.

Not toward the Lantern, not toward the battlefield, not toward the dead we couldn't take with us. She glanced back the way someone glances toward a door they know is closing behind them, and her breath hitched as if she felt the hinge swing. Then she faced forward again and ran harder, as if speed could keep regret from catching her.

The canyon mouth had been there before, but not like this.

Before, it was a scar in the land—a fissure the world carried without explanation. Now it yawned wider, stone grinding low as if the earth were making room in its own throat. The walls rose on either side, dark and striated with pale seams that caught what little light we had. The air changed as soon as we crossed the threshold. Not colder, not warmer. Thinner. As if breath itself had to decide whether it wanted to follow us inside.

The scroll leaned.

Not sharply. Not like command.

Like urgency.

"Keep pace," Nadya hissed, more to herself than to anyone else. She adjusted her grip under Cassian's shoulders, knuckles white, and Eliah mirrored her without needing to be told. Their steps synchronized the way people synchronize under strain. Cassian's body bounced once, a terrible jolt, and Nadya made a sound like she'd been struck. Miriam slid closer, bracing the weight with her forearm.

"Don't," she murmured. "Don't apologize. Just run."

Gillie's breath was ragged now. Not from weakness—from holding too much inside her chest. She kept close to our line, stride steady, eyes forward, as if looking back might pull her apart. For several strides she said nothing, jaw tight, shoulders drawn inward, as though language itself might snap whatever fragile cord was keeping her upright.

Then, without turning her head, Gillie said, "You knew."

It wasn't accusation.

It wasn't even a question.

It was a statement shaped like pain.

The reply came without sound of movement, without breath beside her ear—quiet and exact, arriving the way answers do when you've carried them longer than you've spoken them.

I knew enough.

Gillie swallowed hard. The motion made her throat work like she was trying to force a stone down.

"His name," she said. "You called him—"

Michael.

Something in her broke, but not the way it had before.

The name slid into the air without echo, without drama. It did not change the canyon. It did not make the scroll flare. It simply existed—heavier than it had any right to be—because it belonged to a man who had just died with his eyes on his daughter.

Gillie's shoulders shook once—not with sobbing, but with shock. Some truths don't shatter you all at once; they crack you open in quiet, merciless increments.

She kept running. Her fingers tightened around the grip of the Balanced Blade until the leather creaked.

"And her?" Gillie asked, voice thinner now. "You said—when you spoke to Kaela—"

There was the faintest pause. Not hesitation. Weight.

Ella.

Kaela stumbled at the sound.

It wasn't a full trip—her foot caught on a ridge of stone, her body pitched forward, and Rowan's hand shot out, catching her elbow hard enough to leave bruises later. Kaela yanked free, not angry, just raw, as if being steadied felt too much like being owned. She recovered her stride, but her face had gone pale.

"Don't," Kaela rasped, and no one knew if she meant don't say it again, don't look at me, or don't make me feel this now while my lungs are burning and my hands are empty.

Gillie turned her head slightly, eyes wide, and the look that passed between her and Kaela was not reconciliation or revelation. It was shared grief catching itself midair, realizing it had landed in more than one body.

"I didn't—" Gillie began, then stopped, because there was nothing she could say that wouldn't be either too late or too much.

The answer did not rush to fill the silence. It never did. Truth arrived the way it always had—unadorned, unsoftened.

He left you with me, the voice said, low and steady. Not because you weren't wanted. Not because you weren't loved. Because the world he had chosen… was already eating him.

Gillie's breath broke. A sound escaped her—small, involuntary—like the first crack in ice.

"And her?" Gillie asked, and the question carried years inside it. "Ella—Kaela—she—"

Gillie's gaze flicked to Kaela's back—to the tension in her shoulders, to the way she was running like she was trying to outrun being seen.

She lost him too, came the answer. In a different way. The kind of loss that leaves you alive and still abandoned.

Kaela heard enough to flinch. She pressed her mouth hard shut, like she was biting down on words that would bleed if released.

We ran deeper.

The canyon narrowed, then widened unexpectedly, opening into a passage where the stone walls rose smoother and higher. The ground underfoot changed from frost-slick to dry grit, and the sound of our steps sharpened, every footfall clicking like something counting down.

Rowan glanced back over his shoulder.

Not far. Just enough to confirm what we all felt without seeing.

"They're not behind us," he said.

Nadya's laugh was breathless and ugly. "Yet."

Rowan didn't look away from the canyon mouth. His pace didn't change. But his voice lowered, edged with thought rather than fear.

"He let us go," he said. "Not because we escaped."

Eliah glanced at him sharply. "Then why?"

Rowan's eyes flicked—not back, but sideways. Toward Joshua. Just long enough to measure weight.

"Because he still expects something to return."

The words passed through the line like a cold thread. No one spoke for a beat. Even the canyon seemed to listen.

"You're saying—" Nadya began.

"I'm saying," Rowan interrupted softly, "that some possessions aren't meant to be broken. They're meant to be reclaimed."

Joshua heard it.

He didn't slow.

He didn't argue.

He didn't look back.

But something in his shoulders tightened, the way a man tightens when he knows a debt is being named without his consent.

Gillie's grip on the Balanced Blade shifted—not toward Joshua, not away—but firmer against her own side.

"If he comes," she said, breath hard but steady, "he won't come for us."

Rowan nodded once. "No."

"He'll come for what he thinks is still his."

No one said Joshua's name.

They didn't need to.

The scroll leaned again, narrowing the path as if it were listening too—correcting nothing, offering no judgment, only direction.

Forward.

Behind them, the world began to change.

The Lantern's Grief

They were gone.

Not defeated.

Not hidden.

Gone.

The Lantern remained where the clearing had broken open, light held unnaturally still around him, as if motion itself had been dismissed. Frost no longer crept. Wind no longer listened. The field had become an aftermath—a place where events had already decided themselves and no further argument would be accepted.

Kali lay at his feet.

Her body had not collapsed the way the pilgrims' had. There was no distortion in her shape, no grotesque compression. She lay as she had fallen, precise even in death, limbs aligned, face turned slightly upward as if she were still waiting for instruction.

The Lantern did not touch her.

He stood over her, light drawn inward so tightly it barely escaped the outline of his form. It did not flare. It did not dim. It contained itself—a restraint so absolute it bent the air around it.

"She was mine," he said.

Not loudly.

Not angrily.

Not as a threat.

As a statement of fact.

Lucien stood several paces back, hands folded, gaze unreadable. Julian lingered nearer than caution advised, his usual smile thinned into something restless. Elana hovered close to the Lantern's shoulder, her presence shaped like devotion made flesh. Marcus paced once, boots grinding frost into powder, then stilled.

Raven stood apart.

Not deliberately.

Instinctively.

The Lantern did not yet look at him.

"She did not fail," the Lantern said after a long silence. "She was taken."

Julian opened his mouth—perhaps to agree, perhaps to deflect—and stopped when the frost beneath his boot cracked inward, collapsing just enough to remind him where power still lived.

No one corrected the Lantern.

Grief, in him, did not soften.

It clarified.

Kali had been his cleanest expression—will without interpretation, cruelty without indulgence, obedience without hunger. Where others sought favor or position, she had sought alignment. She had carried his intent without asking what it would cost.

That was why her stillness offended him.

Not because she was dead.

Because she had been removed without consent.

The Lantern knelt.

The act was not reverent. It was evaluative. His light brushed the edge of her form once, twice—not to restore, not to punish, but to confirm what could not be reversed.

Something in the air withdrew. A chain slackened.

Raven felt the break like a breath he wasn't supposed to have—freedom shaped like danger.

He did not move.

He did not smile.

He did not run.

But something that had always pulled him forward—tightened him toward obedience, narrowed his options until even rebellion felt scripted—was gone.

The Lantern rose.

Slowly.

His gaze lifted, not toward the canyon yet, but outward—across the clearing, the kneeling pilgrims, the scattered remnants of order. These were not soldiers. They were adherents. People who had bent because bending felt safer than standing alone.

They watched him now with wide, desperate eyes.

Waiting for meaning.

He saw them clearly.

Spent.

Replaceable.

Useful only as demonstration.

"You mistook patience for mercy," the Lantern said.

The air thickened.

"I gave you rules so you could believe suffering was purposeful," he continued. "I gave you enemies so you would not have to examine yourselves."

A pilgrim nearest him whispered, "Lord—"

The word never finished forming.

Pressure folded inward around the speaker's chest, precise and merciless. Bone compressed. Breath vanished. The body dropped without spectacle.

The others screamed.

The Lantern turned.

This time, his light expanded—not wildly, not chaotically, but with intent sharpened by loss. Cold surged through the clearing, compressing joints, locking spines, sealing mouths mid-prayer.

Julian exhaled something like delight.

Marcus leaned forward, eyes bright.

Elana watched with reverence, lips parted.

Raven watched with something closer to dread.

Not because of the violence.

Because it no longer claimed him.

Bodies fell. Silence returned.

The Lantern walked among them, boots leaving shallow impressions in the frost—not weight, but authority made visible. He stopped where the ground dipped, where the fight had thinned, where absence now felt deliberate.

"They ran," he said at last.

His gaze shifted—not searching—simply acknowledging direction.

"They believe distance is freedom."

Lucien inclined his head. "Shall we pursue?"

The Lantern did not answer immediately.

He thought of Kali.

Of severed control.

Of Joshua.

Joshua was not among the dead.

Not kneeling.

Not captured.

Not crushed.

Gone.

The realization tightened something deep and volatile inside him.

"They took what belongs to me," he said quietly.

That was when grief finished turning into resolve.

"Gather what remains," he commanded. "Strip the field. Leave nothing here that remembers them kindly."

This time, it was command.

The lieutenants straightened as one.

The Lantern turned last to Raven.

Not accusing.

Not threatening.

Assessing.

"You will come," he said.

Raven inclined his head.

"Yes."

The word tasted different than it used to.

Behind them, the clearing cooled into stillness—grief hardened into strategy.

Ahead, the canyon waited.

And the Lantern stepped forward, carrying loss like a blade he intended to use.

The Lantern's Wrath

The world gave way all at once.

Not with sound.

With surrender.

The frost that had once locked the clearing into a false stillness lost its grip in a single, collective failure. It did not melt. It collapsed. The surface sagged inward as if the ground had been hollowed from below, stone groaning under its own weight before splitting open in jagged seams. Fissures raced outward in erratic lines, glowing faintly with a dull, sulfurous light that did not illuminate so much as reveal depth—too much depth, too close to the surface.

The sky dimmed in answer.

Not into night.

Not into storm.

Into pressure.

Clouds sank lower, thickening, flattening the air until it felt as though the heavens themselves had been pressed down by a heavy hand. Light dulled. Distance shortened. The horizon pulled inward, crowding the clearing until there was nowhere left for the eye to rest without touching the Lantern.

He stood unmoving at the center of it.

Grief had finished its work.

Wrath took its place.

The air thickened until breathing felt like drawing smoke through cloth. Heat bloomed and vanished in erratic pulses—not flame, not warmth, but pressure that blistered skin without burning it. The smell of iron and ash seeped into the clearing, carried on no wind at all, as if the land itself had begun to bleed and exhale at the same time.

The pilgrims who had bent the knee felt it first.

Their relief curdled into confusion. Gratitude soured. Hope—thin already—began to shriek quietly inside their chests, searching for somewhere to hide.

One of them stepped forward.

He was shaking so hard his teeth chattered, hands clasped together as if prayer might still be a language the Lantern recognized. His voice cracked before it found its shape.

"My lord," he said. "We only meant to praise you. You spared them. You showed restraint. You showed order. You showed care."

The words were wrong.

Not because they were false.

Because they were mistimed.

The Lantern turned his head.

Just enough.

The man's next breath never arrived.

The air around his skull compressed without sound, without visible force. His eyes bulged, mouth opening in a silent question as blood burst from his nose and ears in thin streams. The pressure intensified, folding inward, collapsing bone and thought together until his head imploded with a wet, final sound.

His body crumpled a heartbeat later, neck reduced to ruin.

No one screamed.

They were past screaming now.

Another pilgrim dropped to her knees, palms slapping against the fractured stone. She sobbed openly, words tumbling over each other in frantic obedience.

"Forgive us. Forgive me. I will crawl if you command it. I will burn if you ask it. I will keep order. I will keep the light."

The Lantern stepped closer.

Where his foot touched the ground, the stone blackened and sank, as if scorched by something colder than fire. The air around her crystallized—not on her skin, but inside it. Her breath caught mid-sob, lungs freezing in expansion. Ice raced visibly beneath her flesh, veins turning white, then brittle.

She tipped sideways.

When she struck the ground, she shattered.

The sound was sharp and final, her body breaking into jagged pieces that skidded across the stone like spilled glass.

A murmur rose from the army.

Not fear.

Approval.

"Yes," Julian breathed, eyes shining as the shards slid to a stop. "There he is."

Lucien's lips curved in something like reverence. "Correction through annihilation."

Marcus straightened, shoulders squaring, armor humming softly as if recognizing a familiar frequency. Authority, long disrupted, was reassembling itself into a shape he understood.

The Lantern lifted his hand higher.

The sky responded.

A tear opened overhead—not a rift, not a wound, but a thinning, as if the sky itself had been scraped too thin to hold. Beyond it stretched a depthless red-black void, lightless and endless. Heat poured down in heavy waves, wilting what little vegetation remained. Weeds shriveled into ash before they could burn. Stone blistered, cracked, buckled as if trying to escape its own surface.

The Lantern spoke calmly, his voice threading through the roar without effort.

"You praised me," he said, "for letting them go."

He turned slowly, light boiling outward now, no longer contained, no longer pretending to be restraint.

"You mistook necessity for mercy."

The words carried.

They carried too well.

Another pilgrim broke and tried to run.

He made it three steps.

The ground seized him at the ankles, stone climbing his legs like liquid iron. Fire erupted beneath his skin—not consuming him, not granting release, but lighting him from within. For a heartbeat, his skeleton was visible, mouth locked open in a scream that never reached sound.

Then the fire collapsed inward.

Nothing remained but a scorched outline burned into the rock.

The army began to chant.

Low at first. Fragmented. Names. Titles. Affirmations twisted into doctrine.

"Order."

"Correction."

"Severance."

The Lantern breathed deeply.

The clearing breathed with him.

"Look at you," he said, sweeping his gaze across the remaining pilgrims. "Still believing proximity is protection. Still thinking survival proves favor."

He paused.

Long enough for the words to settle.

"You think light means kindness," he continued, voice smooth, almost patient. "You think care means restraint. You think order exists to make you comfortable."

His hand clenched.

The air imploded.

Bodies lifted from the ground as invisible pressure folded them inward like paper. Bones snapped. Spines bowed. Blood misted into the air in fine red clouds that froze where they hung, drifting downward in crystalline flakes.

Screams finally came.

They did not last.

"This," the Lantern said, voice almost tender now, "is what obedience looks like when it is named correctly."

Fire bloomed—true flame at last—ripping upward from the fractured earth in jagged columns. It did not spread. It selected. Each remaining pilgrim was claimed individually, fire wrapping around them, lifting them screaming before snapping their bodies apart and dropping the pieces back into the widening cracks below.

The ground sealed itself afterward.

Smooth.

Black.

Finished.

Hell had arrived.

And the Lantern smiled.

The lieutenants were radiant with it.

Julian laughed openly, clapping once as another scream cut off. "Yes. Yes. This is the voice that unmakes worlds."

Elana tilted her head, eyes half-lidded, savoring the devastation. "They wanted to belong," she said softly. "Now they do."

Marcus inhaled deeply, armor humming in resonance with the heat. "Command restored."

Lucien inclined his head toward the Lantern. "The Severing answers you."

Only Raven did not move.

The pull inside him surged—stronger now, louder—but it felt different without Kali's hand closing around it. The obedience rose by habit, not compulsion. The absence where ownership had lived throbbed like an open wound.

"I feel it," he said before he could stop himself. "I feel the hunt waking up in me."

The word I rang like a crack in glass.

The Lantern turned.

Fire dimmed instantly.

Cold slammed into the clearing with crushing force.

Raven gasped as the air drove into his chest, pressure pinning him in place. Frost raced up his boots, locking him where he stood. His vision blurred as light folded inward around him, compressing, crushing.

"You feel," the Lantern said softly.

Raven swallowed, pain burning through his ribs. "I feel the chase," he corrected quickly. "The call."

"You speak from self again," the Lantern said. "Do you miss your master that badly?"

A ripple of amusement passed through the lieutenants.

Raven's jaw clenched. "She is gone."

"And yet you remain," the Lantern replied. "Interesting."

He stepped closer. Light flared violently.

"Listen carefully," he said, voice dropping, every word deliberate. "You are not free. You are unmoored. And that is far more dangerous."

The pressure intensified, forcing Raven to one knee. Frost climbed higher, biting deep.

"Do not mistake the absence of a chain for permission," the Lantern continued. "If you speak as 'I' again, I will remind you what 'mine' means."

The pressure vanished.

Raven collapsed forward, gasping, shaking, the army's eyes burning into him. He nodded once. Stiff. Wordless.

The Lantern turned away.

"They run," he said, staring toward the narrowing land ahead. "They carry their dead. Their names. Their guilt."

Fire rolled outward again, staining the sky a bruised red.

"They think distance will save them."

The army stirred, restless now, hungry.

Lucien spoke first. “Shall we loose the hunters?”

Julian grinned. “Let me go first.”

Marcus flexed his grip. “They will break.”

The Lantern raised his hand.

Silence fell instantly.

“No,” he said. “Not yet.”

The fire settled into a steady, hellish glow. The land reshaped itself—ridges sharpening, paths narrowing, thorns erupting where none had been before.

“Let them run longer,” the Lantern said. “Let hope stretch thin.”

He inhaled deeply, savoring the air as it curdled around him.

“This world remembers how to be Hell,” he said. “And I will teach it again.”

The army answered with a low, unified murmur—reverent, eager.

Raven felt the pull tighten once more.

He followed.

Not because he was owned.

Because the hunt had begun.

The Decision to Hunt

The violence stopped.

Not gradually. Not with a final strike or fading echo.

It stopped the way a hand closes.

The fire withdrew into itself, collapsing downward until the fractured earth no longer bled light. The sky sealed, the red-black thinning smoothing back into dull cloud, though it did not rise again. Heat vanished without cooling. Cold followed without relief. The pressure remained—

heavier now, denser, as if silence itself had learned how to weigh something.

The field was ruined.

Stone lay blackened and smooth where bodies had been. The fissures had sealed too cleanly, as though the land wished to forget what it had opened itself to. No ash drifted. No smoke lingered. Even the smell of iron thinned, swallowed by a deeper, older scent—the raw mineral breath of something stripped down to bone.

No one spoke.

The army stood frozen in the aftermath, reverence and hunger caught mid-breath. Weapons hung useless at their sides. Armor cooled and creaked. A few of the younger ranks shifted their weight and then stilled again, instinctively aware that motion now would be a kind of disrespect.

The Lantern did not move.

He stood at the center of the clearing as if the destruction had never required effort. His light had dimmed—not extinguished, not softened, but narrowed, drawn inward until it was precise again. The excess of fury was gone.

Wrath had completed its work.

It was no longer needed.

Silence thickened around him, settling into the ruined ground like a second skin. It pressed against the lieutenants' ears until even their thoughts felt too loud. The chant that had almost risen died before it could take shape. The army waited, not for permission, but for meaning.

The Lantern finally lowered his hand.

The gesture was small.

Absolute.

What followed was not an order.

It was understanding.

"They were allowed to leave," he said, voice level, unforced. It carried without echo, as if the land itself had decided to hold it. "Because the rule required it."

No one questioned this.

They had all felt the constraint. The tightening that would have snapped had he commanded too early. The invisible line that had held him back when instinct had screamed otherwise.

"Letting them go," he continued, "was necessary."

A pause.

"Letting them stay gone," he said, "is impossible."

The statement did not rise.

It did not threaten.

It settled.

Some chains don't break—they recoil.

He turned, slow and deliberate, surveying the ruined field not with satisfaction, but with assessment. His gaze passed over the sealed stone, the absence where the kneeling pilgrims had been, the faint distortions still hanging in the air where pressure had folded reality in on itself.

Then his eyes lifted—toward the narrowing land beyond the clearing.

The direction they had run.

"They believe distance is escape," the Lantern said. "They believe motion itself is defiance."

A faint tilt of his head.

"They are wrong."

Julian shifted first, anticipation crawling visibly across his expression. "Say the word," he breathed. "We can be on them before the ground finishes forgetting."

Lucien smiled, slower, more patient. “They’re already tired. They carry weight they don’t understand yet.”

Marcus said nothing. His eyes tracked the horizon, calculating routes, choke points, places where terrain itself would do the work of a blade. His posture had changed—less reactive, more certain. The moment of being ruled had passed. He was useful again.

Only Raven remained still.

The Lantern did not look at him.

Not yet.

“The pursuit will not be chaos,” the Lantern said. “It will not be indulgence. What just occurred”—his gaze flicked briefly to the ruined field—“was correction.”

He turned fully now, facing his army.

“What comes next is recovery.”

The word landed strangely.

Not bloodless.

But precise.

“The scroll is not to be destroyed,” the Lantern said. “It is not to be damaged. It is not to be defiled.”

A ripple passed through the ranks—not disappointment, but recalibration.

“It is to be taken.”

His light sharpened a fraction.

“Returned to alignment.”

He did not name Gillie.

He did not name Cassian.

He did not name any of them.

Names gave weight. Names invited resistance. Names created stories.

He had learned better.

"They will be brought back," the Lantern said. "Alive."

Julian blinked. "Alive?"

"For now," the Lantern replied.

Lucien nodded slowly, pleased. "A longer lesson."

Marcus finally spoke. "They will fight."

"They already are," the Lantern said. "They simply don't know it yet."

He lifted one hand—not high, not dramatic—and the land answered. Far off, ridges sharpened. Paths narrowed subtly. Thorns pushed up through soil that had not known them before. Nothing obvious. Nothing immediate.

But the world had begun to lean.

"The hunt will be patient," the Lantern said. "They must believe they are choosing their road."

A pause.

"Hope must be allowed to stretch."

Raven shifted.

The movement was small.

It did not escape notice.

The Lantern turned then, his gaze fixing on Raven with unsettling calm.

"You will go," he said.

Not will you.

Not if you wish.

Raven swallowed. "Yes."

The word came clean. No compulsion pulled it from him. No pressure bent his spine.

The Lantern studied him for a long moment.

"You follow," he said, "but you are not bound."

The words were not mercy.

They were warning.

"Do not mistake that for trust."

Raven inclined his head. "We won't."

Something unreadable flickered across the Lantern's expression. Approval, perhaps. Or interest.

"Good," he said. "Unbound things hunt differently."

He turned back to the army.

"Prepare the way," the Lantern said. "Not with fire. Not with force."

A beat.

"With inevitability."

The lieutenants straightened as one, anticipation settling into discipline. Orders rippled outward—not shouted, not dramatic, but efficient. Scouts peeled away. Ranks adjusted. The ruined clearing began to empty, the army moving with purpose now rather than frenzy.

The Lantern remained where he was.

Alone at the center of what wrath had made.

He looked once more toward the narrowing land.

"They think they are running," he said softly, to no one in particular.

His light dimmed further, sharpening into something colder than rage.

"They are already being gathered."

Far ahead, unseen and unknowing, the world leaned gently beneath fleeing feet.

The hunt had begun.

And every chain we thought we had broken had only gone slack.

The Edge of Deliverance

The Pursuit Begins

We felt it before we saw it.

Not footsteps—those came later—but a pressure leaning against the back of the world, subtle as a held breath. The canyon ahead narrowed and widened in slow pulses, stone shifting with a sound too deep to be called noise. It was the kind of movement you noticed in your bones before your ears agreed. I adjusted my stride without thinking, angling left where the ground dipped and rose again, the Balanced Blade tapping my thigh in a steady rhythm. The scroll rested firm against my back, warmer now—not burning, just awake.

Behind us, the sky began to change.

It did not darken like a storm. No clouds gathered. No wind announced itself. Instead, the light thinned, stretched, as if someone had pulled a veil across the sun and forgotten to finish the knot. Color drained from the far ridges first, leaving the land ahead washed pale while the horizon behind bruised into something heavier. The air tasted of iron again—faint, familiar, unwelcome.

Rowan was the first to look back.

He didn't turn fully. Just a glance over his shoulder, quick and measured, the way you check a wound you already know is there. His jaw tightened. He said nothing.

Nadya caught it anyway. She always did. "They're moving," she said, not asking. Her grip tightened on the strap she carried, knuckles whitening. Cassian's weight shifted against Eliah's shoulder as the ground sloped, and the two of them adjusted together without breaking stride.

"They haven't rushed," Rowan said finally. "That's worse."

Sera's hum faltered, then steadied again, lower now. "The Veins are humming backward," she murmured. "Not calling. Warning."

The scroll leaned—barely—but the pressure was unmistakable. Not a command. A suggestion shaped like urgency.

We broke into a run.

Stone blurred beneath our feet. The canyon walls pressed closer, then fell away again, opening into a long, shallow descent where grit skidded underfoot. Breath tore loose from our chests, harsh and ragged. Somewhere behind us, the land answered with a low groan, like something massive shifting its weight.

Joshua felt it like a hand between his shoulders.

Not pushing. Not pulling.

Claiming.

He stumbled—not from the terrain, but from the certainty that settled into him with brutal clarity. This was not pursuit born of rage. This was reclamation. The Lantern was not coming for us.

He was coming for him.

Shim'on flinched at the same instant—not the way Joshua did, but like a man recognizing the edge of a blade before it touches skin.

Joshua slowed.

At first it was subtle—a half-step lost, then another. I sensed the change and glanced sideways, breath hitching when I saw his face. He wasn't afraid.

That was what frightened me.

His eyes were fixed not ahead, but behind us, tracking something none of us could yet see.

"Joshua," I said, reaching back without breaking stride. "Don't—"

He didn't take my hand.

"I hear it," he said, voice rough with breath and something else—recognition. "It's not stopping."

"We're not either," Nadya snapped. "Move."

But Joshua had already turned.

Shim'on stopped too—but only for a breath. His eyes tracked Joshua's movement with a stillness that felt older than fear, as if he were watching a decision he had once failed to interrupt.

The army crested the far rise then, spilling into view like a tide that had never learned to hurry. They came in lines that bent with the land, armor dull and dark, weapons held low. Lantern-light moved among them—not flaring, not announcing—just enough to show shape and number.

At their center, a figure of compressed brilliance walked without touching the ground.

The Lantern.

He did not quicken his pace when he saw us running.

He smiled.

Joshua stopped fully now, boots skidding on grit. The absence of his steps cracked our rhythm. I spun, heart hammering, and for a heartbeat the world narrowed to the space between us.

"No," I said. Not plea. Recognition.

Joshua met my gaze, and for a moment the years fell away. He looked younger like that—stripped of defense—just a man seeing the cost of what he loved.

"He won't stop," Joshua said quietly. "Not while I'm with you."

"That's not true," Kaela said sharply, though her voice shook. "He'll follow anyway."

Joshua shook his head. "Not like this."

The ground trembled again, stronger this time. Pebbles danced. A crack raced across the stone a dozen paces behind us, thin and bright, then sealed itself like a wound refusing to stay open.

The scroll burned hot for the first time.

I gasped as the leather flared against my back, heat flooding my spine—not pain, but intensity. Urgency. The pressure leaned forward now, unmistakable.

Move.

Joshua stepped backward instead.

"If I go back to the Lantern," he said, eyes already turning toward the dark, "the path stays open for you."

"Joshua—"

"I already did it once," he said, and something in his eyes broke open. "You just didn't know."

The words landed harder than the tremor.

"In the Swamp," he went on, breath tight but controlled, "when you thought I turned—when you thought I chose them—I was already counting how far the suffering would spread if I didn't."

Nadya went still. Rowan's jaw tightened. The scroll flared again, sharp and searching.

"I made a deal," Joshua said. He did not look at the Lantern. He looked at me. "Not with him. With Marcus. I gave them my obedience so they wouldn't take yours."

Memory rearranged itself inside me—the way the darkness had closed around him and not us. The way the Withering had swallowed Joshua whole and left the rest of us standing.

"You weren't spared by accident," Joshua said softly. "You were traded."

The ground shook again, closer now.

Joshua turned fully, facing the dark.

Raven saw him then.

From the far side of the field, from the place where obedience had once been simple and was now merely habitual, Raven's gaze locked onto Joshua's form. Something old stirred. A memory of standing shoulder to shoulder under a different sky.

He did not move.

The Lantern raised a hand—not to strike, but to still his army. They halted instantly, boots sinking into the earth as if the ground itself recognized authority.

"Joshua," the Lantern called. "You remember your place."

Joshua swallowed.

"I do," he said, and the words tasted like ash.

I stepped toward him, the scroll's heat climbing higher. "Joshua, listen to me. This isn't—"

He smiled at me then.

Small. Apologetic. Devastating.

"I left so you could breathe," he said. "I'm going back so you can keep doing it."

The Lantern advanced a single step. The ground rippled outward from where his light touched stone.

"Come," the Lantern said. "You have always understood obedience."

Joshua took one step toward him.

Behind him, the path ahead narrowed.

The pursuit did not begin with rage.

It began with a sacrifice finally being named.

Joshua's Offering

He did not stop at the edge because he was afraid.

The ground ahead of us had begun to fracture—not violently—but with the unease of something preparing to open. The scroll's pressure shifted again, guiding us forward, narrowing the way into a channel of light and broken stone that promised movement, distance, survival. One by one, we crossed into it, bodies slipping through the thinning space with urgency.

Joshua did not follow.

There was no dramatic hesitation. No backward glance. He simply slowed, then stopped, boots settling into the frost as if the ground itself had claimed him.

Gillie felt it before she saw it.

Her steps faltered. The Balanced Blade struck her hip once, then missed its rhythm entirely. She turned, already reaching.

"Joshua—"

He didn't answer.

He had already turned away from the path. From the opening earth. From the light that was beginning to feel like promise. He faced the clearing instead, the ruined field still breathing with the aftermath of the

Lantern's wrath. Smoke clung low to the ground. The sky above hung heavy and bruised.

Joshua took one step back toward it.

Then another.

The Lantern was already watching.

He did not rush forward. He did not need to. His light had drawn inward again, focused now into something colder, more intimate. This was not pursuit.

It was reception.

Joshua walked toward him.

There was no bargaining left in him. What moved him forward was simpler than faith and heavier than despair.

If he crossed, the Lantern would follow.

If he crossed, the chase would begin now—while we were still burdened with the dead, while grief still slowed our limbs.

If he stayed, the Lantern would stop.

Not forever. Joshua was not foolish enough to believe that.

But long enough.

He believed his presence could anchor the darkness where it stood. That the Lantern's fixation on him was strong enough to delay pursuit. He believed his suffering could buy us distance.

Not freedom.

Distance.

The Lantern met him halfway.

Not with violence.

He approached as one approaches something cherished that has wandered too close to escape. His steps did not disturb the ground. His light did not scorch. It folded inward, shaping itself into something almost gentle.

Joshua stopped an arm's length away.

For a moment, neither of them spoke.

The Lantern tilted his head, studying him—not as an enemy, not even as a traitor, but as a possession returned.

"You always do this," the Lantern said at last. "You mistake endurance for choice."

Joshua lifted his eyes.

"I know what I'm doing," he said.

The Lantern smiled faintly. "That is what you tell yourself when you obey without being asked."

Joshua did not rise to it.

"I'm not asking anything of you," he said. "I'm giving you what you want."

The Lantern's gaze sharpened.

"And what do you think that is?"

Joshua glanced past him, just once, toward the narrowing path where we were still moving. The scroll's pressure urged us onward. It did not drag. It waited.

"I left before so they could breathe," Joshua said quietly. "I'm coming back so they can keep doing it."

Something shifted in the Lantern then.

Not rage.

Recognition.

"You confuse sacrifice with authority," the Lantern said. "You think pain entitles you to meaning."

He stepped closer, close enough that Joshua could feel the cold beneath the light.

"Love does not free you," the Lantern continued. "It is simply another chain you consent to carry."

Joshua's jaw tightened.

"Maybe," he said. "But it's the only one I choose."

The Lantern laughed softly.

"You speak as if choice still belongs to you."

His hand lifted and rested briefly at Joshua's shoulder. The touch was light.

"You were always mine," the Lantern said. "Even when you ran. You confuse absence of command with freedom."

Joshua did not flinch.

"I know you want to kill me," he said.

The Lantern's fingers tightened slightly.

"Yes," he agreed. "But possession is better."

He leaned in, voice lowering.

"You will walk beside me," he said. "And they will know they escaped because you stayed."

The words struck harder than any blow.

Because they were true.

Joshua felt the weight of them settle—not as threat, but as sentence. To be remembered as the reason we lived.

He nodded once.

Not in agreement.

In submission.

The Lantern withdrew his hand.

"Come," he said, turning back toward the ruined field. "You understand obedience."

Joshua followed.

Behind him, the path narrowed further. The light dimmed. The scroll leaned harder now, urging us away.

Gillie watched him go.

She did not scream.

She did not chase.

She pressed her hand flat against her chest as if holding something in place, and then—because she had learned this much already—she turned forward again.

Joshua did not look back.

Love had done its work.

And captivity had claimed its offering.

The Ground Remembers

The Lantern advanced again.

Not quickly. He did not need speed. He moved with the assurance of something that believed the world would make room for it simply because it always had.

Joshua walked beside him.

That was when the scroll burned.

Not with flame.

With light.

It did not burst outward. It drove down—a sudden surge of brilliance pouring from my shoulder into the earth beneath my feet, as if the scroll had found something buried there and could no longer remain still.

For a heartbeat, nothing happened.

Then the ground answered.

Stone split—not with violence, but with intent. A single fracture raced forward from the scroll's position, slicing the clearing cleanly in two. It opened as if the land had been holding its breath and had finally been given permission to exhale.

Light welled up from the fissure.

Not white.

Alive.

It pulsed and shifted, gold threaded with deeper hues—blue, green, memory moving beneath the surface. The crack widened just enough to matter. Beneath it, the Veins were visible now—living channels etched through the earth itself, glowing with remembered breath.

Marcus felt it before he understood it.

His shoulders stiffened. His grip tightened. His gaze locked not on us but on the light.

Recognition.

This was not new.

This was the same force that had torn the Swamp apart. The same brilliance that had unmade his armies and rewritten a place he had believed belonged to him.

Now it did not explode.

It remembered.

Elana stepped back without meaning to. Her heel scraped stone. She had been unraveled by this light once. She knew what it did when it was unleashed.

Raven staggered—not physically, but inside. The pull in him surged, then recoiled, like something reaching for a door that refused to open. He had been torn apart by this radiance before. His body remembered even if his mind resisted.

The world did not tear.

It remembered.

I felt it in my bones. The pressure I had followed for so long settled into certainty.

This was not a path opening.

This was a boundary being named.

Gillie crossed without hesitation.

Not because she was brave. Because she was already moving when the ground split, already aligned with the pull that had guided us from the beginning. The light flared softly beneath her boots, steadying instead of resisting.

I followed.

So did Kaela—her cry tearing free as she ran, raw and wordless.

Nadya came next, hauling Miriam across. Rowan's hand locked around Eliah's wrist, yanking him forward as the fissure widened another breath. Sera stumbled, recovered, pressed her palm briefly to the glowing stone as if greeting something she had always known was there.

We crossed.

All of us.

The light held.

Behind us, the army of the dark stopped.

Not because they could not advance.

Because the land refused them.

The first rank reached the edge and slowed, boots scraping against stone that no longer behaved like ground. The glow beneath their feet dimmed, hardened, rejecting their weight. A second line pressed forward and found the same resistance. The Veins beneath the surface twisted away from them, light receding.

Lucien tested it once, carefully, placing his foot at the edge.

The stone did not break.

It simply would not bear him.

Julian laughed under his breath and tried to step forward anyway. The fissure answered by widening another fraction, light surging just enough to force him back.

Marcus growled and lifted his weapon as if authority alone might compel the land to obey.

Nothing happened.

The Lantern halted.

For the first time, he did not command the ground.

He looked down instead.

At the fissure.

At the living light.

At the Veins revealed without his permission.

His expression did not change, but the air around him tightened.

Adjustment.

Joshua felt it then.

His shoulders tensed. His head turned slightly toward us. He had believed his choice would anchor the darkness, delay pursuit, buy us time.

He had not understood the cost.

The ground had chosen us.

And in doing so, it had chosen against him.

"Joshua—" Kaela's voice broke as she stumbled to the edge, hands outstretched. "No—please—"

Joshua took a step toward her.

The fissure flared.

Not angrily.

Decisively.

He stopped short as the Veins beneath his feet dimmed and withdrew. The light that welcomed us would not welcome him.

He looked down at the ground.

Then at the scroll.

Then at Gillie.

Understanding landed too late.

"I didn't mean—" he started.

The Lantern's hand closed around his shoulder.

Not crushing.

Claiming.

"You offered yourself," the Lantern said quietly. "The world accepted."

Joshua went still.

Raven stood a pace behind him, eyes wide, something unfamiliar flickering across his face. He could feel the Veins now too.

And feel that they did not want him.

Shim'on stood apart from the line, gaze fixed on the fissure as if measuring what it would cost to cross—and what it would cost not to.

The fissure settled.

Not widening.

Not closing.

Holding.

A living line drawn through the world.

On one side: light, breath, motion, grief that still moved forward.

On the other: command, possession, memory sharpened into chains.

Kaela dropped to her knees at the edge, pressing her forehead to the glowing stone. Her cry was not a plea.

It was mourning.

Behind us, the scroll dimmed—not exhausted, but complete.

Ahead, the path narrowed into land we could not yet name.

Behind us, something ancient gathered itself to follow.

The Charge

They did not speak.

There was no time left for silence to carry meaning.

The pressure came first—not a sound, not a command, but a sudden insistence that leaned forward through the land itself. The Veins beneath our feet surged, light pulsing hard enough to rattle bone and breath alike. The scroll flared against Gillie's back, heat blooming through the leather in a sharp warning.

Behind us, the dark moved.

Not cautiously.

Charging.

The Lantern lifted his hand—not to restrain his army, but to loose it.

And the lost souls answered.

They surged forward as one body, armor clattering, boots tearing into stone that tried—and failed—to refuse them. The barrier shuddered under the weight of their advance, light flaring and recoiling as ranks pressed against it. Cracks spidered through the glowing stone, sealing only to split again.

The Lantern advanced with them.

Not running.

Walking.

His light cut through the chaos, steady and precise.

"Now," Gillie said—not loud, not calm—certain.

The scroll answered.

The ground ahead of us groaned, a deep splitting sound that rolled through the valley. The mountains before us shuddered.

Then they moved.

Stone did not explode.

It parted.

A seam of light tore down the face of the range, widening as the Veins surged upward, forcing space where there had been none. Rock peeled back in grinding slabs, dust screaming into the air as a narrow valley opened between the peaks—not a path made for marching, but a wound carved just wide enough to run.

Light spilled through it.

Alive.

Far ahead, beyond the narrowing pass, something answered—a resonant glow rising from a stand of Humming Trees, their branches shimmering as the Veins converged beneath them. The light there felt different. Clearer.

Sera gasped. "That's it," she breathed. "That's the Vein. It leads out."

The Lantern saw it too.

And he smiled.

"Run," he said, voice carrying easily over the roar of stone and breath. "Let us see how far the living can flee."

We ran.

No formation.

No dignity.

Boots skidded on broken stone as we plunged into the valley, walls towering on either side, the air thick with dust and Vein-light. Breath tore loose from lungs. Hands grabbed, released, grabbed again as the path narrowed and twisted.

The ground behind us screamed.

The dark slammed into the barrier in a full-bodied charge. Light flared blindingly as the Veins resisted, stone buckling under the force. For a moment, the boundary held—then cracked again.

"They're breaking it!" Nadya shouted.

"They're bleeding it," Rowan corrected. "Keep moving!"

Shim'on ran now.

Not beside us.

Not behind.

Parallel, keeping to the edge of the narrowing valley, eyes flicking between the collapsing barrier and the light ahead, as if measuring cost with every step.

The Lantern raised his hand again.

This time, the ground answered him.

The barrier ruptured.

Light tore open behind us, the Veins recoiling as dark boots broke through, the first ranks spilling forward with a roar. The Lantern stepped through the breach without slowing.

"They're through!" Eliah cried.

The valley narrowed further.

Stone groaned overhead as the mountains leaned inward, slabs shifting, Veins blazing along the walls. Pebbles rained down. Dust choked the air. The passage was closing—not fast enough to crush, but fast enough to terrify.

Ahead, the Humming Trees pulsed brighter.

The sound reached us then—a low resonance vibrating through chest and spine, steady and welcoming. The Vein beneath them surged, a vertical current of light threading upward into somewhere that wasn't here.

Gillie stumbled, caught herself, and ran harder.

"Don't stop!" she shouted. "Don't look back!"

The Lantern's voice rose behind us, no longer calm.

"YOU CANNOT OUTRUN WHAT CLAIMS YOU."

The valley shuddered.

Stone split overhead as the walls began to draw together in earnest, Veins flaring violently as the ground made its final decision. The passage tightened to a single corridor—just wide enough for the living to pass.

The dark howled behind us.

And still we ran.

The light ahead blazed brighter with every step, the Humming Trees bending toward us as the Vein opened fully, roaring now with breath and promise.

Behind us, the Lantern surged forward, light flaring, hand outstretched—

And the mountain moved.

Not sealing.

Holding.

Just long enough.

We crossed the final bend of the valley as stone screamed and light exploded behind us, the dark slamming into a narrowing world that no longer wished to bear them.

The last thing I felt before the Vein took hold was the ground deciding.

And the sound of pursuit cut short.

The Exodus

The Way Opens

The canyon did not welcome us. It tolerated us.

Stone scraped and shifted beneath our feet as we ran, the ground uneven in ways that felt intentional—small rises where breath caught, sudden drops that stole balance just long enough to punish hesitation. Vein-light pulsed along the walls in erratic seams, flaring bright and dimming again, as if the land were struggling to remember the shape it had been forced into.

This was not a road.

It was a wound held open by will alone.

Gillie ran at the front, jaw set, shoulders tight, the scroll pressing hard against her back now—no longer merely warm, but urgent. It leaned into her stride, its weight insistently forward, as if momentum itself had become law. Her breath came sharp and measured, each exhale counted and controlled.

Behind her, the rest of us ran without grace.

Boots slipped on grit. Packs slammed against spines. Someone gasped too loudly—Eliah—and Nadya shoved him forward without breaking stride, her own breath tearing loose in short pulls. Miriam stumbled once, catching herself with a hand against the canyon wall, fingers skidding across hot stone before Kaela hauled her upright again. No one spoke. There was no breath to spare.

The canyon narrowed abruptly, forcing us into a tight line, shoulders brushing stone, ribs scraping as if the passage were measuring us.

"Keep moving," Rowan said, voice low and steady despite the strain. "Don't bunch up."

Sera's hum flickered at the back of the line—broken, breathless, trying to find pitch in a place that would not settle. Even that small sound seemed to agitate the stone. Vein-light flared, then recoiled.

This way would not hold forever.

We all felt it.

Behind us, the barrier screamed.

Not with sound, but with resistance—stone buckling, Veins recoiling, the ground protesting as if pain had finally found a voice. The dark did not rush blindly at first. They pressed. They tested. They learned where the land bent and where it refused.

The Lantern raised his hand.

"Again," he said.

The word did not echo. It landed.

The lost souls answered immediately, ranks surging forward in brutal unison. Boots struck stone in time with his will, armor clattering, weapons low—not raised in fury, but carried with purpose. They did not look at the canyon as an obstacle. They looked at it as something that had made a mistake.

"Break the seam," the Lantern commanded calmly. "Not the walls. The Veins."

Light folded inward around him as he advanced, step by measured step, his presence stabilizing the ground beneath his feet even as it shuddered elsewhere. Where he walked, the stone did not resist.

Cracks spidered through the glowing barrier, thin and frantic, sealing only to split again under renewed pressure. Vein-light flared white-hot, dimmed, then flared again, bleeding brilliance into the dust-choked air.

"Forward," the Lantern said. "Do not hesitate. The ground will yield."

A half-step lagged behind the line.

Just one.

The stone above it shuddered—then peeled away as if the mountain no longer recognized what stood beneath it. A plate of rock dropped straight down, clean and sudden. Armor rang once, sharply, and then the sound ended, crushed flat into a dull thud. Dust burst outward in a choking wave, filling the space where two bodies had been with grit and light and the smell of split stone.

The line closed without slowing.

Boots struck past the fallen place. A shoulder clipped a shattered helm and sent it spinning into the Vein-light. No one bent. No one looked down. The ground settled again, smooth where it had broken, as if nothing had stood there long enough to matter.

The Lantern did not turn his head.

"Press," he said. "They are running because they know they cannot be claimed once they cross."

His gaze lifted, tracking the narrowing canyon ahead.

"Do not let them."

The command tightened the Veins.

Light surged unevenly through the barrier, no longer resisting as a single surface but breaking into channels and fault lines, each one flaring and dimming as pressure mounted from within and without. Stone groaned—not collapsing yet, but loosening, shedding grit and fractured plates that skittered across the ground.

Joshua felt it before he saw it.

The resistance beneath his feet thinned—not vanished, not welcoming, but relenting. The ground no longer pushed back against his weight. It shifted instead, angling him forward as if gravity itself had chosen direction.

Raven stumbled beside him.

Not from the stone.

From the command.

He gasped, a raw sound torn loose from his chest, hand clawing at his ribs as if something inside him had seized. Light flared beneath his boots, then recoiled—unstable.

"No," Raven hissed, teeth bared. "No—"

Joshua grabbed his arm and pulled.

The barrier answered.

Not by breaking evenly.

By splitting.

A seam of Vein-light tore open directly in front of them, narrow and violent, the ground peeling apart just long enough to matter. Stone folded back in jagged slabs, edges glowing hot, dust screaming into the air as the world made a sudden allowance.

Joshua didn't think.

He ran.

Raven was dragged with him, boots barely touching stone as the light surged upward beneath them, hurling them forward through the breach. The resistance vanished all at once, replaced by a breath-stealing drop as they spilled onto ground that did not fight them.

They hit hard, skidding across grit and fractured stone, momentum carrying them several strides before Joshua caught himself against the canyon wall. Raven slammed into him, gasping, hands locked tight in Joshua's coat as if letting go would tear something loose.

Behind them, the breach convulsed.

The Veins snapped inward, light recoiling violently as the barrier tried to reassert itself. Stone crashed down in grinding slabs, sealing the opening behind them with a thunderous finality that shook the canyon floor.

For a heartbeat, the dark surged toward it—

And were stopped.

Joshua twisted around, chest heaving, just in time to see the Lantern halt at the edge of the sealed seam. Light folded inward around him, controlled and contained, as his gaze locked onto the two figures now standing on the far side.

Joshua.

Raven.

The Lantern's expression did not change.

Only his focus sharpened.

"Run," he said, voice carrying through stone and distance alike. "You have only borrowed ground."

Joshua felt the truth of it settle into his bones.

The canyon ahead stretched wide and unstable, its walls already shifting, Vein-light pulsing erratically along the stone. Far ahead—distant but unmistakable—the glow of the Humming Trees flickered, a promise shaped like escape.

Raven wrenched himself free, staggering forward, breath ragged, pain written into every step.

"He's still—" Raven choked. "He's still holding—"

"I know," Joshua said, forcing his legs to move. "Run."

They broke into a sprint.

Behind them, the barrier held.

For now.

Ahead of us, the canyon bent sharply left.

Two figures burst into view at full sprint.

Joshua.

Raven.

They ran as if the ground wanted them gone.

The Veins beneath their feet flared bright where they touched, light rising to bear their weight, stabilizing stone that otherwise shuddered and slid. They were not fighting the canyon the way we were. They were being allowed.

"They're through," Sera breathed. "How—?"

"Because they don't belong where they were," Shim'on said, already adjusting his pace. "And they don't belong here either."

Joshua's head turned as he ran. He saw us.

Relief flickered across his face—quick, fragile—then vanished. He shouted something we couldn't hear and pointed back over his shoulder.

Raven did not look back.

His stride faltered instead—just a fraction. His hand clenched at his side as pain tore across his features. Then his pace surged again, reckless.

"Something's wrong with him," Nadya said between breaths.

"Something's wrong with all of us," Kaela snapped, hauling Miriam around a jut of stone as the wall shuddered inward again.

The canyon convulsed.

A violent surge of light tore down the far end of the passage as the barrier finally failed in cascading fractures. Stone split and peeled back, Veins flaring as the dark burst through at last.

The roar that followed was not triumph.

It was hunger.

Joshua heard the Lantern's voice before he understood the words.

"Forward," it said—closer now, inside the canyon. "Take them."

The command struck him like a blow.

He stumbled, shock jolting through his limbs as the Veins beneath his feet flared and dimmed in rapid succession. Raven cried out beside him, his stride stuttering as something tightened around his chest.

"Don't stop," Joshua said, grabbing Raven's arm. "Don't listen."

Raven gasped. "I can hear him. It hurts—"

Another command cut through the canyon.

"Obey."

Raven screamed.

Not loudly.

Like something tearing loose inside him.

Joshua dragged him forward anyway, forcing speed, gaze locked ahead where the canyon widened—

And there we were.

Still running. Still ahead. Still not far enough.

Gillie turned at the sound of Raven's cry, eyes widening as she saw them sprinting toward her. She slowed instinctively, then cursed and forced herself forward again, hand dropping to the hilt of the Balanced Blade.

The canyon shuddered, stone raining down as the walls leaned inward.

Behind Joshua and Raven, the dark poured through the breach in full force now, armor flashing in the Vein-light, weapons raised at last. The Lantern stepped into the canyon without breaking stride, his presence steady even as the walls groaned.

"Close the distance," he ordered. "Now."

Joshua saw it then.

The math.

The narrowing way.

The dark gaining.

We were slowing.

Whatever this passage had been meant to buy us, it was already being spent.

He shouted again, louder, voice breaking as he waved frantically.

"RUN!"

And Gillie did.

So did the rest of us.

The way was open.

But it was already closing.

The Chase

Joshua ran until his lungs burned, then ran harder.

The canyon resisted everyone else—tilting, narrowing, stealing balance with sudden drops and broken stone—but beneath his feet the ground thinned its resistance, Vein-light flaring just enough to bear him forward. It wasn't welcome. It was allowance: a narrow mercy extended to something that did not fully belong to the dark, but could not yet be claimed by the light.

Raven ran beside him, and every step cost more than the last.

His breath hitched violently, fingers clawing at his ribs as if trying to tear something loose. Each time he thought of slowing—of letting the distance close—the pain surged sharper, driven inward by the Lantern's will.

"Don't think," Joshua said through clenched teeth, dragging Raven forward when his stride faltered. "Just run."

Raven laughed once, broken and breathless. "That's the problem," he gasped. "Every step hurts less than stopping."

Behind them, the canyon thundered.

The Lantern's presence pressed forward through stone and breath alike, his commands threading the Veins, tightening the world behind them. Joshua could feel it like pressure between his shoulders—claim without hands, pursuit without rage.

We ran ahead.

Not together anymore. Not cleanly.

Gillie led, but her pace had slowed, shoulders tight, breath sharp and audible now. Miriam stumbled again, favoring her left side, Kaela never more than a half-step from her. Nadya ran with her jaw locked, blood streaking one forearm where stone had torn her skin. Rowan's stride shortened, controlled but tiring. Sera's hum had vanished entirely, swallowed by breath and fear. Eliah lagged, dragging one foot, eyes wide and glassy.

The canyon had begun to demand payment.

Far ahead, past the narrowing bends and falling grit, the Humming Trees glowed.

Not bright.

Steady.

Their branches shimmered with resonance as Veins converged beneath them, light rising in slow pulses that felt different from the frantic flare of the canyon walls. This light did not strain.

It waited.

“That’s it,” Sera breathed when she saw them, the words torn loose between gasps. “That’s the Vein. That’s the way out.”

Hope surged—and faltered just as quickly when Gillie looked back.

She saw Joshua and Raven sprinting toward them.

Joshua’s face was drawn tight with urgency, fear cutting through the composure he had worn for too long. Raven’s stride was uneven now, his movements sharp and jerking, as if pulled in two directions at once.

Gillie slowed instinctively.

Then stopped.

“No,” she said aloud, turning fully, the word tearing free before thought could catch it.

The Balanced Blade slid into her hand with a sound too clean for the chaos around them. Its weight settled into her grip—familiar, inevitable. She stepped forward, planting her feet against the shifting stone as the others skidded to a halt behind her.

“Joshua,” she called, voice raw but steady. “Stop. Don’t come any closer.”

Joshua did stop—just long enough to hear her.

Raven cried out beside him, doubling over as pain surged hard enough to buckle his knees. He clawed at Joshua's sleeve, breath ragged, eyes wild.

"He's close," Raven choked. "He's inside—"

The canyon convulsed violently.

Behind Joshua and Raven, the dark crested the ridge in force, armor flashing in the Vein-light as the vanguard poured into the passage. Above them all, the Lantern stepped into view, his presence steady even as the walls groaned.

He saw everything at once.

Joshua.

Raven.

Us.

And the blade in Gillie's hand.

"Enough," the Lantern said calmly, his voice carrying through the canyon without strain. "Take them."

The command struck like a hammer.

Raven screamed.

Not in rage.

Not in defiance.

In pain.

He staggered, doubling over as something inside his chest seized and twisted hard, his hands clawing uselessly at the air. Vein-light flared beneath his feet, then recoiled, as though the ground itself rejected what was happening to him.

"I can't," Raven shouted back, the words tearing free raw and unguarded. "I can't—"

The Lantern's head snapped toward him.

For the first time since the pursuit began, his composure fractured.

"OBEY."

The word struck Raven like a blow.

He convulsed, body arching as if wrenched upward by invisible hooks, breath ripped from his lungs in a choking gasp. Light burned along his spine—searing, invasive.

Raven dropped to one knee, shaking.

"I—" He swallowed hard, voice breaking. "I can't do it."

The canyon seemed to recoil.

The Lantern's light flared, sharp and furious.

"BOW."

Raven cried out, clutching his head as if pressure were being driven straight through his skull. His shoulders folded inward, forced low by a weight that was not physical but absolute, his body bending under command alone.

"I'm trying," he gasped. "I'm—please—"

The Lantern took a step forward.

"BEND."

Raven collapsed fully this time, palms slamming into stone as his back arched unnaturally, a sound tearing from his throat that was no longer entirely human. Veins along the canyon wall flared in sympathy, light stuttering as if something ancient were being violated.

I saw it then.

Not Raven.

Jonah.

Not the vessel, not the fractured echo shaped by command and obedience—but the man from the stories, from the worn photographs his family kept folded in drawers and frames. The man who had carried blame that wasn't his. The man who had taken a burden meant for someone else and never set it down.

And the voice—

The voice was singular.

Not they.

Not we.

I.

"I can't," Raven said again, clearer now, shaking but present. "I won't—"

The Lantern roared.

"BREAK."

The command detonated.

Raven—Jonah—screamed as something inside him tore loose, the sound ripping through the canyon with such force that stone cracked outward in jagged lines. Light surged from his chest, then recoiled, as if ripped free and forced back by sheer will.

Joshua staggered as the Veins beneath his feet flared and dimmed in wild pulses, something inside him answering—stirring—recognizing what was happening too late to stop it.

The Lantern's fury was incandescent now, focused entirely on the figure at his feet.

The disobedience had been spoken.

The singular named.

And the curse already laid could not be taken back.

I saw it all.

Raven's hesitation.

Joshua's flicker of light.

Gillie's blade poised for a killing she believed was mercy.

And in that suspended breath between command and violence, I understood.

I saw my family's long shadow—the blame Jonah had carried, the curse that had bled forward through generations. I saw how obedience had hollowed Joshua, how love had been mistaken for weakness, how death had always been offered as the solution.

But not this time.

Jonah could still be saved.

Not by killing.

Not by command.

Only by love.

The canyon held its breath.

For a heartbeat, Raven remained still, shaking, hands pressed to the stone as if the earth were the only thing keeping him whole. The singular voice had been spoken. The fracture had occurred.

The Lantern felt it.

And he would not allow it to stand.

His light snapped inward, collapsing from brilliance into something dense and punishing. The Veins recoiled as his will drove down through them—not persuading, not commanding—but seizing.

Raven screamed again.

This time, there were no words.

The sound tore out of him as his body convulsed, muscles locking, spine bowing under a pressure that had nothing to do with pain and everything to do with possession. The singular presence—the glimpse of Jonah—was shoved back violently, buried under command and curse and force.

"You will not speak as one," the Lantern snarled, voice no longer measured. "You will not choose. You will not be."

Raven's head snapped up.

His eyes burned—not with light, not with darkness—but with something trapped and furious behind both.

The dark vanguard surged forward, closing the distance in a rush of steel and hunger.

The Lantern raised his hand.

"NOW," he commanded.

The Offering

Raven lunged.

There was no warning left in him. No hesitation to betray the motion. The Lantern's command still burned through his bones, searing muscle and sinew into obedience that hurt more the harder he resisted it. His body moved first—shoulders snapping forward, boots tearing loose from the stone, arms extending with the inevitability of something thrown.

Gillie did not scream.

She did not think.

Her body answered before her heart could argue.

The Balanced Blade rose in her hands with a smoothness that terrified her even as it steadied her. The weight of it was familiar—too familiar. It had been with her since childhood, shaped by stories of protection and balance, carried through grief and promise. Her grip tightened instinctively, knuckles whitening as her stance adjusted, feet grounding into fractured stone.

She saw Raven's face.

Not monster.

Not enemy.

A man being broken from the inside.

His mouth was open—not in rage, not in hunger—but in a soundless cry that pulled at something deep and unhealed inside her. His eyes were wide, glassy with pain, veins of light and shadow tearing themselves apart beneath his skin.

But he was still coming.

The distance between them collapsed.

Gillie thrust.

Not with hatred.

Not with cruelty.

With the terrible precision of someone who believed—truly believed—that this was the only way left to save someone.

The blade cut forward through the air, parting dust and Vein-light alike, its edge catching the glow of the canyon walls as it moved. Every inch of its path felt inevitable, ordained by every failure that had come before this moment.

Time slowed.

Not metaphorically.

Actually.

Sound dropped out first. The roar of the canyon, the Lantern's fury, the scream of stone and breath—all of it fell away, leaving a vacuum so complete that I could hear my own pulse, loud and solitary, beating against the inside of my ribs.

The blade advanced.

Raven's chest expanded as he drew a breath he would never finish.

The space between Gillie and Raven tightened, heat gathering there.

For an instant, the world felt exactly as it had in that square—the fire waiting, patient, certain it would be fed. A memory surfaced—not as words, but as weight: fire doesn't take those who walk beside it. It waits for silence. And I understood, with a clarity that didn't need words, that this was the moment silence costs blood.

And I stepped forward.

Not in panic.

Not in confusion.

In recognition.

The space between Gillie and Raven was already claimed by motion, already promised to violence—but I entered it anyway, stepping directly into the path of the blade as if the world had finally revealed the one place I had always been meant to stand.

Gillie saw me too late.

Her eyes widened, breath tearing loose in a sharp, broken sound as my back filled her vision—my shoulders, the slight turn of my head as if I were bracing myself not against pain, but against consequence.

Someone tried to say my name.

The sound did not reach me.

Because I already knew.

In the suspended stillness between strike and impact, understanding flooded me—not as memory, not as deduction, but as truth finally allowed to surface.

If Raven died, the cycle would continue.

Jonah would be freed by death, not healed by love.

Joshua would remain fractured—restored in strength, perhaps, but forever broken where faith and love had failed him first.

The blade would do what blades always did.

It would end something.

And endings were not what the world needed anymore.

I stepped fully into the strike.

I did not raise my arms to shield myself.

I did not shout to stop her.

I opened my chest.

And the Balanced Blade struck me instead.

The impact was not sharp.

That was the first thing I understood.

I had expected pain to arrive like violence always did—clean, bright, immediate. A tearing sensation. A white edge. Something that would split me apart fast enough that I would not have time to regret the decision.

Instead, the blade entered me with weight.

A deep, unbearable pressure drove the air from my lungs in a single, involuntary rush. The sound that came out of me was not a cry. It was the collapse of breath, hollowed and dragged out as the Balanced Blade drove inward and stopped—caught, lodged, held by bone and muscle and whatever part of me refused to let it pass through.

The world lurched back into motion.

Sound returned violently, crashing into me all at once—the roar of the canyon, the shriek of grinding stone, Gillie's scream tearing loose now in full and unrestrained horror.

"No—no, no—"

Her hands were still on the hilt.

I felt them there—the way her grip trembled, how the strength left her fingers in uneven pulses as understanding struck her harder than the blade had struck me. She tried to pull back, to undo the motion that had already completed itself, but the blade did not move. It was anchored inside me, fixed in place by more than flesh.

Her knees buckled.

She dropped the hilt as if it had burned her.

The Balanced Blade remained.

I swayed—not backward, not forward—but inward, my body folding slightly around the wound as if trying to remember how to hold itself together. Heat spread outward from the point of impact, not searing, not consuming, but vast. A presence rather than a sensation.

Blood followed.

Warm. Real. Shockingly ordinary.

It soaked through my tunic and into Gillie's hands as she reached for me again, this time without purpose, without training, without any idea of what to do next.

"I didn't—" she gasped. "I didn't mean—"

Her voice broke completely.

I wanted to tell her it was all right.

The words formed clearly in my mind, shaped and ready, but my lungs would not answer. Every attempt to draw breath met resistance now, as if the air itself had thickened, refusing to enter me without permission.

Around us, everything slowed again—but differently this time.

Not suspended.

Attentive.

Raven froze mid-lunge.

The Lantern's command still echoed through the canyon, but it fractured as it reached him, splitting into discordant threads that no longer aligned with his body. His forward momentum collapsed into a violent stumble as his feet skidded on loose stone, arms jerking as if pulled by competing forces.

He screamed.

This time, the sound was unmistakably human.

Not fury.

Not hunger.

Pain.

Pure and unfiltered.

I felt it resonate through the blade embedded in me, felt the Balanced Blade respond as if recognizing the sound. Light flared along the weapon's edge, not blinding, not destructive—clarifying.

The Lantern shouted something then.

An order. A correction. A reinforcement of will.

It did not land cleanly.

The Veins beneath our feet surged erratically, light stuttering as if struggling to decide which command to obey. The canyon walls groaned in protest, slabs of stone shifting, dust raining down in choking waves.

Joshua moved.

I saw him out of the corner of my eye, staggering forward a step as if pulled by something invisible, his hand clutching at his chest. His face contorted—not in pain exactly, but in recognition so sudden it stole the strength from his legs.

"No," he breathed. "No—what are you—"

He did not finish.

Because the light had begun to move.

It rose first from the wound.

Not spilling.

Not leaking.

Emerging.

A concentrated thread of brilliance surged outward from my chest, flowing along the length of the blade still buried inside me. It followed the metal as if the weapon were a conduit, a channel long denied its true purpose.

The light did not burn.

It lifted.

It struck Raven squarely in the chest.

The impact folded him backward with brutal force, his body arching as if caught on an invisible hook. A scream tore out of him, ripping through the canyon walls—not rage, not command, but something raw and uncontained.

Something inside him broke.

The air warped around his torso, thickening, resisting, as if reality itself balked at what was being forced into the open. Light burned white-hot at the point of contact, searing through flesh and Vein alike, and then—

It came out.

The thing that tore free was shaped like a man only by mockery. Limbs too long, joints bending where no joints should bend, skin stretched slick and thin over something that had never been human at all. Its face carried the suggestion of eyes, a mouth, but twisted beyond recognition—hatred etched into every angle as if it had learned loathing before language.

It screamed.

Not in pain.

In fury.

In loss.

The sound clawed at the canyon, setting the Veins screaming in response as the creature thrashed against strands of light that burned through it without mercy. It reached back toward the body it had worn, shrieking Jonah's name like a curse, like a claim being torn away.

Raven collapsed.

He hit the stone hard, limbs slack, breath tearing in ragged, uncoordinated gasps. His eyes fluttered wildly, unfocused, as if he had been thrown back into himself too fast, too suddenly, without warning.

The Lantern screamed.

Not in pain.

In fury.

His light flared violently, folding outward in jagged pulses as he reached for control that no longer answered him. The command that had once flowed so effortlessly through the Veins now met resistance at every turn, splintering, rebounding, failing to anchor itself.

"NO," he roared. "YOU DO NOT CHOOSE—"

The light surged again.

This time, it did not strike to tear away.

It wrapped.

It flowed into Jonah.

I saw him—not as he had been moments before, twisted and broken beneath possession—but as he had been before the weight of generations crushed him. The man from the stories. The man in the faded photographs my family kept tucked away like relics.

The light did not erase him.

It returned him.

Jonah cried out—not in agony, but in release—as the darkness that had hollowed him for so long burned away, stripped from him layer by layer until nothing false remained. Light spilled from his skin in trembling waves, his body shaking as breath returned fully, painfully, rightly.

He collapsed to his knees, hands pressed to his chest, sobbing openly—not broken, not possessed, but present. His limbs folded awkwardly beneath him, as if he no longer remembered how to inhabit his own body. His eyes darted wildly, unfocused, the world rushing back into him all at once.

Behind him, the creature screamed as the light tightened, dragging it farther away, its form buckling and unraveling.

The Lantern roared.

Not in command.

In outrage.

His light lashed outward as he reached for control that no longer answered him. The Veins recoiled, their glow spasming as his authority slid off them, unanchored.

And still the light flowed—into Jonah, around him, recognizing him.

That was when I felt it leave me.

Not all at once.

Steadily.

Like a tide receding from ground it had only borrowed.

The weight of the blade deepened immediately, pain crashing in where the light had been. My body swayed as strength drained with it.

I was no longer standing on borrowed breath.

Jonah was alive.

And the cost was not finished being paid.

The canyon roared around us, stone grinding against stone, dust choking the air as the collapse gathered speed. Gillie's sobs pressed close to me, her breath hitching against my shoulder. Jonah's gasps tore raggedly through the noise somewhere nearby. Even the Lantern's fury still raged in the distance, his voice breaking against the failing ground.

And then, beneath all of it—

Something else.

Not louder.

Clearer.

It passed through the other sounds, steady and unmistakable, like a current beneath a river's surface. It did not belong to the canyon or the Veins or the Withering at all.

It belonged to me.

A sound.

Not the canyon.

Not the collapse.

Not Gillie's sobs or Jonah's ragged breathing or the distant fury of the Lantern tearing the world apart behind us.

This sound did not belong to the place at all.

It came from above the moment, from behind it, from somewhere that did not need stone or air to carry it.

A voice.

It spoke once.

My name.

Not the one I had worn.

The one I had waited for.

It didn't shake the canyon or break the Veins or demand attention through force. It filled everything instead, warm and absolute, the way a presence fills a room when you step into a place you have always belonged.

"Caleb."

The sound wrapped around me.

It did not startle me.

It comforted me.

Something inside my chest loosened at the sound of it, the way a clenched fist finally releases after holding too long. The pain did not vanish, but it no longer frightened me. The weight of the blade, the tearing in my lungs, the dimming of the world at its edges—everything settled into place.

Just completion.

I had never heard my name before—not because it had been kept from me, not because it had gone unspoken, but because it had never been mine to hear.

The voice did not explain.

It did not praise.

It did not command.

It welcomed.

I breathed.

"Names are for saying," I said.

And for the first time, I said mine.

"Caleb."

The truth of it moved through me, deeper than bone, deeper than breath. The name did not replace who I had been; it gathered every fragment and held them together, whole at last.

I had been afraid that if I said my name, it would be written down and I would be kept.

I hadn't known there were houses that don't lock their doors.

This one opened them.

I whispered it again.

"Caleb."

The sound barely left my lips.

But Gillie heard it.

Her breath caught sharply as her head snapped up, eyes searching my face with sudden, terrified hope. She did not ask. She did not need to.

She knew.

Her hands tightened around me, trembling, slick with blood and tears she hadn't yet noticed were falling.

"No—" she whispered. Then again, broken. "No. No, no. I didn't—"

Her breath hitched hard enough to shake her shoulders. She pressed her forehead against mine as if closeness might undo what had already happened, as if the world could be rewound by touch alone.

"I was trying to stop him," she said, the words rushing out unevenly. "I was trying to stop Raven. You stepped in—"

She pulled back just enough to look at me. Horror widened her eyes—not fear of what was happening, but of what she had almost done.

"You shouldn't have done that."

I nodded.

Just once.

The effort burned. The edges of the world were already dimming, but her face stayed clear—closer than the pain, closer than the ground beneath us.

For a moment, she said nothing.

Her hands hovered, unsure where to go—whether to hold me, or hold herself together.

Then, softer. Almost to herself.

"You stepped in front of it."

I drew a shallow breath. "I had to."

Her mouth opened again, closed. She swallowed hard, as if her body needed time to catch up with what her eyes were seeing.

And then—only then—did the other realization reach her.

"You..." Her voice faltered. She searched my face again, slower this time. "You have your name."

She didn't say it like a declaration.

She said it like something fragile, something she was afraid to touch too hard.

I swallowed. My breath came shallow, rough.

"Yes," I said.

The word seemed to land between us and stay there.

I shifted slightly, breath thinning. Something pressed against my ribs from inside the tunic—not pain. Memory.

"Gillie," I said softly.

She leaned closer, as if the world were already too loud.

I slipped my hand between us and pressed something small into her palm. Metal. Warm.

"Carry this," I whispered.

She looked down, confusion flickering—but her fingers closed around it without asking why.

"I don't—"

"It belongs to Cephas," I said quietly.

She stilled.

"It shouldn't be with me anymore."

Her eyes lifted to mine, searching. "Then why—"

"Because it remembers," I said. My breath caught, then steadied. "It was never meant to buy anything. It's a witness."

Her throat worked.

"Witness to what?"

I managed a faint, breathless smile. "That love didn't trade him away."

Her fingers tightened around the metal, as if it might slip through her grasp.

"Keep it," I whispered. "Until it finds its way back to where it belongs."

She nodded once—not because she understood, but because I had asked. She tucked it into her pocket, as if the motion itself were enough to keep me there.

Her hands tightened—not around the wound, not yet—but around me, anchoring herself to something that still existed.

We stayed like that for a breath. Maybe two.

Then she shook her head slightly, as if remembering something she hadn't meant to remember yet.

"You used to say…" She stopped, breath catching. "You used to tell me what your father said."

I waited.

She didn't meet my eyes.

"It's necessary to go through the fire," she said quietly now, the words no longer breaking but heavy, deliberate, "to be tempered and refined."

Silence followed. Not empty. Considering.

She shook her head again, slower this time. "I never thought—" A breath. "I never thought this would be the fire."

"Maybe it wasn't meant to spare us from it," I said softly. "Maybe it was meant to show us who we are inside it."

Her eyes lifted then—searching my face, not for reassurance, but for truth.

"It wasn't," I said.

"This wasn't your choice," I whispered. "It was mine."

Her shoulders folded inward. Not collapsing—yielding.

"I didn't think," she said. "I just moved."

"So did I."

I lifted my hand with what little strength remained and rested it against her wrist. She froze—not from fear, but from the weight of what even that small touch now carried.

"He's my blood," I said quietly. "I didn't know how to do anything else."

I drew another breath, thinner than the last.

"I knew Jonah was still in there. Raven didn't resist—Jonah did."

The words settled into her—not accusation, not absolution. Recognition.

"I stepped into the blade," I continued. "The fire followed."

She closed her eyes.

"I didn't want this," she said.

"I know," I said. "Neither did I."

I drew a breath that barely stayed with me. "But this is your fire now."

Her eyes opened sharply.

"No," she whispered. "I don't want it."

"I didn't either," I said. "That's how you know it's real."

She stared at me, trembling—not resisting now, but standing at the edge of something she could no longer deny.

"My father used to say the fire doesn't just change the blade," I went on. "It changes the hand that holds it."

Her breath caught.

"He never meant it only for me," I said. "He meant it for whoever stayed."

The chaos around us softened—not gone, not undone—but finished.

And then I saw him.

He stood at the far edge of the canyon, just beyond where the light had burned brightest moments before. Falling stone did not disturb the air around him. He stood calmly, hands folded, watching.

The Silent Child.

He looked as he always had—small, still, unafraid. But his eyes were gentle now. No longer searching. No longer waiting.

He was watching me.

And he smiled.

Not wide.

Not triumphant.

Just enough.

Understanding passed between us without words.

He had never been watching the end of the story.

He had been watching the moment I would finally understand who I was.

Gillie saw him too. I felt it in the way her breath stuttered, the way her grip tightened as her gaze shifted past me.

"The child," she whispered. "I see him."

He lifted one hand—not in farewell, but acknowledgment.

Then he stepped backward, and the light behind him folded inward, closing softly.

He was gone.

The world rushed back in.

The canyon groaned as the collapse accelerated, stone screaming as it tore free from the walls. Voices shouted—movement, now, live.

Gillie shook as she held me, torn between staying and surviving.

"I'm sorry," she whispered, her forehead pressed to mine. "I'm so sorry."

I smiled. It surprised both of us.

"This," I breathed, every word costing me now, "was never death."

Her tears fell harder.

I reached up—slowly, clumsily—and brushed my thumb across her cheek, wiping one away. My vision was dimming fast, but her face stayed clear.

"For life," I whispered. "Not for death."

Her breath broke completely.

"You didn't take life," I told her. "You gave it back."

My strength failed then.

The canyon tilted, darkness pulling inward from the edges of my sight—but there was no fear left in it. Only warmth. Only rest.

The last thing I felt was the ground—not rejecting me, not resisting—but receiving me gently.

The last thing I heard was my name.

"Caleb."

And then—

Home.

The Way Closed

The canyon began to close as if it had been waiting for permission.

Not from the Lantern.

From the ground.

It started at the center, where light had burst through flesh and truth had been torn from Jonah's ribs. Stone groaned deep in its own language, a low grinding that rolled through the mountain and made the Veins flare in answer. A seam split beneath the dark vanguard—not wide enough to swallow them yet, wide enough to warn.

Then the warning became motion.

Rock peeled loose from the canyon walls in plates the size of doors. Dust erupted in choking waves. Pebbles rained first, then fist-sized shards, then entire slabs that dropped without drama—only weight. Vein-light embedded in the stone flashed when it fractured—bright, alive for a heartbeat—then snapped out, as if breath had been withdrawn.

The Lantern threw his hand forward.

"Advance!" he screamed, and the word did not behave like sound. It struck the army like a whip. "Forward—FORWARD!"

The lost souls lurched into motion.

Some obeyed instantly, boots pounding stone that was already bending. They ran like a single body trained for fear, armor clattering, weapons low, faces blank with obedience. They did not look up. They did not look down. They ran because command was the only language left in them.

Others faltered.

They looked at the walls.

They looked at the ceiling.

They saw the canyon folding inward and their bodies remembered what minds were too slow to name: this place wanted to kill them.

A slab dropped.

Two figures vanished beneath it, crushed so completely they were not thrown or pinned—they were simply erased, armor folding under the weight. The sound was short and ugly. Then the dust swallowed even that.

The line broke.

Half surged forward.

Half tried to pull back.

The Lantern's light flared, furious and surgical.

"No!" he roared. "You do not retreat. You do not—"

Lucien turned anyway.

He was already moving backward, already dragging Julian with him, boots scraping for traction as the ground shifted underfoot. Elana ran with them—running as if she had seen this kind of judgment before and knew better than to argue with it.

The Lantern's gaze snapped to them.

His hand clenched.

Pain answered.

Lucien jerked as if struck from inside, his shoulders locking, his spine bowing. Julian stumbled hard, a strangled sound tearing from his throat. Elana cried out through clenched teeth, one hand flying to her chest as if something there had been grabbed and squeezed.

The Lantern raised his voice, each syllable landing like a nail.

"BOW!"

Lucien's knees buckled. He caught himself on sheer will, teeth bared, eyes wild.

"BEND!"

Julian's arm twisted at an angle it should not have twisted, not breaking but threatening to. His scream echoed once, thin and shamed.

"BREAK!"

Elana collapsed to one knee, shaking, breath chopped into ragged pieces. The Veins beneath her flickered like a candle in a storm.

They did not stop.

Lucien grabbed Elana by the wrist and hauled her upright. Julian stumbled forward again, half-limping, refusing to turn back and face the Lantern's wrath. Their retreat became a sprint, pain trailing them over stone.

The Lantern's army saw it.

Saw disobedience.

Saw punishment.

And still, the instinct to survive rose in some of them anyway—untrained, ugly, sudden. Bodies shifted backward. A few turned fully.

The Lantern's face contorted, not with fear of collapse, but with offense.

"FORWARD!" he screamed again. "The ground will yield to me. It always has! It always—"

A rock the size of a cart wheel broke free overhead and slammed down among the wavering soldiers. It crushed three at once. One was thrown hard enough to bounce, armor ringing like a bell, before he disappeared under a second fall. Dust blossomed and was swallowed by more dust.

Marcus stood in the middle of it.

Not running forward.

Not retreating.

He stared at the closing walls, then at the Lantern, then at the retreating figures—Lucien's limp, Julian's bent posture, Elana's shaking hand still clutched around her ribs.

His jaw worked as if chewing a decision.

He had seen the punishment.

He had felt the canyon's judgment beginning.

And still he wanted to live.

He shifted backward a half-step.

Then another.

The Lantern's attention flicked to him.

Marcus froze.

The Lantern did not punish him yet. That was the cruelty of it—letting him feel the leash tighten without snapping it, letting hesitation become its own torment.

The Lantern looked past them all then.

Forward.

Toward the narrowing path where the living were fleeing.

He could see them—small now, distant, bodies moving through dust and Vein-light toward the glow of the Humming Trees. He could see the opening where the Vein rose like a vertical river, bright enough to stain the air with promise.

Rocks fell around him.

Stone shrieked as the canyon folded inward.

He did not flinch.

And then he saw Joshua.

He saw Jonah.

They were getting up.

Not crawling away.

Not collapsing.

Rising like men who might run.

Raven—no longer within Jonah, no longer hidden—moved near the Lantern like a shadow given legs. It stalked forward on twisted limbs, hunger written into its shape. Its mouth opened as if to speak, but what came out was a wet rasp, a sound made of spite and need.

The Lantern snapped his gaze to it.

"No," he hissed. "Not here."

Raven flinched.

The Lantern pointed toward the fleeing eight.

"Go," he commanded. "Go to them. Bring me the blade-bearer. Bring me the ones who think they can escape."

Raven turned.

And ran.

The Lantern lifted his hand again, light blazing.

"ADVANCE!" he screamed, voice cracking with rage and arrogance. "Advance! I am the ground's master. I am—"

He stepped forward as debris fell around him, as stone shattered, as the canyon tightened like a fist.

He believed the walls could not touch him.

And he advanced as if belief were armor.

Joshua's feet found purchase only because he forced them to.

His lungs burned. His throat tasted like iron and dust. His body still carried the aftershock of what had happened—light tearing, truth moving, the world shifting under the weight of a sacrifice he could not undo. He looked at Jonah as Jonah hauled himself upright, and for a moment Joshua's face held something almost childlike: disbelief that he was seeing him whole.

Jonah's eyes were clear.

Not wide with possession.

Not fogged with absence.

Clear—like a man who had returned to his own name after years of being called something else.

He swayed once, then steadied.

Behind them, the Lantern's scream cut through the canyon.

"ADVANCE!"

Rocks fell.

The canyon groaned.

The Veins in the stone flickered and recoiled as if pulling back from something poisonous.

Joshua reached for Jonah's arm. "Come with me," he said, voice ragged. "We can make it—"

Jonah shook his head before Joshua even finished.

"No," he said.

Joshua's grip tightened. "Don't do this. Not now. We're—" His voice broke. "We're finally—"

"Finally what?" Jonah snapped, and there was no cruelty in it—only grief sharpened into clarity. "Finally free? Finally forgiven? Joshua, listen to me."

The Lantern advanced.

Raven ran ahead of him, closing distance, driven by command.

The dark army churned behind them—some surging forward, some scrambling back—caught between obedience and panic as the canyon judged them.

Ahead, the glow of the Humming Trees pulsed brighter.

Gillie's voice carried back through the dust. "Joshua! Move!"

Kaela shouted something after her—prayer, warning, both. Nadya's voice cut through the chaos like a curse. Rowan was already turning his body to guard the rear. Eliah kept Miriam moving. Sera's hum—thin, strained—clung to the air like thread.

Shim'on ran with them now. Not beside them. Not behind. Near enough to be counted.

A crack sounded above us that wasn't thunder.

Shim'on looked up once—only once—then shoved Rowan forward with his shoulder.

Stone sheared loose from the wall and struck him along the outer leg. He went down hard, breath leaving him in a clean, brutal cut.

He didn't cry out. He hooked his hand into the rock, hauled himself up, and ran again—one step true, one step borrowed—as dust swallowed the blood before it could fall.

Joshua's feet wanted to follow.

His hands wanted to drag Jonah with him.

Jonah wrenched free.

He grabbed Joshua by the front of his shirt and hauled him close enough that their foreheads nearly touched.

"You broke the Law of Faith and Love," Jonah shouted, and the words came out like confession and indictment in one. "But I let you."

Joshua froze.

"I didn't stop you," Jonah continued, voice cracking as stone thundered overhead. "I watched you do it. I watched Grace get crushed under your choices and I called it loyalty. I called it silence. I called it anything but what it was."

"Jonah—" Joshua tried, voice raw.

"I was just as unfaithful to her," Jonah said, eyes burning now, wet with fury and grief braided tight. "Not because I struck the blow—because I stood there and let you swing."

The Lantern's shout rose again behind them. "FORWARD!"

The canyon convulsed.

Joshua looked past Jonah and saw it—the dark pressing, Raven running, the Lantern walking as falling stone came down around him.

He looked forward and saw Gillie at the edge of the Humming Trees, Balanced Blade gone from her hands now, her arms out as if she could pull him across distance by will alone.

"Come!" she cried.

Jonah's grip tightened.

"I need to do this," Jonah said, every syllable absolute now. "For me. For you."

Joshua shook his head hard. "You don't have to pay for—"

"Yes," Jonah snapped, cutting him off. "I do."

He shoved Joshua forward.

"RUN!"

Joshua stumbled, caught himself, turned back again—

Jonah screamed it a second time, louder, tearing his throat raw with it.

"RUN!"

Joshua ran.

He ran because Gillie was calling. Because the canyon was closing. Because the rest were moving and the prophecy was not a riddle anymore—it was a path being counted by feet and breath.

He ran—and behind him Jonah turned toward the Lantern.

The change in Jonah was immediate.

He did not hunch like prey.

He did not brace like a man expecting to be crushed.

He stood upright.

Light—faint but real—gathered around him, not flaring outward, not attacking, simply present, a shield made of truth.

The Lantern saw it.

His face twisted, rage spitting through his composure.

Jonah lifted his hands—not in surrender.

In readiness.

The Lantern advanced anyway, arrogant enough to believe he could break light the way he broke men.

They collided.

It was not an explosion.

It was a transfer.

The light in Jonah surged—one clear, decisive pulse—then moved.

It left Jonah.

And it entered Joshua.

Joshua staggered mid-run as if struck from inside. His breath hitched. His spine arched as something sealed, something ancient and broken finally re-knit. A sound tore from his throat—half sob, half gasp—as his lungs filled like they had never fully filled before.

He did not stop running.

But he ran differently now.

As if the weight that had hollowed him out for so long had finally lifted.

As if his footsteps belonged to him again.

Behind him, Jonah stood alone.

And the canyon began to close in earnest.

Stone slammed together with deafening finality.

The sound was not a single impact but a convergence—layers of the world colliding with themselves, pressure resolving into judgment. The canyon sealed from the center outward, not collapsing chaotically but closing, as if the mountain had reached a decision and was now enforcing it.

Walls that had once leaned apart with trembling restraint folded inward with unstoppable force, slabs of ancient rock grinding together in violent alignment. Dust detonated outward in choking clouds, light splintering as Veins withdrew in jagged flashes, then vanished altogether.

For a brief, terrible moment, the Lantern and Jonah were visible through the storm of falling stone.

Two figures locked in motion—one blazing with furious authority, the other standing fast in light that did not burn but held. Jonah's feet slid as the ground convulsed beneath him, yet he did not retreat. He braced, shoulders squared, body set against the advance not as a challenge but as an offering already given. The Lantern surged forward, light flaring violently as he reached, fingers clawing through dust and falling debris, his voice tearing through the chaos in a scream of command that the mountain no longer obeyed.

Then the walls came down.

A slab of stone spanning the canyon like a fallen cliff-face tore loose and fell between them, obliterating the space they occupied. Stone struck stone with a thunder that swallowed all other sound. Light flared once—bright, furious, defiant—and then disappeared beneath crushing weight and blinding dust. The struggle vanished, consumed not by victory or defeat, but by closure.

The mountain reclaimed its shape.

Marcus ran.

He had hesitated too long, caught between obedience and instinct, between the certainty of command and the undeniable truth of falling stone. He turned at last, sprinting hard toward the narrowing gap as the canyon devoured itself behind him. Armor clattered. Breath tore loose from his chest. He did not look back—not because he was brave, but because he was afraid of what he would see.

He was almost clear.

The final collapse came without warning, without mercy. Stone folded inward in a violent surge, the ground heaved upward as if struck from below, and the passage behind him vanished in an instant. The mountain slammed shut with a concussive force that sent Marcus sprawling forward, skidding across broken rock as dust and debris engulfed him.

The sound was immense.

Then—gone.

Silence fell.

Not the fragile silence of aftermath, but something heavier. Complete. As if the world itself were listening to what it had just done.

Where the canyon had been, there was now a mountain.

Whole.

Unbroken.

No seam. No scar. No trace of passage or fracture. The stone stood smooth and ancient, as if it had never parted at all. Whatever struggle had taken place within it was sealed away, buried beneath layers of rock and weight and time. The land did not mourn. It did not rage. It simply remained.

On the far side, the nine who remained reached the Vein.

They did not arrive together.

Gillie stumbled to the edge first, breath ragged, blood streaked across her hands and sleeves where she had gripped stone and flesh alike. She did not cross. She stopped short, boots skidding on grit as the ground beneath her feet changed—no longer straining, no longer fleeing, but steady in a way she felt immediately.

Miriam reached her side next, face pale, eyes wide with shock that had not yet found words. She stood frozen for a heartbeat, as if afraid that one more step might wake whatever horror they had just outrun.

Sera came next, one hand pressed hard to her ribs, her hum broken at last into uneven gasps. Even so, the sound lingered faintly in her chest, a fractured echo of what she had carried for so long.

Rowan and Nadya emerged together, hauling Eliah between them as his steps faltered. He sagged briefly, then steadied, teeth clenched, refusing to collapse while the world was still deciding whether to let them keep breathing.

Shim'on arrived last, not running now but slowing deliberately, as if the urgency had finally loosened its grip on him. He stopped a few paces back from the others, eyes lifting once toward the newly formed mountain behind them, measuring it the way one measures a sealed door—accepting without trusting.

Joshua reached the edge after them.

He staggered as his feet found the same unmoving ground, the light beneath the surface flaring faintly at his arrival—not in challenge but in recognition. He dropped to one knee, breath tearing loose from his chest as the weight of what had been lost—and what had been given back—crashed through him all at once.

Kaela came in just behind him, one hand still at Miriam's back out of habit, as if her body hadn't realized the running was over.

No one spoke.

They did not need to.

Behind them, the mountain stood whole.

Unbroken.

Where the canyon had been, where the world had torn itself open to choose sides, there was now only stone—ancient, immovable, indifferent to pursuit. No light leaked through. No sound followed. The way back had not merely closed.

It had been erased.

Ahead of them, the Vein rose.

Not a path yet. Not an opening.

A presence.

The light gathered upward in a steady, vertical current, threading itself through the roots of the Humming Trees that stood just beyond, their branches trembling with quiet resonance. This sound was nothing like the violence they had fled. It did not roar or split or burn.

It hummed.

Low.

Steady.

Alive.

It was the sound they had longed for without knowing how to name it. The sound of something holding instead of chasing. Of breath returned to the world instead of stolen from it.

Kaela stopped.

Not from exhaustion. From recognition.

She turned slowly, as if turning were a sacred act the world would punish if rushed. Her eyes moved from face to face with the quiet precision of prayer.

Gillie—hands still stained with what she could not undo.

Miriam—pale, breathing like someone learning again.

Sera—broken hum still trembling in her chest.

Rowan—standing because he refused to fall.

Nadya—blood on her arm, jaw set against grief.

Eliah—held upright by will and borrowed strength.

Shim'on—arrived at last, not as an addition, but as a return.

Joshua—kneeling, breath in him like a miracle that hurt.

And herself—still standing, still counting, still here.

Her lips parted.

"Nine," she whispered.

The word did not echo. It settled.

Not into air, but into ground—into Vein-light—into the roots of the Humming Trees that trembled as if they had been waiting to be named correctly.

Kaela lifted her voice, and the prophecy came out of her like something remembered rather than spoken.

"Nine shall walk the broken path."

Gillie understood then.

The count had never been about who started.

It had always been about who remained.

Not as loss.

As fulfillment.

The grief did not vanish—but it rearranged itself, taking on a shape that could be carried without breaking her. The blade was gone. The blood was still warm on her hands. But the purpose that had driven her forward for so long now stood complete, revealed not in victory, but in balance restored.

This was always meant to be this way.

The Humming Trees answered, their resonance deepening, roots glowing faintly as the Vein gathered itself more fully—preparing, not yet opening, but acknowledging.

Behind them, the mountain did not move.

Ahead of them, the light waited.

They stood there together, breathing at last, listening to the sound they had been running toward for longer than any of them could remember.

The pursuit was over.

The path had been walked.

And the world, finally, was ready to let them go.

The Crossing

The Vein Waits

He had laid the scroll down by dying, and I had lifted it by killing. The ache of that truth still burned my hands.

My name is Gillie. The scroll rides my shoulder now.

I did not take it because I wanted to. I took it because it would not remain on the ground.

That was the first honest thing I could admit to myself once the running stopped.

The leather strap cut into my collarbone as I shifted, the weight unfamiliar in a way that felt wrong, like wearing someone else's coat too soon. The scroll rested against my back, quiet and awake. It did not ask if I would carry it. It simply remained, as if the world had already decided something I was still refusing to understand.

I stood at the edge of the Vein and did not move.

None of us did.

The Crossing

The Humming Trees rose before us, ancient and luminous, their roots threaded with Veins that pulsed in a slow, steady rhythm. The sound filled the air—not loud, not demanding—but constant. This was the sound we had been running toward for so long. The sound that had pulled us through terror and doubt and blood.

Now that we had reached it, it waited.

The Vein did not pull.

It did not open wider.

It did not rush us.

That was how I knew this wasn't an escape.

It was a choice.

Behind us, the mountain stood whole, the canyon sealed as if it had never existed. No crack. No seam. No path back. The way we had come was gone—not erased, but finished.

I could still hear it, though. Not the collapse. Not the screams.

The moment before.

The moment that mattered.

I swallowed hard and felt my throat tighten.

Caleb should have been standing here.

The thought came sharp enough to steal my breath. I turned instinctively, already knowing what I would see.

There was space where he should have been.

Not a void—just a space shaped by his presence and now holding its outline. My chest constricted around it, the ache immediate and merciless.

I staggered, knees buckling, and dropped to the ground.

The scroll shifted with me, its weight pulling me forward until my palms hit the earth. The impact jarred my arms, but I welcomed the pain. It grounded me in a way the grief refused to.

"No," I whispered.

The word did nothing. Still, it tore itself out of me.

I pressed my forehead to the dirt and squeezed my eyes shut.

This wasn't how it was supposed to end.

We had been together. Through fear and fire and silence. He had been there when I doubted myself, when the weight of the Blade felt too heavy to lift. He had stood beside me when the scroll stirred and the world pressed in. He had spoken when I couldn't. Listened when I wouldn't.

He had believed.

And I had—

My hands shook as the memory surged up unbidden. The moment of impact. The resistance giving way. The sound—too soft, too final—as the Blade found flesh that was never meant to receive it.

A sob ripped out of me.

"I didn't mean to," I choked. "I didn't—I was trying to save—"

My voice broke.

Someone knelt beside me.

Miriam.

I felt her before I saw her, her presence steady as she reached for my shoulders. She didn't pull me upright. She didn't tell me to breathe. She simply rested her forehead against the side of my head and stayed there, her own breath uneven against my ear.

"You did save him," she whispered.

I shook my head violently, tears soaking into the dirt.

"I killed him," I said. "I killed him with my own hands."

Her grip tightened—not restraining, but anchoring.

"No," she said, firmer now. "You didn't."

I let out a jagged laugh. "Then whose blood is still on me?"

She didn't answer.

None of them did.

The silence stretched, heavy with shared loss. Around us, the others stood or knelt, each caught in their own reckoning.

Sera sat with her back against one of the Trees, her hum fractured into soft, broken notes that wavered with every breath. Her hands were clenched in her sleeves, knuckles white.

Rowan stood a few paces away, staring at the ground with an expression I had never seen on him before—unguarded. Nadya hovered near him, her hand close to his elbow, not quite touching.

Eliah sat heavily on a root, head bowed, lips moving silently as if counting or praying.

Shim'on remained standing, watchful even now, though his gaze lingered longer than usual on the empty space where Caleb should have been.

Joshua knelt near the Vein.

He had not crossed it.

The light beneath him pulsed faintly, recognizing him without pulling him in. His shoulders were hunched, his hands braced against the earth as though the weight of what had been returned to him was threatening to crush him all over again.

He looked up when my sob broke into something harsher.

Our eyes met.

And whatever composure he had been holding collapsed.

He rose unsteadily and crossed the distance between us, dropping to his knees in front of me. His hands hovered before settling on my forearms—gentle, reverent, as though afraid I might vanish if he held too tightly.

"I'm so sorry," he said.

The words were simple. Inadequate. Honest.

"This was never meant to cost him," he continued. "This was never meant to be his burden."

A sound tore out of me.

"But it was," I said. "Because of you. Because of me. Because of everything we failed to stop."

He bowed his head.

"Yes," he said quietly. "Because of me."

The admission hung between us, unadorned.

"I broke the Law of Faith and Love," he went on. "Not once. Not accidentally. I broke it knowing what it would cost, and I let others pay that cost for me."

I clenched my fists, nails biting into my palms.

"You paid too," I said fiercely. "You paid more than anyone."

He looked up at me, eyes wet.

"And he paid more than all of us," he said.

Silence fell again.

I forced myself upright. The scroll shifted against my back, its presence impossible to ignore. I reached up without thinking, my fingers brushing the worn leather.

The contact steadied me.

"He can't carry it anymore," I whispered.

Joshua followed my gaze.

"No," he said softly. "He can't."

The truth struck clean and hard.

"He laid it down," I said. "He laid it down by dying."

Joshua nodded.

"And you lifted it," he said. "Not by wanting to. By being willing."

Fresh tears spilled over.

"I don't want it," I admitted. "I don't want to be the one who survives him. I don't want to leave without him."

The words came raw and unguarded.

"He was with me," I said. "Every step. Every doubt. He believed when I couldn't. And now the world just expects me to walk forward like that doesn't matter?"

"It matters," Joshua said. "It matters more than anything."

He hesitated.

"But listen to me, Gillie. What you did—what we did—was not for death."

I flinched.

He held my gaze.

"For life," he said. "Not for death."

The words settled into me, echoing Caleb's final breath.

"You didn't take his life," Joshua went on. "You gave it back. You gave it meaning. And the Blade did what it was made to do."

I pressed my hands to my face.

"I still feel it," I whispered.

"I know," he said.

He placed his hand over his heart.

"So do I."

We stayed there, kneeling at the edge of the Vein, surrounded by grief and light and the low hum of the Trees.

No one rushed us.

The Vein waited.

Not because it had to.

But because crossing meant accepting what had been lost.

And what had been entrusted.

I drew a long breath and let my hands fall.

"I'll carry it," I said at last.

Joshua's eyes lifted.

"I don't know how," I continued. "And I don't know where it will take us. And I don't know if I'll ever forgive myself for surviving him."

I gripped the strap of the scroll.

"But I'll carry it," I said. "Because he can't. And because someone has to."

Joshua bowed his head.

"So be it," he said quietly.

The hum deepened around us.

Not behind. Not ahead.

Beneath.

The Trees did not surround the Vein—they were the Vein, risen into form. Their roots threaded through the same living channels that had carried us here. What hummed was not wood or leaf, but passage itself.

The light did not beckon.

It listened.

And for the first time since the world had broken open around us, I understood that salvation was not an ending waiting to receive us.

It was a crossing that required consent.

A weight taken up.

A burden borne forward—not because it was demanded, but because it had been given.

What Has Been Decided

The hum changed.

Not in volume. Not in force. It did not rise or swell or demand attention. It clarified, as if a thousand overlapping tones had quietly agreed to become one. The sound sharpened into something steady and precise, vibrating through root and stone and breath alike. It was no longer the sound of pursuit. It was the sound of alignment.

I felt it first in my chest.

Not as pressure, but as release.

The ache I had been carrying since the Bell rang—the constant tightening, the sense that something remained unfinished—loosened without warning. It did not vanish. It settled. The difference mattered: pain that fights, and pain that has found its place.

The world did not move.

But time did.

It folded inward, compressing so tightly around us that the present moment felt impossibly small. I knew, then—without permission from doubt—that what we had just endured had not happened after the Swamp.

It had happened within it.

The memory rose without invitation.

Not the Swamp as we left it—burned open, silent, emptied of dark—but the Swamp in that final instant. Mud trembling. Light fracturing through water and shadow. The God-Forsaken Bell still ringing, its toll vibrating through every realm at once. I felt again the precise moment Joshua dropped the scroll, the way the ground seemed to inhale, as if the world itself had flinched.

And then his cry.

REDEMPTION.

The word did not echo the way memory usually echoes. It compressed, folding into a point so dense it felt capable of holding a lifetime inside it. I understood, then, that everything we had lived through since—the Withering, the path, the sacrifice, the canyon—had not followed that cry.

It had unfolded inside it.

I sucked in a sharp breath, my hands curling into the dirt. My pulse thundered as the realization settled with the force of truth finally named.

This was the judgment.

Joshua reacted before I could speak.

His entire body locked, spine bowing as if struck by something intimate and unbearable. A broken sound tore out of his throat and he dropped to his knees, palms slamming into the earth hard enough to jolt his shoulders. The Vein-light beneath him surged—not violently, not in attack—but insistently, threading upward around his forearms and chest like breath forcing its way back into lungs that had forgotten how to expand.

"Joshua!" I shouted, already moving.

I scrambled toward him without thinking, boots skidding against root and stone. I stopped short only because I felt it—saw it—washing over him.

Warmth.

Not heat. Not fire. Something deeper, as if the air itself had softened. The light did not accuse. It did not measure. It did not demand accounting. It poured into him with quiet authority, filling spaces that had been hollowed out long before this journey began.

All I could see was him shaking.

All I could hear was his breath breaking apart as he gasped, raw and unguarded. He folded forward until his forehead struck the ground, shoulders heaving as something inside him finally gave way.

"Stop!" I cried, panic slicing through my voice as I dropped beside him. "Please—stop!"

I didn't know who I was yelling at. The Trees. The Vein. The Law itself. Whatever unseen force had seized him so completely it had driven him to the earth.

"He's had enough," I shouted, hands hovering uselessly over his back, afraid to touch him and afraid not to. "He knows what he did. He knows. You don't need to—"

My voice broke.

"You don't need to tear him apart to prove it," I pleaded. "If this is judgment, then judge me too. My soul is tied to his. Take what you need from me instead."

Joshua let out a strangled sob, fingers clawing into the dirt as if the ground were the only thing keeping him from coming undone.

"I don't deserve this," he choked, the words scraping out like confession and accusation. "I don't deserve—"

"Yes, you do," I snapped back, tears streaming. "You do. You're still here. You're still trying. That has to count for something."

The warmth did not withdraw.

It did not intensify.

It settled.

Joshua gasped again—a full, wrenching inhale that caught halfway through his chest before breaking loose in a sound that was half sob, half breath reclaimed. His shoulders shook, every defense collapsing under the weight of what he had carried for so long.

"I thought it was over," he whispered into the ground. "I thought I'd missed it. That whatever chance I had… I threw it away."

I leaned forward, pressing my forehead against his back, no longer caring who saw or who heard.

"It wasn't too late," I said fiercely. "It's never been too late. Not if you're still here."

Something shifted—not outward, not visibly, but within him.

The shaking eased, not all at once, but gradually. Joshua's breath slowed, deepened, each inhale less ragged than the last. The warmth no longer surged; it remained, steady and encompassing, as though it had always known exactly how much he could bear.

"I didn't know it could still… reach me," he whispered, disbelief threading every syllable.

I pulled back just enough to see his face.

Tear-streaked. Broken open. Unhidden.

"It can," I said quietly. "Because I'm here. Because Caleb was here. Because love doesn't stop just because someone fails."

Joshua's body sagged then, not in collapse, but in surrender. His forehead rested fully against the earth now—not in shame, but in reverence, as if he finally understood the weight beneath him and was willing, at last, to let it hold him.

The warmth held.

And I knew—without words, without proof—that whatever was happening was not being done to him.

It was meeting him where he had finally stopped running.

Around us, the hum deepened.

Miriam lifted her head slowly, eyes unfocused as if she were listening beneath the sound. Sera's fractured notes steadied at last, her breath aligning unconsciously with the Trees. Even Rowan—skeptical, guarded Rowan—went utterly still, his posture shifting as though the ground had finally decided to bear his weight without question.

"The Bell didn't decide," Nadya murmured, the words leaving her not as argument but as revelation. "It asked."

Joshua bowed forward again, forehead to the earth.

"Yes," he said hoarsely. "And this—" He gestured weakly around us, to the Vein, the Trees, the space Caleb should have occupied. His voice shattered. "This was the answer."

The truth landed in me with crushing clarity.

Caleb had not died because redemption failed.

He had died because redemption required completion.

Not blood demanded.

Not obedience enforced.

Love chosen freely, eyes open—refusing to let death have the final word.

That was the judgment.

Not spoken.

Not pronounced.

Fulfilled.

The Vein did not flare or widen or claim us. It remained utterly still. No resistance. No sorting. No pressure.

And in that absence, we understood.

Joshua lifted his head, tears streaking his face, and met my gaze. Something in his eyes had changed—not erased, not absolved of memory, but clean. Grounded. Present.

"I have a choice," he whispered.

"Yes," I said.

"For the first time," he continued, voice trembling, "I actually have one."

The Vein waited.

And judgment, at last, was complete.

The Crossing

No one moved at first.

The Vein waited, light rising and falling in a slow rhythm that no longer urged or resisted. The Humming Trees stood rooted in that light, their branches trembling softly as the resonance steadied. The urgency was gone. The strain was gone. What remained was simple and patient.

The pilgrims were the first to go.

They did not speak. They did not look back. They moved in small groups, faces drawn but calm, as though something long clenched inside them had finally loosened. Each step into the Vein was deliberate but unafraid. The light accepted them without ceremony. No flare. No sorting. Just passage. One by one, they crossed, dissolving into the hum until only the sound remained.

The rest of us watched in silence.

The scroll settled more firmly against my back as stillness returned to the world. My breath deepened. The ache in my shoulders made itself known again. My hands trembled faintly where tears had not yet dried. The Withering was loosening its hold—not dramatically, not suddenly—but steadily, as though it no longer had reason to keep us.

Miriam stepped forward first.

She paused at the edge, hands clasped tight. When she turned back to us, her eyes were wet but steady.

"I carried fear longer than I knew," she said. "I thought it was mine. I thought it was who I was." She swallowed. "It wasn't. I chose to hold it because I thought it kept others safe."

She looked at me, a small, tired smile touching her mouth. "Thank you for showing me I can put it down."

She stepped into the light.

The Vein brightened briefly, then settled. She was gone.

Sera followed.

She rested her palm against one of the Trees, her hum wavering once before finding its pitch. When she turned, her voice was thin but sure.

"I learned to want without taking," she said. "To feel without consuming."

Her eyes flicked to Joshua—not accusation, not apology. Recognition.

"I forgive what I carried for you," she said. "And I forgive myself."

Her hum aligned fully as she stepped forward and dissolved into the light.

Rowan went next.

He stood rigid at the threshold, jaw tight, hands clenched.

"I don't like faith," he said bluntly. "I trust what I can test."

He glanced toward the Vein. "But this worked. I won't pretend it didn't."

His gaze met mine, then Joshua's. "If there's a world beyond this, I intend to live in it honestly."

He stepped into the Vein without ceremony.

Nadya lingered only a moment longer.

She knelt, pressed her palm to the ground, then rose.

"I was angry," she said. "At the world. At the laws. At you." She nodded toward Joshua. "At myself."

Her voice steadied. "Anger isn't a weapon. It's a wound."

She gripped Eliah's hand once. "Come back alive."

Then she crossed.

Eliah followed, lips moving in a quiet blessing. He paused just long enough to look at the scroll.

"Carry it gently," he said. "It remembers."

Then he stepped into the light.

Shim'on remained.

He stood slightly apart, not watching the Vein, but listening. His gaze lingered once on the sealed mountain where the canyon had closed. There was no grief on his face now. Only clarity.

When he turned toward us, something in him had settled.

"I was never meant to stay," he said quietly. "But I was meant to stand."

He stepped closer to the Vein—and stopped.

His breath caught. His hand lifted to his chest.

He closed his eyes.

None of us spoke.

When he opened them again, there was awe in his expression.

"I heard it," he said.

Joshua looked up sharply. "Heard what?"

"A name," Shim'on replied. "Not the one I was given."

He swallowed, then spoke more clearly.

"He said I would be a stone. That I would hold when others falter. That what is built will rest not on certainty, but on faith that stands even when it trembles."

He looked at Joshua. Then at me. No pride. No claim.

"I didn't ask for it," he said. "But I won't refuse it."

The Vein brightened beneath him—not claiming, simply acknowledging.

He inclined his head toward me. "You will not walk alone."

He shifted his weight, favoring the leg the canyon had marked, and stepped forward.

As the light took him, I heard him murmur, "Cephas."

Something warmed in my pocket—steady, certain.

Caleb's voice returned to me: It belongs to Cephas… it will find its way back.

I pressed my hand to the coin through the cloth. It pulsed once, then stilled.

I did not need to look.

I knew.

The Vein closed behind him without sound.

Only three of us remained.

Joshua stood nearest the light. It brushed his boots without drawing him forward. His shoulders were squared, but his hands hung loose, as though he were still learning how to stand without bracing.

Kaela stood a few paces back.

She was not facing the Vein.

That was what caught my attention first—not as realization, but as unease. The Vein hummed steadily, open and patient, and Joshua stood at its threshold, clearly meant to cross. But Kaela had angled herself away from it, her posture turned not toward release, but toward me.

I felt the shift before I understood it.

"You're not coming," I said.

The words weren't sharp. They weren't even loud. They surfaced the way truth sometimes does—uninvited, fully formed, already past denial.

Kaela met my eyes.

She did not hesitate.

"No," she said.

The sound of it struck deeper than any explanation could have. She didn't soften it. Didn't justify it. She didn't dress it in prophecy or necessity.

She simply stood there, hands loose at her sides, shoulders relaxed in a way I had never seen before, and let the word be what it was.

Final.

I took a step toward her without thinking, the scroll shifting against my back as I moved. The leather strap pulled against my collarbone, grounding me in the weight I now carried, but my focus narrowed to her face—older than I remembered, gentler than I expected.

"You don't have to stay," I said. I didn't know why I said it. I only knew I needed to hear the answer.

Kaela shook her head once.

"I do," she said. "Just not the way you think."

She stepped closer—not toward the Vein, but toward me. The hum of the Trees deepened slightly as she moved, the resonance steady and untroubled, as if the world itself recognized the choice being made and found no fault in it.

Up close, I could see the strain she had carried without complaint. The faint lines at the corners of her eyes. The set of her mouth, disciplined by years of silence. She lifted her hand as if to touch my shoulder, then stopped herself, fingers curling inward before settling lightly against my arm instead.

"I should have protected you better," she said.

The words landed without ceremony, heavy but honest. Not rehearsed. Not prepared. Just spoken.

"I thought," she continued, her voice tightening just slightly, "that if I stayed where I was, if I held what needed holding, you wouldn't have to carry as much."

I felt my throat close.

"You don't need to ask me for that," I said.

She inhaled sharply, as though the sentence had caught her off guard.

I shook my head, the motion small but firm. "You don't need forgiveness from me. Not for this."

Her eyes searched my face, uncertain now in a way she hadn't been moments before.

"You were there," I went on. "Even when I didn't know it. Even when I didn't understand what you were doing—or why you couldn't do more."

I swallowed hard.

"You were there."

Something in her expression broke open then—not grief, not relief, but release. Her shoulders sagged, just slightly, as though she had been holding herself upright against a weight that was finally allowed to fall away.

She smiled.

Not the careful smile she used when words failed her. Not the distant one she wore when duty came first. This was smaller. Truer. A smile that didn't ask anything in return.

"I've always been with you," she said.

The Vein hummed on, unperturbed.

"I know," I replied.

She stepped back.

Not abruptly. Not as retreat. Just one measured step, placing distance between herself and the Vein's edge. The light brushed her boots and did not follow. The resonance did not tighten around her. It let her go.

"I'll see you again," she said, already turning away.

I believed her.

Not because I understood how, or when, or where. But because the certainty of it settled into me without resistance, the same way the scroll had—quiet, undeniable, complete.

Kaela walked back into the Withering.

Not swallowed. Not erased.

Simply choosing a different road.

I watched until the light no longer touched her, until the hum reclaimed its previous balance, until the space she had occupied resolved into absence without ache.

Then there were two.

Joshua turned toward me.

"This is where I choose," he said.

I nodded.

"For the first time," he continued, "I'm not being pulled. Not by fear. Not by debt."

He met my eyes. "I don't know where I belong."

"I don't either," I said. "I just know I'm not done walking."

A faint smile touched his mouth.

"Then we trust the road."

He stepped toward the Vein.

I followed.

We paused at the threshold together. The light rose around our feet without urgency, without demand.

For a single heartbeat, we stood side by side.

"Whatever waits," Joshua said softly, "thank you. For believing I could still choose."

I tightened my grip on the scroll.

"For life," I replied. "Not for death."

He nodded once.

And then we stepped forward.

Together.

The Vein accepted us without flare or resistance.

And somewhere behind us—faint at first, then unmistakable—the God-Forsaken Bell finished its toll.

Not beginning again.

Ending.

The last note thinned, held, and finally vanished into the hum, as if the world had been waiting for that sound to stop before it could let us go.

After the Bell

I woke alone.

There was no jolt, no sharp breath, no sense of being pulled back into myself. Awareness returned quietly. I lay on my back beneath an open sky and did not move for a long moment. I listened—not for voices, not for danger—just to be sure the silence was real.

The ground beneath me was cool and firm. When I lifted my hand, grass bent under my fingers, soft and alive, carrying the clean scent of growth instead of rot. My throat tightened at that alone. I rolled to my side, then pushed onto my knees as sensation returned fully—the weight of my body, the ache in my shoulders, the soreness in my arms from carrying something too long.

The scroll rested against my back.

I had known it would be there. Before I reached for the strap across my chest, before I felt its pull, I knew. It didn't feel foreign.

It felt settled.

"I'm here," I whispered, unsure who I was speaking to.

The field stretched in every direction, open and unscarred. Distant trees stood upright and unburned. Wind moved through the grass in steady waves. The sky was clear—not harsh, just clear—as if something that had long dimmed it had finally lifted.

I stood.

That was when it struck me—not all at once, but in pieces sharp enough to stagger me. The quiet. The absence of urgency. No one shouting my name. No ground splitting beneath my feet.

Caleb was not here.

The thought stole the air from my lungs. I turned, though I already knew what I would see. Open space. No familiar figure. No steady presence at my shoulder.

My knees buckled.

I sank back into the grass, pressing my palms into the earth. It smelled clean. Alive.

And something inside me gave way.

I sobbed. Not quietly. Not carefully. The sound tore out of me as grief finally found room to exist without being outrun. I cried for Caleb first—for the way he had looked at me before stepping forward. For the certainty in his eyes. For the trust he placed in my hands.

"I didn't want it to be you," I choked. "I wanted us to walk out together."

The names followed.

Cassian's crooked grin. Tomas laughing at something small and stupid. Years I hadn't realized I was still carrying. I cried for Micah too—not as mystery, but as father. As loss.

A broken laugh slipped out at the memory of Caleb mangling a place name so badly we all groaned. The laugh folded back into tears.

I let it all come.

Time passed. I couldn't measure it.

Eventually the sobbing eased. I sat back on my heels, hollow and spent, and looked out over the field.

The world was still here.

Not fractured. Not dimmed. Marked, perhaps—but standing.

I rose slowly and turned in a circle. The colors seemed deeper. The air clearer. I could see farther than I remembered being able to before.

"This is what he died for," I murmured.

The words did not comfort me. They did not accuse me. They were simply true.

I reached back and touched the scroll. The leather was warm beneath my hand—not hot, not pulsing. Present.

"I'll carry you," I said. "I don't know how yet. But I will."

The wind shifted.

I turned.

A figure crested the rise at the far edge of the field.

My heart slammed against my ribs.

I stood so fast the world tilted. For half a second hope and terror collided so violently I thought I might fall.

Caleb.

Joshua.

The thought wasn't formed. It lunged.

The figure kept walking. Not toward me. Just along the ridge.

As the distance closed, truth settled in. The posture was wrong. The stride unfamiliar.

It was only a man.

A traveler—dust on his boots, a pack over one shoulder. He slowed when he noticed me and lifted a tentative hand.

"You all right?" he called.

The ordinariness of it nearly undid me.

"I think so," I managed.

He nodded, satisfied. His gaze drifted toward the distant trees.

"Strange day," he said. "Those humming trees been sounding different since morning. Like the ground's awake."

My fingers tightened on the scroll's strap.

"That's one way to put it."

He shifted his weight, glancing around the field as if orienting himself again. "You heading toward town? Path runs just over the hill there." He jerked his chin back the way he'd come.

Relief and disappointment tangled together in my chest. "Thank you." Then, before I could stop myself: "Did you see anyone else pass through?"

He frowned, thinking. "One fellow. Came over the ridge not long ago. Asked where the path went."

My pulse jumped.

"What did you tell him?"

"The same thing I told you." A faint smile tugged at his mouth. "Though I did ask him why everyone suddenly seems so concerned with paths."

My breath caught. "What did he say?"

The man shrugged. "Didn't answer. Just smiled and thanked me." He turned to leave, then added over his shoulder, almost idly, "Strange thing to worry about, paths. When it feels like the world's finally figured out where it's standing."

Something in his tone made my chest ache.

He took a few more steps, then slowed again—not stopping this time, just letting the words trail back toward me as if they barely mattered.

"People are already starting to say it happened because of him," he said. "That the dark broke because Clay finally bore it. Guess folks like having a name to put their weight on."

He lifted one hand in a loose, half-formed gesture that might have been a wave.

"In his name," he said.

Not as a blessing.

Not as a warning.

Just as a goodbye.

Then he walked on, boots crunching softly against the grass.

I opened my mouth to say more, but he was already gone.

I didn't wait.

I broke into a run, boots tearing through the grass as I sprinted toward the rise of the hill, heart pounding with a hope I didn't dare name yet. I crested the ridge hard, breath burning in my lungs—

And saw him.

Joshua stood on the far side, sunlight catching his shoulders as he turned at the sound of me.

We stared at each other.

He looked younger—not untouched by sorrow, but no longer hollowed by it. The weight that had once defined him was gone. What remained was steady. Whole.

When he smiled, it wasn't triumph.

It was recognition.

"Gillie," he said.

And this time, when my heart stopped, it was because it had finally found what it had been reaching for.

The sound of my name carried across the field, gentle and unmistakably human. It grounded me in a way nothing else had since I woke.

I took a step forward. Then another. My legs felt unsteady, but I didn't stop.

When we stood a few feet apart, I could see it clearly now—the absence of fracture. The way his eyes no longer flinched from the world. The way his breathing had settled into an easy rhythm, unforced.

"You look—" I stopped, unsure how to finish the thought.

"Like myself," he said softly. "For the first time in a long while."

"I didn't know if I would see you again."

"Neither did I."

Silence settled between us—not heavy. Full.

His gaze shifted to the scroll.

"He trusted you with it."

"He trusted me to keep walking."

Joshua's eyes brightened.

"He saved me," he said. "And Jonah. And more than that—he saved the part of the world that still believed I could choose."

"It cost him everything."

"Yes," Joshua said. "And he paid it willingly."

The field stretched wide around us.

"I don't know what comes next," he admitted. "Only that I've been given permission to walk forward. Either into the world I broke… or somewhere beyond it."

"Wherever you go," I said, "you won't walk alone."

A small, determined smile touched his mouth.

Together, we turned toward the horizon.

The Bell did not ring again.

It didn't need to.

What had been asked had been answered. What had been broken had been mended—not erased, but made strong enough to carry what comes next.

I adjusted the scroll on my shoulder.

Joshua walked beside me.

And the world moved forward.

Epilogue: In His Name

The world did not return all at once. That was the lie people told themselves later—that everything snapped back, that the ground healed cleanly, that the dark retreated and stayed gone. What actually happened was quieter and more dangerous. The world resumed. Slowly. Unevenly. With memory still lodged in the seams.

Fields took seed again. Rivers ran without tasting of iron. Nights grew dark without pressing too close. People breathed without feeling watched.

And almost immediately, they began to speak.

They spoke first in relief. Then in gratitude. And finally—in certainty.

Stories gathered the way crowds do, drawn not by truth but by shape. People wanted an ending they could carry. They wanted a name they could repeat when the ground felt uncertain beneath their feet.

Joshua Clay gave them one.

He heard it before I did. Not the praise—he had learned to flinch at that—but the tone. The way his name began to replace other words. The way people said it the way they used to say *safe* or *chosen* or *answered*.

Epilogue: In His Name

They said it when the harvest came in stronger than expected. They said it when a child recovered. They said it when fear loosened its grip for reasons no one could explain.

In his name.

Joshua tried to stop it. He corrected gently. Redirected often. He spoke of the scroll, of the Law, of the choice that had nothing to do with him. Most listened politely. Some nodded. A few even believed him.

But belief is not the same as obedience.

Shrines appeared where he had passed through—not grand ones, not at first. A stack of stones by a road. A ribbon tied to a post. Marks scratched into wood. Memory hardening into object.

I watched the scroll when it happened.

It did not burn.

It did not warn.

It did something worse.

It went still.

Joshua noticed that too.

One evening, a man thanked him with trembling hands and eyes too bright with relief. The words were ordinary, but the meaning beneath them wasn't.

"Say it again," Joshua asked, quiet enough that only I heard.

The man blinked. "Say what?"

"The reason you think you're safe," Joshua said.

The man's smile widened, eager and certain. "You."

The scroll did not move.

Joshua turned away.

I followed him until the road bent out of earshot. "It's starting," I said—not afraid, not surprised. Naming something only becomes dangerous when it's avoided.

"I know," Joshua replied. His voice held no pride. Only weight. "I can feel it leaning."

"Then you don't let it rest on you," I said. "You don't become load-bearing."

Joshua stopped walking.

"That's exactly what they did to me before," he said. The words were not accusation. They were memory. "They built a god out of a man so the Word wouldn't have to cost them anything."

A presence moved at the edge of the road—quiet, unhurried, as if it had been walking alongside us long before it chose to be seen.

I felt it first. Not threat. Not warning. The strange steadiness of something that did not need recognition to remain.

Joshua lifted his eyes.

Cephas stood a few paces off, dust on his boots, pack slung loose, posture plain enough to be missed by anyone who wanted spectacle. The kind of person you didn't notice until you realized the ground felt firmer when he was near.

"You're early," Joshua said, voice low.

Cephas's mouth twitched—almost a smile, almost nothing. "The stones have been listening," he replied. "They don't like what they hear."

My fingers brushed the strap across my chest. "They've started using his name like a handle," I said.

Cephas nodded once, as if this were not news but weather. "Handles become idols," he said. "And idols become cages."

Joshua stared down the road where village smoke rose thin and steady. "I keep telling them," he said. "I keep pointing away from myself."

"Yes," Cephas replied. "And they keep pointing back."

Joshua's jaw tightened. "What do we do when correction isn't enough?"

Cephas held his gaze—steady, unromantic, without reverence. "Then we outlast the lie," he said. "Not with volume. With weight."

I watched him carefully. "Weight of what?"

"The Word," Cephas said simply. "The kind that holds when names are taken away."

The scroll warmed against my back—just slightly. Not approval like fire. Recognition like a pulse.

Cephas glanced at it, then back to Joshua. "They'll try to make you the crossing," he said. "But crossings aren't foundations. They're passages."

Joshua exhaled—a slow, controlled breath, like a man refusing both pride and despair.

"They're already carving it into doorframes," he said. "Already saying it like a blessing."

In his name, Cephas murmured. The phrase sounded different in his mouth. Not worship. Diagnosis.

Behind us, somewhere out of sight, someone laughed. Someone else prayed. Someone else stacked a stone upon a stone and called it gratitude.

Joshua did not turn around.

I adjusted the scroll on my shoulder. "Then we keep moving," I said.

Cephas fell into step without fanfare—not ahead of us, not behind—but beside us, like a brace the world did not yet know it needed.

And the world—no longer broken, not yet wise—kept pace with us.

Not toward a monument, but toward the reckoning that comes when devotion forgets what it is for.

As the road bent away from the villages, a lone house stood back from the track with its shutters open to the night. No lamp burned there. None was needed. The air moved freely through the room, touching a sleeping child's brow and a plain iron frame left ready but unused. No mark hung on the lintel. No name had been carved into the wood. By morning, no one would remember to speak of it. But the house would breathe easier, and something quiet would take root where spectacle could not reach.

And so the day came when the living were required to choose whom they would serve—whether the name they held, or the truth that had been holding them.

For throughout all their journeys, the Presence walked ahead of them—

and the road was not finished.

Next in the Scrollbearer Saga

The Silence of Joshua Clay: A Story of Devotion and Deception

Book Three of The Scrollbearer Saga

After the Light returned,

the world wanted a name.

They spoke it with gratitude.

They spoke it with certainty.

They spoke it until they stopped listening.

But redemption does not belong to the redeemed.

And the Word does not answer to devotion alone.

When silence is mistaken for absence,

truth must learn how to stand without a voice.

Coming soon.

Enter the World of

The Scrollbearer Saga

The Darkened Light of Joshua Clay

Book One of The Scrollbearer Saga

This is where the witness is first given.

A tale of broken light, fractured faith, and a burden no one was meant to carry alone. Step into the shadows that first revealed the scroll, the Withering, and the cost of grace.

Available wherever books are sold.

www.ingramcontent.com/pod-product-compliance
Lightning Source LLC
LaVergne TN
LVHW050908080826
845145LV00001B/8

* 9 7 8 1 9 6 8 0 2 3 1 0 2 *